JACKPOT BLOOD

Also by
Jimmy Fox

Deadly Pedigree
Lineages and Lies

JACKPOT BLOOD

A Nick Herald Genealogical Mystery

Jimmy Fox

iUniverse, Inc.
New York Lincoln Shanghai

Jackpot Blood
A Nick Herald Genealogical Mystery

All Rights Reserved © 2004 by Jimmy Fox

No part of this book may be reproduced or transmitted in any form or by any means, graphic, electronic, or mechanical, including photocopying, recording, taping, or by any information storage retrieval system, without the written permission of the publisher.

iUniverse, Inc.

For information address:
iUniverse, Inc.
2021 Pine Lake Road, Suite 100
Lincoln, NE 68512
www.iuniverse.com

Jackpot Blood is a work of fiction. The author has herein created imaginatively a nonexistent world containing characters, inanimate entities, places, events, and more, and he has used these and all other elements of the book fictitiously. Any resemblance between anything in this novel and anything in actuality is completely coincidental.

ISBN: 0-595-30886-4 (pbk)
ISBN: 0-595-66216-1 (cloth)

Printed in the United States of America

Chapter 1

"Get out, you bum!" the infuriated man at his opulent desk shouted. "And take this crap with you!"

The judge hurled the offending final report at the genealogist responsible for discovering the bad news.

Nick Herald ducked just in time.

Sitting in a comfortable leather chair in front of the judge's desk, Nick hadn't expected so violent a reaction. His painstakingly researched family history grazed his brown hair and fluttered on to knock over some costly antique clutter behind him. Exquisite Scotch from the heavy crystal glass Nick held splashed his new-to-him Hickey Freeman houndstooth sport coat—a Goodwill-store find—and his crisply laundered khakis.

He'd even sprung for a fashionable coiffure at a tony barbershop catering to big shots like the judge, a departure from his usual beauty-school haircut, which, though it wasn't always symmetrical or bloodless, was cheap…and the girls nervously wielding the scissors were sweet.

A waste of time and cash, all his efforts to look the part of the respectable professional.

This big client of his—make that "former client"—was a Louisiana Supreme Court justice and a member of the tight circle of old-line New Orleans families still clinging to remnants of tainted fortunes, obeying secret social codes, guarding endangered privileges, and getting quite testy with those who have the gall to cross them.

Talk about killing the messenger! Nick thought bitterly, on his feet now, retreating across a massive, splendidly complex rug of Caspian provenance toward the door of the book-filled study, in which he happily could have spent the rest of his working days.

Months of research down the drain, and I can't even finish my drink!

For the past two hours, things had gone quite well in the air-conditioned chill of this scholarly refuge. Judge Chaurice had hung on every word and had seemed delighted with Nick's presentation. Then Nick reached the dicey part, the facts that would certainly keep the judge's son from marrying the daughter of the captain of New Orleans's most prestigious Mardi Gras krewe. This marriage was the event the judge had hoped to celebrate with a lavishly printed family history flaunting the Chaurice clan's illustrious deeds and spotless origins. Nick, however, had uncovered a spot. A great big spot.

Family honor is a life-and-death matter in New Orleans, as the Dueling Oaks in City Park would confirm if they could speak, although these days, injured pride is usually dealt with in the courtroom or at the business end of one's own pistol. What hasn't changed is that the laurels go to those who can sip champagne in white tie or ball gown while lugging around a filthy burlap sack full of inherited lies.

Usually in the courtroom, Nick reassured himself, for at this moment the judge looked capable of an old-fashioned murder born of pure pique.

In 1728, France began to ship young women of allegedly good character to New Orleans for marriage to the female-starved, morally challenged men of the wild new settlement hacked from a swampy crescent of the Mississippi River. These *filles à la cassette* arrived carrying a small chest, resembling a casket, of belongings and were promptly put under the care of Ursuline nuns.

But the judge's immigrant matriarch on the paternal side wasn't a "casket girl." Family tradition had rouged reality: Nick found that she was, in fact, a prostitute and later a bordello owner, who, when her professional days were done, devoted her considerable fortune to a charity hospital for women of all walks of life. The judge had heard enough before Nick could mention this particular tidbit of meritorious ancestral philanthropy. The family burlap sack of lies was already spilling far too much accurate family history for the judge's taste.

Nick stooped to retrieve his splayed spiral-bound report. Another missile came his way, this one a check the judge had angrily scribbled and wadded up.

"Two hundred?!" Nick complained with some heat, looking up from the crumpled check in his hand. "Hey, Judge, if you weren't ready for the truth, you shouldn't have asked me to find it. Do you have any idea how much work I—"

The thickset man's face turned the color of a boiled crawfish, and his gray jaw-line beard quivered with a prairie prophet's ire. "Sue me!!!"

◻

The butler slammed the front door in Nick's face.

Nick took off his wool coat, flipped it over his left arm, and impulsively raised his right fist to pound on the door. But he stopped himself.

Sue a judge? Yeah, right. Doesn't Louisiana have more lawyers per capita than any other state? Fat chance finding one for that case.

Trying to calm down, he breathed deeply for a few seconds, staring at his distorted reflection in the glittering curves of the big brass fleur-de-lis doorknocker.

He peered down a mirrored corridor of his own family history...his thin face took on the emaciated look of his father's Jewish ancestors living hand-to-mouth in an eighteenth-century East European shtetl he had yet to pin down; and his light brown eyes had grown huge and luminous with medieval mysticism and a wandering poet's forever unrequited yearning, the spiritual legacy of his mother's Catholic, Provençal line—or so he'd always liked to speculate.

Doubt. Doubt everything. The surface version can't be trusted: it is but a misleading version of the past. Just look at the judge. The cream of New Orleans aristocracy? *Ha!*

Nick touched his eyebrows—thick, but not a mink stole draped across his forehead, as his distorting reflection showed. His nose?—still the same straight triangle. And his cleft chin did not in fact slope to insignificance, as the golden, surreal image before him suggested.

He grinned; stumbling on a metaphor that helped him connect the dots always gave him goose bumps. The true genealogist fearlessly runs his hands across the face of the past, using imagination and methodology to feel the mysteries of ancestry, who we were and who we think we are.

Yes, this was the crux, the mission, the glory of his vocation.

Nick had always been curious about the inside of the judge's Second Empire mansion, which was a star of the Garden District. At least he'd accomplished that much this morning.

He closed the heavy black wrought iron gate behind him and walked to his car. The sun bathed bustling Prytania Street in muggy October afternoon heat.

Two hundred dollars. Up yours, Judge!

Not enough to keep the wolfish creditors at bay or to satisfy his chronically underpaid assistant, Hawty Latimer, who'd used her phenomenal computer and research skills in preparing the top-notch presentation for the judge. Enough, though, for a late lunch for two of oysters en brochette, Crabmeat Yvonne, heavenly bread, and a bottle or two of Montrachet at Galatoire's! His companion: a pretty young woman who worked at the Historic New Orleans Collection in the French Quarter. Veronique—she was of French birth, and, like the Quarter itself in its Gallic hauteur and pleasure-loving insularity, had shrugged off the late national exasperation with mother France. Nick had been trying to charm her for weeks, and the time seemed ripe for a higher level of intimacy. Culinary indulgence is a hallowed New Orleans form of foreplay.

As he tried to get his battered white MGB/GT to start, he thought about the possibility of serializing the rejected project in a genealogical or historical journal. That would show the pompous SOB! Or maybe he could persuade his occasional sponsor, the eccentric treasure hunter Edward Coldbread, to publish it. Four other extended works of genealogical scholarship by Nick had scored a pair of prizes and moderate, but short-lived, financial success.

At forty-two and in the second career of his life, he wasn't much bothered by assaults on his self-esteem. He'd learned to be resilient, and perhaps too cynical, in the years since his "resignation" from the English staff at Freret University, a.k.a. "Yale on the Bayou," actually on St. Charles Avenue, where the judge's son attended law school—naturally.

A false, anonymous, ultimately circumstantial charge of plagiarism, exacerbated by departmental backstabbing, had ended Nick's promising career as an upwardly mobile assistant professor of English. His stalwart friends, Professors Una Kern and Dion Rambus, helped him climb from the ensuing emotional morass by suggesting genealogy as a worthy use of his over-educated mind. Una offered some willing cousins as Nick's genealogical guinea pigs.

The new calling had been good for his soul, if bad for his net worth. And now he wouldn't give up being a certified genealogist, even if that scheming bastard Frederick Tawpie—presently the head of Freret's English department, then the leader of the plagiarism investigation—offered him a full professorship on a silver platter.

Well, maybe if he threw in tenure.

The coupe's engine finally coughed to life in a cloud of blue smoke. Doc Cheatham was in the tape player. The great virtuoso's sweet, lyrical trumpet notes filled his musty car—classic New Orleans jazz, a purer version of the Bourbon Street touristy product that drifted nightly on the river breeze to the balcony of his Dauphine Street apartment. He rummaged around in the debris on the passenger-side floor and came up with a Frank Sinatra cassette.

Ah, "Indian Summer." Love and loss. Just right.

Nick pulled out onto Prytania in the direction of a nearby Hibernia Bank to cash the judge's check before the jerk could stop payment.

Something else would come up.

And something did, that very night, two hundred miles northwest in Tchekalaya Forest.

Chapter 2

Tommy Shawe turned toward the vehicle dipping in and out of sight on the undulating road. Headlights glimmered in the distance, disappeared, then glimmered again. Eyes of an ancient stalking beast crouching and then advancing each time the prey drops its guard, Tommy thought. Then he laughed wearily at himself for being so edgy. It had been a good day, and his solitary stroll in the darkness, though not of his choosing, had allowed him time to reflect and to plan. Wasn't this his forest, the forest of his ancestors? He had nothing to fear.

Let it be a friend. Otherwise, he wouldn't much blame the driver for not stopping to pick up a stranger in the dead of night, in the middle of Tchekalaya Forest.

He felt more than he heard something whiff past his ear from the black wall of pines behind him. The bugs were bad this warm fall night; they'd clotted his windshield earlier. But this was no insect, he sensed, no gust of wind, though a storm was building.

Puzzled, he faced the dark woods. A pain slapped him in the chest. Not deep, but sudden and fiery, more like a wasp sting. *At night? Could be a nest of yellow jackets disturbed somewhere near.*

His left hand cautiously, nervously probed a thin, straight object, jutting out just below his right collarbone.

Syrupy coldness spread quickly through his body.

In a flash of dim light from the approaching vehicle, he saw a dart stuck fast through his shirt, in his flesh. He recognized it as he would know the tongue-wagging face of a favorite dog from his innocent childhood. The dart was a six-inch strip of sharpened river cane wrapped with thistledown. Just like the ones he and his brother had used as kids, hunting squirrels and birds with their blowguns of hollowed-out cane as tall as they were. Just like the ones his Katogoula Indian ancestors used...

Tommy imagined himself sliding through a canebrake of time, and on the other side he opened his eyes to the dazzling daylight of a vanished world, centuries before the white man came to these Louisiana hills and woods.

It was beautiful. Beautiful! He wanted to stay forever.

Chapter 3

That morning, Tadbull sawmill had closed down.

Paychecks had never been much to brag about, but they were all the men who worked here had.

The pine woods hissed in the saturated October heat as the subdued men lined up below the concrete loading bays for their final payment. Word had spread. The last of the year's cicadas wailed like an echo of the silenced saws.

Chain-smoking Clara, the dried-up white woman who'd been the company secretary since Noah's time, barked out the names. No apology, no explanation—merely a strip of paper announcing the closure: "Tadbull Lumber Company, LLC, has ceased operations." No representative from the family that owned the land and the sawmill made an appearance. Not even Wooty Tadbull, who managed the mill and everything else for his father.

It wasn't the Tadbulls' fault, the men agreed. Just the way things were. Computerization, automation, consolidation, tree-huggers and owl-lovers, NAFTA, politics—each man had a pet scapegoat. The only certainty was that there would be no more steady jobs, soon or ever, in this hardscrabble enclave of west-central Louisiana.

Most of the men at the mill were descendants of the Katogoula Indians who had settled here before recorded history. The Tadbulls had always been paternalistically inclined toward the Katogoula and had hired from their ranks almost exclusively. Nobody knew Tchekalaya Forest better than the Katogoula.

The men at the mill and their families loved the forest as the one remaining tangible link to the vanished way their ancestors lived. Without the mill, it would be nearly impossible to live here at all. Too many years of encroaching white civilization, too many alien laws, too much discrimination had not yet killed their cherished identity. But closure of Tadbull Mill just might.

For generations the lumber trade had fed them and served as one of the threads holding their fragile social fabric together. They had turned cutting and processing trees into a highly specialized art form. Lumbering was all the Katogoula knew.

After Clara had distributed the checks in the slanting October morning sunlight, Tommy Shawe had lingered at the old mill for a while to cheer up his friends. Many men talked of leaving, going to look for offshore oil jobs; younger ones spoke of the armed forces.

Then Tommy drove the swaybacked truck that had been his father's to the Three Sisters Pantry. He cashed his check and promptly blew some of it on beer and five-dollars' worth of scratch-off lottery tickets.

"Your brother was just in here," Luevenia Silsby said. "That boy is looking scarier every day, I tell you. He don't even speak when you say hello anymore." She tore off the tickets and handed them to Tommy. "I hope you win one of them, I surely do. I don't know how we're going to make it when the mill checks are gone."

She swallowed a lump of sorrow and adjusted her thick steel-rimmed glasses. One of the purer blooded of those who called themselves Katogoula, Luevenia was a small woman with a round face the color of a paper grocery bag; she kept her ash-gray hair pulled back and secured in a neat bun. When she was young, most of the whites had regarded her and her family as mullatoes and had treated them to the racism built into Louisiana's elaborate caste system of the time. She spoke succinctly, and like many folks of different heritages around this part of

Louisiana, she gave her sentences a French inflection. Her grammar was a bit off; she'd been denied the benefits of a complete education, as had most Katogoula her age.

Even though she shunned a leading formal role in the affairs of the tribe, Luevenia's opinions carried great weight.

At the front of the store, six stools were arrayed before the plate glass windows facing the gravel parking lot. On one stool sat an elderly man in suspenders. With great enthusiasm he was telling a story to Felix Wattell, a slightly younger man in denim coveralls. Both men wore baseball caps with the Tadbull Lumber Co. insignia.

"So, when that fight was over, the poh-lice came in the barroom and ask what all them muscadine grapes doin' on the floor. I say, 'Them ain't muscadines, them's eyeballs!'"

The teller of the tale, old Odeal Caspard, laughed in his high-pitched, uninhibited, childlike way and slapped Felix on the back.

Luevenia said to Tommy, too low for Odeal to hear, "How many times you heard that story?" She smiled affectionately at the old man who spent most of his days just where he was.

"I grew up on his stories, Miss Luevie. We all did." It hurt him to think that their tribe would be gone soon, forever, leaves in the wind, just as would Odeal himself, whose family had been one of the six core kinship groups which had stayed during the forced marches to Oklahoma, beginning in the 1820s. Tommy wished he'd paid more attention to Odeal's corny tales.

"I saved you a sweet potato-and-acorn pie," Luevenia said. "Tell Brianne it's my great-great-grandmother's recipe, from before the Trail of Tears. You just remember where you bought them lottery tickets, now, and spend a little of that jackpot when you win, you hear? I'm going to need the business."

"Yes'm, Miss Luevie." Tommy knew that the seller of a winning ticket reaped a small payment; but any meager one-shot payoff he might win wouldn't be enough to buy a future for Three Sisters Pantry or for the tribe. "Thanks for the pie."

◻

Tommy sat on the porch of his family's house. From inside, he heard Brianne cleaning up after lunch. He had not joined them; Brianne hadn't pressed him. His baby daughter didn't understand why he was home at this hour. But she'd sensed something bad was on the horizon, and now she was unusually subdued, like her mother.

They'd never had trouble like this, even when she'd gotten pregnant in high school (she and Tommy having ignored a thousand parental and priestly warnings). She'd lost that child, and the next, but she'd refused to give up. And now she'd matured into a strong woman, a good mother to their twin boys and daughter. Another kid on the way. Tommy loved her so much it sometimes literally took his breath away.

What am I going to do? he asked himself desperately. Welfare? Food stamps? Would his family have to leave the forest, too, as the others were talking of doing? His parents had helped through past rough patches; but they were gone now. He was the head of his family, and, in fact, the head of the tribe, such as it was. He didn't feel much like a leader now. His family tradition was about to stop with him; he must be unworthy of it.

The remaining beer cans swam in an ice chest next to his rocker. Finishing the can in his hand, he crushed it easily and laid it quietly in the paper sack with the other empties. Then he popped another one, shielding the wet explosion with his hand. He didn't want Brianne to know how many he'd drunk.

Tommy was not a morose person by nature, but this hunting season he was thinking he might take his shotgun on a short walk into the woods and bag some very familiar prey. Himself.

He fought off the horrible image of his family at his funeral and began to tote up his possibilities for income. There was the guiding he did during duck season. Not bad, but it all depended on connections, an elaborate servant-master relationship with certain powerful men in the area. He hated that part of it. One of these days he would tell off some fat, pampered, son-of-a-bitch. He knew he had a temper, when pushed.

At least he stayed on the right side of the law, unlike his brother, Carl. Funny, how Carl seemed to get along with the rich hunters: he couldn't get along with most other people—especially his own brother.

Tommy had bought out Carl's share of the family property for eighty thousand dollars. When Tommy defaulted, as seemed inevitable now, the bank would take his and Brianne's home away. Carl, as usual, had squandered the money in no time; now he blamed Tommy, accused him of something shady. The brothers avoided each other.

Tommy forced his fuzzy attention back to thoughts of future employment. What else could he do on a regular basis that wouldn't require him to grovel? Drive a school bus, deliver newspapers, cut yards for the few affluent residents of Cutpine? Not very appealing or rewarding, and he'd be fighting for the same jobs with every other ex-mill worker and logger. Fellow Katogoula men.

And then he thought about a frequently suppressed idea that lurked in the shadows of his mind: he could start running drugs.

Some of the local young white men had chosen this dangerous way of life; a few guys he knew boasted incautiously about their wages of sin. They were sneaking the stuff through the forest at night on logging roads and then on the sparsely traveled state highways, away from heavily patrolled I-10 and I-49. Tommy had seen forest airstrips, too. They were booby-trapped. It was hardly safe to walk in the woods anymore.

It would be easy for Tommy. He was as good a backwoodsman as anybody around here—with the exception, maybe, of his brother. But a guy could get killed in that line. He would be dealing with rough characters who'd just as soon shoot you as look at you; and then there were the cops.

Best stick to the guiding, even if humiliating and seasonal. Carl would just have to share a little more of the work with him. Tommy was the favorite of a couple of rich old Shreveport men with Range Rovers and Hummers, jewel-encrusted Rolexes, $50,000 shotguns, and more gear than a Marine squad. Who knows?...if things worked out, he could build a high-class lodge, train some pure-bred Labs, and offer nearly year-round hunting and fishing for a king's ransom.

He tried to filter out the mournful dirge of the cicadas, concentrating instead on the discordant voices of the ages in his soul. *Think, listen!* he commanded himself. *What are they trying to tell me?* He had to come up with something, or his family would starve, the tribe would fall apart, and their age-old dream of rebirth die. How could he face his ancestors, if he let this happen?

The Golden Trace meandered by his house, at one edge of his property, about fifty yards away from where he sat now. His father had cut a deal with the Office of State Parks for use of the trace, reserving for his family an island of private property in the midst of the forest. Tommy remembered how careful his father had been with the details of the agreement, having seen in his time many unlettered Katogoula lose their land to unprincipled white men. His father had always believed that no human being could own the Golden Trace. And now, though it was officially under the administration of Tchekalaya State Forest, Tommy, like his father before him, considered himself only its caretaker.

Tourists, people from everywhere, strolled down the Golden Trace, just about all year. Harmless, friendly people, with money to spend. Brianne often fed a group, giving them fine memories—and a few pounds around the waist—to take back home.

Tourists. The voices were trying to say something, but that one word was all he could make out so far.

There were many stories about why the forest path was called the Golden Trace. Some said there was hidden gold, buried by the French, the Spanish, the Confederates, or the Yankees. But he believed the story passed along by his tribe: that it was the ancient Katogoula hunting trail, and that the name came from the way the morning sun caught diamonds of dew clinging to countless pine needles.

Blood! the voices sang in magnificent harmony, startling Tommy and making him look around his front yard where the kids' toys were dwarfed by towering longleaf pines.

Blood? Yes, of course, blood. He knew he had it, American Indian blood, Katogoula blood. He had felt that blood coursing through his veins as a boy, when, watching the first morning sunlight pour across the Golden Trace, he imagined that his own bare feet were those of his ancestors as they moved along without noise, to hunting grounds, or to battle. Blood. He could feel it as a presence in the pre-dawn darkness at the boat dock on Lake Katogoula, as the rich white men drank their bourbon-spiked coffee from gold-plated thermoses. He was with the stars above, with the pintails, the mallards, the geese; he was inside the cold blackness of the lake with the sleeping bream, perch, and bass. The white men had to ask him things twice; probably thought he was stupid.

And it was his blood that connected him to all these things. He could feel it when he and Brianne made love, and his seed sought out in her womb the river of blood that had been flowing for eons through their people.

His parents had been brought up to avoid the subject of Katogoula blood. Being an Indian in their day was no glamorous thing. Few whites, then or now, realized there still were Indians in Louisiana. Sure, they'd heard of the Plains Indians and reservations out west. Everyday in Louisiana, whites rattled off tongue-twisting place names in Indian languages now dead. They flocked to one of the Indian casinos that dotted the state. But the flesh-and-blood Indians at their doorsteps, still honoring their ancient ways, had always been invisible—often by choice.

For much of their lives, Tommy's parents had suffered from this desire to remain invisible. But the damage had been done: grandparents had told them of the old magical times of *their* grandparents. And slowly, an interest in their heritage was born.

Golden Trace! Tourists! Blood! The voices drowned out every other thought. *Golden Trace! Tourists! Blood!*

A woodpecker cackled crazily deep in the woods. The voices sank back into a murmuring babel. Tommy opened another beer.

Shortly before his birth, during a national flowering of ethnic pride in the early sixties, his father had spearheaded the effort to obtain official recognition from the Bureau of Indian Affairs.

Hopes ran high. Some initial genealogical work was done on a few families. The governor of the day, seeing a painless, cost-free way to get some votes, quickly gave state recognition to the tribe. But eventually the enthusiasm faded. The BIA never actually rejected the application, but merely suggested that the tribe's claims had been "misinterpreted."

Budget reductions, probable fraud, sporadic assimilationist policies, and pressure from already recognized tribes were the real reasons. The BIA, long viewed as the most inefficient federal agency, faced a dwindling amount of cash to support a sloppy bureaucracy and paltry benefits already earmarked for existing tribes.

Tommy himself had pretty much forgotten about the application, in the frenzy of adolescence and then the press of family life. He couldn't remember the last time anyone had mentioned recognition. There was a box of paperwork somewhere in one of his garage closets.

Jackpot! the voices shouted. *JACKPOT!* even louder.

Tommy jumped up from the rocker.

OUR JACKPOT BLOOD! Our salvation!

Now the strange chorus ceased. He could hear his own inner voice again.

Yes! Tribal recognition. It would be like winning the big one, the lucky once-in-a-lifetime score!

Thoughts now rolled across Tommy's mind, whirring like the symbols in a slot machine's windows. He would get on the phone, fly to Washington, triple mortgage his house and his land...whatever it took. He would devote all of his time to getting the application back on the front burner. The Katogoula could form some kind of charitable group, a foundation; solicit donations, take out loans, sell their hand-made baskets door to door, whatever they had to do. And finally, when they had federal recognition, they would open a casino, like the Chitiko-Tiloasha.

Tommy ran unsteadily to the garage, tripping over a plastic tricycle. He ricocheted off his truck and his wife's '91 Pontiac as he charged to the closets. He didn't have the key to the closet he wanted, so he kicked in the hollow-core door and groped for the string of the light. He pulled it so hard the ceramic fixture fell on him. The box that held the files for the application with the BIA...*where the hell was it?!*

Tommy dug through layer after layer of family junk.

"Please, God, I hope it's not thrown away!" he said, his voice slurred by alcohol, his throat choked with fear, his shirt sticking to him.

"Tommy! What are you doing?!" Brianne stood in the garage between the two vehicles, holding something. She looked disapprovingly at the mess. "Have you lost your mind?! You're soused to the gills. And you're soaking wet."

"I'm looking for our people," he said. He couldn't explain now.

"Floyd just delivered this." She held up the thick manila envelope their mailman had brought. "He had to come all the way back here from the highway to get a signature. He wasn't happy. Here. It's addressed to you. I bet you can't even read it."

"Shhure I can," Tommy protested, trying to stand up like a sober man, which only made him look drunker. "Lemme see it."

Looked official. Addressed to him personally, from the BIA, Branch of Acknowledgment and Research.

He ripped into it. Dozens of forms spread across both hands; some fell to the oily garage floor. He read the first few words of the cover letter. He shook his head vigorously and read the words again.

"...*happy to inform you that a final determination of acknowledgment of the Katogoula Tribe of Cutpine, Louisiana, has been reached.... actual tribal recognition did not result from actions of this agency, but through the Omnibus Congressional Funding Resolution....*"

Tommy let out a whoop. He grabbed Brianne and twirled her around until they fell against the Pontiac.

"Tommy! The baby! I'm pregnant, dear. Be careful."

"Yeah. Right. Uh. I've got to, uh..." Shock and confusion momentarily immobilized his tongue.

"What does all that mean?" She tried to read the letter Tommy held in his shaking hands.

"Brianne, the BIA is giving the Katogoula tribal recognition!"

She inhaled sharply and put her hands over her mouth.

"Don't cry, honey. Don't cry." He hugged her, gently now.

"Well, I'm so happy," she said. "I can't help it."

Tommy tried to rub sobriety into his face. "I'm not sure what happened, exactly." He read more of the letter, and as he did clarity sharpened his words. "Says here our senators and congressmen snuck some bill through that gave us official recognition and funding. The BIA's got to take it from there. Look, I need to talk to Chief Claude. I'll call you from the casino. See if you can find a beat-up blue cardboard box of tribal records in there, about newspaper size, six inches high. Don't lift anything too heavy; get the boys to help you when they get home from school. Call Miss Luevie, too.... And don't worry, honey. All our problems are over."

The white people of Cutpine had shunted the last of those who still called themselves Katogoula to the southern edge of the piddling municipality and beyond, where the longleaf pine forest, the Indians' ancient home, grew thick again after the clear-cutting of the late nineteenth century. Their dirt-yard neighborhoods of ramshackle wood-frame houses had become their ghetto, their de facto reservation, and would probably be their deathbed if the gradual cultural extinction continued.

A hodgepodge of legends now little more than superstition, a stubborn pride, and a vague hope for rebirth were the feeble remaining elements of Katogoula identity. This complex of beliefs and emotions made them feel different, wronged, alienated, proud; it was both a curse and a treasure.

Cutpine was a good hour's drive from the immensely successful Chitiko-Tiloasha casino, but more like two hours the way Tommy had to drive his old truck. Tonight, he didn't mind; he had a lot to think about.

Before setting out for home that night, Tommy called his wife from a brightly lit gas station on the Chitiko-Tiloasha reservation, fifty miles outside of Lafayette, in the southwestern corner of Louisiana. He'd spent hours at the tribe's Bayou Luck Casino. But he hadn't been gambling. Today, the luck of his own tribe had changed forever.

He apologized to Brianne for being so late—it was after midnight now. He touched the thin silver chain and small cross around his neck; she'd given it to him for their twentieth wedding anniversary. He glanced up: the blade of the old moon shone dully through a thick haze of fugitive clouds. Chief Claude had talked and talked, Tommy told his wife; the old man had seemed almost as thrilled about the Katogoula finally receiving federal tribal recognition as Tommy himself.

"The chief treated me to the biggest, best steak I ever had," a last surge of excitement stirring his words through exhaustion. "You ought to see that place, Brianne. We can do it, just like them. We can bring our tribe back to life. Like I was saying this afternoon."

"Dear, you said a whole lot that didn't make much sense to me," Brianne said, with characteristic patience.

"No, honey. Listen. I haven't had a beer since I left. I know what I'm saying now. More than I ever have. I'm talking about our jackpot blood. We're going to win, Brianne, *our* tribe's finally going to win, just by being who we are!"

He didn't have the energy to go into the details of his meeting with the highly respected Chitiko-Tiloasha leader, but he briefly explained that Chief Rafe Claude had urged him to hire a genealogist. The chief recommended a good one from New Orleans, who'd done competent work for the Chitiko-Tiloashas.

Tommy looked down at a business card in his hand: "Jonathan Nicholas Herald, Certified Genealogist, Ph.D. No charge for initial consultation."

Brianne listened and spoke at just the right moments to encourage Tommy, while cautioning him to control his emotions, at least for the long drive home. It had all happened so fast: they'd soared from crisis to elation in the space of one day. Her vague unease came through the line.

Executives from four casinos had each called several times; functionaries in the offices of State Senator Augustus Bayles and State Representative Rufus Girn were also trying to get in touch with Tommy.

"Word's spread like chicken pox," she said. "Everybody around here from Luevenia to Odeal's looking for you. We haven't had a moment's peace since all this started this afternoon. The baby can't sleep, what with the phone ringing. Are you sure tribal recognition is a good idea, dear? I don't know why, but I feel like I do when a hurricane's heading our way."

He assured her that everything would settle down eventually, in a few months, at the most. She told him she'd not yet looked for the box of records and then cautioned him again to drive carefully. He swore on the Bible that he hadn't been drinking. She loved him, she said.

Tommy bought a large coffee. Blearily pondering the long, dark road ahead through swirls of bracing coffee mist, he hoped his old truck would make it all the way back to Cutpine.

The Shawe family had always done a little better than the rest; it was said that leadership ran in the family. Tommy was soft-spoken, steady, and polite. His twin brother, Carl, was far from identical in either body or personality. Carl was raucous, hotheaded, and rude. Marital bliss had made Tommy look younger than his thirty-six years; debauchery and a tendency toward petty crime had made Carl into a wild hermit. Tommy was thirty pounds heavier than his stringy brother—Brianne's excellent cooking. Both men were shy of six feet and had straight medium-blond hair; Tommy favored a clean-cut look; Carl emerged from the woods with a scraggly beard and shoulder-length, matted locks.

The brothers and most of the other Katogoula living in and around Cutpine weren't stock Indian characters from Remington's paintings or Hollywood films. The Katogoula had less of a white-reaction problem in the skin-tone and facial features department. A stranger probably would see the Katogoula as ordinary Louisiana rural poor with few modern skills and a muddled lineage nobody cared enough about to mention.

But they did mention it, at least among themselves. The injustice of it all was often a topic at the Three Sisters Pantry, where Luevenia Silsby presided. The whites had destroyed their tribal life because they *were* Indians, and then refused to grant tribal recognition because they claimed the Katogoula *weren't* Indians anymore. Too much dilution of the blood line, the Bureau of Indian Affairs alleged, for the three decades and more that their application had been pending.

But that frustrating situation had changed today—yesterday, now, Tommy realized, in the midst of a big yawn. The coffee was long gone.

Bouncing over potholes that shook his truck, he wanted to stretch out the momentous day, so important would it be to the future of the Katogoula. In a few hundred years, maybe a future generation would enshrine Brianne and him and their kids in a new Katogoula sacred story. They would be called saviors of the tribe.

Oncoming headlights momentarily revived him. The Shawe family's characteristic deep blue circles under his tired eyes stood out in the light. The car sped by, and Tommy's truck rattled down the road, solitary again, at the rip-roaring speed of 45 mph.

What an incredible day! He could compare the roller coaster ride of emotion only to the mingled fear and elation he'd felt during the birth of his three children.

The jerking steering wheel and the thumping of his flat right-front tire saved Tommy from falling completely asleep and running off the road.

He stopped the truck on the weedy shoulder, amid bottles and cans and a dead possum. You had to be awful stupid to get hit by a car around here, he was thinking; hardly any traffic at this time of night. He found a flashlight; it gave off a dim amber glow.

The tire had five nails in the nearly smooth rubber; the back right had at least three, and was slowly deflating. Tommy used the fading beam to search behind the truck, just to see what else was left from the fool who must have driven by earlier with an untarped load of construction debris or plain junk.

Cursing the careless driver—probably someone he knew—he stepped down further into the weeds. He saw a splintered two-by-four, about three feet long, studded with nails that hadn't stuck in his tires.

At that moment, the flashlight gave out.

His truck predated emergency flashers, so he left his parking lights on. He knew these wouldn't last long; his truck battery had dead cells.

He began walking the way he'd come. For half an hour, only his footsteps, the freshening northwesterly breeze, the occasional cry of an owl, and the pulsing of cricket and frog calls competed with his thoughts. His only visible companions were several freshly exploded road-kill carcasses, unidentifiable in the cloud-blocked moonlight. Dog? Possum? Skunk? No telling.

Three miles back he'd passed Three Sisters Pantry. The store was closed, but there was a pay phone outside. Luevenia and Royce lived in a trailer in back; they'd let him sleep there or borrow their truck, if he asked, but he didn't want to bother them.

Headlights. Somebody coming. Good.

Brianne was probably a nervous wreck. He could call her soon.

His attacker saved Tommy the price of that call.

Chapter 4

As Tommy Shawe, fighting fatigue, was driving unwittingly into ambush on the lonely highway home, three figures, only a few miles away, toiled in the dense darkness that held Tchekalaya Forest hostage.

Wooten Tadbull IV was one of these men. Usually he trusted the night, gratefully accepting its blindfold of depthless shadows and its gag of heavy, humid stillness. Nighttime had long been his partner, his best friend, his brother. Tonight was different. He wondered what ransom of pain or death would be due before sunrise.

Through sheer will he held back a building compulsion to pull out his pistol and start shooting into the living danger he sensed. Instead, he continued hefting cardboard box after box of neatly shrink-wrapped marijuana bricks. Street value of tonight's load: around three million.

The last-quarter sickle moon had risen through the pines but couldn't slash a hole in the thick shroud covering central Louisiana. In this pocket of the Deep South, the transition from summer to fall was violent and unpredictable. Even in October the thermometer could read ninety degrees one day, twenty the next. Storms packing brute cyclonic force could just as easily rampage up from the warm moist Gulf as rip across Texas with an arctic blast and winds that could drive splintered pine limbs right through a human body.

Some violent change was very close now, Wooty felt; and it wouldn't be merely a shift in the temperature.

His two friends helping him unload the customized van—a family vehicle, he reflected, with a twinge of guilt—didn't seem to understand their utter vulnerability; he didn't expect them to. Nice guys, Mancel and Travis. He'd known them for twenty years, since junior high, maybe even before that; but they were going to live and die unnoticed, unnoticing, never having gone anywhere or been anybody special.

A cold front was moving in quickly. Wind hissed through countless pine needles; sudden gusts made stout limbs groan. Was that why the sweat chilled on his skin? His heart wasn't racing and pounding because of physical exertion; he was in great shape, and Mancel and Travis were doing the hard work at the moment.

The Katogoula—back when there was a tribe to speak of—used to call this month The Moon of Rains. They understood Nature, but they miscalculated the evil and power of their fellow man. Wooty didn't plan to repeat their fatal mistake; and he wasn't going to be a nobody, like Mancel and Travis. Ambition, more powerful than any earthly storm, raged in his unsatisfied soul. And ambition required that he stay alive.

For a moment he watched the menacing sky, trying to discern the amorphous outlines of the murky clouds he knew were there. Hit men in black trench coats, hiding in a crowd, he thought. The sky winced with electric-blue flashes. Distant rumbling, almost too faint to hear, sounded like feral growls. It would let loose pretty soon; he could smell it already, a violent tempest galloping in from the Texas plains and before that from Canada and the top of the globe.

"How many more you got, hoss?" Mancel asked Travis, who was shifting boxes inside the van with his customary bottomless strength and stamina. Mancel straightened up, stretched his slight shoulders, and wiped his face with a handkerchief.

"You dumb coonass pip-squeak," Travis said, laughing, from inside the van. "I'm in this pitch black oven sweating like a damn pig and you asking me 'How many?' Shitfire, boy, I don't got no idea. God didn't give you the sense he gave a worm. Ask our college graduate out there. He always was good with numbers back in high school, ain't that right, Wooty? Four, thirty-two, seventeen—*hike!*"

A heavy box of Mexican weed came flying out of the van just as the sky quivered with indistinct lightning deep within the storm clouds. Mancel had to use his flashlight to find the box on the road, fifteen feet away. Travis thought this was the greatest joke in the world.

"Cut it out, you crazy redneck," Mancel said to Travis, with the lilting Cajun cadences of southwest Louisiana. He was the smallest of the three men and clearly didn't enjoy such tough manual labor; he took frequent breaks for sips of beer, much to Wooty's annoyance. "That stuff's too valuable to be throwing around, yeah," Mancel chided. "Wooty, how many more we got? Wooty?"

Wooty didn't respond; he was listening and watching with his woods sense.

Mancel shrugged. With no enthusiasm and plenty of grunting, he resumed hefting the boxes Travis had stacked up in the meantime at the back of the van.

This chunk of Tchekalaya Forest had been Tadbull land for over a century and a half. Wooty knew these woods as intimately as he knew the female body. He knew all the pulses and scents that should be here on an early fall night, on a logging road in the middle of nowhere—and all the ones that shouldn't. The night hunters were at work, and only the crickets and mosquitoes were too stupid to cower for their lives.

Wooty, standing stock-still in the pale moonlight, couldn't shake off the feeling that something was out of place, dangerously out of place. His woodsman's skills were something of a local legend, though his new enterprises left no time for the old outdoor pursuits he once so enjoyed.

When he was younger, the Katogoula men at the mill and on the plantation used to kid him, saying that he must be part Indian, so adept was he in the ways of the woods. Eager, like most boys, to throw himself into make-believe, Wooty began to take the affectionate joking of the Indian men to heart. By the time he turned eight, he could hunt, fish, and trap as well as any Katogoula his own age—with the exception of Carl Shawe, and maybe Carl's twin brother, Tommy.

He had always been certain exactly who his parents were, of course—thoroughly white and wealthy Mr. and Mrs. Wooten Tadbull III. Lately, he wished he could change that fact of parentage; his mother was dead, but the mere presence of Wooty's father was beginning to drive him crazy. Wooty was determined never to be the ineffectual, unadventurous fool he thought his father to be. That vow was one of the reasons he was out here tonight, risking a lifetime of incarceration, or death—which, now that he thought about the choice between the two, would be preferable.

Mancel noticed that Wooty's normal high-strung skittishness had given way to alarm. "Travis, hold up a second, you hear," Mancel said. He had to repeat the request a couple of times until big Travis, caught up in his task again, cursed him liberally and asked him what the hell he wanted now.

The two men stopped unloading the van. The trailer behind Wooty's Honda four-wheeler was three-quarters full.

"Wooty? What's going on, man?" Mancel asked nervously. Following Wooty's gaze, he looked into the black void of the forest. "You want us to shine the flashlights?"

"No," Wooty snapped. "Just shut up a second!"

Wooty walked a few steps away along the raised road that felt so familiar under his feet from years of camping around here, of trekking to and from Lake Katogoula with a day's bag of fish or ducks, of parking here with the giggling girls of his adolescence. In the daylight he would have expected to see a built-up crude logging road of distinctive red dirt crawling through the thick longleaf pine woods.

Sight was of no use to him now, though. He had to decipher the forest's warnings, as a blind man would sense something deadly in his path.

Early geese fleeing northern cold honked somewhere in the dark sky, the old leaders turning and rallying the flock's broken V for the descent to Lake Katogoula, an important flyway stopover.

Wooty thought about patterns, the ancient imperative the geese obeyed. He felt stripped of volition, a mere animal machine without the advantage of a human brain. The invisible force using the forest for cover now controlled his actions, drawing him into conflict. Like the geese, he had only instinct as his imperfect armor.

Travis stooped out of the van. "There somebody out there, Wooty?" he asked. His silhouette in the night was larger than that of the other men, mostly chest and shoulders dwarfing a small cube of head. "I'll take care of the bastard. Just point the way and I'll block for you, like we did in the division game against the Dry Spit Braves, remember Wooty?" Travis now held something that gleamed dully in the glow filtering through the low, scudding clouds. His voice betrayed his fear.

Wooty knew that big Travis did rash, violent things when he was afraid—which was precisely how they'd won that epic football game twenty years before. "Epic," that is, by the standards of this nook of rural central Louisiana, which Wooty considered to be a hopeless wasteland where feeble aspirations evaporated like sweat in August. That famous game between the high-school teams of Cutpine and Dry Spit...Travis had been terrified by their principal, who told the huge center that if the team didn't bring home the division trophy, he would be expelled because of his miserable grade point average. Four members of the opposing team ended up in the hospital, mangled by Travis's charge.

"This is more serious than any high-school game, big guy," Wooty said, in a calm, low voice, as if to a spooked horse. "No need to do anything crazy. We're operating in a new league, different rules. Probably just a coon out looking for dinner."

More rustling from the darkness, this time on the other side of the road.

"I don't think it's no coon, Wooty. That's human," Travis insisted. "Must be two of 'em. They got us surrounded!"

"Oh, man, if we get caught with this stuff out here. Oh, man," Mancel whimpered. "I ain't goin' to jail, Wooty, that's all I got to say. I ain't goin' to Angola. I'm gonna go down to the marsh to my cousins that got the shrimp boats and hitch a ride to Mexico—"

"Shut up, Mancel!" Wooty growled.

But the jumpy man couldn't remain silent. "Maybe we better get the hell out of here. Like, now!"

"Come on, you bastards!" Travis blurted out.

And before Wooty could stop him—about as likely an undertaking, he realized, as stopping a charging bear barehanded—Travis had bounded off into the darkness, brandishing his revolver.

Wooty jumped into the van. "Come on, Mancel!" Wooty shouted. "We have to get this done! Forget about him for now. He can take care of himself."

The two of them worked like madmen, Mancel grunting and complaining, Wooty feeling even his honed muscles starting to tire.

Travis's angry roar echoed through the trees, silencing the myriad crickets. Then there was nothing.

Wooty and Mancel stumbled through the woods, tripping over downed pines, fending off thorned tentacles that latched onto their skin and clothing; they collided with scaly trunks or matted walls of vegetation before their dancing flashlight beams could warn them. Mancel had a tougher time of it than Wooty and had fallen behind.

Wooty stopped abruptly. Mancel, panting heavily, still a few yards back, staggered up beside his friend.

"Jesus!" Mancel cried with the little strength he had left.

Wooty said nothing. Sweat streaming down his face, he walked up to the edge of the pit that yawned before him. His chest continued furiously to pump air, though his expression showed that his winded condition did not affect his thinking.

Travis lay at the bottom of a pit trap, a deadfall. Roughly six feet square, six feet deep. Not a very skillfully made one, either. Travis would have seen it by daylight.

"Watch it, Mancel," Wooty said. "May be other pits around."

But Mancel had retreated to a tree trunk behind Wooty, which held him up while he vomited repeatedly.

Wooty assumed poor Travis must have been running when he fell in; hit the far side of the pit and his head was pushed down into his chest until his stubby neck snapped. His sloping wrestler's shoulders were now hunched over his upside-down face. It was a horrifically unnatural posture, a bizarre, sickening sight. His fixed, surprised eyes told Wooty he was undoubtedly dead, and his mouth was open in the act of uttering that final roar of defeat as he fell. Sharpened broomsticks protruded from his back.

The trap was designed not for game, but for human beings. A booby trap. Wooty directed his light ahead and saw, as he expected, what was being guarded: a good-size plot of healthy marijuana plants. Fairly common out here in the woods, where the remoteness of the location made even spotting by helicopter nearly impossible. Free-lancers probably, growing the stuff for themselves or for their local turfs, thus bypassing the big operators, like the Tijuana cartel which had recruited Wooty—but the locals were just as ruthless, as Travis had fatally learned.

Wooty was certain that someone had known of this trap and had led Travis right into it. Someone who wasn't here because of them, not here to stop or bust them, but someone who didn't want to be seen, who did not want a confrontation.

Was it that crazy son-of-a-bitch Carl Shawe, Tommy's twin brother? He had rare talent in the old ways of the woods, that was for sure. And he was a well-known poacher, especially fond of breaking game laws at night. But Wooty couldn't think of Carl as the murdering type—and this was murder, wasn't it? Besides, Carl would surely have made a better deadfall, as a matter of pride, considering it was an ancient Katogoula hunting method.

No, the cultivated patch and the trap didn't belong to Carl. An alcoholic loser, his brain rotted by booze, sure, but he wasn't a dope farmer or particularly fond of grass, as Wooty recalled from their adolescent years.

Who had led Travis on a race to his death? If not Carl, who had it been out here in the woods, watching them? Watching them still.

Anger got the better of rational analysis.

"Hey!" The word fled into the darkness. "Hey, you asshole! What did you have to let him get killed for?"

Wooty didn't expect an answer.

With great difficulty they lugged Travis's body back to the road and the vehicles. Neither man had spared breath to speak in the woods. They placed the body gently on the ground.

"How much this mother weigh?" Mancel complained, bent forward, his hands on his knees.

"Let's put him on the boxes, in the trailer," Wooty said, after an interval of rest. He grappled with Travis's limp arms and torso, while Mancel awkwardly wrestled the massive rubbery legs. Blood dribbled on the cardboard.

"Make me think of a dead alligator, yeah," said Mancel. "The big fool. Calling me dumb, too! How you like that?"

Wooty secured the body with black rubber tie cords. "I'll put him where he'll never be found: over in the Katogoula burial mounds. They don't let anybody dig around there anymore."

"But what about his folks? Ain't they gonna look for him?"

"They'll be glad he's gone," Wooty said. "When he went to Alaska, they threw a goddamn party, remember? I had to bail him out after that pool-hall fight last year; nobody else would. Look, it was an accident. Some independent pothead dug that pit. Travis's luck ran out. There wasn't anybody out there tonight. Just my imagination, that's all. We're not at fault, we're not busted, so we got to make the best of it. That's what he'd want us to do."

"You right, you right. Like always. And you know what? Since there only two of us now, that mean we split up his share, yeah?"

"Let's don't worry about that right now, Mancel. I've got a lot of work to do, and the only thing you should be concerned about is getting the hell out of here and not running off the road or getting a ticket. I'll let you know what happens in a few days. Don't speed, and remember to keep your lights off until you hit pavement. Oh, and Mancel."

"Yeah, Wooty?"

"These guys we're dealing with aren't Boy Scouts. Keep your goddamn mouth shut for a change, will you, buddy? We'll both live a lot longer."

Mancel had lately taken to showing off his newfound wealth at bars; for the first time in his life, he had more women than he knew what to do with vying for his attention and his wallet. He was in heaven, in spite of the hazards of his new line of work.

"Yeah, okay, Wooty." The little Cajun looked down sadly at Travis. "Say a prayer over him for me."

▣

Through a fleeting, jagged deadfall of black sky that had opened in the clouds, the sliver of bone-white moon shone on the burial mounds and a solitary standing human form, at momentary rest.

Wooty had dug a hole big enough to contain his friend's body. He was almost completely exhausted. Before taking care of Travis, he'd unloaded and hidden the marijuana at his family's rustic hunting cabin, deep in the pine woods, where in years past his father had entertained state politicians and business bigwigs with booze, prostitutes airlifted from New Orleans, and plentiful wildlife to be blasted.

The dope had arrived via a clandestine network of couriers. Now it would wait in a dry raised cistern beside the cabin for another crew to start it on the next leg of its malign journey to America's pushers and users. Wooty didn't know—didn't want to know—who his contacts were; identities were compartmentalized for security reasons.

"You played your last game tonight, you big idiot," he said to the corpse as he started the final stages of concealing Travis's body.

Wielding his folding field shovel to make as little soil damage as possible, he threw more dirt into the almost-filled grave. Sudden gusts of high wind carried a fine, cool mist, but down in the meadow a thin layer of fog was already starting to cohere, blurring shapes and multiplying shadows. There would be no major rain tonight, he thought. That was lucky. Give the dirt time to settle back into this particular ancient hump of bones and tribal trash. When he was through, it would appear that some night forager had pawed this area and given up.

Tadbull property, though today only a remnant of the family's original empire, still enclosed several different types of distinctly Louisiana terrain. Here, the pines reluctantly ceded the higher, drier ground to sweetgum, pecan, magnolia, hickory, and live oak. The trees were very old. Some of the oaks might have been here for centuries, might even have stood sentinel over the fires and drums and dances of the Katogoula burial ceremonies once held down there on the meadow, in front of these mounds.

Wooty wiped his face across his short sleeve and noticed the burst water blisters on his hands.

"Damnit!" he said, and threw the shovel into the empty trailer behind the ATV. He was something of a dandy and had his hands manicured when he got his hair cut in Baton Rouge, New Orleans, or Dallas. He visited each of these cities at least once a month on business for his father—and for himself.

Spectral movement down on the meadow caught his eye. He crouched low to cut his silhouette. The heart-pounding wariness he'd felt on the logging road instantly returned, banishing the aches of his joints and muscles.

A hundred-and-fifty yards away, he estimated—a deer! A big whitetail buck. Two-hundred pounds, minimum.

He relaxed a little. Just a deer. It was the rutting season and deer were very active, devoting most of their daylight hours to the mating game, marking territory and sniffing out does.

The antlers were huge, perfect, maybe fourteen points. But he couldn't be sure: perspective and color were leached out of the landscape by the darkness, the low mist set aglow by moonlight, and the subtle graying of the eastern sky.

Probably returning to his bed after a night of feeding, Wooty thought. But this was no time to dwell on the dream of bagging a fine deer. He had only his pistol and Travis's revolver, and even if he had his rifle with the night scope he wouldn't dare fire it. The noise of a shot would carry for miles.

"Old buck," Wooty said to the deep-blue shadow outlined in phosphorescent white, as it soundlessly entered the indigo woods, "you're too smart for me tonight."

Then, just as he was about to climb onto his four-wheeler, Wooty saw another animal emerge stealthily from the dark forest and follow the path the deer had taken.

He rubbed his forehead and eyes and shook his head. Could he believe what he thought he saw?

He trained his gaze on the second animal now moving across the meadow.

"That's a damn cougar," he said, his voice no more than an awed whisper, as if he were witnessing a sacred event.

Though protected animals these days, cougars around here had been hunted nearly to extinction in the nineteenth and early twentieth centuries by the white settlers, partly in self-defense, partly for sport. They'd been a favorite prey of Wooty's own Tadbull ancestors. Now cougars were extremely rare in the Tchekalaya Forest. There were still plenty of bobcats, though; Wooty's father, in fact, had a few mounted in his study. This was definitely no bobcat.

The cougar stopped and turned in Wooty's direction. Was it aware of his presence? Wooty held his breath as the cougar seemed to be deciding what to do. He hoped that the distance between them made him an unappealing meal and a minor threat.

And then the big cat did an incredible thing: it rose several feet above the ground fog and appeared to fly rapidly at that height across the remainder of the meadow and into the opposite woods.

Wooty took a few involuntary steps backward. *This was downright spooky!* An icy chill seemed to come up from the burial mound and squeeze his heart.

He'd always known that the cougar was important in Katogoula mythology. In his youth he'd played with the Katogoula boys, particularly the Shawe brothers, Tommy and Carl. The fragments of legends he'd absorbed piqued his young imagination; but since then, he had come to see them as no more than primitive artifacts of a culture that had gone the way of the slaughtered cougar.

Yet, what he'd just seen was almost enough to make a guy a Katogoula in his soul.

◻

A bulbous van with darkly tinted windows sped by Tommy Shawe's truck, which sat dark and abandoned on the opposite northbound shoulder of the deserted country highway.

Half a mile south of the truck, a spooked armadillo scurried through a new gap in the weeds; at this very spot, Tommy, unconscious, had just been dragged from the shoulder of the road. The armadillo blundered onto the asphalt-and-gravel pavement and paused unwisely, raising its pointed snout to sniff details that its poor eyesight didn't provide.

Mancel's van slammed into the animal, disintegrating it in a spray of leathery shell, blood, and viscera.

Barely swerving, the van accelerated until its taillights dipped out of sight several miles away and the shriek of its engine subsided into the deceptive peacefulness of the dark forest.

Chapter 5

Carl Shawe could have killed for some hot coffee—well, at least hurt somebody real bad.

He'd finished his pint of bourbon about four that morning and had flung the empty bottle into the dark, murky waters of Lake Katogoula. Now he watched through bleary eyes the first eruptions of dawn set molten purple-and-orange fire to the clouds above the trees on the eastern shore.

Boy, a good cup of strong brew sure would clear the bats from his brain! He hadn't seen his old, dented thermos for years; besides, domestic tedium like making a pot of coffee in advance wasn't his style. Woman's work, that was.

Probably best he didn't have any. The deer he stalked would smell the swirling, pungent, delicious cloud of coffee steam and would leap away into the thicket.

Carl took a few gulps from his water canteen. A piss-poor substitute for coffee. Quietly, very quietly, he spit a mouthful out. He knew this deer had hearing even better than its sense of smell. It was a big one, a survivor. Survivors don't get that way by being stupid, by letting their guard down.

Some hunters covered their noisiest gear in camouflage felt. Not Carl. An Indian hunter knew how to be quiet when necessary, without fancy precautions.

Indian, my ass! He shook his head ruefully at his own delusions, delusions he'd used to hold together his wasted life of gloomy reclusiveness, rabid substance abuse, and undirected rage.

The question of which part of him was Katogoula, which part white, Carl had never been able to resolve. He had long before given up the effort to arrange a truce in his warring soul, erecting instead a stockade of bitterness around his confusion of identity. At certain times he hated the white man within him for his cutthroat cultural victory; at others, he despised his Katogoula heritage for allowing itself to be so shamefully defeated.

Carl sat concealed in the blind he'd fashioned close to the deer tracks leading to the water's edge. He'd stuck cattail, palmetto, and long grasses in the mud around a clumping of cypress knees, which had served as a pleasant enough backrest during the dark, drizzly hours he'd already waited. Using the same itchy materials, he'd festooned his clothing to break up his human form, as if he were awaiting communion with some guardian spirit bird—the kind of superstitious crap he thought he'd outgrown. Deer don't see colors the way humans do, but shapes that stand out as unusual can send them running, even in moonlight. Carl's forest sense had not abandoned him.

Carl pictured what he hoped would happen.... The deer would cautiously emerge from the stand of willows and cottonwoods, and step out onto the buff-colored mixture of clay and mud that sloped into the lake. He would saunter right by him, muscles twitching, tail erect in alertness, rack of antlers poised for challenge. He would lower his proud and graceful neck for a long drink from the lapping lake water and, eventually, turn back toward the thick woods, where he bedded down before resuming his own hunt for does, this being prime rutting season hereabouts. And as the buck drank, Carl would strike, sending an arrow through the great unsuspecting beast's heart.

"Come drink, my friend!" Carl said. "I been hunting you for near a week. Ain't no way around it: one of us gotta die this morning."

A hunter showed respect for the prey by putting himself in danger. Carl considered it an insult to an animal to kill it from hundreds of yards away. He remembered several close calls when wounded deer had charged him in their death throes and almost gored him with their sharp antlers. He'd won those battles and hung the racks outside his ramshackle cabin on stilts over his slope-tail travel trailer, which he'd acquired from a junkyard six years before for the price of a totaled Harley-Davidson motorcycle.

His personal fort was on his brother Tommy's land. Just let that wimp try to throw him off!

Carl was the bad seed of the Shawe family, everyone had always said. The accepted opinion around Three Sisters Pantry was that his parents died of grief and shame after he went to prison the first time for repeated, flagrant out-of-season hunting, and selling of game. That was before Nooj took over as the area Louisiana Wildlife & Fisheries agent.

Carl had no use for laws and those who enforced them, but he and Nooj had a deal. Nooj—Nugent Chenerie—was from these parts. He had more Indian in him than many of the old folks; looked Indian, too, much more so than the twins Carl and Tommy. Nooj often sat and drank beer with Carl, amid Carl's hoard of scavenged possessions and hand-lettered "NO TRESPASAN" signs.

When he was assigned to this district a few years back, Nooj flat out told him, "Carl, I don't mind you taking what you need, but don't be letting those white fat cats you guide break the rules. Or we'll have everybody and his cousin in here thinking they can take advantage of us. Like in Mexico, with the white-wing dove. Those greedy bastards'll shoot till there's no ducks left, and then spit and leave, the way the oilmen and the lumbermen always done us. Carl, they'll ruin our lake, forever."

Carl had stuck to the agreement. It was turning out to be a cozy understanding of winks and nods. Just keep his hunters in line, and Carl could go a little over the limit on mallards or pintails, take a deer every now and then when the calendar said no. Which was why the rich bastards kept using him.... Nevertheless, today he would use his bow. No sense asking for trouble with a gunshot.

Besides, using his bow just felt right; more natural, more attuned to something that defied translation, but which he knew to be his Katogoula inheritance: a way of living, thousands of years old, that like instinct had passed to him without the need for words and lessons.

Like the way he *understood* how to make a pirogue by hand, burning away the cavity in a cypress log and then chipping it out perfectly with an ax; he would never auger it for thickness, the way the Cajuns fashioned their version of the traditional Louisiana canoe. Once, when some LSU archaeology students were hanging around asking damn fool questions and snapping pictures, one of them noticed him making a gourd scoop, with the circular cutting motion he had always used. She asked him why circular, and he couldn't answer her.

He made a little money when those college folks came up here, showing them around the woods. He rather enjoyed being a curiosity.

Carl went out of his way to appear slightly crazy, but he knew he wasn't. It suited him that most people walked to the other side of the street when they saw him coming. Yet he was sane enough to know that truth doesn't always speak with a human voice.

He crafted his own bows and arrows, too, using the old methods, and arrowheads that were all over the forest floor, like fruit just for the picking—though the archaeologists raised hell with him for disturbing sites. Hell, everywhere was a site around here! Sometimes he did make his own arrowheads, patiently chipping away at a native stone or a piece of obsidian he'd stolen from some shop, until it was sharp enough to cut paper. That was tough work, but he felt good about it afterward, somehow complete and cleansed.

Carl couldn't help feeling, in spite of his determined skepticism, that a spirit directed his movements; he couldn't explain what happened if he wanted to.

The bow beside him today was his favorite, made from Osage orange, what most local Indians tribes preferred in their heyday. The outside of it he'd covered in baby alligator hide. He'd sold a few bows to the fat cats to put on their walls, but that was too much like real work for his taste, too close to being a pitiful living anthropological display. You'd never catch *him* demonstrating Katogoula handicrafts at malls for city housewives and their bratty kids.

Boy, could he use some hot coffee! The front that had just passed through without dropping much rain had dropped the temperature to forty-five degrees. Carl was shivering now, even under his quilted, ragged camouflage hunting coat.

Aw, quit your whining. You sound like one of them old men hanging around Three Sisters Pantry.

He started thinking about the deer again. It had looked like a fresh bed up there in the woods, in that tangle of honeysuckle and briars, the grass pressed down, the droppings. All the right signs. But maybe he was wrong; maybe this deer wasn't coming back after a night of feeding.

Towering over him, moss-draped cypress trees caught the coppery blaze of the sun, which was still a few minutes below the horizon. With the first really good extended cold snap, those cypresses would turn rusty red.

His mind began to wander now. Maybe he was dreaming. He wasn't sure. *You're thirty-six, Carl,* he thought, *through drooping eyelids; a real no-count in this white man's world. You were born a few centuries too late.*

But hell, he wasn't such a bad guy. At least he wasn't into killing human beings, like those Mexican and Mafia badasses who ran drugs up and down the pitted parish roads to avoid the interstates. He'd hidden in the woods many a time, watching them transfer the stuff to little Cessnas and Pipers that had put down on makeshift airstrips in Tchekalaya Forest.

Oh, yes, he knew lots of things he shouldn't. He knew for a fact Wooty Tadbull was in on it. Wooty had gotten a big head, nowadays thought he was better than everybody else, what with his fancy clothes, fast women and cars, and Tadbull money—though people said they didn't have as much of that as they used to. Carl and his twin brother, Tommy, had been pretty close to Wooty years ago. But damn, whatever you thought about him, that Wooty could sure hold his own in the woods, for a white boy.

Carl himself didn't mess with drugs anymore. Budweiser and bourbon were all he needed now; cheaper, too. He sighed groggily at the absence of those two liquids, as well.

He really didn't give a damn what people said about him, he'd long ago decided. Just let him hunt whenever and however he pleased, scrounge up enough cash for food and booze and a piece of ass now and again with a favorite whore, and they could say whatever the hell they wanted. Even Tommy, his brother.

Now, Tommy…there was a real chump! Worked hard all his life and what does he get? Kicked out of the only job he ever had, thrown out on his butt without so much as a "sorry" by them Tadbulls. Serves the self-satisfied bastard right. He and Tommy might look alike—Carl never did agree that they did, and everyone called him the "crazy twin," with his long pony-tail, scraggly beard, and bloodshot blue eyes an old girlfriend had dubbed "raper's eyes"—they might look alike, slightly, but they were world's away in attitude.

Carl wasn't into this tribal thing. Just play-acting, in his opinion, those meetings the "tribe" held in the spring and fall at Three Sisters Pantry. Family reunions, is what they were; and the "business" transacted there was mostly gossip. He didn't bother to attend.

He'd heard about the federal tribal recognition; everybody had by nightfall. Another big joke. He didn't believe for a moment that the powers-that-be had all of a sudden turned benevolent. Somebody was going to get screwed. The fat cats would triumph in the end, at the expense of chumps like his brother, Tommy. The past was dead and buried; everything had changed and there was no changing things back.

But at this moment, the past *was* alive for Carl....

◻

It was nighttime, many years before. He and Tommy were with their mother's father at the brush arbor they used on their summer hunting trips. The twins were still in the Katogoula grade school, just a spare room in a teacher's house, because they weren't allowed in the white public schools—this was before anybody in Louisiana had to pay serious attention to Brown vs. Board of Education. Fortunately, Katogoula kids had never been considered Indian enough to be shipped off to some government Indian boarding school, where the guiding principle was traditionally "kill the Indian, save the man." And they couldn't afford Catholic private schooling. Their grandfather, at least, was happy with this muddled state of educational affairs: he didn't want his grandchildren learning the ways of the white man first. It was he who celebrated with the boys when each killed his first deer, smearing their faces with the deer's hot blood dripping from the arrowhead.

On this night Grandfather was telling a story. He told wonderful stories. Carl and Tommy—at this point in their lives looking very much alike—lay on blankets around a small fire. Grandfather began to tell them about the Sacred Cougar, in more detail than they'd ever heard before.

The tribe had come here, Grandfather related, from what the whites call today Alabama and Mississippi, after being uprooted by a more powerful tribe, centuries before the Europeans arrived. They had even forgotten their tribe's name and language, so long had their wanderings been. But the stories the tellers told kept the essential memories alive.

They had roamed aimlessly for decades through alien lands, until they came to a beautiful calm lake that reminded them of their lost homeland. Their chief and his best warriors went ahead to scout out the lake and the land around it.

And then the advance party saw a cougar on the far shore, walking toward them from the rising sun. The cougar had just killed a big deer, a buck, and seemed to be dragging it somewhere to eat. The cat walked onto the surface of the dark glassy lake. Yes! He walked across the lake and did not sink into the water. And then he dropped the deer at the feet of the astonished scouting party, turned, and walked back the way he had come.

The chief declared that this was a place of plenty, blessed by the Sacred Cougar, which had, through its offering, invited the wanderers to make a new home here. And in a new language that sprouted at that moment, all at once, in their minds like corn from sacred seeds, the tribe began to call itself the Katogoula, or "people of the sacred big cat."

◻

Carl had dozed off, his back to a cypress knee, facing the woods. He awoke now, stiff and hungry. A cold northwesterly wind had blown up countless small crests on the lake, changing its color from black to pewter.

"Kapasa yako netak," he muttered. Then he laughed. "It's cold today," he had said. It surprised him that he remembered so much of the old language, enough to originate a thought in it, without translation first from English. He must still mentally be with his grandfather, under that brush arbor, so many years ago. "Too damn cold for me," he said, in English.

To hell with that deer! He'd probably missed it anyway while he slept; if not, this weather's got him too spooked to leave the safety of the heavy brush. He reached for his bow and deerskin quiver and started to get up.

At his back, something came between him and the sun, between him and the lake. Had the deer sneaked behind him? He felt its presence before he saw the branching shadow on the muddy clay in front of him.

For an instant he thought it was the huge rack of antlers atop the monster buck's head.

But something else cast that branching shadow, something Carl struggled to remember from his childhood.

Pivoting on his left arm, he got his legs under him in a squat and turned toward the lake, feeling another cypress knee behind him. He brought his right hand up to blot out the blinding early morning sun streaming through his inadequate shield of fingers.

He froze in fear. Silhouetted by the inferno of the sun, the Sacred Cougar of Katogoula legend loomed over him, ready to pounce!

Carl yanked his right hand down to the handle of the hunting knife in the scabbard on his belt, but sharp death plunged into his neck before he had a fighting chance.

Chapter 6

The Twins of the Forest
A Katogoula Sacred Story

 A Maiden journeyed from the Sleeping Moon to the Land of the People of the Sacred Cougar. Her hair was a great black river with shining white rapids; her teeth were pearls; and her eyes shone like stars in the winter night. She was naked and beautiful and unafraid, for strife and shame were not known yet. There was no cold and no hunger, no pain and no sorrow.
 A handsome Warrior appeared from the smoke of the sky. His eyes were like falling hail in hot summer, his sweet breath like the morning wind through the Golden Trace at the Awakening Sun, his speech like distant thunder, his speed a sailing, sharp spear from the atlatl.
 The woman and the man lay together in the Forest. And from the place where the pine straw cushioned them sprang two twin plants, in the shape of men: The Twins of the Forest
 The Twins of the Forest sang to all the animals, beckoning them to gather and to eat of their arms and legs and heads.
 But only two raccoons ate of the plants, and then there was no more. One raccoon learned the secrets of healing and of birth and of making dance for the gods and of planting the Three Sisters; this one lives in the daylight. The other raccoon learned to kill; this one hides in the trees of darkness. Both were unhappy with their knowledge, envying the other. When one sleeps, the other tries to steal his stripes.
 And if they meet when awake, the Chief of the People must slay one of them.

Thus came Life and Peace, and Death and War into the World, from the Twins of the Forest.

Chapter 7

"I won! I won!" exclaimed the woman who had ridden a sleek deluxe tour bus from Texas to gamble at Bayou Luck Casino in Grosse Jambe, Louisiana.

She set her drink down and clasped her trembling hands together.

"Thank you, Lord, I won!" she said, to some indefinite point in space above her. Then she raised her arms and did a little circular tap dance as she shouted, "Sue Ann! *Sue Ann! I won!*"

Her friend, nine slot machines away, leaned out of the row of gamblers' hunched backs, waved, and gave a thumbs-up sign, but soon returned her undivided attention to the mesmerizing mechanism before her.

"I'm so excited I hope I don't wet my pants!" the woman tearfully confided to a man slumped on the chair beside her.

The wrinkled, cadaverous man gave her a cockeyed scowl through the smoke streaming up from a cigarette stuck in his colorless, thin lips. Without comment he grimly returned to pumping the arm of his own stingy machine.

Quarters still clinked rhythmically into the chrome lip of the fortunate woman's slot machine, as if they would never stop—a mere trickle of the great river of crime-tainted currency that had flowed through the fingers of losers throughout the country, to settle like contaminated sludge here, in the small town that Bayou Luck Casino, the most successful Indian gaming enterprise in the South, had put on the map.

Nick Herald watched the bedazzled woman scoop quarters into her plastic coin cup. He pegged her as a mid-level office worker, a smart shopper at factory outlet malls, on a short holiday from her job, kids, and husband. And cats, lots of cats.

Have fun, lady; the rest of us are paying for your luck.

Personally, he could live without gambling, and any other situation that put him at the mercy of rigged rules. Only a sap thinks he deserves a fair shake in a casino—or in a college English department, for that matter. His days as a sap were over. He'd decided that Ben Jonson, the literary lion of seventeenth-century England, had it right: life is a big con, and the greatest rogue wins.

And yet, look at that ecstatic woman over there, he told himself. At this moment he understood what the addicted gambler must feel: a free-floating optimism, as irresistible as lust or adrenaline, that quickens the heart and clouds the vision.

A few more hands of blackjack couldn't hurt. His number was bound to come up sooner or later, wasn't it?

The casino interior conceded nothing in gaudiness or size to its models on the famous Strip in Nevada. In spite of his innate scorn for what he'd always considered a front for organized crime, Nick was just a bit awed by the casino's theme-park, over-the-top version of self-indulgent, fake Edwardian luxury. A few stylized American Indian touches hid in the background here and there, but the decoration was not intended as a history lesson. Mirrored ceilings and walls made it difficult for Nick to tell where the dim, hazy, glitzy reality ended and the illusion of good times began. Massive chandeliers dangling countless strands of tiny lights dwarfed players, tables, and machines. The multi-level room seemed to have no physical limits.

"Busted!" Nick said and slapped down his cards. He watched the dealer smoothly sweep away his chips. She was good, too good. Gritting his teeth, he pushed a few more chips forward for yet another hand.

Like zombies, men and women clutching their coin cups, narcotized by the syncopating lights and the ceaseless, almost subliminal music, drifted amid the long rows of slot machines and clusters of gaming tables and open-air bars and cafés. Nick simultaneously admired and resented the subtlety of the deception: lull gamblers into a mental zone in which they freely traded their individual will to become suckers in a shell game that allowed them an infinitesimal chance at phenomenal wealth. Today, he was just another unlucky sucker.

A Vegas gambling mega-corporation, Luck o' the Draw, was the managing minority partner of the Chitiko-Tiloasha tribe's Bayou Luck Casino. A first-class place, the pleased, but fleeced, patrons left saying.

It was Tuesday afternoon, two weeks after the peculiar death of Carl Shawe. Outside, a cool, moist breeze from the Gulf of Mexico and the marsh blew north across the prairies of southwestern Louisiana. Acadiana it was called, fabled as the refuge of the ethnically cleansed French of Nova Scotia, the Acadiennes, or Cajuns.

The Chitiko-Tiloasha tribe had been here for at least half a millennium before 1757, when the first verified sizable group of Cajuns arrived.

In modern times, sugar cane, then rice, then oil had each reigned as king of this flat, ancient Mississippi River floodplain; but only a few powerful families had prospered from any of these enterprises. For centuries, the Cajuns had been reviled as backward interlopers, and the Indians had been hounded for being in the right place at the wrong time. Lately, the Cajuns had witnessed an about-face in their fortunes: they were the darlings of Louisiana's tourism industry, and anything with Cajun attached to it was an instant success. Now it was the turn of the Chitiko-Tiloasha Indians, who, armed with an arcane tomahawk of federal law, had established a new kingdom of interlocking corporations and gambling wealth.

Each month, thousands of people traveled the interstate highways across the few miles from Texas or made the longer journey from

Mississippi and Arkansas, to throw their money into the tax-exempt casino's coffers. These gamblers were Middle Americans, not the standard Vegas habitués—gold-bedecked lounge lizards, gaudy women on the make, or overweight conventioneers on expense accounts looking for a faceless lay. The Chitiko-Tiloasha had succeeded in making a day at their casino as wholesome as a trip to the mall.

The buzz in the gambling industry was that Bayou Luck raked in more cash than many of the bigger and older casinos in Las Vegas—but nobody knew for sure because the tribe's enterprises were legally shielded from complete public scrutiny.

Tommy Shawe had asked Nick to meet him here, roughly midway between Cutpine and New Orleans, on the Chitiko-Tiloasha reservation, twenty miles southwest of Lafayette.

The Chitiko-Tiloasha had received federal recognition in the thirties. For decades, nothing much changed for the tribe: life continued to be a meager, isolated affair in the teeming marshland, on and near Bayou Grosse Jambe. Subsistence fishing, trapping, and farming remained the major means of support. They wanted it that way. To fight prevailing bigotry, the tribe even more resolutely turned its back on the white economy and the twentieth century. Their small reservation, hemmed in by new cities and highways, went begging for residents. Stagnation followed. The young ones of the tribe, seeing the empty future, fled their decaying heritage.

Things had changed dramatically in the last dozen years, and Bayou Luck Casino was both symbol and agent of the tribe's resurgent vitality.

回

"So you're a gambler?" Tommy Shawe asked Nick. "You look like you know what you're doing."

Tommy stood at the side of Nick's chair, intently following the flow of the game.

"Everyday's a gamble, when you live in New Orleans," Nick said, peeking at his hidden card on the green baize of the blackjack table as other players received their cards. "Really, I'm no good at this. Blackjack's the only game I'm comfortable with. Usually I try to stay out of casinos altogether. To paraphrase W. C. Fields, it's not a game of chance the way *they* play it. I lose every time." He'd made sure the dealer heard his half-joking barb.

Tommy put his hands in his pockets and looked down at the carpet.

Whoops. Wrong thing to say.

Nick had really stuck his foot in his mouth; the last thing the guy needed was the tribe's newly hired genealogist talking down casinos and gambling—which would soon no doubt be paying his fee. And, of course, it couldn't have been pleasant to have a brother killed, and then to be questioned by the local sheriff as, if not a declared suspect, a "person of interest," in the way cops put it, so diplomatically and falsely.

Nick had heard about the peculiar murder of Tommy's brother, Carl, from Chief Claude, before Tommy arrived at the casino.

No wonder he's touchier than a moody teenager.

Nick's dealer was a young woman with gingerbread skin and jet black hair in bangs. He'd been flirting with her and was under the delusion that he was making some progress.

"Maybe you should think of this as charity, not gambling," she said. "Don't you like helping out a worthy cause?" She dealt cards around the table with beautiful fluid movements, keeping her hands visible for the surveillance cameras hidden in tinted hemispheres on the ceiling and for the stern Vegas pit bosses cruising the aisles. "We're just one big happy family here, sir."

"If you say so," Nick replied. "But I've never had a relative pick my pocket before. Hit me."

Busted again, over twenty-one.

Chief Claude had given him a twenty-five dollar credit; within an hour he'd lost that and twenty of his own. Now nearly out of chips, he was more eager than ever to tackle the job he'd been hired to do: helping Tommy's tribe sort out the dozens of requests for enrollment that were coming in as a result of the federal recognition. Lots of people wanted a seat on the gravy train.

Proving individual Indian descent was one thing, difficult enough even in the most clear-cut cases; but proving the heritage of a whole tribe of individuals whose collective history had been mostly forgotten...

Well, we're talking BIG genealogical bucks.

The thought brought a slight smile to Nick's face, despite his losses. Since he was going to be rolling in cash soon, he blithely shoved the last of his chips forward.

The dealer gave Nick a queen on top and a ten face down, "in the hole." A strong hand—twenty. He motioned that he would stand with these. She had a six of hearts showing. When she flipped her hole card, Nick saw a ten of hearts.

"Dealer must draw." She dealt herself a five of hearts. "Twenty-one," she said with chirpy dispassion. She collected Nick's chips.

"Great," Nick said, disgusted. He hopped off his chair. "Tommy, pull me away from her table right now, before I lose any more and have to start calling my losses expenses."

He waved at the pretty dealer. She smiled back, still dealing. Maybe another heart awaited him in a different kind of game.

"Chief Claude's office is this way," Tommy said.

"Yeah, I know where it is. I should have been there fifty dollars ago."

回

Tribal Council Chairman Rafe Claude's quiet office was a welcome haven from the low-level but nerve-racking pinging and dinging that was the sound of millions being made every hour.

Chief Claude had thrown lots of genealogical projects Nick's way, mainly research for individuals wishing to enroll in the Chitiko-Tiloasha tribe. Two hours earlier, over lunch in his office, the chief had told Nick, "Carl Shawe didn't die in a hunting accident, like people thought at first. Sheriff Higbee says it was murder, and a real strange one at that." Tommy had been found wandering delirious in the forest near the crime scene. All he claimed to vaguely remember was being hit by a blowgun dart. The murder weapon was apparently an atlatl—a spear thrower used in ancient times by many American Indian tribes. And the atlatl had belonged to Tommy; he had confirmed that damning fact, even though he couldn't explain it.

Now the three men sat at the round conference table where Nick and the chief had eaten their corned-beef sandwiches. Pictures of Chief Claude with Louisiana governors and other officials vied for wall space with paintings and drawings of Chitiko-Tiloasha life and history.

The chief had served twice as commissioner of the state Office of Indian Affairs, but he still looked like the man who had spent most of his sixty-four years on the bayous and the marsh of South Louisiana. He was short, stocky, and bowlegged, with tobacco-colored, leathery skin and just enough white hair to form a long ducktail. His facial features were fleshy and elongated, typical of many Chitiko-Tiloasha. He wore a dark-gray three-piece polyester suit, and a bolo tie with a handsome silver-and-turquoise clasp, a sixtieth birthday gift from the tribe. Medallions of beadwork decorated his cowboy boots.

Splendid examples of traditional tribal crafts, some ancient, some modern, lay on tables and shelves and the chief's desk, accessible to curious hands. Chief Claude encouraged this kind of direct contact with his tribe's past. The office was clearly not a personal preserve, but that revered term in the modern Indian lexicon, a public trust.

Chief Claude had told Nick once, "The knowledge of our past is more fragile than these relics. We are not them, but they are us. I want them to be handled, as long as it brings one person closer to our past. If we lose one now and again, so it goes; if we lose the knowledge, we are truly dead."

A young, pimply waiter with glittering braces on his teeth distributed coffee from a tray.

The chief said to his two guests, "Stu, here, is over at USL studying to be an engineer."

"UL at Lafayette, Chief Claude," Stu corrected.

"That's right. UL Lafayette…I'll never get used to that. We're awful proud of Stu." As if grading him, the chief eyed the obviously embarrassed Stu. "Thank you, son."

When the young man had gone, the chief continued. "He'll come back to the tribe with new skills this casino paid for. Because there's something for him to come back to. Today, gambling is our buffalo; it provides for us in many ways. And now it's the Katogoula's turn to join us."

"Chief Claude says Indian gaming accounts for almost ten percent of gaming revenue in the U.S.," Tommy said. "We want to get in on the party before someone yanks away the punchbowl."

"Your casino's going to put us over ten percent," said the chief with complete conviction. "Since the great victory we won in 1988, with the Indian Gaming Regulatory Act, the white man has tried to take even our gambling away from us. Just another treaty to break." Chief Claude sipped his coffee, shaking his head as if in disappointment at a friend who had double-crossed him once too often.

He continued: "Most states are at war with us over reservation gambling. They talk about 'states rights' and 'devolution.'" He gave a wise old grin. "Greed, that's what it is. Now some in Congress are scheming to ambush us, kill the spirit of the IGRA. And the Supreme Court decision against suing states that don't make compacts with us hurt, too. See, they all want to get at our tax exemption somehow, they want those tax dollars. Well, I tell them, every dollar we make is taxed 100%—by us! We're a sovereign nation and decide how to help our people with our money."

Federal law stipulated that tribal income earned from reservation sources could not be taxed; individual Indians paid income tax, like all Americans, but most reservation-derived income was exempted, with the exception of per-capita distributions of casino profits, a big gray area that cloaked constant experimentation—critics called it questionable accounting—by tribes partnered with non-Indian casino companies.

Chief Claude was one of the first American Indians to realize the potential of the tribal-tax-exemption loophole when combined with the landmark 1988 legislation, which required states to negotiate the issue of reservation gambling. In succeeding years, he led his tribe from small-time weekend bingo to big-league casino profits.

"My genealogist friend here," Chief Claude said, "is one of our great weapons against the envy of the white man. He helps us in our rebirth. We call Nick the Midwife-of-Yesterday Man."

Nick had never been overly fond of the title. But in spite of the slight revulsion he felt at being the midwife of anything—the sight of blood made him queasy—as a former teacher of literature he admired the chief's evocative style.

Tommy had lapsed into a reverie over his coffee cup. He shifted in his chair and sat up straighter. "Chief Claude—"

"'Chief' implies power that's hereditary or oligarchic," the older man interrupted. Nick knew him to be unflappable, sometimes irritatingly dogmatic and didactic, but good natured in even the hottest debate. "These days we're democratic. I'm elected, and any adult can be. Your tribe ought to be set up the same way, like a business with a board of directors accountable to the stakeholders. People are supposed to call me 'chairman,' but nobody does."

Nick said, "It's a sign of respect, Chief."

"Respect, my foot!" the chief exclaimed. "You ought to sit in at one of our council meetings."

The three men laughed.

"As far as your business analogy goes," Nick said, "the titles 'chairman' and 'CEO' have become synonymous with 'crook' in my mind. Every time I look at my IRA statement, I feel less like a stakeholder and more like a 'shameholder'! You might want to stick with 'chief,' after all."

This amiable interlude seemed to help Tommy vocalize what was on his mind.

"It's all sort of overwhelming," he said. "I mean, I've worked in a lumber mill all my life, and now I'm supposed to be, well, the chairman. How do I get started? I'm not really sure we *are* a tribe, now that the government says we're one. Some of my people are having second thoughts. They're saying recognition isn't a good thing. Especially since my brother was"—he looked down at his work-toughened hands—"since Carl died. I've had some requests to get our congressmen to reverse the recognition bill. Most of us didn't even know about the old pending application."

Chief Claude grinned at Nick. "We Louisiana Indians are a superstitious bunch. You mix the old Indian ways with Catholicism, see what you get? A mighty jumpy critter, that's for sure. They had a meeting, Nick. It was a slim margin to go on with establishing a proper tribe and start looking into building a casino."

"Irton and Grace Dusong broke the tie," said Tommy.

"That close, was it? I remember good old Irton from Korea. Nick, we used one of our ancient languages, *Yama*—the Mobilian Jargon, you whites call it. Used it to talk in code over the radio, like the Navaho Marine Code Talkers of World War II. Except we never got as good a press as they did. Maybe you can write up one of your articles on us." A twinkle in his eyes, he turned to Tommy. "How'd you vote, son?"

"For, of course," Tommy stated, slightly offended. "But my wife, she voted against. Brianne's kind of a headstrong girl, worries about what gambling will teach our kids about life."

"They should learn from all of this," Chief Claude said, "that fighting a bear needs a trick or two."

Nick hoped Tommy was only momentarily dispirited; he felt yet another handsome paycheck slipping away. "I've heard of tribes being terminated by the government—the Miami of Indiana, the Menominee of Wisconsin, dozens of tribes in the fifties and sixties."

"The Menominee got it back, though," Chief Claude interjected.

"Right. Nineteen seventy-three, I believe it was," Nick confirmed, silently admiring the chief's depth of knowledge about Indian matters. "But I've never heard of a tribe refusing recognition. Does recognition have to mean a casino? If it were my tribe, I'd take the BIA assistance money and run, and worry about the casino issue later."

"You have good people on your side," the chief said to Tommy. "It will all fall into place. Some of us Chitiko-Tiloasha were afraid, too, at first. Now, as far as being an Indian, if you think you are, that's a big first step. The Census Bureau says that anyone who asserts they're an Indian, is an Indian. But to get into a tribe, or to form one, you got to prove it to the BIA. Y'all got lucky; that limited research your daddy commissioned didn't tip the scale. No, I believe somebody pulled strings up in Washington."

"Do you know who?" asked Tommy.

"No, not even with all my connections. These politicians can hide inside their legislation or get out front when it suits 'em. You'll find out, I guarantee," answered the chief. "He'll hit you up for a big contribution to his reelection campaign, his party, and his favorite think tank. Could be a her, for that matter. That's how they do. Anyway, I wanted to be in on this first meeting to help you and Nick get acquainted, since I recommended him. He's proven the lineages of many of our tribe members.

Once he gets going, you won't need me anymore. But I'll be here, all the same."

"I guess I'd better ask you, then, Nick," Tommy said. "What do I do first?"

Nick said, "The classic approach is to start with the known, Tommy, your own family, and follow the line back. Once you've done that, you move on to the others who've remained in the traditional tribal group. One important thing is to begin getting the testimony of the oldest tribe members, to learn what they remember."

"Six families I know of go pretty far back," Tommy said. "They all hid out in the forest during the Removals. I can start with the elders of those. The ones that are left."

"Meanwhile, I'll tackle the written records," Nick said. "I'd like to review the documents from the previous effort to get recognized."

Tommy cleared his throat. "I did have them. They're...missing. We think somebody got into a closet out in my garage. Stole some other stuff, too."

"I'll check with the BIA acknowledgment branch," Nick said, making a note. "Maybe they can send me copies of what's on file, though they always tell me they're swamped by recognition cases and legislative mandates. You've had a rough time of it, lately. Does the theft of the records have anything to do with the death of your brother?"

"I don't know," Tommy said. "Some say that all that important stuff going missing is another sign recognition is going to cause us more grief than it's worth." He pushed his cold coffee away. "Look, if you don't mind, let's stick to the genealogy. How long will it take? I mean for all the Cutpine folks to be enrolled. We have thirty-five families, twenty-three with men who lost their jobs when the sawmill closed. When the BIA payments start, I want everybody to get their share as soon as possible. Maybe that'll change some minds about recognition. We all got doctors' bills to pay, house notes, car notes...this is real tough on us."

Tommy had recently been informed, by way of an onslaught of paperwork, that the federal government provided assistance payments to needy Indians. And, it turned out, some of Tchekalaya Forest was tribal land still held in trust by the United States, a bizarre arrangement lately discovered to be riddled by bureaucratic mismanagement and political manipulation dating back to the late nineteenth century. As a result of the recent recognition and the subsequent discovery of a dusty packet of apparently authentic documentation, the Katogoula were in line to receive accumulated logging and natural-gas revenues. No one was sure yet how much was forthcoming. And the divvying up of the proceeds all depended on who was in, and who was out, of the tribe.

"You got to get off on the right foot with a system, son," the chief advised. "Today the government allows you a lot of freedom to say who's Katogoula and who's not. But even so, you're going to find that some of those families won't qualify. Either they should belong to another tribe, or they're just plain wrong about having any Indian heritage. I know from experience, it's a painful thing....You need a Katogoula system, not anybody else's, so there's no room for favors and abuse—or anger. Nick will help you with the blood-quantum technicalities."

"What's the deal with that?" asked Tommy, frustration evident in his voice. "I been studying up on it, but...well, it's confusing."

"Simply put, blood quantum is the percentage of Indian ancestry in an individual," Nick said. "It's just a mathematical result. But political and emotional elements are even more important and need to be factored into the equation. Requirements vary from tribe to tribe; by and large, it's their call."

"25 CFR Part 83," Chief Claude said. "That's the code of federal regulations dealing with tribal acknowledgment. The BIA works with this authority and uses seven mandatory criteria to decide what teams are in the league. But—and this is an important 'but'—the tribes pick the players."

"Good analogy, Chief," Nick observed. "The Ute Mountain Ute of Colorado require a blood quantum of five-eighths; but the Cherokee Nation of Oklahoma requires descent from any person named on the 1906 Dawes Commission roll. Today, with all the casino development, blood quantum is hot topic."

"And a hornets' nest," Tommy said, "from what I been reading on the Internet."

"Exactly," Nick agreed. "The controversy is causing the Indian community to turn on itself. Some tribes hate the idea as the government's patient, sneaky plan for ultimate Indian assimilation. Other tribes use it as bureaucratically approved racism to keep rolls small and gambling payments large."

"This man speaks his mind," Chief Claude commented with a chuckle. "No offense taken."

"None intended," Nick said. "Blood quantum for federal tribal recognition—which has already happened in the Katogoula's case—is different from blood-quantum enrollment issues at the tribal level. The BIA uses blood quantum to establish the 'purity' of some base tribal roll or petitioning group. Personally, I think you're spinning your wheels if you go to the BIA these days for initial recognition with a tribal blood quantum of less than one fourth. But the old one-quarter rule for individual enrollment in an established tribe seems to have fallen by the wayside. There have been successful court challenges and some tribes have unilaterally lowered blood-quantum requirements; some have done away with it altogether. The BIA still has tremendous authority on what tribes get recognized, and it still has the power of the CDIB—"

"The what?" Tommy asked.

"Certificate of Degree of Indian Blood" Nick said. "But now tribes seem to have the upper hand in deciding who can be a member."

"Won't be so easy for us Katogoula," Tommy said, "deciding on membership rules and blood quantum and all. Nobody ever took a census of our tribe, that I ever heard of. The tribal leaders refused to cooperate with the white officials, didn't trust them on anything. I want every Katogoula to benefit, no matter what his CDIB might say."

Chief Claude spoke now: "The BIA, over the years, has created a monster of crazy regulations. People don't fit in boxes on a piece of paper; we aren't horses you buy or sell based on our bloodlines. Sometimes the confusion looks like bad faith or worse, but in general these BIA folks mean well. Lot of times, they're Indians, like us. I want to tell you a story, Tommy. You know of the Jena Choctaw?"

The chief was referring to another central Louisiana tribe, which had fought a long battle for recognition.

"Sort of," Tommy said. "I think they got recognition not long ago, didn't they?"

Chief Claude nodded. "In 1901, the government told the Jena Choctaw they maybe could have land in Oklahoma, Indian Territory. A group went on up there to meet with a federal commission, but they came back two years later without any agreement. Then the government up and tells them, yes, they do qualify for land, no doubt about it; but they got to go back to Oklahoma. They said forget it and stayed. About sixteen years ago, they made a formal application for recognition, and it was approved in '95. How you like that story? Almost a hundred years jumping through the government's hoops. This blood quantum rule was another sneak attack by the white man: he knew that scattering us would weaken us, that intermarriage with whites and blacks and whatnot would one day make the Indian blood just a drop in a big lake."

"I guess history answers a lot of questions," Tommy said.

"That's my job in a nutshell." Nick placed several sheets of paper on the table. "Have a look. I've come up with some suggestions for qualification of applicants. You start fairly wide and after a generation, narrow it a bit to a one-parent descendancy requirement, to ensure commitment to the tribe without harping on blood quantum."

Chief Claude excused himself, allowing Nick and Tommy a good hour of work.

◙

Later, as Nick stuffed his papers into his battered soft-sided leather briefcase, the chief returned.

"May the Great Spirit bless you and keep you out of New Orleans parking tickets," he said to Nick as he slapped him robustly on the back several times. The Chief had often heard Nick complaining about the city's draconian traffic-law enforcement.

"I almost forgot." Tommy dug in a pocket of his jeans. He pulled out a wad of cash. "Here's a small down payment, Nick. Three hundred dollars. I won five hundred on a scratch-off lottery ticket. Guess maybe I'm not all bad luck."

◙

Nick left the two men and walked into the secretary's smaller office. He looked back to see Chief Claude conducting Tommy around the room, pointing to the shelves crowded with artifacts, helping the younger man understand how to build a new identity for the Katogoula. He envied Tommy his opportunity and his courage. To few was it given to cross the impossible gap of years and mortality, to form, as much as is humanly possible, a living link with the past.

Faint sounds of the casino filtered down a hallway lined with photographs of big winners. Did he actually hear prehistoric chants and the pounding of drums emanating from the chief's office, mixing with the muted electronic tintinnabulation of the casino?...No, this was merely a figment of his rampant imagination.

I'm the bridge keeper.

Now, there was a title he could live with. He stood between two worlds, serving as the bridge keeper between white and Indian, between clock time and endless cycles, "modern" religion and ancient animism, between the individual bloodlines and the tribe. And he decided who crossed the millennia.

Seldom was so much at stake in his genealogical work, and he felt the responsibility as never before.

He took a deep breath that broke the spell.

"You okay, Mr. Herald?" the young Chitiko-Tiloasha woman asked. The monitor of her computer displayed spreadsheets thick with big numbers no doubt generated by the packed casino.

"Yeah, fine, Sally. Thanks." He found himself near a photo of a ceremony at the White House. "What was the occasion here?" he asked, trying to show he was not daydreaming but instead studying the photo.

"That was 1994. First time all federally recognized tribes were invited to the White House. Chief Claude's up front, because he's short. On the right of President Clinton."

Nick suspected it was the chief's skill in gaming the system that ensured his proximity to power.

"Sally, do you gamble?"

"Oh, no sir." She made a disapproving face at the foolish idea. "All *my* extra money goes into the tribe's retirement plan."

◻

Free drinks for gamblers was a Vegas trick to persuade people they were actually getting something for their money. Nick savored another cup of strong, delicious black coffee, trying not to think how much it had actually cost him. He'd decided to hazard just a few more dollars on the slots before hitting the highway back to New Orleans.

The last of twenty dollars' worth of quarters barely covered the bottom of his plastic change cup, which was festively decorated with cartoon alligators, armadillos, crawfish, and pelicans cavorting around the casino's slogan, "Big Luck on the Bayou!"

Nick had heard that high rollers were rewarded with free food, complimentary rooms at the adjoining hotel, and golf and tennis privileges on the courses and courts of this growing resort complex. He wondered if the perks—or comps, in industry parlance—included illicit sex, as was the reputed practice in some gambling Sodoms elsewhere in the country.

Nah, not here! he told himself. *This is a moral outfit, all for a good cause, untainted by the standard depravity of the industry!*

"May I get you some more coffee, Mr. Herald…or anything else?"

Nick looked up and saw a woman with lots of blonde hair swirling onto her shoulders. Early thirties, he supposed, attractive even under a showgirl's load of makeup. Her stunning blue eyes had an arctic brilliance. She worked for the casino, and not in an inconsequential capacity, Nick instantly sensed, from the penetrating appraisal she was giving him.

"No coffee, thanks, but you could explain to this machine that I'm a really nice guy who hasn't won a dime all day."

She gave him a warm, obviously practiced smile. Nick read her nametag: "Val, Management Team." Val wore a variation of the dealers' costume, though she looked anything but institutional: frilly white shirt with bow tie, tailored red blazer, tight black stylized riding pants, tall black boots.

A stripper on a foxhunt, was Nick's immediate impression.

Val propped one glossy boot on his chair. She leaned close. Her perfume, strong even from a distance, hit him like a sadist's kiss. He could hear the subtle jangling of her silver-and-rose quartz earrings—a product of the reservation's crafts business, Nick recalled. He'd seen them in the casino gift shop and had considered buying them for his French friend, Veronique—but, dreaming of piles of lucre, he'd chosen instead to gamble away his inchoate thoughtfulness.

"You're the genealogist I've heard Chief Claude speak so highly of, aren't you? Chief Claude's a sweetheart. A very—oh, I don't know—a very *proper* man." She waited a beat and then continued. "My company does business a little differently than the Indians. We're aggressive, and we usually get what we want. And if our partners don't like it, fuck them."

She seemed proud of her dirty brusqueness. "We'd like to do business with you, Mr. Herald."

"Sorry, but I don't see where I fit in."

"You'd be surprised just how easily you could…fit in." Her white teeth glittered viciously. "Our president is absolutely fascinated by genealogy," Val explained. "He's authorized me to hire you to work on his family history. Of course, he'll want *exclusive* access to your time. That would mean dropping any other projects that might interfere. All of them."

Nick stuck a quarter in his slot machine and pulled the handle.

"Projects, for instance, like helping the Katogoula get their families enrolled?" The slot windows whirled for a few seconds and then jolted to a stop on a lemon, an orange, and a bunch of cherries. He tried again. "Maybe I'll have better luck at their casino…if they're able to build one."

Her mane of golden ringlets tilted as she took in a new perspective of his face. "Luck o' the Draw International pays its contractors very well, Mr. Herald. *Very* well."

Nick's instinct for self-preservation shouted an alarm and rushed forward to shield him.

"Let me sleep on it, Val."

"That's the best offer I've had in a while."

"What I mean is, I'll get back to you, okay?" He, too, was a cardsharp in psychological games of deceit. Holding up a coin, he said, "This is my last quarter. After this one, I'm outta here."

She stopped him with a frigid hand on his wrist. Working in air-conditioning for hours on end will do that, but Nick was already convinced that Val had ice water for blood.

"This machine has been giving us some trouble," she said, releasing his wrist with a lingering, cold touch. "A few minor adjustments should make your visit more enjoyable."

She used a key attached to a security bracelet of coiled, plastic-coated green wire to open a panel on the side of the machine. A moment later she'd completed her adjustments.

"I'm in New Orleans all the time," she said. "We have a riverboat casino down there, the *Crescent Luck*. Maybe we could go out for dinner, or something." She slipped a card in his coat pocket. Her lips brushed his ear as she whispered, "I'd enjoy getting to know you *much* better, Nick. Especially since we'll be working together soon."

Nick dropped his quarter in the slot machine and pulled the handle. The wheels seemed to spin an unusually long time.

But what did he know about the mechanics of gambling, about odds and payoffs and mob connections, about the game Val was playing? His place was among dusty, mildewed archives, or in front of an archaic microfilm projector, attempting to match pieces of history for a genealogical jackpot. A scholarly hermit gets into trouble only when he leaves his monastic cell. Too many times in the past he'd forgotten this cardinal rule of his order.

The three wheels of symbols settled after much internal clanking and ticking. A trio of pots full of gold showed in the windows. Lights on the machine began to pulse, and a siren whooped. Other gamblers gathered, forming a small crowd, some patting Nick on the back, others grumbling about their own paltry payouts.

He looked around for Val, but she'd vanished like a light frost at sunrise.

Another casino functionary appeared, spoke into a walkie-talkie, and snapped Nick's picture.

"Congratulations, sir!" the young man said with a cheerleader's gushing good humor, pulling the photo from the camera and handing it to the flash-blinded Nick. "You just won *fifteen hundred dollars!*"

Chapter 8

Freret University graced an idyllic, verdant rectangle shoehorned into one of the most beautiful uptown areas of New Orleans, on the fringe of the Upper Garden District. Founded in 1839, Freret was a charter member of the ivy league of academically excellent Southern private colleges—or the "Kudzu League," as Nick and his friends used to say, substituting the creeping weed of the Deep South for the aristocratic ivy of the North.

Along with the fine education and high teacher-to-pupil ratio it offered, Freret also dished up a sanitized taste of the addictive decadence of New Orleans. For those who survived this expensive, protected bohemianism, a Freret diploma commanded great respect, and sometimes prompted salacious assumptions, on a résumé. Prospective employers were wont to view a Freret graduate as a cross between Marco Polo and Marquis de Sade, or Sally Ride and Janis Joplin, who had journeyed to a mysterious, magical, perverted kingdom and returned unscathed—except for alcohol-induced brain-cell loss—to tell about it.

The New Orleans elite treated Freret like a distinguished ancestor who brought honor to the lineage. If you didn't have a Confederate officer with a high-caste French or Spanish surname in your pedigree, a Freret graduate in the clan would go a long way toward redeeming that deficiency.

Early Friday morning Nick boarded one of the old green streetcars downtown at Canal for the twenty-minute rocking ride through the splendors of the Garden District, and finally to the St. Charles Avenue side of the university. The impressive trio of rough-stone buildings anchored by Gibbon Hall—called the Fortress for its neo-Romanesque massiveness—seemed to give him a surly welcome as he stepped down from the streetcar onto the palm- and crape myrtle-lined grassy neutral ground dividing the traffic lanes of St. Charles.

When he resigned from the faculty of the English department at Freret, more than ten years before, dispirited and indignant over a baseless allegation of plagiarism, he thought he was glad to be rid of the place and of his accusers, still unidentified to this day. But he'd been a teacher too long to quit the academic life cold turkey without emotional consequences. Soon he fell into a yawning intellectual and spiritual void that dwarfed even the temporary emptiness he'd felt after his brief marriage ended in divorce, years earlier in graduate school.

Genealogy rescued him from a cancer of cynicism that might have turned suicidal. His passion for the new discipline was the reason that today he walked Freret campus as simply a tourist, and not an updated Jude the Obscure, Thomas Hardy's tragic casualty of defeated aspirations.

In no hurry to reach his destination across campus, the library, Nick strolled past the Fortress, relishing every familiar aspect of the well-manicured, compact campus that now spread out before him.

This first-of-the-semester walk had become a ritual of fall for him, different from his regular, usually hurried, visits to the campus for research. The balmy New Orleans air; a St. Charles streetcar's distinctive lazy clamor in the distance; sunlight slanting through the old oaks; the hulking Italianate buildings, like waking giants, with only a few windows illuminated in this orientation week...all the recollected sensations of twenty-five years in academia, as student and teacher, brought him as close to melancholy as he would now let himself come. For this one moment of each year, he could again be one of those rare and great teachers, believing in endless possibilities, hoping for the imminent birth of genius from a seed he planted in a receptive mind.

Enough mental loafing. He picked up his pace. Hichborn Library would be opening about now.

Still, he enjoyed the way the few wandering students glanced at him with mingled respect and dread, their eyes as clear and innocent as the morning dew on the inviting, lush grass. His bulging briefcase, scholarly slovenliness, and enigmatic smirk must have given the impression that he was a faculty member, probably in the midst of planning a diabolically difficult course. He wanted to reassure these kids, break through their fears, urge them to be bold, tell them of the new worlds of knowledge and new ways of thinking that were hanging like ripe fruit within their grasp.

◙

"That's my reader!" a woman's voice protested to Nick in a grating whisper. He'd just finished loading a reel on an apparently free machine in the library's second-floor microfilm-reading room. It was an old machine, but a motorized model, essential when one had to examine many reels.

He turned to see the owner of the voice: a short, thin woman posed in a combative hands-on-hips stance. She had a helmet of dull leaden hair, as if the roots had grown through an inner layer of acid. Her glasses were oversize squarish lenses of considerable strength. The white light reflecting upward from the reading surface of the microfilm machine cast her face into a monstrous abstraction of bleached skin, black shadows, and floating gray-blue eyes. Her wheeled lawyer's briefcase was supremely ordered, revealing folders of different colors, and enough pens and notebooks to stock a small office-supplies store. When the final days of Civilization-As-We-Know-It came, she would be taking notes and applying Post-It Flags.

Nick recognized her immediately as a genealogical survivalist—one of the peculiar personality types that the study of genealogy attracts. Or maybe produces. He himself was turning into something of a genealogical hermit, periodically shunning the affairs of the world for days or weeks in pursuit of the elusive answer to a research problem.

With keenly honed skills the genealogical survivalist fights an information battle every working day, determined to get those microfilms and books she needs, and get them *first*, at any cost. It's scoop or be scooped. And what she doesn't need, she tries to keep from others; for every discovery by someone else diminishes her own accomplishments, her years of unappreciated toil on her own family's history.

Nick had known several genealogical survivalists who, having no real research project at all, engaged in a demented campaign of silent sabotage and obstruction. Very unpleasant people, usually.

He glanced at the stack of census-index books and piles of white microfilm boxes this woman had sequestered in a corner of her microfilm compartment.

"I beg your pardon, lady," Nick began, bluffing, "but no one's been on this reader for twenty minutes. I've been watching it from the stacks, over there." He pointed across the dimly lit room to a door leading to the bookshelves. In fact, he'd just noticed the empty reader and had hurried over to take possession.

"*Sir*, I have a bladder condition, if you *must* know," she said, her voice louder than library etiquette allowed. "But I've been in the ladies' room only *eight and a half* minutes. I time myself." She took out a small spiral notebook from a blouse pocket; there were her bathroom visits, neatly chronicled. She pointed triumphantly to a sign on the wall: READERS UNUSED FOR 10 MINUTES ARE CONSIDERED OPEN.

"Kindly remove your film," she continued. "I have this one reserved until 5pm. I'm working on a very special project."

There were twelve machines in the room, but seven were out of commission; three crank models and one other motorized one were in use by grad students or professors—he could tell by the cowlicks and inside-out shirts—oblivious in their research.

Nick glanced at the reservation sheet on the partition. "Muriel" had obviously been waiting at the front door when the library opened at eight, in her baggy hiking pants, marathon runners, and pink ankle socks. Her name was indeed first on the list, but two other names below hers were scratched out; in the same ink, a line detoured around those expunged persons, to continue Muriel's unfair possession of the projector.

Nick apologized with convincing deference.

"I'll just take down this microfilm and get my things together—if you don't mind." He turned his back to Muriel.

She smelled victory in the air and imperiously held up her chin as she waited, checking her watch every fifteen seconds or so.

It was a simple, speedy matter for Nick to jam an inconspicuous paper clip into the spool-and-lens assembly at the base of the unit. He'd been bullied once too often by genealogical survivalists. Payback time.

Moving out of the way with exaggerated graciousness, he relinquished the now useless machine to Muriel.

The library was at the moment operating under an austerity budget. Eight months before, a political scandal with Freret at the heart of it had infuriated the state's citizenry. As usual in Louisiana, when the shoe fell, the politicians instinctively scattered like guilty roaches. Freret took the rap.

Scholarships for the steep tuition at the prestigious school had been thrown like Mardi Gras doubloons to children of the well connected, in the time-honored, oligarchic Louisiana way—secretly. And not merely for a year or two; but since 1876. For over a century, no newspaper or other media organ had dared break the silence (possibly because many media-owning families had benefited, too). Louisianans are wary of pointing their crooked fingers at each other.

But a Republican cattle and natural-gas centimillionaire and philanthropist from north Louisiana, incensed that his state senate candidate had lost the election through gerrymandering machinations of the traditionally Democratic legislature, purely out of spite bought a rural weekly and spilled the beans in a hyperventilating month-long series that gained the notice of the New York papers.

Now there were rumors that further tax breaks were quietly being offered to Freret's for-profit, joint-venture biotech and computer-sciences divisions as a sop for the punitive cuts in state grants that the embarrassed legislators had inflicted on the private institution from which so many of their children had graduated, tuition paid. And for all the heat the university president personally had to take, the bond commission stealthily approved a tax-free issue for the renovation of a St. Charles Avenue mansion as his new official residence. The good times would roll on as discreetly as before, and everybody would soon be happy again.

Except Muriel. She lambasted an already stressed-out young woman from the library staff, who scribbled "Out of Order" on a yellow sheet of paper, placed it on the reader, and beat a hasty retreat. Muriel, gathering her things and threatening legal measures to an audience that couldn't care less, left in a huff. Five minutes later, Nick returned to the abandoned machine. He removed the "Out of Order" sign, repaired his sabotage, and got to work.

Nick and Tommy Shawe had agreed on a three-pronged strategy. He would prepare a short tribal history; update and verify the pedigrees of the six core families back to the time of French rule; and formulate guidelines for future admission based on a study of other tribes' practices. This basic work would help the tribe in establishing its enrollment office, the in-house genealogical department that, in most tribes, reviews the claims of applicants for tribal membership.

Of course, many of the applicants would want as their genealogist someone familiar with the case, someone who could work on a friendly basis with the tribe—namely, Nick. He hoped he'd finally found his own oil well that would pump cash for years to come. Few people got rich in genealogy; Nick wouldn't mind being one of them.

This morning, he planned to travel back two centuries to colonial Louisiana. He looked around to make sure no library worker lurked about, and poured a steaming cup of black coffee-and-chicory from his thermos.

◻

Nick was well versed in the standard works of Louisiana history. He had riffled through two of his favorites, Le Page du Pratz's *Histoire de La Louisiane* and Giraud's *A History of French Louisiana*, which were in his own library at his office—he'd bought them for a dollar each at a garage sale some years before. He had also browsed through archaeological and ethnographic periodicals for more recent investigatory leads.

The earliest description of the Katogoula that he'd found was in a 1771 narrative by the French explorer Jean-Bernard Bossu. He also had reviewed the accounts of Thomas Hutchins, William Bartram, Baudry de Lozieres, and other explorers and soldiers of various nationalities, who, in official reports and memoirs, told of later contacts with the tribe. These men wrote that the Katogoula were part of the Sangfleuve Confederation, dominated by the Chitiko and the Tiloasha, powerful tribes which had been in existence centuries before the arrival of the Europeans.

French-Canadian missionary priests who visited the Katogoula gave up trying to learn the tribe's original language, though it was apparently Muskogean in character, superficially akin to Choctaw. U.S. Indian Agent John Sibley, President Jefferson's friend and appointee, reported in 1808 that he made himself intelligible using Mobilian

Jargon, a composite language based on Choctaw, Chickasaw, and loan words from the European tongues. With the Katogoula, as with many other tribes forced to deal with the colonial powers, Mobilian Jargon—more precisely, Mobilian K, an evolving variant—became the accepted language around the middle of the eighteenth century, during the last years of the French regime.

Leaning back with his head wedged in his palms, Nick squandered a few minutes staring at the wall, pondering the ancient helix of chance and determination weaving through the new and strong friendship that had formed between Tommy and his Katogoula tribe, and Chief Claude and the Chitiko-Tiloasha...

At length he sat up, shook his head, and flexed his shoulders. Another bout of aimless philosophizing wasn't getting him anywhere. He forced his attention back to the slanted viewing surface of the microfilm reader.

The Internet was certainly a boon to the modern genealogist; yet, Nick took perverse pleasure in the fact that all the servers in the world couldn't hold the century upon century of genealogical material contained in courthouses, places of worship, governmental agencies, libraries, attics, basements.... The day might come when the world's genealogical source material would be captured in bytes, but it wasn't here now. Real genealogy still required the researcher to physically venture into the field for patient spade and brush work, just as any good archaeologist would think it necessary to crawl around on hands and knees in an excavation. In both disciplines, part of the art was knowing where to dig and what to seek.

Hichborn Library, despite the cutbacks, was an excellent facility, as long as you knew your way around the hundreds of microfilm drawers, and the special manuscript collections that weren't listed in the library catalog—and Nick did know his way around. It was still a great place to research French colonial archives, and no slouch either when it came to the vast assemblage of Spanish colonial records collectively known as the *Archivo General de Indias,* the lion's share of which was housed in Seville, Spain. Of especial interest to Nick was one of the *Archivo* subdivisions holding a wealth of Louisiana materials: the *Papeles Procedentes de Cuba.* Louisiana as a Spanish colony fell within the administrative sphere of the viceroyalty of Cuba, and that's where great quantities of Louisiana records of the time were sent and stored, before most of the surviving records were ultimately transferred to Spain.

Unfortunately, the Hichborn lacked an important part of the *Papeles*: the *Legajos de Luisiana,* "bundles" of documents that were themselves a newly rediscovered portion of the famous *Fondos de las Floridas,* which contained material relating to East and West Spanish Florida. The *Legajos de Luisiana* included documentary details even more useful to researchers interested in the colonial history of the area which became central Louisiana.

The *Fondos* and the smaller *Luisiana* were left in Havana after most other colonial records had been removed to Spain in the late 19th century, as the former superpower gradually lost its New World foothold. In the 1990s, the Historic New Orleans Collection created an academic sensation by gaining permission from Cuba and the U.S. government to microfilm the *Fondos* on-site at the National Archives of Cuba, where conservational conditions had always been wanting. THNOC pulled off another major coup by returning to Havana, during a time of renewed diplomatic tension, and capturing on microfilm nearly 20,000 pages of the deteriorating *Legajos de Luisiana.*

Since the *Luisiana* microfilm set had not been released for sale and was expected to be very expensive when it finally was, scholars from all over the world were swarming to the Collection's beautiful complex of landmark buildings in the French Quarter for a crack at this newly available trove of historical information. Nick had lately treated his friend from THNOC, vivacious Veronique, to quite a few expensive, cholesterol-laden dinners, during which he subtly mentioned how grateful he would be if she could use her influence to move him up the waiting list of researchers. Chills ran up and down his spine as he thought about getting his hot hands on THNOC's *Luisiana*.

Was genealogy replacing sex as his primary source of excitement? he asked himself...*C'est la vie!*

Today Nick was exploring the *Papeles* and the *Fondos*, having first consulted several guides and articles that directed him to productive fishing grounds amid this ocean of information. For hours he slogged through hundreds of microfilmed pages of beautiful script, vowing to himself to brush up on his Spanish and French during his next slack period—the *Papeles* and *Fondos* contained records in both languages, a fact highlighting the peculiar political reality of the colony: the French would be French, no matter whose flag flew over them.

Each page lay projected before him like an insubstantial slice of a core sample drilled down into history itself.

He discovered several references to a devastating intertribal war that nearly wiped out the Katogoula and probably destroyed their ally, the smaller Yaknelousa tribe. The enemy tribe, the Quinahoa, was utterly extinguished, according to the colonial officials who were trying to understand the convoluted power politics of dozens and dozens of tribes. But precisely when this war had been fought—if it had been fought at all outside the mists of legend—Nick was unable to discover.

He did find evidence that the Katogoula were well established in Louisiana when the infamous Removals began in earnest, in the 1820s. Ironically, these times of trouble were relatively good for the Katogoula, and the tribe's numbers increased.

The territory of the Katogoula was one of the last stops on the mournful trip to the government-selected reservations. Fleeing individuals and family groups of many Southeastern tribes peeled off and sought shelter in the wild backwoods of central Louisiana, avoiding the forced marches to Oklahoma and other frontier lands. Many walked back from Indian Territory, finding life unbearable there, separated from the familiar sky, sun, animals, forest, and waters of their traditional way of life in the Southeast.

◙

When Nick surfaced again, he realized it was late afternoon. He returned his films and books to the appropriate carts, and took the stairs to the third floor—Literature and Languages, faculty carrels, and Hawty Latimer.

Chapter 9

"How can you read this chicken scratch?" Hawty Latimer asked, the expression on her brown face somewhere between teasing and contempt. "If you'd gone to grade school where I did, up in north Louisiana, they'd have broken you of this left-handed writing. One run-in with the principal's wooden ruler—that would have been *that*."

After a few more silent moments, she tossed back the pages of cramped scribbling Nick had produced. He suspected she would make a good principal herself—and wouldn't spare the ruler. She was a formidable young woman, in both mind and body, with more drive and joy for living than anyone—in or out of a wheelchair—Nick had ever known.

"But you can't fault the content, right?" Nick asked hopefully. "Even if the form isn't up to your lofty standards of penmanship."

Sarcasm was their normal mode of communication. That Nick employed Hawty in his genealogical firm wasn't immediately obvious; a person could be pardoned for thinking it was the other way around.

It was past six now, and they sat in Hawty's carrel on the third floor of the library. The carrel was a drab seven-by-five-foot study area, painstakingly constructed, Nick often thought, to exclude any naturally occurring material. A silvery plastic grid suspended over the carrel's walls filtered fluorescent light from a higher coffered acoustic ceiling that extended over all of the carrels. It was too cold and too dry in here; too bright, yet not bright enough; and there was the restive silence of unseen people straining to overhear conversations or muttered secrets. Still, a carrel was a nice perk for grad students and for professors too busy to return to their offices; if you were the kind of person who could lose yourself in your work, then the facsimile of privacy would become real. Hawty had added a few comforting touches: a lamp here, a family photograph there, the odd sentimental tchochke.

Her volcano-orange wheelchair mocked the sterility of the enclosure. This wasn't her usual chair, which she referred to as her "chariot." Normally she rode a motorized, gizmo-crammed computer-lab-on-wheels that made Nick wonder how he'd missed the leap from present-time to science fiction.

"Oh, I suppose 1771 isn't bad. For a start," Hawty said.

Nick had found references to the Katogoula that far back and was proud of having done so.

"Just so happens I ran across this thesis." She held up a slim pamphlet. "Nineteen twenty-two. A girl in one of Herbert Bolton's classes, out in your neck of the woods—Berkeley. She did some really outstanding work on Louisiana Indians."

"Bolton, Bolton. Sounds vaguely familiar. Refresh my memory." He knew she loved to do that.

"Herbert Bolton was the scholar who broke ground with studies of the relationship between the Spanish and the Indian tribes in Louisiana and Texas."

Hawty handed him the thesis and continued. "This student quotes from an unpublished journal of 1768. She says she studied it in the possession of descendants of the writer, in southwest Texas. The journal's author was a clerk of Athanase de Mézières. Mézières, as I'm sure you know—and if you don't I'm going to tell you anyway—was a Frenchman, son-in-law of St. Denis, and later, during the Spanish period, commandant of Fort St. Jean Baptiste—"

"Natchitoches."

Louis Antoine Juchereau de St. Denis was a daring French officer in Sieur de Bienville's command, now remembered in Louisiana primarily as the founder of the picturesque city of Natchitoches, in 1714.

"You got it," Hawty confirmed. "Mézières, in his spare time, mediated for the Spanish between feuding Texas tribes—"

"Oh, come on, Hawty," Nick said, interrupting her. "Sounds to me like a transparent imitation of another well-known journal. I bet she'd read about Jean Penicaut, St. Denis's carpenter—"

"I know, I know. St. Denis's carpenter, who later wrote about the expeditions to the Red River area and into Spanish territory. I understand where you're coming from," Hawty said. "But I think our clerk's journal gives us a reliable earlier Katogoula sighting than you found."

Nick had begun shaking his head even before she finished. They were in the habit of defending mutually exclusive positions, eventually moving to some midpoint of compromise.

"She decided to create her own source," he said. "Happens all the time. Look at the *New York Times*. Academia, and especially genealogy, aren't any different."

"Don't be dissing my newspaper," Hawty warned.

"Sorry. No great mystery here. She was trying to please the great man, Bolton, her professor. A simple case of fraud brought on by a raging need for approval. Maybe she had a thing for the old guy."

"I'll ignore the sexism implicit in your allegation. And look who's accusing somebody of intellectual dishonesty. Don't you even want to hear the facts? Reminds me of the case of a certain English professor wrongly accused of plagiarism."

Chastened, Nick readjusted himself in his chair and slowly exhaled in an attempt to expel any remaining opinionated cantankerousness. She had a knack for keeping his feet on the ground.

"Hush up and perpend," Hawty said, doggedly sticking to her point, mixing down-home gruffness with higher-ed decorum. "Maybe you'll get something useful in that overstuffed head of yours. Besides, there's more to this journal than simply moving three years further back than your date."

"I'm all ears."

She'd begun to finger her elaborate arrangement of six-inch-long braids. "Do you like my hair? Took *four* hours." It was her third new look of the month.

Ah, youth! Nick thought. *All innocent narcissism, gullible idealism, blissful self-absorption!*

Not waiting for an answer, Hawty quit bothering her braids and plowed on. "You say there in your notes that scholars believe there was a big intertribal war over inland salt sources and rock deposits for projectiles."

He nodded. "Among other causes: horse trading with the Wichita, slave trading in Apache captives—"

"Excuse me, please! I have the microphone. This young scholar says in her thesis that following the war, the remaining Yaknelousa allies merged with the Katogoula, and that the few surviving defeated Quinahoa were kept as slaves. The Katogoula and the Yaknelousa shared a lot of folkways, even before the war. She also says that Mézières's clerk spoke with some old men of the tribe, using *yama*—what's that, sign language?"

"*Yam-AH*, accent on the last syllable. The Indian name for Mobilian Jargon." Seeing Hawty's eyebrows rise for more of an explanation, Nick added, "*Yama* was a Chickasaw-Choctaw pidgin of the central Gulf Coast, with French, Spanish, and English loan words. It became the trade language many tribes used to communicate with each other and the Europeans."

"Oh. Well, these old tribe members placed a definite date on the great battle. Nine years before 1768. That would mean the battle was fought about 1759." She smiled in triumph. "Now *that's* a significant advance backward, I'd say."

Nick rubbed the stubble on his chin. "Hmmmm," was his only response. His rapt gaze drifted around the cubicle.

Hawty wanted his attention. "A-*hem*! Our young scholar is probably close to a hundred now, if she's alive."

"Definitely a long shot," Nick said, still processing the information Hawty had given him.

"I'll track down her family in California, see if she left any notes or other clues."

"What about the 1768 journal?" Nick asked. "Any chance of unearthing that jewel? We might find some new family lines that aren't part of the Cutpine group."

"Nobody at the Texas genealogical libraries and the universities I called knows anything about it. So I posted some queries on my favorite genealogy websites. We'll hear something soon."

"Good work, Hawty. But…oh, forget it. Maybe it won't be a problem."

"What, extending the timeline back for the tribe? Isn't that the point of genealogy, to go as far back as you can?"

"It's not so much the timeline," Nick said, "as this new wrinkle about the other tribes. We have a close-knit community of people here, with a treasured identity. They've taken care of their own for centuries. They've maintained a central decision-making body. They honor their ancient traditions."

"Even if they don't practice them in any meaningful way anymore," Hawty said. "But I won't tell the BIA."

"That's politics, and we avoid it like the plague. What I'm saying is, all these years, belief has sufficed for written genealogy. These people *believe* they're Katogoula. Not Scots-Irish, not French, even though this blood runs in their veins, too. You don't need a pedigree chart to see that. They've *chosen* their identity. What happens when, on the eve of their greatest victory in modern times—tribal recognition—some of them find out they're not Katogoula, but of another tribe, maybe even a tribe that was an enemy?"

"I'd say some applicants are going to be on the warpath, because they won't be getting the expected invitation to the Katogoula pow-wow."

"You got it," Nick said. "I learned a lesson from the Judge Chaurice incident: if you mess up somebody's family jigsaw puzzle, you better know another way it fits together." He waited for her to pick up on his idea. She didn't disappoint him.

"The bylaws of the tribe," she said. "Use phrasing that will include descent from the other two tribes, if that's all the lineage under examination shows."

"Exactly. This is one of the few instances when a genealogist can create instead of merely define." Nick tilted back in his chair and thumped against a wall of the carrel. There was an answering thump. "What the hell was that?"

"Oh, I have a new neighbor with hyper-sensitive hearing. I don't even know who it is, but she's always thumping somebody's wall when anyone so much as coughs. Pisses me off. I mean, I have ears too, and she makes plenty of noise. The *nerve*. I don't think it's a guy, unless he's fond of really expensive perfume."

"Hey, this is New Orleans," Nick said in a lower voice. "You never know.... As I was about to mention, at least the six old core families check out as genuine Katogoula. And we have living representatives of all but one of the surnames." He read a portion of the BIA records he'd obtained. "Royce and Luevenia Silsby; Odeal Caspard; Felix and Alberta Wattell and their family; Irton and Grace Dusong; the Shawes; and the Bellarmines—the mother of a current tribe member, a man named Nugent Chenerie, was a Bellarmine. Only this guy's Bellarmine cousins with other surnames are still around locally.

"Most of the others from Cutpine can trace some connection to these core surnames; so I don't really foresee any qualification problems for the local families who haven't had genealogical work done on their lines. But we're sure to have applicants from beyond this area who think they're Katogoula, and turn out to be Yaknelousa or Quinahoa. Let's say their ancestors left decades, maybe centuries ago, didn't hang around to marry a Katogoula. This is where a little creative qualification writing will come in."

Nick explained that Tommy Shawe wanted to build a vibrant tribe with five hundred initial members. The Cutpine group was small, barely more than a quarter of that; many were elderly, without children. By broadening the criteria to include the other two tribes linked with the Katogoula in history, perhaps more people could be admitted. Nick admired Tommy and the other tribe members for their willingness to share the federal bonanza and their heritage. But he wondered how welcoming the Katogoula would ultimately be to those of the two lost tribes; he had learned through his genealogical work that ethnic pride is a first cousin of racism.

"Sounds like a lot of intermarrying to me," Hawty said. "I get claustrophobic just thinking about it."

"It's not really that bad. In the nineteen-twenties and thirties, some of the Oklahoma Katogoula came back to Louisiana. Many of these immigrants weren't related to the six core families, but claimed roots to other, as yet undocumented, earlier tribe members. So this was new blood, new sets of ancestors. Their paths to the past were different from those of the six Cutpine families. And then we have unions with non-Indians, which have increased in recent years."

"How are we going to find out who's descended from the Yaknelousa and the Quinahoa? What do we use for evidence?"

"A good genealogist never gives up," Nick said. "There's always the next book or microfilm that may reveal the answer."

"Sure would be nice if you could get at the *Legajos de Luisiana*."

"Yeah, I'm trying. Maybe nothing about those tribes survives in written form. Maybe the Katogoula swallowed them completely, without a trace."

"That would simplify matters, wouldn't it?" Hawty suggested. "Everybody who thinks she's Katogoula turns out to be just that. You might not have to change the invitation list to the pow-wow after all."

"True, we may never use information on the other two tribes, but we need to keep our eyes open for any references."

"Well, I have faith in the Jesuits, and the French and the Spanish bureaucrats. I bet you somebody with a quill pen left a breadcrumb trail of unpronounceable names for us to follow, for all three tribes."

They heard more thumping from the adjacent cubicle. Nick brought his chair down on all four legs. "Jeez! What's with that woman? A real pain in the ass. Can't you get another carrel?"

Hawty waved off his suggestion. Nick knew that below her brusque manner was a tolerance for the emotional foibles of others; her physical limitations had taught her that we all have our handicaps, though most are on the inside. This was one of the traits that made her such a good teacher, and such a good friend.

He'd reluctantly hired her a few years after starting his business, at the insistence of his best friends and former Freret colleagues, Una Kern and Dion Rambus. Working alone was the way he thought he preferred things. Last year, Hawty had earned a B.A. with honors in English and a B.S. in computer science; now she was pursuing her M.A. in English. The Freret English faculty was crazy about her and had given her plum teaching assignments. She'd also caught the genealogy bug and had qualified as a CGRS—Certified Genealogical Record Specialist.

Nick relied on her brilliance, her organizational talents, and her loyalty. One day, he knew, a great job or a wonderful man would steal her from him. He hoped, for his sake, that it would not be soon, but for hers, that it would.

"There's another development that bothers me," Nick said. "Tommy Shawe's twin brother, Carl, was found dead on the bank of a lake. Looks suspicious to the local fuzz."

"Oh, Lordy! I hope you're going to stay out of *this* one. Can't you just leave some skeletons in their closets?" Then, her irrepressible curiosity aroused, she asked, "So what happened?"

"I've always liked what another Shaw—George Bernard—said about family skeletons: if you can't get rid of them, make them dance. Carl's death undoubtedly wasn't a hunting accident; could have been a fight, but probably was murder."

"And," Hawty prodded, impatient with Nick's pace.

"An ancient Indian weapon was used, an atlatl. The weird thing is that it—or at least the spear used—belongs to Tommy, who says it was stolen from a garage closet."

"That's spooky. The spear thrower," Hawty said. "I remember it from my background reading. Paleo-Indians used it to kill big game, mammoths even; now modern Indians are bringing it back, sort of as a living cultural reminder."

"Kwanzaa for the Red Man," Nick said.

"Oh, that's real cute. You think his brother's death has anything to do with the tribal recognition?"

"I don't know. But I get the feeling there are some powerful forces trying to discourage the Katogoula from opening their own casino." He couldn't help thinking of Val and the powerful force of her body touching his. He mentally shoved aside the image and the sensations. "Tommy wouldn't talk about the death when I saw him last week, but it seems he's being questioned as a suspect. I just read the coverage in the *Daily Bagpipe*."

"The *who*?"

"The newspaper of Armageddon? On the Sangfleuve River? Parish seat?" Nick snapped his fingers, playing the badgering grade school teacher. "Come on, Louisiana girl."

"All right, all right, now! I'm with you. I just didn't remember the newspaper right off the top of my head, that's all."

Then Nick told her what else he'd gathered. "The morning of the murder the police found Tommy's abandoned truck on the highway. Tommy turned up wandering near the body, in a confused condition. Claims to have been hit by a drugged blowgun dart."

"And this is the guy who hired us?" Hawty asked. "You really know how to pick 'em."

"Tommy doesn't remember what happened to him the previous night and that morning, when the murder probably occurred. Chief Claude—"

"Of the Chitiko-Tiloasha? See, I'm getting the hang of these crazy tribal names."

"Good. Chief Claude told me that Tommy and his brother argued quite a bit; but then, Carl didn't get along with anybody. Personally, I don't think our guy did it."

"You mentioned the sheriff," Hawty said. "Is he black?"

"Never met him."

"Sangfleuve Parish...uh-huh, he's a brother. John Higbee. First black sheriff there. His daddy and my granddaddy used to sharecrop on the same plantation back in the twenties, up in the north of the state, my stomping grounds. Tell him who I am if you see him. You're going up there this week, right?"

Nick gave an affirmative nod.

"I've never met him either," Hawty continued. "But our families looked out for each other when times got rough.... I see that look on your face. What do you want me to do?"

Sheepishly, Nick pointed to his scrawled notes. "Think you can distill something meaningful in the way of a tribal history from this?"

"Are you joking?! I don't know why you don't let me get you one of those little notebook computers. See how much more efficient we are in the office since you bought our new desktop to replace that old dinosaur we've been using. You need to join the modern age, boss...."

He stood up to leave and backed toward the door. He'd expected another attack on his aversion to modern technology.

"We can't afford it," he said, his hand on the cold door handle.

"Don't I know it. You can't even afford to pay me my overtime. When's the last time I got a paycheck instead of a handout? Not to mention a raise? Never mind. Just rhetorical questions."

"Hey, that's a new chariot, isn't it?" he said, hoping to distract her, appeal to her vanity. "Pretty wild. I like it."

"Oh...you noticed. I'm shocked. We women bust our butts trying to look nice for you men, and most of the time you're belching in front of the TV, scratching yourself, and watching the Saints get whipped from one end zone to the other. Yeah, it's a little reward I gave myself, since my boss doesn't seem to appreciate me." She paused significantly. "I sold a couple of articles to a computer magazine. And no, there's none left for the firm's penny jar."

"Hey, just trying to be nice. Want to go out for poboys later? I think I can swing that."

The Folio, only a few blocks away, served some of the best in town, at almost any hour of the day or night, as befitted a college hangout.

"Got a basketball game at seven. That's why I'm in this." She grasped the wheels of her chair, as if ready to propel it forward. "A high-performance model, ultra-light tubular aluminum. Some women buy new earrings, some new shoes. This is what *I* do for myself."

Nick noticed her sweat suit for the first time.

"Hawty."

"What."

"I do appreciate you."

Looking away, she straightened a book on the desk.

"Yeah, I know. And I know we're going to get some money from this project. But sometimes, sometimes...*boy*, I'm telling you, it's just too much." She gave a long-suffering sigh. "You can come watch the game, if you feel like it."

"And then poboys and beer?"

Her smile broke through the pout. "You got it! Oyster for me."

◻

Nick closed the door gently. He didn't want to rouse the ire again of Ms./Mr. Radar-Ears in the next carrel.

Standing between two monoliths of shelved books that seemed to stretch to tiny infinity, Nick felt the old longing for the academic life waft through him like heartache on seeing a former girlfriend. He ran a hand across the spines nearest him: 18th-century English comedy.

Sex, money, and status, and the base things we'll do to get them.

He took down a pocketsize leather-bound edition of Sheridan's *School for Scandal* and began leafing through it. As he chuckled over the scathing social satire, his mind drifted to Hawty.

He knew her well enough to understand what she'd hesitated to say; they'd danced around the topic before, more frequently, of late. She loved genealogy, but decision time was approaching. Either Nick offered her more of the paltry, erratic profits, or she would go into teaching or some computer-related field full time. It wasn't a matter of money, wholly, but of her estimation of self-worth. He'd shared his gambling winnings with her, but he still owed her.

Nick didn't want to repeat the bad management he'd witnessed at Freret. Certain unenlightened school administrators, foolishly hoping to keep talented minds forever on substandard pay, never did understand why the turnover in their departments was so high. Yet, in spite of his good intentions, and after performing accounting misdeeds that would be the envy of any corporate CFO, he never seemed to have quite enough left for Hawty.

The door of the adjacent carrel opened. Professor Frederick Tawpie emerged. His coat and tie had undergone some recent crushing, and his wiry pumpkin-colored hair, usually sprayed into tentative submission, was in disarray. His attention directed downward, he hiked up his trousers below his roll of self-indulgent flab. He had yet to realize Nick was there, observing him.

Tawpie spent big bucks on trendy clothes and appurtenances; he was a walking billboard of designer logos, all surface without substance. Nick had an image of a golf-tournament official whenever he saw him. Even the new affectation of faux tortoise-shell glasses didn't help Tawpie look like the scholar he never would be.

"Hello, Frederick," Nick said, trying to mask his distaste. Una, Dion, and he called him "the Usurper." "Don't tell me the English department head no longer rates one of those plush offices over in the Fortress."

Gibbon Hall, a.k.a. the Fortress, was the center of Freret's Arts & Sciences division.

"Oh!—" Tawpie put a hand over the place his heart should have been. "You startled me, Nick." He fiddled with his glasses. His jowly neck flushed crimson. "I was just...just in a meeting with a—another staff member. What brings you here?"

"What else? Genealogy."

By now Tawpie had rallied a bit. "I never got the chance to thank you properly for that marvelous work you did for me. I was certainly glad to get all *that* cleared up."

A bit over a year before, during a scandal involving genealogical fraud and an eighteenth-century New Orleans immigrant ship, Tawpie had feared that one of his ancestors was a transported convict from England. Nick found that Tawpie's true ancestor was in fact another person with a similar name who arrived in New Orleans on another boat decades later. Since then, the old animosity between the two former colleagues seemed to have cooled; but Nick would never think of him as anything else but a self-serving phony.

The old guile returned to Tawpie's beady eyes. "Pity that plagiarism thing lingers on in the collective memory. I rather think you'd be an asset to the faculty. But alas, we have the reputation of the department to consider." He gave his gaudy watch a fake glance. "Must run."

Tawpie took off at a brisk pace, taking the first turn he could.

Head of the English department. What a joke! They had to bump him up to full professor just for the desk job. Always a mediocre teacher, Tawpie had finally found his niche as a sycophantic, pompous bureaucrat.

Una had told Nick countless times that he held a grudge too long. He didn't agree. The only thing he hoped to regret at death would be the necessity of giving up his grudges. Nick would never forgive Tawpie for his silence, or worse, during the controversy that lead to his dismissal. A word from Tawpie—then, as was Nick, an assistant professor, but also head of the departmental-affairs committee—might have tilted the scale in his favor. Time, the exigencies of his business, and a certain mellowness of middle age had assuaged the sharpness of Nick's rancor, but the poison still burned deep within him.

He looked around, a feeling of contentment again settling over him in the midst of the collected wisdom of the ages. The Tawpies of the world leave behind them nothing more than outlines, in which they themselves are merely passive participants. Better men and women leave the elaborations of their souls.

A door opened...the same carrel. A young woman emerged. She registered momentary surprise, but collected herself immediately and approached Nick.

Now he knew the source of the thumping. It certainly hadn't been someone protesting noise from Hawty's carrel; Tawpie and this associate English professor had been much too busy for that!

"Have a good meeting, Brigitte?" Nick asked. She was new to the faculty. He had met her once before over drinks with Una at the favorite student-faculty hangout, the Folio; he'd admired her conversation, and, even more so, her looks. Brigitte was small and shapely, with chestnut hair and an almost-ripe red-apple complexion.

"Fair," she said, flicking a corkscrew strand of hair back, returning Nick's searching gaze. She brought a black leather portfolio to her chest and hugged it. "It's so frustrating when a colleague doesn't have, shall I say, the equipment to reach a certain satisfying conclusion to his argument."

He pointed to the buttons of her sky-blue sweater vest. She gave him a blushing, thank-you smile as she re-buttoned them correctly.

"You know, Brigitte, I've found that a cross-disciplinary approach sometimes works quite effectively in these nagging literary quandaries."

"Really?" she said, in a tone that betrayed considerably more than professional interest.

"Whitman's your area, isn't he?"

"You're familiar with my…area, Nick?"

"Not nearly as much as I'd like to be." He recited a few favorite lines from the great nineteenth-century American poet who had captivated him as an undergraduate.

"Very impressive," she said. "Stanza five, 'Song of Myself.' It would be nice to have a real scholar's input—for a change. Give me a call, why don't you."

She walked down the same aisle of books that Tawpie had used for his escape, paused, gave a frank, appraising backward glance, and continued walking straight.

Nick silently thanked her for the fine view of her swishing, short black dress that hugged her pert body underneath.

And then, behind him, fists pounded in unison on carrel doors. He preferred to think they were applauding his method rather than protesting the noise.

He located the anti-theft strip in the binding of the little 1928 edition of Sheridan's play, removed it deftly with his Swiss Army Knife, and dropped the book into his briefcase.

Chapter 10

Only six hundred acres of prime forest and cropland remained to the Tadbulls from their antebellum heyday, when the family's empire sprawled across more than four thousand acres of central Louisiana.

Bayou Fostine ran through Tadbull land, a fact that in the past had guaranteed the family political and economic power. Before the modern era of flood plans and Corps of Engineer projects that robbed the bayou of much of its natural flow, steamboats plying the Sangfleuve River could still travel up Bayou Fostine as far as the landing at Tadbull Hall, enriching the brash Anglo-American Protestant families who'd barged into the French and Spanish Creoles' territorial parlor.

From the old cypress-beam landing on the bayou the "great house" known as Tadbull Hall was visible, half a mile away down a long corridor of well-tended landscape. Once, bales of cotton, stacks of lumber, and barrels of sugar waited for loading here, to be exchanged for the products of the glittering industrial world of New Orleans and beyond. Now the still-solid landing on the atrophied stream was used only for fishing and crawfish boils.

The corridor connecting the landing to the house was bordered by a double windbreak of hundred-and-fifty-year-old live oaks, and between these venerable trees ran an oval road of bleached, crushed mollusk shells. Legend had it that during Mardi Gras season, the early Tadbulls and friends dressed up as Romans and conducted wagon and buggy races on the oval. These revels, for their time, allegedly reached shocking levels of debauchery.

Arthur Tadbull, the founder of the Louisiana dynasty, was a failed merchant from Virginia, who married a socially prominent young woman from New Orleans, Mignon Frusquin. In 1810, he managed to take part in the successful revolt in West Florida that resulted in the capture of Baton Rouge from the Spanish. Later he played an important role in Territory of Orleans Governor Claiborne's occupation of the disputed land between the Mississippi and the Peal Rivers.

Arthur began accumulating property in what is now the center of the state, near the old French settlement of Post du Sang. The town that grew up around the colonial fort on the banks of "le fleuve Sang," or Blood River, eventually became Port Sangfleuve, and finally the present-day city of Armageddon. At some point after the Louisiana Purchase—according to the perpetually aggrieved French Creoles—the uncouth Americans, having taken everything and turned it on its head, began to refer to the muddy red waterway as the Sangfleuve, even adding the redundant "River" in their clumsy language. Armageddon acquired its forbidding name as a result of a fiery Civil War skirmish that destroyed most of the original town. Though this battle was a tactical footnote in the greater conflict, it imbued the river's accidentally appropriate name with a meaning that seemed, in the eyes of townsfolk then and now, fated.

How Arthur Tadbull ended up with so much property was a topic of debate by locals and historians. Most of land had been guaranteed through the Louisiana Purchase to various Indian tribes by the American government, the usual, ultimately empty, promise in territorial acquisitions. These tribes had bought the land from the French or the Spanish, who had persuaded them, through treaties and threats, that they were not entitled to claim the forests and lakeshores they'd occupied for millennia. Arthur Tadbull used his wife's dwindling fortune and his political clout to acquire some of his land, but undoubtedly he tricked the trusting local Indians out of a much larger portion.

The family home was an Anglo-American raised cottage of two-and-a-half generous stories, built primarily by slaves in 1821. Even though technically correct, the term "cottage" didn't do the lovely house justice. It was white with green shutters and a chimney on either end, outside the walls, following the English building ways. The first story was of bricks made of clay and mud from Bayou Fostine; the second was of huge cypress and pine boards and beams from the vast property, a kind of lumber that became extinct with the old-growth forests that had provided it. Four simple square brick columns supported the second-story gallery, matched by four wooden colonettes below the gabled roof and the rambling attic. The strongest hurricanes merely glanced off Tadbull Hall.

Unlike many other great plantation houses of the era, Tadbull Hall was no classical temple of ostentation. It spoke of a family that loved life's pleasures but knew the danger of overreaching, that believed the winner in the game of wealth and power was he who took his modest winnings and left the table to the double-or-nothing fools.

◻

On the gracious front porch of Tadbull Hall, state representative Rufus Girn impatiently hammered away with the arm-and-tomahawk brass doorknocker.

"Damn nigger's probably watchin' that Oprah woman," he muttered dyspeptically. "Shit. Niggers all over the state 'cept where you need one."

Girn wiped sweat from his forehead with a stained handkerchief. Louisiana fall weather was as faithless as his campaign refrains. He wanted to blame the heat, too, on African Americans, but couldn't come up with a satisfactory conspiracy theory at the moment.

Scowling, he looked around him at the signs of established affluence and removed the stubby cigar from his mouth. He stared at the cigar with loathing, as if it had spattered him with some of the spit he'd soaked it in all day. With a vindictive flick, he sent it tumbling into the nearby thick dwarf yaupon hedge hugging the perimeter of the porch. A disc of ash lay on the lapel of his shiny blue suit—one of several he'd purchased for a song from the widow of an old colleague who'd died sleeping in his chair on the House floor. He brushed off the ash, but succeeded merely in creating a silver smudge on the dark silk.

It had not been a good day. That lamentable state of affairs was about to change. He'd put in too much work on this project—which just might turn out to be the achievement of his corrupt career—to let such minor irritations distract him.

Representative Girn had just been re-elected to serve his sixth four-year term in the Louisiana House; two four-year Senate terms in the middle had allowed him to get around constitutional term limits. He was a bit past sixty-three, hard of hearing, with a touch of prostate cancer and gonorrhea, and due for another angioplasty. But Rufus Girn was still as mean and wily and determined as an old Blue Channel catfish. In fact, friends and enemies alike knew him as "Catfish."

There was a certain facial resemblance to that ancient denizen of the state's lakes and rivers: flat, broad nose that had been broken in fistfights on the House floor during the desegregation era, bushy gray mustache, indignant goggle eyes, and irascible bulldog scowl. In behavior he earned his nickname by being a consummate bottom-feeder, eagerly foraging for personally enriching legislative deals that were too risky or too unprofitable for the flashier fish.

Girn had been the gofer for a rapacious, dictatorial governor, one of the great exemplars of the political tradition that feeds the image of Louisiana as a veritable banana republic. The young Girn had been adept on the ukulele and had composed a campaign song for the governor, which became quite popular. In the sad last years of the administration,

Girn proved indispensable, even zipping the failing governor's pants after his increasingly disappointing dalliances with Bourbon Street strippers. For this unwavering loyalty and cunning, the governor loved him as medieval kings loved their most ruthless bastard sons. Girn was one of the few parasites who narrowly escaped federal indictments and prison after the governor was committed to a psychiatric hospital.

And just before the governor lost his wits completely, he saw to it that Girn got his reward: the 120th District, drawn specifically through corridors of five parishes to include the poorest and most uninformed of Louisiana's electorate. Except, of course, for the Tadbulls.

The secret of Girn's strangle hold on power in his district was also the reason for his relative failure to be stinking rich. The soil of his garden was simply too played out. There were few wealthy constituents to offer juicy bribes for his influence in the legislature, and fewer industries he could hit up for plump rake-offs and silent partnerships on state-contracted business. At a time when most of his contemporaries in state government had already made fortunes through such strategies and were kicking back on their hunting camps in the coastal marshes or in their condos in Tahoe and Aspen, Rufus Catfish Girn was still sifting mud for his elusive big score.

A less bitter man would not have struck the Tadbull door so violently. Girn pounded away, as if desperately trying to break into a vault loaded with gold.

At length, a black woman in a white uniform opened the tall paneled door.

"Mr. Girn, come on in, sir," she said cheerfully, moving with the sweep of the door out of Girn's way as he charged in. "So good to see you again. Mr. Tadbull's in the study. I'll take you on back."

But he was already striding down the cypress-lined main hall, his second-hand alligator Guccis thudding dully on the old Persian runner. "I know where it is," Girn said sourly over his shoulder. "Don't bother."

Chapter 11

"*Got*damn, Catfish, where *have* you been?"

Wooten Tadbull III sat at a graceful pearwood gaming table; new fuchsia baize covered the playing surface. He held a screwdriver in one hand, and a cheap plastic wristwatch in the other.

"We waited lunch on you as long as we could, boy," Mr. Tadbull said. "Is it still hot as a horny whore out there?"

Mr. Tadbull was a stout, dapper man, with a horseshoe of gray hair around his shiny, healthy pate. Mischievous blue eyes hid a punch line, perhaps, but nothing much deeper. He favored the English country squire's sporting look, augmented with lighter-weight fabrics for the Louisiana climate. His Norfolk jacket had suede elbow patches. A bright red silk handkerchief sprouted from a breast pocket and complemented the muted plaid of his coat. The toes of his velvet slippers, emblazoned with a golden-threaded fox, barely grazed the floor as he swung his legs.

Though stuffed game birds and other animals perched or snarled here and there about the room, Wooten Tadbull III didn't seem to be the man who had left the comfort of Tadbull Hall to kill them.

"You damn right it's hot," Girn said. "And I got lost, as many times as I been coming, here. Can you believe that? Had to stop at that Indian woman's store, ask directions. There's some kind of a meeting there tonight. Some of them Las Vegas boys'll be there, I understand, pitchin' a casino contract. We best be gettin' our shit together."

"That'd be Luevenia, you're talking about," Tadbull said, engrossed in tinkering with his wristwatch. "A good woman there, boy, let me tell you. Known her all my life. She been good to this family." Mr. Tadbull squinted at the watch with new determination. He went to work with the screwdriver again, apparently trying to pry open the back cover. "Why don't you get you a chauffeur, like you used to have? And one of these sale-you-lahr phone thingamajigs."

Girn stood before a beautiful tall cabinet of pale and satiny pearwood matching the table; lozenges of glass echoed the panes in the bay window behind Mr. Tadbull. Girn poured a heaping tumbler of fine bourbon. Then he used silver tongs to remove ice from a small silver bucket. One, two, three. The ice cubes tinkled musically.

Girn took a big swallow and smacked in pleasure for a moment. "Tadbull, them times is gone. I tell you, it just almost don't pay to sacrifice for the public good no more. Nowadays, somebody's forever gettin' to the trough first or snappin' at my butt. And 'bout the last thing I need is some pain-in-the-ass constituent callin' me while I'm on the crapper."

"Say, Catfish, pour me one, will you, boy?"

As Girn ranted on about the myriad barriers in the path of today's crooked politician, Mr. Tadbull again became absorbed in dissecting the watch. Suddenly, his screwdriver slipped and shot out of his hand, hitting a Tibetan gong that had arrived at Tadbull Hall in the baggage of a globe-trotting ancestor.

"*Got*damn! The gotdamn rice-eating bastards! Can't even change the battery in the gotdamn thing," Mr. Tadbull complained, as if the watch were a microphone to Asia. "You got to buy a whole new one. You know what these things cost? *Fifteen* dollars! Now that's plenty smart of the slant-eyes, isn't it? Lots more than a measly old battery, but not so much you're gonna lose sleep over it. Say, I ever tell you that story about my daddy and the time he sold the scrap iron from our sugar house?"

"I can't call it to mind, just now," Girn said, delivering the drink to his old friend and retrieving the screwdriver. He then sat in a sloping, fringed Edwardian chair recently re-covered in a fabric of golden leaves falling on scarlet ground.

The cozy room was crammed with other museum-worthy furniture in various nineteenth-century styles; with Indian and Civil War artifacts dug up on the property; with fine old books; rare Marlin and Winchester rifles, vintage L. C. Smith, Parker, and LeFever shotguns; hand-carved duck decoys; excellent paintings and watercolors of the local Indians by a Tadbull forebear; and with curious gimcracks from many world tours.

Someone in the family had obviously been an antiquarian or an amateur anthropologist. This scholarly pursuit of knowledge seemed to have degenerated into Mr. Tadbull's manic absorption with his timepiece.

"Was 1960, maybe '62," Mr. Tadbull said, now using the screwdriver to excavate earwax. "We just plum stopped planting cane, because nobody wanted to work hard like that anymore, in the fields and boilerroom and such. A lot of the niggers done moved to Dee-troit to build cars for the unions. So we closed down the place with cane still on the carrier, that's what we did. Yessiree. That's just what we did."

Mr. Tadbull examined the screwdriver head for a moment, and then bent down, grunting, and wiped it on the carpet.

"My daddy had the sugar house and all the other buildings stripped of everything he could sell," he continued. "And these scrap-iron fellas from out West sent a special train over to the lumber mill to pick up the stuff. Well, my daddy heard it was the Japs gonna buy that iron. He went right on out on the tracks and stopped that gotdamn train with nothing but his bare hands! Stood right there in front of it till they gave up and went home. How you like that, Catfish? See, he lost a brother at Pearl Harbor, that's what it was."

"Maybe I have heard that one," Girn said, "once or twice. Look here, Tadbull. Les us get down to business. I been talkin' to Pokie, Coondog, Boo-Boo, and Gumbo, down in Baton Rouge." These were just a few of

Girn's legislative buddies. "They don't have no problem movin' a bill with what we need in it through their committees. 'Course, we got to make it worth their time and effort. But that ain't no problem, neither. They just have to get certain things out of *my* committee, and their usual consultancy fees. We can handle all that. If *our* casino deal comes through, there ought to be plenty for everybody—after we take care of you and me." He winked, one bushy eyebrow closing like a sly flytrap over a bloodshot eye. "Now, here's what's been goin' on since last time you and me talked."

"Hold on, Catfish. When you get to jabbering about what y'all do at the legislature, it's like reading the Bible or listening to a lawyer; I don't understand one nor the other. Let me get my boy in here."

Mr. Tadbull padded hurriedly to the door of the room. "Wooty! Ho, Wooty!" he shouted for his son. And then to Girn: "He's the smart one. But you know that. You the one got him that full scholarship to Freret, and then sent him on to business school. Now that's what I call real statesmanship!"

Both men laughed.

"I'm glad you remember that, Tadbull. We ever settle up on that little arrangement?"

Mr. Tadbull, still chuckling, walked past Girn and patted him on his lean leg. "Don't you worry none, Catfish. We going to take care of you real good in *this* deal. *Got*damn, where is that boy?!"

Wooty filled the doorway. "Sorry, Pop. I was in the office, on the phone." He wore multi-pleated charcoal pants, a gold crinkly silk shirt, and black suede brogues with aggressive soles and rivets.

His studied hipness clashed with his father's imitation of a country gentleman.

"How are you, Rufus?" Wooty said, entering the room and shutting the door behind him. The rubber soles of his shoes squeaked on the oft-polished wood for a few steps before he hit the old carpet. He shook hands with the representative. "Please, don't get up. Enjoy your drink. I think I'll have a Coke, myself."

Wooty stood just short of six feet. He was square of face and fit in body. His black hair flowed in one long salon wave on top, becoming short at the temples with hardly any sideburns. His brooding, speckled blue eyes were darker than his father's. A certain cast of his full lips suggested frustration, perhaps disgust, with the life he had led thus far. Yet, even though his high-school quarterbacking days were over, he still had the peremptory, condescending air of a man accustomed to being obeyed, of a star player stuck on a team below his abilities.

Mr. Tadbull's expression showed that he was proud of his son, of Wooty's arrogant bearing and arresting good looks.

But Mr. Tadbull said, "Wooty, you look like some gotdamn wop, son. These styles today, Catfish. Got-awful, I tell you. Your pants, son…you're tripping over the gotdamn things." The father shook his head in displeasure. This was obviously a scene repeated in variations over and over again. "And what's that fairy shirt you got on? I tell you Catfish, once they get a taste of New Or-leenz, they hooked. Wooty, how come you never wear those good-looking wing-tips I bought you in Armageddon?"

"You know how I hate to shine my shoes, Pop," Wooty said, with sarcasm lost on his father but not on Girn. He sat down in a chair matching Girn's, released a sigh of heroic forbearance, and had a sip of his drink. "Rufus, I understand you've made some progress. Fill us in, why don't you, before Pop really gets going on me. Ever since that watch of his stopped, he's been crankier than a newborn. Like I can't do anything right."

Girn's mustache jumped as he limbered up his mouth. "Well, here's the deal. Them pointy-head Jew pinko faggots in Washington gave these here Katchatoula Indians—"

"Katogoula, Rufus," Wooty interjected.

"Whatever," Girn said, waving his drink in front of him to clear away any further petty objections. "Why this recognition shit happened now, I don't rightly know. But somebody got paid off real fine, you can bet your ass. I only wish I could take credit for it, but our Washington delegation don't ever tell me jackshit. Didn't even get an in-vite to the Mardi Gras ball up there this year." He worked his jaw around, chewing on this slight. "Anyways, it's our fault if we let this chance get away from us. First thing is the question of an initial reservation for them Indians. Now I ask you, where the hell they gonna get one, huh?" He paused a moment for effect.

"They poorer than a tick on a dead man's pecker," Mr. Tadbull said, on cue.

"'Specially now that your mill's done so conveniently closed." Girn turned to Mr. Tadbull, a big, satisfied smirk of complicity stretching his fishy lips.

Mr. Tadbull cleared his throat. He retrieved the screwdriver and began to pry vainly at the watch, avoiding his son's eyes. Apparently, Girn had brought up a touchy subject.

Wooty forcefully set his glass down on a side table crafted of a slice of pecan trunk supported on a tangle of deer antlers.

"Rufus, I never thought much of that idea," he said, an edge to his voice. "Sure, I have no problem with making some money out of the Katogoula's recognition, but I don't want those people hurt anymore, okay. That's all I'm asking. We shouldn't have closed that mill. It was doing okay, providing most of them a pretty good living. I said it then, I say it now, it was wrong."

"Son, we done explained it all to you," Mr. Tadbull blurted out, in apologetic exasperation. "Old Catfish and me, we not getting any younger. We don't got many days to mess around. So, we had to turn up the pressure, that's all. Rufus heard about the recognition through the grapevine, and closing the mill sounded like the best idea at the time.

Remember this, son: when it comes to making money, you can't go worrying your head over right and wrong."

"Them Indians can't hold out long with no jobs or income, now can they?" Girn added. "They got to build this thing, and soon. And we'll just happen to have all our ducks in a row, ready to help 'em out, like the nice folks we are."

"Gotdamn!" Mr. Tadbull exclaimed. "This casino's gonna be something else, son. Class 3 gaming! It's a gotdamn gold mine for us. You watch and see. And the Katogoula'll jump on it."

"Like flies to shit," Girn seconded. "We're talking yearly revenues of two hundred, maybe three hundred million dollars, Wooty. It'll draw suckers in from all over the South. And we'll get a good fat chunk of the net profit!"

"What is it, Rufus," Mr. Tadbull asked, "thirty percent for our group, and half of that for us? You hear that, boy? Fifteen gotdamn percent! We don't have to do a gotdamn thing but count the money." Mr. Tadbull's tone pleaded for understanding. "Son, I'm only doing this for you, so's you can have it all when I'm gone. I know you grew up with those Indians. Hunted with them, played that ball game—"

"Stickball," Wooty said peevishly. He sat hunched forward, contemplating the faded geometry of the fine old Turkish kilim carpet, his hands wedged beneath his thighs, as if to stop them from doing something he'd regret.

"*Got*damn, Catfish. You ought to've seen this boy of mine playing with those Indians, knocking each other silly. All bloody and sweating. Sometimes the whole day, twelve hours at a stretch. They had the women with switches beating their men when things got slow. I say that went a long ways to making him into the all-state quarterback he was."

No one spoke for an awkward minute. Outside, a gang of blue jays noisily harassed some enemy.

"Well, it's done now, anyway," Wooty finally said.

Girn swallowed the bourbon he'd been savoring in his mouth. "Boy, your Indians gonna be so rich they can wipe their asses with hundred-dollar bills. And don't you forget, young fella, not for one minute, that these Krapafoolas are my constituents." The politician held up his left hand, a solemn swearing-in expression on his face. "I look after those that look after me."

For nearly two hours, the three men mapped out their strategy to lock in control of the Katogoula casino they were sure the tribe wanted to build. Wooty, apparently having knuckled under to the persuasive talents of his father and the representative, took notes while Girn held forth.

The initial reservation of a hundred acres was to be carved out of Tadbull land and placed in trust with the federal government, as required by law. The tribe would then have the coveted tax-free status that had recently become so controversial, now that tribes across the nation were scooping up unprecedented amounts of gambling revenue that was technically off-limits to governments.

A tribal casino had tremendous resources to plow back into the operation, and to share with non-Indian partners, who salivated at the chance, even though they would owe taxes on their enhanced earnings. But clever things could be done with profit and expense figures to ease that sting, since Indian casinos weren't required to open their books to the public. Governmental sanction, secrecy, huge tax-advantaged cash flow: a no-lose proposition, Girn assured father and son Tadbull.

Even though the current governor was loudly siding with the anti-gambling, Bible-thumping forces, he'd privately communicated to Girn that the state would sign a seven-year compact, with a rollover clause, giving the Katogoula permission to establish reservation gambling. This treaty would also guarantee the state and the parish a nice chunk of the casino profits, "rendered in good faith and voluntarily," beginning two years after the opening. In fact, either the tribe agreed to pay this back-door tax, and, by the way, to hire the governor's wife's law firm for all legal advice, or there would be no treaty, and no casino.

The alternative was unsavory: a lengthy bureaucratic battle, with the state as probable winner, because tribes could no longer sue it in federal court for refusing to negotiate. The Katogoula's only hope without a state compact would be special intervention by the Secretary of the Interior; but that was big-league politics, and Girn was certain the tribe wasn't up to that yet.

"Sure enough, we got 'em by their red balls," the legislator gloated.

As all of these machinations proceeded under Girn's expert hand, the first of the federal benefits—roughly $300,000 in grants from various agencies—would soon help the tribe set up an administrative structure, and programs for job training, education, housing, and health care.

In stage two, if things worked out, Girn and his cronies would push for the elimination of gambling in the state.

"Eliminate gambling?!" Mr. Tadbull said in utter astonishment.

"That's 'gaming,' Tadbull," Girn said, winking. "And don't you forget it. Louisiana constitution tells us we got to suppress gambling, but gaming's just fine and dandy. So that's what we called it, gaming. And see what happened? There's more video poker machines than urinals, and everybody but me's gettin' rich. That's fixin' to change."

"Gotdamn, Catfish, I don't understand," Mr. Tadbull persisted. "We're going to all this trouble to bring the casino here in the first place."

Wooty closed his eyes and shook his head, embarrassment and impatience twisting his mouth into a grimace.

Girn hastened to clear up Mr. Tadbull's confusion.

The breathless predictions of the benefits of gambling had proved hollow. Retail dollars were disappearing from local economies, gambling addictions were soaring, gambling-related organized crime was spreading like kudzu. Even traditionally blasé Louisiana voters grumbled about video-poker "truck stops" that didn't sell enough diesel fuel to fill a pickup; about casino riverboats—some without engines—that never sailed, in spite of the asinine requirement to do so, which was soon quietly repealed in a special governor-called legislative session; about a land-based casino fiasco in New Orleans that had cost taxpayers many millions; about videotaped payoffs to legislators in Capitol elevators and bathrooms.

Louisiana, always a laggard in most quality-of-life rankings, had one more dishonor to add to its sleazy reputation: first place on the FBI's public-corruption list. Suddenly, "ethics" was all the rage in Baton Rouge, and every bill was sure to pass that contained that magic buzzword. A politician with the odor of gambling on his breath could expect his reputation to be flogged in newspaper editorials and his seat to be stolen by any minister willing to pay the filing fee. Because it seemed to be everywhere, video poker was the special target of the anti-gambling movement.

But Girn and his cronies had a trick or two up their sleeves to take advantage of the new moral tone, while improving their personal balance sheets: a state constitutional amendment abolishing gambling, and even gaming—except for *existing* Indian casinos.

The legislators planned to spread fear about probable decimation of local and state economies if the casinos were closed. Business confidence would be shaken by repudiating contracts with the national companies running the tribal casinos. These operations had required huge investments, and unlike video poker machines and riverboats, couldn't be moved to other markets, the legislators would solemnly point out.

The amendment, as usual in Louisiana, would be so impenetrable, so stealthily handled, that the voters would have no idea of several important provisos until it was too late. The poor fools would think they were immediately voting out all gambling, under every euphemistic guise. And yes, video poker would indeed have to go. A scapegoat.

But actually, any other form of gambling too good to give up, that brought in lucrative payoffs or helped balance the profligate budget or pleased a substantial number of powerful vested interests, these could be finessed into legality. Charitable bingo, horse racing, and the lottery, for example, were to be simply reclassified as "tests of skill."

And thus, Girn explained, established Louisiana Indian casinos would enjoy a relatively protected market—for which favor he fully intended to hit up the other tribes and their corporate partners. Timing was crucial, though. Until the passage of the amendment, Girn's legislative allies would need to kill any conflicting applications for new Indian casinos; there was talk of one or two in the works. No reason to let more competition in under the wire.

Moreover, the amendment had to hang fire until the compact between the state the Katogoula was finalized.

Wooty's first job was to lock Tommy Shawe and his tribe into an agreement with their group.

"Congratulations, boy. You a lobbyist, now," Girn told him. "Don't let a little thing like friendship with that chief of theirs get in your way."

The Katogoula would have to accept a land transfer that would be structured in the form of an exclusive option. The Tadbulls would donate the land for the initial reservation (assuring a nice tax break), in exchange for the irrevocable right to manage the Katogoula casino. The company that the Tadbulls and Girn would form would then hire an Atlantic City group, which was eager to build and run the casino.

Girn's legislative pals would receive regular, substantial "campaign contributions" from the Tadbulls, and standing high-roller invitations for "comped" weekends in Atlantic City.

Girn lit a new cigar with a fireplace match and returned to his chair.

"Gotdamn, Catfish," Mr. Tadbull said, with evident admiration. "You boys down there sure are earning your pay."

"Ain't no problem we can't fix, if'n we put our minds to it," Girn bragged. "Worked out a lot of it at the Blue House."

This was a remodeled residence in a run-down neighborhood of downtown Baton Rouge, a few blocks from the soaring Capitol, Huey

Long's monument to unbridled ego and graft. At the Blue House, lobbyists and legislators met to nail down quids and quos.

"'Course, we still got enemies," said Girn. "The video poker boys would dearly love to kill our casino, 'cause the reservation machines won't be theirs and that's where everybody's paycheck's gonna be spent when it opens. But they can't touch us. And when they hear about the no-gambling amendment, look out! Now, that MaxiGelt Casinos bunch putting on the shindig down the road at the Indian store sure as hell would like our contract. And the Luck o' the Draw bastards in Grosse Jambe, with them Shithouse-Tallywhackers…"

"The Chitiko-Tiloasha," Wooty said.

"Yeah, them folks. I ain't sure what they up to, but they usually play hardball. Spotted their lobbyist yesterday in Baton Rouge making the rounds. They got a lot goin' on already, what with that Bayou Luck casino, and the riverboat in New Orleans. I don't expect they like the idea of a big casino opening in their backyard, neither. I'll have to explain the mutual benefits to their man, next time I catch him in the elevator."

"Probably just trying to run our batteries down," Mr. Tadbull said, now applying himself with renewed vigor to his watch.

Wooty had walked to the fireplace, where big logs lay, ready to be burned when it finally got cool enough outside to turn off the air conditioning inside. He stood with his back to the two older men.

"Pop, what land are you planning to give the Katogoula?"

"Oh, just that scrub acreage down around the old hunting camp. You know, where those burial mounds are. We haven't used that old camp in years, and I think my granddaddy would be proud of me giving back something the tribe dearly loves."

"Say, Wooty," Girn said, "when we start getting all them millions, do me a favor: buy your daddy a new watch."

Wooty turned and stalked to the card table. He snatched the watch from his father and drilled it into the trashcan, a hollowed, painted cypress knee which two centuries before had served as a Katogoula ceremonial drum.

"Well, I can't help it, gotdamnit," Mr. Tadbull said. "That's just the way I am. Now, don't be like that, Wooty. One day you'll be old and crotchety, like me. Catfish, give him the list of our Baton Rouge boys. Wooty, you go on down the hall to the office and write up these checks for us. That temper of yours needs something to do. Use the sawmill's checkbook. Memo 'em...what do you think, Catfish?"

Girn leaned back in his chair and studied the blue smoke rising from his cigar. "'Fertilizer.'"

Mr. Tadbull laughed heartily. "'Fertilizer'! *Got*damn, that's good, Rufus. Yessir, I like the sound of that! Do it like he says, Wooty. When you're finished, come on back and have a few drinks with us. We got big old steaks to grill for supper, son."

Wooty left the room quickly, without a word.

"'Fertilizer'!" Mr. Tadbull said, still chuckling as he rooted around in the trashcan for his watch. "Your boys down there at the Capitol sure done prepared the ground for us, they sure have."

"When you got the best bullshit in the South," Girn said, "you ought to spread some around on your friends' fields."

"That's the *got*damn truth!"

Chapter 12

LIVE BAIT—HOT FOOD—ROLAIDS.

A few minutes after seven P.M., Nick read that appetizing invitation spelled out in black letters on a lighted signboard, and knew he'd finally found Three Sisters Pantry. There was no oncoming traffic, and he suspected there seldom was out here in the boonies of the piney woods of central Louisiana. He downshifted and steered from the gently rolling, two-lane parish road into the crowded gravel-and-dirt parking lot of the general store.

His old MG scraped the rutted ground as it clattered past the sign.

Nick had to grin. Either Luevenia and Royce Silsby, the couple who ran the store, had a good sense of country humor, or else they needed serious tutoring in the mysteries of marketing. He felt sure the former was the case.

He'd driven for five hours from New Orleans, with two bathroom and coffee stops; for the last hour, he'd cursed his way back and forth on wrong roads that led him on an unwanted scenic tour of the pine wilderness of Tchekalaya State Forest.

The green and gold and blue of the forest afternoon had given way to an otherworldly orange dusk. Now the pine woods hugging the back and sides of the store looked to Nick like a giant Irish setter towering over the building, the gas pumps, the dumpsters, and the venerable but well-kept mobile home in the rear.

Most of the parked vehicles were old pickups with a pair of rubber hip waders stuck soles-up between cab and bed; gun racks hanging inside back windows held shotguns, rifles, and fishing rods. In the rural parishes of Louisiana, when fall deer, duck, and squirrel seasons open, towns empty as men and their sons head for the woods; the Katogoula weren't any different, Nick reflected, except that their passion for the outdoors was much older than hunting licenses and bag limits.

He pulled into a narrow space between a rattletrap International pickup and an old Volkswagen van. The van was plastered with decals and stickers of almost every liberal advocacy group he'd ever heard of, and some he hadn't. Definitely an outsider. The locals' trucks displayed stickers declaring "Rush—Right On," "Don't Blame Me—I Voted for O'Reilly," variations on the theme of "pry my cold, dead fingers from the trigger," or even stronger sentiments from beyond the fringe of normal conservatism. The Rebel flag was also popular as an emblem of the local complex of attitudes.

As a general rule, Nick had no interest in airing his own Machiavellian brand of moderately liberal beliefs to proselytize or antagonize those on the opposite end of the spectrum—especially when they were clients. He wasn't a picketer, a marcher, or even a complaint-letter writer. What was the point? Anyone with an opinion strong enough to be objectionable to someone else has no interest in changing teams. And besides, out here in the sticks, they probably settled ideological conflicts with those ubiquitous guns. The wisdom of taking a bullet for a bumper sticker escaped him.

He killed the engine, and in the process, a fading signal of National Public Radio.

As he stepped from his car, the hypnotic, strangely plaintive and foreboding whine of cicadas enveloped him. The fat bugs had slept silently for years in the ground, and now, having shed their old skin, they clumsily crawled and flew around looking for mates of the same cycle, uncomprehending actors in an ancient script penned on their chromosomes.

Nick walked across the parking lot toward the store, scaring up puffs of red dirt. His briefcase seemed heavier; it must be, he supposed, the weight of the responsibility of exhuming and releasing long-slumbering family histories among the present generation. What would the living tribe hear in the songs of their ancestors?

In front of the store sat three sparkling rent cars and a van, parked in spaces that obviously had been saved for them; their flashy newness seemed to make the sturdy frame building, constructed of weathered, unpainted cypress, look like a cut-out from a Depression-era photograph. Nick wondered if a similar clash of cultures was occurring inside.

The raised porch stretched across the front of the store below a slanting, tin-roofed overhang propped up by thick posts. Nick walked up steps of well-worn planks onto the porch, where a bare bulb overhead and a large neon Lotto sign above the entrance provided weak light. A cardboard sign stuck in the frame of the screen door informed the visitor: TRIBEL MEETING TONITE. INVITED GESTS COME ON BACK. CUSTOMERS JUST HOLLER.

The screen door squealed like an animal in agony as Nick opened it and entered the store. A customer wouldn't need to holler after being announced by *that* rural doorbell.

He found himself standing in a rectangular open area, fifteen by ten feet; five long shelving units, filled on both sides with merchandise, started where the open area ended. A walkway between the two central units led to the rear of the store, where, as he judged from the indistinct sound of people mingling, the meeting had yet to begin. More bare incandescent bulbs with dented metal reflectors hung from rough-hewn rafters. Nick looked behind him and saw six stools under the large windows flanking the front door. One for each of the six core families—a physical manifestation of the tribe's genealogy?

A nice place to spend the day drinking coffee and talking about nothing very important, Nick decided. He couldn't put his finger on exactly why, but the pleasant clutter of the store had a soothing, private aura, even though it was a public place. Like a house of worship, this place seemed to emanate unshakable solidarity and faith. The comforting smell of home cooking wafted through the air. Nick thought of the family kitchens of his childhood, where many troubles had been weathered and a few triumphs celebrated; and he had a fleeting vision of something even older: a cave, a procession of generations, innumerable fingers reaching for warmth from a flickering fire, for sustenance from offering hands.

The construction of the old store confirmed to Nick that trees and the lumber industry had been the mainstay of this community for a long time. Hunting and fishing, too: almost every inch of wall space not dedicated to commerce sprouted stuffed specimens of the local wildlife, once dangerous or benign.

To his left Nick saw the cash-register counter, festooned with hundreds of small useful, tasty, or frivolous things for sale, as if it were a nineteenth-century peddler's wagon. Down the wall on that side was a set of venerable coolers that certainly contained lots of banned refrigerant. The wall on the other side of the store was a jumble of long-handled implements, stacked bags of feed and seed, columns of tires, ladders, and other supplies for people who fixed and built things for themselves. Nick had no clue what much of this stuff was.

"Used to be the company store over at Tadbull Lumber Mill," a female voice said. "The present Mr. Tadbull's father donated it to us back in the sixties. We moved it out here. They don't build them like this anymore."

He hadn't heard her approach. "You must be Luevenia Silsby."

"Yes."

"I'm—"

"I know who *you* are, too." She looked him up and down for a moment—an awkward moment, for Nick. Her steel-framed glasses sparkled over dark brown eyes; Nick had a vague recollection of a childhood dentist who'd worn similar specs. "The genealogist," she said at last, unenthusiastically. He had an irrational, unsettling idea that she'd been watching him for some time.

Nick offered his hand; she hesitated, and then quickly clasped and released his fingers, as if he had some disease she was worried about catching.

He tried to maintain a semblance of politeness: "Tommy was right on the money with his description of you. He also said you've held the tribe together for years."

"That boy's been talking a lot of foolishness again," she said. Her apparent modesty was mixed with a certain condescending air that grated on Nick. Or was there downright hostility in her cool reception? What could Luevenia Silsby have against him, or his trade? he wondered. Maybe when he got to know her better, she would warm up to him, and he to her. According to Tommy, she was an extraordinary woman, strong-willed, smart, and fair, whose opinions held great sway with the other tribe members.

He imagined she seldom got taken in by sharpsters. Luevenia Silsby could surely cut off the glibbest of salesmen in mid pitch. Yet she seemed uncomfortable without the insulating barrier of her cash-register counter. Her hands drew Nick's attention. They were lovely, not the hard-working hands of a storekeeper in her fifties; they seemed to radiate health and fastidious cleanliness and sempiternal youthfulness. She held them crossed at her trim stomach, rare jewels on display. A surgeon's or a priest's hands, Nick was thinking. The brief touch of her fingers had felt like a benediction.

"I didn't know you had any sisters," he said affably. "Not a very good refection on my abilities as a genealogist."

She looked briefly puzzled, and then smiled, revealing a faint glint of gold fillings. He got the distinct feeling she was laughing *at* him, not *with* him.

"You mean the name of this place, don't you?"

Nick nodded.

"*We* all know what it stands for. Just never occurred to me that...oh, I'm not making fun of you. It's just that nobody's ever asked that, and lots of folks been asking plenty around here, lately. All of a sudden, everybody wants to poke their nose into our business."

She drew up her shoulders, subtly growing a bit in height, as if ready to let some transgressor have an earful; but with a sniff she relaxed. Her sudden peevishness was gone.

"The three sisters are corn, beans, and squash—the crop staples of the Indians in the Southeast. That's what we call them."

"Oh, I see," Nick said, feeling suddenly ignorant of the American Indian tradition, in spite of his recent concentrated study of the subject.

He'd noticed Luevenia's pride in relating facts of tribal history; she must have taught Tommy's generation a great deal about the Katogoula heritage. It was people like her, with their unwritten stock of remembrances, who could transform the story told by colorless genealogical charts into a human mosaic of inimitable and timeless beauty. She would probably be a good choice as the new tribe's historian and genealogical director. He'd have to mention his idea to Tommy.

Nick recognized a kindred spirit, a teacher at heart, who would never refuse to share her cup of learning. He was beginning to like Luevenia Silsby, in spite of her prickly personality. He would enjoy the challenge of working with her.

"I guess you better come on back, then." She made a half-turn and added, "You can have some coffee and persimmon bread. A Katogoula favorite. My girls make it real good...no, I don't have any daughters, either. I'm talking about my *cooks*. Or maybe you'd like some supper?"

Her instincts as a hostess cut through whatever had bothered her about Nick's arrival.

He told her he'd already eaten, but the coffee and persimmon bread—whatever it was—sounded good.

"Tommy'll be glad you're here," she said. "These business folks, he's not used to dealing with them. And he's got too much on his mind, what with his brother's death and all." She shook her head. "Find you a seat and I'll bring your coffee and bread. You'll need *something* to keep you awake with these Las Vegas screwballs and their cockamamie ideas. They don't know diddly-squat about us. Even less than you do."

Ignoring the gratuitous insult, he followed the bespectacled little woman, who wore jeans and a cowboy shirt. And moccasins, which helped explain how she'd surprised him a few minutes earlier. Nick could see from her stiffness that she had some arthritis, and a question jumped into his consciousness: could a person with that handicap have sent an atlatl spear through a man's body?

Now was not the time to ask her what she knew about Carl Shawe's murder, even though his intuition was telling him that finding the killer was vital to the tribe's continued existence. From the moment he stepped from his car, he'd felt the presence of a murderous tragedian thousands of years old, standing just behind the gauzy curtain of reality, rehearsing for the next violent act of the present. Nothing was unconnected here.

Hawty would not be happy at the macabre direction of his thoughts. She always accused him of seeing murder in everyone's heart. But he had discovered that he was right: murder is coded in our souls, waiting for just the right catalyst that will motivate the machinery of self-justification. And this inherited potential for homicide that we all share fascinated him as much as the nonviolent, merely documentary aspects of genealogy.

Luevenia's gray hair was pulled back and woven into a bun as intricate as the pine-needle baskets that hung for sale from the rafters above them. She would not have appeared Indian to him, he thought as he followed her, if he hadn't known for sure that she was. Her coloring was more the café-au-lait variety—called locally "high yellow"—of the Cane River Creoles from the area around the old French settlement of Natchitoches, just forty miles to the northwest. Yet, she was supposed to have more Katogoula blood than anyone else in the tribe.

The Katogoula were fortunate that recognition had finally been given, Nick concluded. Race and ethnicity are slippery concepts constantly rewritten in the wet clay of human history. It all boils down to what we want to believe, not what genealogists and the Census Bureau say. In another generation, maybe two, the tribal heirs might look in the mirror and no longer consider themselves Katogoula. The human herd would then be poorer for the extinction of another species of identity.

Luevenia led Nick to the smoky dining area, where a hundred or so people sat at mismatched tables; others chatted in six green-vinyl booths along the back wall. The room was crowded to capacity; most of the tribe seemed to be here.

Tobacco was one Indian tradition that had remained strong: most adults held a cigarette; quite a few men had the telltale cheek bulge of a chaw.

The gangly younger men wore Western clothes; the pot-bellied older ones favored overalls and jumpsuits. The women had gone to more trouble for the occasion: young wives and daughters showed off their figures with flattering blouses and pants, while plump matrons wore full-fitting tunic or shirt dresses. Judging from the plentiful, handsome beadwork and embroidery, Nick figured most of the women's clothing was handmade.

A service window, about three-feet square, framed a view of the well-ordered kitchen, where two young women Nick assumed were also Katogoula served up his coffee and bread to Luevenia, and then leaned forward on the window shelf, ready to listen to the Las Vegas show that was about to begin.

Nick spotted Tommy waving him over to a booth. A woman and three children scooted to make room. Tommy introduced his pregnant wife, Brianne, and as Nick shook her hand a man just to the left of the kitchen began to address the group.

"Here we go again," complained Brianne. She propped her chin in a palm.

"Ladies and gentlemen, good morning," the man said. He had a face like an organizational chart—a grid of symmetrical furrows and compartmentalized muscles that in unison seemed to shout the corporate mantra, "Sell! Sell! Sell!" His beaming cheerfulness made Nick nervous, even at this distance.

"It's evening here, Hal," a woman said irritably from the nearest booth, where she sat with two other business types, a man and a woman, both appearing at least twenty years younger than the first woman and Hal.

Nick instantly saw the dynamic of the team: Hal did the smooth-talking, probably got all the glory back in Vegas, while the rest of the crew handled the wearisome details. Especially the woman, whose heavy make-up did not hide the puffy red rage of long subordination. He discerned a certain haggardness at odds with her pantsuited professional image, and he suspected that only lots of money and booze had so far kept her from strangling smiley-faced Hal.

Will Hawty one day snarl at me for analogous reasons? Nick felt this question roll over him in a sweaty wave of self-loathing as he sipped hot coffee and broke off pieces of persimmon bread, which was a delicious spicy cake flecked with bits of dark red fruit and the tender, rich meat of pecans. *You're so wise when it comes to the inner landscapes of strangers, how can you be so willfully blind to the feelings of those you care most about?* He vowed to mend his ways, but knew he wouldn't.

"Oh, boy," Hal chuckled, rubbing his eyes, and shaking his head playfully, as if someone had just thrown a bucket of cold water on him. "You bet, Connie. I'm jet-lagged, still on Hawaii time, folks; just got back from our newest property out there. And we've already synergized with three other groups on this trip. My apologies. Let me tell you, lots of folks are eager to nexus a value-added, win-win, proactive relationship with MaxiGelt Casinos." Hal polished his business-speak with a big, toothy grin.

"Slick as a water moccasin, ain't he?" Tommy said to Nick.

The MaxiGelt Casinos team had come equipped with laptops and projectors and mini-printers, graphs and maps and aerial photos on foam board, brochures and pamphlets and sample contracts. In a round-robin presentation, the other team members followed Hal. They spoke of cash flow, depreciation, slot-machine take, square footage, payroll, and security. In that spartan back dining area, they constructed a mirage of a casino complex that left the audience with open mouths and blinking eyes.

The plan called for four restaurants, a nightclub, two hotels, a live-entertainment theater, a golf/tennis complex, three swimming pools, a skeet range, a go-cart track, a multi-level shopping mall, a Native America theme park and museum, and a two-year accredited junior college with a well-funded sports department and an e-cubator, this last a program to nurture Internet-based business ideas. And there was more: a new super-warehouse store to anchor the fabulous mall. It would be the first of a nationwide chain. Three Sisters Pantry! It all seemed so easy.

The younger MaxiGelt man dramatically yanked a cloth from a stunning architectural rendering of the proposed development. He began explaining every angle.

After twenty-five minutes, Connie stood up to cut off her colleague. She deftly handed the ball to Hal for the grand finale.

"We're proposing a paradigm shift, here, my friends," Hal said, as he strutted excitedly before the attentive audience. "With MaxiGelt Casinos at your side, optimizing wallet share, market-focused on reinventing the event horizon, you will headlight into success, helicopter over your competitors—and well we know there are plenty in this part of the South! Oh yes, we need to imaginize the mission statement *together*." He flipped to the next board on the easel beside him and used a laser pointer as he read off each word: "Grow self-sustainancy through profitizing your new knowledge workers in collaborative commerce solutions. The Katogoula Indians and MaxiGelt Casinos"—another board—"Change agents for OUR future! Thank you."

Nick saw puzzled faces among the Katogoula. He himself had been tempted to reach for the pocket dictionary in his briefcase.

Scattered applause began.

"At least he got the name right," Brianne observed to Tommy and Nick, as she stopped her daughter from collecting the few remaining crumbs on Nick's plate with a mouth-moistened tiny index finger. "That's more than some of the others did."

Brianne had thick, long, beautiful brown hair, gathered in a loose twist hanging down her back; Nick thought of Mary Pickford, from her films of the 1920s.

"This is the third presentation this week," Tommy said. The circles under his eyes were darker than the last time Nick had seen him. Tommy stood up. "Let me go get these people on the road, or else they'll just move in with us. And I don't think I'd like that. How 'bout you, boys?"

His fidgeting twin sons giggled and made disapproving faces.

Tommy joined the Las Vegans as they packed up. Off to the side, Hal and another man stood chatting. Hal brayed in laughter.

"Who's that?" Nick asked Brianne.

"Talking to that man from Las Vegas? Oh, that's Irton Dusong. The woman's Grace, his wife. They run our little tribal museum over on the Golden Trace, not far from our house. He retired from the mill a few years ago after he got hurt. They were the ones that broke the tie."

"On the vote to continue the casino process?"

She nodded. Brianne, as Nick recalled, had voted against it.

Vegas Hal was playing tribal politics, trying to suck up to those who favored the casino. Nick watched him as he put an arm around Irton like an old buddy, guiding him to the front of the store. Nick heard him loudly promise first-class treatment if Irton ever came out to Las Vegas.

Nick turned his attention to the twins. He liked children; and he was mesmerized by their mystical power, their omnivorous nature, their connection to a boundless reality adults can no longer access. How many baptisms and bar mitzvahs had he attended? Too many to remember. Sometimes, as now in the presence of these children, he felt the stinging pang of being childless, of having muddled through life chasing superfluous goals that paled beside the amazing grace of a child's love.

A line from Yeats's poem "Among School Children" came to mind. Had he become a ludicrous, slightly scary old man to children—as the twins' expressions hinted—condemned to be merely an awed observer of the magical creatures other people brought to life, bequeathing a measure of glory to the collective human experience? Was he to be the last of his line, a recusant of four billion years of Earth genealogy?...

"You guys excited about being government-approved Indians?" he asked the twins, thinking that he should kick this bad habit of thinking too much.

The boys waggled their heads in wild meaningless agitation, and then frogged each other in some never-ending, secret war that had just flared up anew. It was as if each boy were striking his image in a mirror.

"*Boys*," Brianne warned, still somehow sounding as calm as a fall morning. "Tonight they're eleven going on six. Thank heavens for school."

Nick had always marveled at the few people he'd known who seemed to sip from a spring of serenity.

"I used to be a teacher," Nick told the twins, "now I travel around making sure boys and girls are studying hard and getting ready for college."

Their faces grew wary at this revelation. The enemy in their midst! He remembered aunts and uncles who'd played this age-old teasing game with him. Empty, cruel drollery, he'd once thought; but now, having fun doing it himself, he saw it as nourishment for the budding skeptical sense.

"Boys, go out on the porch and play with the other children," Brianne said. "Wait!"

They'd already bolted toward the front, as if some huge sno-cone of badness awaited them in the darkness outside.

"Sam, Matt, you be good, or else *somebody* I know won't be riding horses this weekend."

And they were gone, in a flurry of loose limbs.

"This should be a happy time for Tommy," Brianne said, her voice worried and uncertain, the loving sternness directed at her children now missing. "We buried Carl yesterday. Took an awful long time for the autopsy and all."

"Where?"

"The tribal graveyard. It's on state forest land, but we have rights to use it however we want. Tommy's father worked that out. It's a nice place. Quiet. Just the sound of the wind through the pines."

She folded a green cloth napkin into a small, neat square and placed it on the table even with the edge.

"Carl wasn't all that bad," she said. "He just didn't like people telling him what to do. If anybody'd asked him, I bet he would've been against the casino. Sometimes I think he was the sanest of any of us. Our tribe might not a had to go through all we did if more of us been like him from the start."

She turned to check on the sleeping two-year-old girl beside her.

"This graveyard," Nick said, "I'd like to see it." He was mentally salivating, picturing the feast of information such a place usually had in store for the intrepid genealogist willing to brave the elements and assorted biting, blood-sucking creatures—fleas and ticks, mostly, not vampires.

"See that man over there," Brianne said, pointing to a man in a uniform. "That's Nugent Chenerie."

"Nooj?"

"Yes, that's what everybody calls him. Tommy's told you about Nooj, then? He's the one you want to talk to about the graveyard. He's always taking people on tours out there and on the Golden Trace. Or he'll point you in the right direction, at least."

The baby had awakened and was whimpering. Brianne gathered her up and rocked her. That did the trick; the baby drifted off again.

Brianne had something else on her mind. She spoke softly as her daughter slumbered on her chest. "I feel I know you, Nick. Like I can talk to you." Her apologetic hesitation gave way to the boldness of a woman doing what she thought was right. "Tommy's told me all about you, how hard you're working for us. How much you care. All this"—she meant the presentation—"doesn't matter one way or another to me. What's best for Tommy and our kids, that's what I worry about. I didn't want him to have this responsibility, but he wanted it, and they gave it to him."

Her next words carried a burden of anxiousness: "People say you—well, I'm not sure how to say this—you untangle things. Not just family trees. I mean, bad things. Murders. Find out who killed Carl. If it *was* a 'who.'"

She looked down at her sleeping baby and then back up at Nick, some deeper force urging her past hesitation. "Some are saying our tribal spirits are unhappy with what we're doing. There's evil behind Carl's death. I can feel it, like a cold wind. Evil that wants to destroy my family and my tribe. Don't ask me how I know that, because I'm not sure myself. You can stop it."

Nick, too, could have sworn he felt a cold wind at his back that raised goose bumps on his skin.

"You don't believe in our ways," Brianne said, "so you're not afraid. And maybe these spirits won't hurt you."

Unafraid? Right now, dear lady, I'm terrified.

"Sure, I'll..." he stammered, "I'll do what I can."

Brianne patted his hand on the table in thanks. Nick had the feeling she had known he wouldn't disappoint her. "Will you be staying with us?" she asked. "I can make up the couch real nice for you."

"No, but thanks for the offer. I understand there's a motel not far away. That would be best for me, since I may be here for a few days and my hours are a bit unpredictable."

"We'll be counting on you for supper, then, whenever you want."

Nick threaded his way through the gathering. He met Royce Silsby, a low-key, paunchy man who seemed relieved that his wife, Luevenia, had things well in hand. Odeal Caspard was an elfin bachelor in his eighties; he immediately launched into a corny joke about a short man who sued the state for building the sidewalk too close to his ass. Nick also spoke with Irton and Grace Dusong, Felix and Alberta Wattell, and other Katogoula who sounded familiar from his research.

He began to get a feel for the mood of the tribe. The Katogoula, like an individual, had elements of conflict below the outward unity. An unspoken tension, as thick as the hanging layer of smoke, permeated the dining room; faces showed uncertainty, furtive eyes avoided contact. Nick was sure there must be the usual smoldering feuds here that every close-knit group has; but he gathered that this casino question was a new and serious wedge splitting the grain of this tribe, as nothing had for decades or centuries. There should have been elation over the long-delayed tribal recognition, but Nick saw only ill-disguised angst.

It was after ten thirty now. Most adults were ambling toward the front of the store. Odeal Caspard still rattled on with his silly jokes, but the others couldn't muster similar bonhomie. The men, their hands stuffed in pockets, shuffled singly, contemplating their steps; the women walked cross-armed in twos and threes or gave herding spanks to their weary but still obstinate children.

Only Nooj Chenerie, standing just outside the back door, on the porch that faced the sentinel pines, seemed in no hurry to leave.

Nick had been hoping for a chance to talk to the wildlife enforcement agent, and this looked like it.

Chapter 13

Nooj Chenerie smoked a cigarette and gazed out into the night. He leaned on a leg propped on a massive old cypress stump.

The stump apparently served as a chopping block, Nick judged from the clinging feathers and dried stains. He had trouble picturing Luevenia—she of the lovely hands—remorselessly chopping the head off a chicken, duck, dove, or quail.

At Nick's approach, Nooj put both feet on the porch and straightened up. He wore the Louisiana Department of Wildlife and Fisheries uniform: gray short-sleeve field shirt, black epaulettes over departmental shoulder patches, and black pants. If he stepped a few feet off the porch, Nick thought, he would blend easily into the shadows of the pine woods—except for his glittering state-shaped badge and the departmental pins on his collar. His black-billed gray cap repeated the embroidered LWF shield patches on the sleeves, each featuring a mallard flying over, and a wary buck standing below, the word "ENFORCEMENT."

The man was two inches shorter than Nick, but barrel chested and ridged with muscle from neck to shoulders. His hips were slight and his arms were thick. The body of a wrestler and weightlifter, Nick decided—not that he spoke from any first-hand knowledge. Nooj's hair was jet black, straight, shiny, and short; his face was round with a deep cinnamon tint below the surface glaze of constant exposure to the elements. He appeared to be somewhere in his early thirties.

It had turned cool unexpectedly. Nick wondered what was keeping the enforcement agent warm.

Nooj's genes had come together in a noticeably Indian way. His personality was not so open to examination. Nick thought he had the look of a man who could go weeks or years without seeing or speaking with anyone, and not care—certainly a plus in his line of work, though he probably had a partner and a team he had to work with.

Nick introduced himself, offering his hand. Nooj tamped and squashed the glow on his cigarette between the tips of his thumb and index finger, and then jettisoned the unfiltered butt into the darkness, in no particular hurry. "Fire hazard," he said, as he turned to shake hands, keeping the shadow cast by the bill of his cap in a line just below his eyes.

"What did you think of the presentation?" Nick said, still a little distracted by the cigarette trick. Was it macho ostentation, or did this guy simply like pain?

Nooj shrugged and draped his powerful right hand on the big stainless semi-automatic on his right hip, as if it were his sweetheart. "Don't know that I have to think anything. Or tell you about it, if I do."

Tommy had his work cut out for him; this was one cranky tribe. Nick recalled Luevenia's less than ecstatic reception, and briefly considered suggesting to Tommy that he hire a psychologist rather than a genealogist for the Katogoula.

"Are you opposed to gambling?" Nick said, undeterred by the man's aloofness.

"Not for it or against it," Nooj said, again looking into the night-shrouded forest. "I buy my Lotto every week. Somebody wants to waste his money, guess that's his business."

"But you don't think the casino's a good idea? Could be the chance this tribe's been waiting for. I've heard that a casino is a big factor in determining whether a tribe lives or dies these days. It could make you self-sufficient. Like the Chitiko-Tiloasha."

"A tribe can die in more ways than one."

Nick was about to ask him what he meant by that cryptic reply when Nooj turned to him, now seemingly ready to engage fully in a conversation that might give Nick something he could use—either to fill in the story of the tribe's history, or to get closer to the murderer of Carl Shawe.

Nooj cocked his head at an inquisitive angle. Light from the dining room slanted across his eyes. Striking eyes—dark blue, mostly, but chameleonic, like a spellbinding paperweight that reveals a new view of glittering mineral jaggedness locked inside each time you turn the icy globe of glass.

"Look," Nooj said, "we got along without the government and without these Las Vegas hucksters for a long time. Now we're federally recognized. We're gonna regret it, mark my word. When you get the government involved and you belly up to the trough, things get messed up real fast. I know. I've seen what fuck-ups and crooks run our state government. All governments. Always have, always will. Nothing changes."

"You take a paycheck from the state. Aren't you biting a little too hard the hand that feeds you?"

"They don't buy what's in here," Nooj said, beating his chest as though it were a ceremonial drum; Nick felt the percussion from where he stood. "What do we have to become, in here, to get this casino? This ain't just about gambling and money." He smiled bitterly. "It's like the old days, when the whites boozed and bamboozled us, got us in hock with contracts we couldn't read or understand if we could, and then stole our lands before we could decide to fight back. That's what I don't want to happen. It looks too good to be true, because it is. We're human, just like other people. We're getting greedy.

"Leave things like they were," he continued. "Sure, the mill closed, but these men can find work eventually. The economy's ups and downs don't matter so much here. The state's always got a project on the shelf, a prison or new state recreation area. I been talking to the highway department about maybe using a local crew to do some major road work that's budgeted. But that ain't gonna happen. They'll use Green Card Mexicans for that highway, like always, and the Katogoula casino'll be built. Too many in Baton Rouge got a stake in gambling. Now we'll get more of these outsiders coming in, until they own us."

He paused a moment. The resentment in the blue eyes eased. "I don't mean you, so much, 'cause you're just trying to help. Or her over there; she's on our side, too. I don't have nothing against whites, just 'cause they're white. I work with them all the time."

Nick looked across the room and saw a remarkably attractive young woman, a redhead, shouldering a video camera. He'd noticed her before—how could he not?—but he'd thought she was part of the Las Vegas group.

Nooj said, "Look, I just think all this development and recognition crap is bad for us, dangerous for our souls and tradition. You can take that for what it's worth."

"Hey," Nick said, "I know where you're coming from. Maybe the Great Spirit is trying to tell you something with Carl's death." Nick had tried to make it a joke, but actually he was fishing for some reaction. "Maybe the gods are angry."

No sign of guilt struggled to the surface on Nooj's face. "You won't get many around here to say they follow the old religion. Sure, we do the Green Corn Ceremony, leave sand and corn at graves."

"*La Fête du Blé?*" Nick asked, throwing out the name the Katogoula used, until modern times, for the sacred festival. "Marriage vows renewed, the year's arguments resolved, houses swept clean."

"Yeah." Nooj looked at Nick with new interest. "You're up on your Indian customs. Impressive. But all that's just superstition now, when you get down to it. Kind of like Halloween, just going through the motions. Catholicism's too strong. You're going to find that's what these folks believe in. Most of our ancestors went to mission schools, if they went at all. The conversion process started a long time ago. We really lost the battle then."

"I understand you found Carl's body out by the lake." Nick had learned firsthand from New Orleans detectives the value of a sudden shift of direction during an interview.

Nooj lit another cigarette with a disposable lighter, casting the near side of his face in murky orange relief. Nick got a disconcerting glimpse of cold eyes, watching him. Nooj's profile, sculpted from the darkness in the momentary flare, was a totemic silhouette, older than written history.

"Carl, he had lots of enemies," Nooj said, exhaling a strong stream of smoke. "You don't have to go looking to gods in the forest for his murderer. My job's policing the killing of deer and ducks, not people. You best talk to the sheriff, if that's what you're interested in tonight."

"That's not *my* job," Nick said. "Just curious, that's all. I'm sure the sheriff doesn't need me interfering in his affairs. A genealogist usually looks at death from the distance of decades and centuries, not days; I prefer grass on the grave before I start digging around. Besides, I don't see how Carl's death has anything to do with the genealogy of the tribe…do you?"

"Not hardly," Nooj said, without elaboration.

Nick believed precisely the opposite, but he wasn't sure if Nooj simply didn't see it or if he was hiding something. He decided to play unsuspecting genealogist.

"Speaking of genealogy," Nick said, "I'm researching the family histories of the six core families, and I'm having a little trouble with your paternal line, the Cheneries. Your parents weren't included in the original genealogical work for recognition, back in the sixties, right?"

"My daddy was in the Army. We didn't move back here for good until the early seventies. We missed out on Mr. Shawe's tribal-recognition project."

"I see. So no one's formally documented your Chenerie Katogoula roots?"

"Don't expect they have."

"I'd like to locate your Chenerie grandparents. I've checked the censuses for this parish and beyond, actually, but I haven't found your surname during the likely periods."

Nooj hesitated—long enough for Nick to read that he'd hit a sensitive nerve.

"That don't surprise me," Nooj said. "My daddy's folks moved around a lot, too, between here and Oklahoma. Sort of a family tradition, like avoiding government officials asking questions."

Censuses were a mercurial friend to genealogists. In them, Nick had stumbled on lies and omissions as he sought facts and revelations.

"Like I wrote down on that questionnaire you gave us," Nooj continued, less hesitantly, as if he'd suddenly recalled the details of his family history, "I don't know my Chenerie grandma's maiden name, and my granddaddy was kind of an orphan. Didn't know for sure who his own parents were; no one talked about it. My daddy always suspected a white man fathered his daddy, and my people run him off. Mighta been love, migtha been rape. Story was my Chenerie great-grandma died in childbirth. See, us Indians used to be ashamed of white blood, like whites were of Indian blood. Used to call 'em 'breeds.' Now, most everyone's a breed." Nooj gave an arid smile. "Prob'ly something like that, I expect. Wasn't a Katogoula reservation set aside in Oklahoma, so my granddaddy grew up with a Choctaw family that musta been friends with us."

Nick's pen hovered over a full page of his notebook. "So, you think your grandfather inherited the Chenerie name directly from his mother?"

"And the heritage," Nooj said, as if responding to an insult.

Nick succeeded in prying more information from Nooj about the Cheneries. According to family legend, his Katogoula ancestors of the paternal line left Louisiana with the refugee Choctaw in the 1830s on the long slog to the promised peace of the federal reservations. Over the years, other branches of the Chenerie family married into different tribes, into the general populace, or died out. But a few of Nooj's line kept the forests of central Louisiana in their hearts, and whenever they could, they returned to live with their struggling brethren hiding in wooded isolation from the overwhelming onslaught of white culture.

"I never looked myself, never much cared, but I think you can have a better conversation with my Chenerie cousins up there, in Oklahoma, like I said. They're probably all Choctaw by now. If any are left."

He pointed northwest—Nick supposed, for he had no idea otherwise. Nooj would know compass directions intuitively, as part of his job, as part of his heritage. He knew the lay of the land as well as any duck that cupped its wings to land in this major stop on the Central Flyway, a knowledge passed down through generations.

"Thanks. You've been a big help," Nick said.

A bit of an overstatement. Nooj had been long on generalities, short on specifics. It would be exceedingly difficult to get beyond his Chenerie grandfather, if the family lore proved true. But at least now Nick had a specific tribe and a general location for his search of the bewildering number of Indian censuses and other Indian records the U.S. government had compiled since the early nineteenth century.

"Your mother's family is well represented in parish censuses locally and in Chitiko-Tiloasha tribal censuses from the 1840s and on," Nick said. "The Bellarmines consistently state that they're Katogoula, even when they're living with another tribe in another part of the state."

"Would've been easier if they'd just lied and said they were Chitiko-Tiloasha," Nooj said. "They could've gotten on the tribe's official roll, pocketed a nice handout, maybe taken some allotment land. But the strong ones in my family've never been much on selling out. Either side."

"Don't worry," Nick said, "you're a bona fide Katogoula. What we already know about your mother's line proves that."

"I'm not worried. I know what I am," Nooj replied.

"Yeah. I can see that. But I'll keep working on your paternal line. Thoroughness—that's what I'm getting paid for.... I wonder, would there be anything useful for me in the tribal cemetery in the forest? Can you take me?"

Nooj shrugged. "Sure. You won't find any graves more than about a hundred years old. Katogoula didn't use the white's burial practices before then. We were still mound builders. I'll show you the mounds, if you want; but those don't come with headstones."

A small gibe to put him back in his place as a permanent outsider, Nick supposed.

"The cemetery's on state forest land, but the mounds are private property."

"Tadbull property?" Nick asked.

"Um-hmm," Nooj confirmed through a last puff of his cigarette. He crushed out the glowing end with fingertips as tough as leather. Smoke streamed from his nostrils. "Call me when you're ready to go out there. Keeping tourists safe is my job, too."

He handed Nick a business card, and without another word walked to the edge of the porch and hopped down two feet to the ground. He strode into the dark woods, making no sound on the carpet of fallen pine needles.

Nick pocketed the card and entered the quiet, empty dining room, wondering about the Tadbulls, who seemed to pop up in most conversations delving into Katogoula history.

Chapter 14

Hurrying to their next road-show venue, the Las Vegans had departed Three Sisters Pantry; most of the tribe members had left, as well.

The Shawe twins, possessing apparently inexhaustible energy, chased each other with fallen pine branches on, off, and under the front porch. Their mother, Brianne, visible through the store windows, cradled her sleeping infant and chatted with Luevenia and Royce at the cash register.

Two men stood beside a car in the middle of the nearly deserted parking lot. Above them, a mercury-vapor light on an aluminum arm arched out from a pine tree and cast a bone-white glare around them.

Dodging the darting twins, Nick deposited his briefcase in his car and headed for the two men, an easy stone's throw away. He recognized one man and had no doubt who the other was.

Tommy Shawe talked with a mahogany giant. Strongly disagreeing or denying, Tommy shook his head repeatedly. The big man reached in a pants pocket and handed Tommy something that caught the light momentarily. Tommy held the item in a tight grasp before carefully depositing it in his own pocket. The big man propped one massive arm on the open door of a white police-model Chevrolet, emergency lights on the inside.

"Sangfleuve Parish—Sheriff," Nick read on the car door.

The big man Nick presumed to be Sheriff Higbee wore a businessman's semi-casual clothes—large ones, to get around his three-hundred-plus-pound body: button-down, long-sleeve striped shirt, neatly pressed and unencumbered by a tie; dark-gray trousers; and dressy Rockports of double-digit size.

Nick's first impression suggested that the sheriff was a self-assured, dynamic man aspiring to higher positions than chief ribbon-cutter of a parish in the sticks.

Higbee wasn't packing a gun, Nick could see as he got closer—at least not a visible one. Why should he? Sheer physical intimidation was probably sufficient in most tense situations, and in others that weren't destined to end violently, words—a politician's weapon of choice—would do the trick. The sheriff's badge gleamed on his belt. That, too, struck Nick as an unnecessary reminder of authority: who wouldn't know this walking mountain of a man?

"Well, if it isn't Mr. Jonathan Nicholas Herald, genealogist extraordinaire," the sheriff said in a booming voice that shattered the nuanced sighs of the forest night. His tone was full of jovial sarcasm, but the beaming political grin put Nick at ease as the man's large hand surrounded his. "Your fame precedes you, Mr. Herald. I take the *Times-Picayune*. Seems like you're regular front-page material in New Orleans. NOPD won't make a move without consulting with you first, I hear."

Nick's body shook as the sheriff pumped his arm a few times.

"A left-handed compliment, but I'll take it," Nick said. "Genealogy's usually a pretty sedate field. But, hey, I do what I have to do. It's a living, you know."

"Not for some of your clients," the sheriff countered. "Seems like when you point to somebody's family tree, it gets struck by lightning." His practiced smile and probing stare waited for a reply Nick didn't offer.

"This is Sheriff John Higbee," Tommy broke in to say. "But I guess you already figured that out." Tommy's preoccupied eyes wandered to the darkness as he lost the thread of the introduction.

Tommy's good humor was more anxious and forced than it had been earlier in the evening. The two men apparently were friends, but unsettling words must have passed between them before Nick arrived. Maybe Brianne, Luevenia, and Chief Claude were right to be concerned about how Tommy was handling all of this. He looked a bit dazed, but determined to retain control of himself, like a drunk man trying to act sober. Nick considered the possibility that Tommy might have a drinking problem.

After an awkward moment he himself didn't seem to notice, Tommy said, "Big John, we call him. You remember, Nick, he played defense for LSU awhile back? Intercepted a pass in the conference semi-finals and ran it for the winning touchdown."

"Oh sure," Nick lied. "Who could forget *that*?"

Tommy leaned closer to Nick, in mock secrecy. "Just don't call him 'boy,' and you'll get along fine. Last guy who did is missing a few teeth. And he was the coach."

"Now hold on, Tommy, you're giving Mr. Herald the wrong idea, and some wrong facts. I hit the *assistant* coach, and it wasn't anything racial. He wouldn't put me in another big game. That's all it was. You know as well as me this is the *new* Louisiana, where a black man can get elected sheriff right in the middle of redneck country."

Tommy managed a self-conscious laugh. "Yeah, Big John. Sure. *Everything* is racial in Louisiana, and don't tell Nick no different? The state where the only thing worse than being Indian is being black. John's main opponent in the election was a senile old white man who'd been sheriff going on fifty years. Only reason Big John got elected was the old geezer died during the runoff."

"And it was still close!" Higbee exclaimed. "Some folks preferred to vote for a dead white man instead of a live black one. *Blazing Saddles* always was one of my favorite movies."

"'Round here, Nick," Tommy said, "they wouldn't put white and dark meat chicken in the same bucket until a few years ago. Big John sure got lucky in that election."

"No," Higbee declared, "I got Katogoula power. My family and this tribe go back a long ways, back to the bad old times of slavery and segregation. When I was young and radical, I marched with 'em down at the Capitol, in '72, I think it was, huh, Tommy?"

"Nineteen seventy-four. I remember 'cause my parents let me take off grammar school to ride our buses down there."

"Yep, Katogoula power," Big John said, patting Tommy on the shoulder, "that's what put me over the top. And I'll never forget it. That's partly why I'm out here tonight. I don't take kindly to someone knocking off my loyal supporters. Now that I've asked my friend Tommy, here, a few questions, I got one or two things to ask you, Mr. Herald."

"Me?" Nick said, choking slightly on the word. When would he learn not to expect a normal conversation with a cop, even a seemingly nice guy like Big John Higbee?

"Yep. Tommy, I think Brianne and the kids are about ready to go home. You look plum tuckered out, yourself." It was a gentle dismissal from a skilled manipulator. "You let me know if you see anything funny going on around your place. Y'all drive careful; it's late. And watch your ass, you hear?"

"Got my shotgun in the rack, Big John," Tommy said, with the slight hesitation of a man who would never fire first at an assailant. "Nick, can you use a guide tomorrow?"

"Could I ever!" Nick answered, relieved. "I'd like to start working with the courthouse records in Armageddon, but I'll just end up lost again. All these trees start to look the same after an hour or two."

He was grateful for the cool, humid openness of the parking lot, recalling the disoriented despair he'd experienced a few hours earlier among the dense pines. Like a Greek chorus witnessing the struggles of a doomed character on stage, the trees had watched him, their enigmatic prophecies soughing in high branches.

"The Katogoula once knew how to listen to the forest," Tommy said dreamily, his tentative easy spirit now gone. "Each tree, the sky, the clouds, the ground...they all spoke to us." His hand made a quick pass across his face. "Listen to me. I must be tireder than I thought.... Nick, tomorrow at eight okay by you?"

They agreed eight was fine; Tommy would take him to Armageddon, the parish seat, site of the courthouse, and, Nick hoped, the home of a trove of useful genealogical records.

"I like his style," the sheriff said, as Tommy gathered his family and loaded them into the truck. "He's got backbone, knows when to make a stand, when to back off. He cares about folks. Maybe too much. He'll be a good chief."

"'Tribal president,' Nick said. "They're organizing things according to the Chitiko-Tiloasha model. Decisions democratically voted on, the president or chairman basically first among equals. Lots of checks and balances."

Nick and the sheriff waved as the Shawes drove off in their old truck.

"'S'at right?" said Big John. "You sure know an awful lot about Indian stuff, Nick." The admiration in his tone sounded devious.

Without apology, the sheriff had slid easily into familiarity. Clearly he was used to directing conversations toward destinations he chose, Nick concluded. How many criminals had he cracked with that disarming affability?

"I can do a competent Indian ancestor search. You interested in hiring me? Lots of black and white Americans have Indian blood and don't even know it. Especially around here, I would imagine."

"No, thank you just the same. But let me ask you, how much you know about ancient Indian hunting methods?"

Odd question. This wasn't a genealogical inquiry; it was detective work. The sheriff studied Nick's face intently as he waited for the reply.

"Only what I've read in passing," Nick said. "Anything specific on your mind?"

"How about the atlatl, the old Indian spear thrower?"

"Oh, you mean the weapon that killed Carl Shawe?"

Big John shook his head and scratched one stubbled brown cheek. "Should've known you'd pick up on details of the case. The NOPD detectives I talked to warned me about you. But they said I could probably trust you, call on you to help. And that's what I'm doing."

So, he'd vetted him. Nick wondered if the sheriff had talked with Shelvin Balzar, a newly minted detective on the New Orleans force and a friend of Nick's. They'd met a few years before during a case involving deadly secrets lurking within the history of Shelvin's family.

"Yep," the sheriff continued, "Carl Shawe was nailed to a cypress knee with an atlatl spear. Went right through his neck. Just like that." Big John snapped thick fingers. "I tell you, though, that wasn't the worst way to check out, even if it was one of the strangest. I seen some pretty bad deaths in my uniform and detective days, down in Baton Rouge and over in Armageddon. Drownings, burnings, beatings, shootings, stabbings, overdoses, a couple of lynchings, even."

A one-eyed pickup ambled down the road, mud tires thrumming loudly. Conversation would have to wait for a few seconds. Big John's attention turned inward. Nick's thoughts turned to the sheriff.

This man had seen the most awful aspects of human nature, but he fought on, determined to make a difference. His heroism lay in knowing that he could never truly win against evil. Nick had already learned that Big John earned a law degree while working on the force in Baton Rouge. And though Nick was fonder of flesh-eating bacteria than lawyers, he couldn't help admiring the sheriff's drive. Sheriff Higbee's political ambition was not an end in itself, Nick suspected, but a means to do good. A rare bird in Louisiana.

The noise of the truck tires diminished into the omnivorous night.

Big John took in and slowly released a titanic breath. "When we want to be, we are truly disgusting animals, you know that? Well, at least Carl's exit was quick.... You able to shed some light on my predicament, here?"

Time to clear the air.

"If you're asking whether I had anything to do with Carl's death—no. If you're asking me do I know who did—not yet. But I intend to find out."

Though Nick felt a growing respect for the sheriff, he still didn't appreciate being treated like a suspect or being prodded like an informant who could be shunted out of the loop when he was no longer needed. *Either we work together as equals, or we each chase the killer separately.*

"Not much gets past you, I'll admit that," Big John said. "Ever consider a career in law enforcement?"

"Never. I've had my radical days, too. Misguided silliness, most of it, but I retained a healthy distrust of the establishment."

"I hear you, man." The steely glint of suspicion had left Big John's dark eyes. "In Louisiana, you best be looking over your shoulder for the little man with a lot of power; slavery may be dead, but you can still wind up in bondage for a handful of cash.... Tell you the truth, I don't think you're the murdering type. But I had to feel you out, you know what I'm saying? I didn't get where I am today being fooled by too many folks. I can usually see a lie coming from a mile away. Nope, I got you pegged as more your petty-criminal type, white-collar perpetrator of so-called victimless crimes and such."

"Hey, thanks a million," Nick said.

Big John leaned back against the Chevy, his arms crossed over his expansive torso. "Tell me something, Nick: anything you know of in this ancestor-hunting game might give a person cause to kill Carl Shawe? I mean, speaking hypothetically. That Carl, he was a man with barbed wire wrapped tight around his soul. One *difficult* son-of-a-gun. But I never knew anyone around here wishing him any worse than a day in my jail to sleep it off." A deep bass chuckle rumbled from Big John. "He sure had his share of those."

The sheriff appeared to understand the difference between foibles and felonies. He seemed to share Nick's belief that the truly scary malefactors—other than the fifty or so serial killers wandering the U.S. on any given day—were the grass-mowing, car-pooling, burger-grilling citizens who exploded into violence with unpredictable ferocity.

"Genealogical motives are relatives of the kind you handle every day," Nick said. "Greed, pride, fear, love, hate, only with a slower burn—centuries, sometimes. The fuse gets lit when a cherished identity is threatened."

"Identity. I can just hear the DA bust out laughing over *that* motive. But go on. I want to hear what you got to say."

Nick kicked absently at rocks in the dark red dirt. One rolled over and for a moment he imagined a miniature skull's face in the shadowy lumps and gouges, leering at him. He shivered, looked away, and jammed his hands into his coat pockets.

"Genealogy is a magnifying glass over the past. That's how the hobbyist and the professional see it, at least. Normal people."

Nick pretended not to hear the sheriff's skeptical harrumph. He seemed to have a jaundiced opinion of addicts of family history.

"Normal people," Nick repeated, slightly piqued at the unstated slur. "*We* search for the truth in the historical record, whatever it is, pleasant or disturbing—you have to take the bad with the good. That's a major part of the fun. Trouble starts when people use genealogy as a mirror. A distorted mirror. They try to bend it, warp it. They insist on seeing the image of the mask they wear."

"Mask?" Big John asked. "I hope you're speaking figuratively. All I need is masked killers running around my parish. We been through that phase already, and I hope to God it's through for good."

"The mask I'm referring to may be a hallowed family tradition or a more recent delusion. The point is, it's what the individual thinks of himself, his identity."

"Now I'm catching on. You're saying genealogy turns into an obsession for people like that. An unhealthy one. And what we see on the outside isn't what they think of themselves."

"Yeah. And they'll fight to the death for the family lie."

"Or kill?"

Nick nodded. "I've seen it happen before. What makes you so sure this involves genealogy?" As usual when dealing with law enforcement, Nick had the feeling the sheriff held back more than he was revealing.

"I'm not sure of anything," Big John said, holding out his arms to embrace the confusing universe. "The murder went down not long after the tribe got word of federal recognition; that's what put me onto genealogy. Maybe somebody's trying to hide something in their family tree."

"Possibly," Nick allowed. "There's going to be increased scrutiny of everyone's family history during the initial enrollment period."

The sheriff began to count off on his fingers: "But Carl's murder also happened at the start of this big argument over the casino, after Tadbull Mill closed down, right in the middle of hunting season, and during one of our periodic surges in dope running through this area. Shoot, man, I could name you a dozen suspects, from the mob, to the Mexican and Colombian cartels, to Louisiana legislators, to poachers—I mean other poachers, besides Carl—to these here Indians or ones from another tribe, to the man's own family! The murder weapon—the business part of it, at least—belonged to Tommy."

"So I've heard," Nick said.

Big John nodded, casting a narrow-eyed glance down his wide nose at Nick. "I figured. The atlatl was a family heirloom, pretty old, I understand. His granddaddy gave it to him. He says somebody stole it and an unknown number of spears from his garage storage closet. He identified the spear as one of his. But I just can't believe Tommy did that murder, any more than you did. He and Carl had their run-ins, like most brothers, no doubt about that. But I've known those two since we were all kids.

"No, Nick, I'm not sure of anything at all. I was just hoping if I could get your help on this genealogy angle, I could pursue a few others. My chief of detectives is at a doggoned forensics conference in Miami."

Nick didn't buy Big John's whining. Louisiana sheriffs seldom left the courthouse, except for the occasional fund-raiser. Most were paper-pushers, accountants with sidearms, or slick political climbers, demi-dukes of patronage. Not this one. Big John liked to get his hands dirty in real law enforcement, whenever he could find the excuse.

"This isn't a garden-variety murder, Sheriff. Something weird's going on here, something ritualistic, with roots deep in Katogoula identity. At least, that's what some of the tribe members I spoke with tonight think. A few are even whispering about angry spirits roaming the woods."

Big John didn't laugh. "I've known the Katogoula a long time. They're scared, all right." He raised an eyebrow as his mind focused on concrete details. "But excuse me if I keep looking for a human suspect. The atlatl isn't all that hard to use. We could be talking about an Indian of any tribe around these parts; most of 'em used it before the bow and arrow. Even a non-Indian could figure it out. And it doesn't take much muscle, either."

Nick walked a few steps toward the road. He looked into the black wall of longleaf, loblolly, and slash pines on the other side. The radio in Big John's car warbled as voices began and ended pithy coded messages. He returned to face the sheriff.

"How familiar are you with the ancient traditions of the tribe?"

"Not very. Got my hands full just trying to be a good Baptist. What ancient tradition might you be talking about?" Big John asked, displaying the keen interest of an open-minded detective.

"Twins," Nick said. "Tommy and Carl were twins."

"Yep, I'm aware of that fact. So?"

"According to the mythology of many American Indian tribes, and of the Katogoula in particular, twins are figures of special significance."

In many ancient Indian belief systems, Nick explained, twins were either beneficent or evil. If judged a manifestation of good, they were honored during festivals or given ceremonial duties during planting, harvesting, and war. If evil, they were seen as perversions of the natural order, bad luck, scapegoats. The whole tribe suffered when nature was in an unbalanced state. A ceremonial, or actual, purging was necessary. Sometimes a twin was cast out into the wilderness, sometimes parents killed one twin outright at birth.

After Nick briefly sketched the Twins of the Forest Story, Big John meditatively rubbed his bulbous forehead at the line where his short black-and-gray coils were eroding backward.

"You're saying one of the Katogoula believed killing the evil twin—that would be Carl—could ward off something bad that's been happening or is about to happen to the tribe?"

"Maybe someone believed that, or wanted others to believe it," Nick said. "According to the myth, it's the chief's responsibility either to perform the deed himself or to officiate. But you've already told me you don't think Tommy did it."

"So far.... I guess you go in for that voodoo stuff in New Orleans, too, huh?"

"Hey, at least you have a human suspect according to my theory. The message could be: no more outsiders, no more tribal organization, no casino." Nick was thinking of what Brianne and Nooj had said, of the grumbling opposition that had made the casino vote so close. "Money isn't everything, Sheriff."

"Who you tellin'! *I'm* the one in public service.... Why kill Carl? Why not Tommy?"

"The killer bagged two birds with the atlatl spear. First, he emotionally hobbled the leader of the Katogoula, slowing the tribe's momentum toward becoming a soulless corporate entity rather than a group of spiritually linked people; and two, he—or she—called on the traditional beliefs to inspire fear among the others. Carl's death was a symbol, a warning from someone who doesn't want change, for some pathological reason. Our killer may actually think he's protecting the Katogoula. After all, Carl's death wasn't a great loss to the tribe."

"A murderer with heart. That's awful comforting."

"Or maybe Carl was simply an easier target. Tommy's a family man, active in tribal politics. He's surrounded by other people most of the time."

"Now hold on," Big John objected, "things have never been this good for the tribe. Federal recognition. Legislators, casinos, financial people knocking on the door with contracts and wads of money. I'd take a little of that kind of bad luck. These Katogoula are in high cotton, man!"

"Look at almost any tribe's history," Nick said, "at all the worthless treaties Indians have signed with the white world. These treaties meant the end of thousands of years of Indian civilization. Couldn't someone perceive federal recognition and a gambling compact as more of the same? A few years ago, the Arizona Hopi voted *not* to build a casino because they felt their culture, their privacy, their spirituality would be jeopardized. Maybe we're seeing that here. Someone could be powerfully motivated by such beliefs, don't you think?"

"Hard for me to imagine the Katogoula would do something like that to their own folks. But I think you're onto something about the set up. Tommy's tires were flattened on his way home before dawn the morning of the murder. He turned up incoherent, wandering by the lake, not far from where Nooj, the wildlife agent—you meet him?—found Carl later that morning on his regular boat patrol. We found Tommy's necklace near Carl's body; has the date of his marriage and 'Love, Brianne' on the back of a little silver cross. Tommy says he remembers getting hit with a blowgun dart, but that's it."

"The cane blowgun. Another ancient hunting method of the Katogoula," Nick said.

"You *are* up on your Indian ways," Big John said. "Could be he was drugged by that dart. I've read about a trick from our Colombian friends. They mix a powder called *Burundanga* to turn a man into a zombie; slip it to him in a drink or food or even a cigarette, and he wakes up in some emergency room after they've used him as cocaine mule or cleaned out his bank account. Main ingredient is from a shrub of the nightshade family, I recall, scopolamine. But up here? Well, I just don't know."

The sheriff snicked his tongue in perplexed sadness. "Sure was a nice, quiet parish, till that doggoned recognition came through. Let me ask you something else. Would a big cat enter into the picture? No housecat, I'm talking real big, cougar size. Reason I'm asking, we found lots of claw marks on the cypress knees around where old Carl was killed."

Nick explained the Story of the Sacred Cougar, the story of the wandering Katogoula and the divine sign that revealed to them their new homeland in the pine forest.

"I can't say I agree with all your ideas," Big John said, "supernatural or otherwise. But I thank you, sir. You've been a big help. Now you remember what I told Tommy. We got a murderer on the loose. You give me a call if you get a bad feeling about something you notice. And stop by my office tomorrow. I won't take no for an answer. If you don't, I'll send a deputy after you. We got some good coffee. New Orleans blend. You'll feel right at home."

"An offer it would be wise to accept," Nick said. "Oh, yeah, I'm supposed to deliver greetings from a mutual friend. Hawty Latimer says hello. She's an instructor at Freret University, and manages to make herself indispensable to me in her spare time."

"Hawty Latimer," Big John said, smiling broadly. "Well, I'll be. Haven't seen her since she was this tall"—he marked a spot on a massive thigh just above the knee—"before she had her sickness. She was a firecracker, even in diapers. Guess I was right about you after all: you can tell a lot about a man by the company he keeps."

The unmistakable purr of a Volkswagen engine interrupted the crickets' responsorial calls. The van that had been parked to the right of Nick's car lurched out at a steep angle. The front bumper crunched into his passenger door.

"Sorry!" shouted the red-haired woman who had wielded the video camera inside Three Sisters Pantry. Then she drove off, shifting unhurriedly down the highway, the van's one functioning taillight winking with each pothole.

"Did you see that?!" Nick sputtered in anger. "She hit my car! She...who the hell is she?"

He raced over to his MG and looked at the dent. "Damn!" He kicked a rear tire in frustration.

"Name's Holly Worthstone," Big John said calmly. "Been filming some kind of video about the Katogoula for months now. I don't know what she calls herself—amateur sociologist or anthropologist, one of them people-ologists, anyway—but she used to work for the TV station in Armageddon. My parish has to pay for every unfunded mandate Baton Rouge can think of, but they can still find the taxpayer dollars for that! It's enough to make me want to try for ol' Representative Girn's seat in the legisla—"

Nick ran back to Sheriff Higbee. "She hit my car, blatantly, and drove off! Aren't you going to do anything about it? Give her a ticket. You saw what happened. That car's a classic."

"Looks like a classic piece of junk to me, man, and I didn't see nothin'. Consider yourself one lucky genealogist. Didn't you notice how pretty that woman is? You crazy or gay or something? The ice been broken, you know what I'm saying? And my information is she doesn't have a steady man.... Reminds me of how me and my wife met. She ran a red light over in Armageddon, plowed into a cattle trailer. I was on motorcycle duty that day, if you can believe it." He slapped his substantial belly in self-mockery. "Nobody hurt, 'cept a few cows. But man, I never seen such a beautiful woman in my life. Now…" he glanced longingly at the stars, his smile of pleasant reminiscence fading, "now she look like a doggoned UPS truck. Big, brown, and noisy. They ought to put one of them beepers on her for when she backs up!"

Nick laughed with the sheriff, and forgot his anger.

"You're right, Big John. It *is* a piece of junk."

Sheriff Higbee dropped into the driver's seat of his car, which dipped substantially with his weight.

"Say, Nick, keep that about the claw marks under your hat, all right? No sense getting everybody riled up about something that might not even exist. They might've been there before." He started the car. "I'm thinking about what you said a minute ago, about that tribal myth, and something worries me. Tommy and Brianne got twins."

He slammed the door and drove off in a hail of gravel and red dust, leaving Nick alone in the parking lot.

The lights inside Three Sisters Pantry went out.

Like a pale apparition, Luevenia Silsby's face appeared in a window of the darkened store and then was gone.

Chapter 15

Nick spotted Holly Worthstone's van as he searched for his room at Greensheaves Court Motel. He'd convinced himself to take Sheriff Higbee's advice on matters of romance—and on self-preservation.

It was well past 11 p.m., but he saw lights on behind the seedy curtains of what he took to be Holly's room.

There were few other guests. The Greensheaves had seen much better days. He drove on according to directions the owner—a blowzy, ill-tempered woman in a frilly robe—had given him as he checked in.

The motel consisted of three carelessly placed, boxy sections, each room named for a figure from pioneer and Western lore. For fifty years or so, the Greensheaves had served the area's minimal lodging needs; now, in expectation of a casino-driven boom, at least eight hotel chains had surveying teams stealthily triangulating likely properties. Nick noted two out-of-state trucks, conspicuously logo-less, bristling with storage tubes and compartments that no doubt hid high-tech measuring equipment. The front-desk woman had reason to be testy: she was about to be inhospitably put out of business by the national hospitality industry.

Nick parked in front of "Daniel Boone." He opened the hatchback and grabbed his briefcase and his much-battered suitcase from the litter atop the folded-down backseat. The room door had been damaged many years ago. With a shoulder he shoved it open and then understood why trespassers weren't a problem.

"Daniel Boone" was water-stained, chilly, very small, and as musty as a two-hundred-year-old coonskin cap. Half a century's dust, hair, and flaked paint caked at the baseboards. Husks of countless insects gave Nick a gothic chill of mortality. If the Western-kitsch decor was ever truly in vogue, he was thinking, now it was simply depressing—too depressing to remain in alone.

He washed his face, splashed on some cologne and gargled mouthwash. Then he grabbed the cracked plastic ice bucket and two bottles of wine from his suitcase, slammed the door several times until it stuck, and set off toward the ice machine he'd seen near the office.

◙

"Who's there?" the guarded voice said from the other side of crossed wooden-pistol cutouts on the door of the room dubbed "Annie Oakley."

"Nick Herald. The guy you ran into over at Three Sisters Pantry." He stopped himself from adding "literally."

The window curtains moved. She opened the door as far as the chain allowed.

He could have sworn he'd seen her on the back of a magazine, advertising hypoallergenic cosmetics. She radiated that kind of wholesome beauty.

Holly Worthstone stood about three inches shorter than Nick. She wore tight black leggings above thick gray socks, and a long blue fleece pullover dotted with fanciful snowflakes. Her lustrous long hair was sunset red and gold in the deficient light of the room. She'd worn it tied back in a practical ponytail at the store, but now it cascaded freely to the front over her right shoulder to frame a high, full cheek and strong jaw line; on the left it fell straight back behind her ear, tossed there probably by habit. Through the narrow aperture she allowed him, Nick had a fleeting image of her dimpled mouth as two oversized, coalescing teardrops.

Below graceful, thin, sorrel brows, her eyes were light green, like translucent quartz, repeating the motif of her pretty mouth. Eyes at once vulnerable, longing, and relentless. Nick felt himself getting lost in them. He concentrated on her slightly mannish nose; it alone saved her from being impossibly drop-dead gorgeous.

He had no trouble deciding that her room was much more pleasant than his. Even though the decor was about as ugly, the company was the deciding factor. Now, if he could only convince her not to brain him with the wooden coat hanger she held raised in one hand.

"I don't think you'll need that. See?" he said, holding up the ice bucket containing the tapered green bottles. "I bring a gift of good will."

"Wow! You scared me." Her relief was audible.

She undid the chain and flung the coat hanger on a chair, where her faded blue jeans rested in a heap like cast-off lovers. A pair of well-used hiking boots lay abandoned on the floor. "Come in, Nick. I'm the one who should be making peace with you."

She stepped aside, shivering at the cool air flooding into the warm room. A lot warmer, in a different way, than his.

"We haven't formally met," she said, closing the door and chaining it again. "I'm Holly Worthstone. But you know my name already, obviously."

"The obvious is vastly overrated." They shook hands. Nick liked the feel of her firm, forthright grip. *A modern woman, and you damn well better not forget it!* "I wouldn't be a very good genealogist if I settled for the easy answers, for hearsay and tall tales."

"Yes, digging in other people's business seems to be your forte. You've made a lot of people nervous."

"That's normal when family histories are dusted off," Nick said. "I'm used to it."

"I suppose it's a tribute to your abilities. And something tells me you like to stir things up. I don't know, must be that naughty look in your eyes." She nodded approvingly at the wine. "This place has room service? Why didn't I know that? And the waiter isn't half bad, either."

"I never travel without the little comforts that ease the nagging anxieties of existence."

"When a man whispers sweet existential nothings in my ear," she said archly, "I go all mushy inside. What do you do now, quote Sartre to complete the seduction?"

"Shakespeare usually works: 'I shall see thee, ere I die, look pale with love.' *Much Ado about Nothing*."

"Ooh. You're right. But before I throw myself into your arms, you mind giving me a taste of that...whatever it is."

"New York Gewürztraminer," Nick said, already using his indefatigable Swiss Army Knife to open a bottle. "Finger Lakes region." He poured wine into two smudgy water glasses Holly held out.

"Sounds like a rare breed of dog." She took an exploratory sip. "Yum! Spicy. I like it." She finished the glass. "More porridge, please."

"You may need the *hair* of a rare dog tomorrow. This stuff is deceptively strong. Best to drink it slowly," Nick advised, sensing at the same time that she wasn't the type to take her pleasures in moderation.

"Oh, give me a break! You're talking to an LSU sorority girl. I minored in shooters, stomach hoses, and vomit buckets. And I *despise* being patronized. So don't."

"Hey, just trying to be helpful. You don't have to prove anything to me. I've seen you in action. Your hit-and-run style shows great confidence."

She blushed deeply and sought refuge in the wine, which she nevertheless sipped more daintily.

"See all that?" she said, diverting the conversation from the uncomfortable subject. She walked over to two videotape machines hooked up to an editing controller and two monitors, all on a cheap table too flimsy for the load. "I set all this up, all by my ditzy lonesome. I'm living here, temporarily, trying to finish my Katogoula documentary. What a place, huh?"

"Charming, for about half a second." Nick had noticed the mess of extended motel habitation: dirty clothes spilling from luggage, bottles and tubes and a hair dryer crowding the tiny basin counter beside the bathroom, greasy boxes of recent fast-food meals stacked by the trash can.

Holly said, "I wanted to talk to you earlier tonight, but I never got the chance. Except, of course"—she pursed her lips, a contrite little girl—"when I apologized for hitting your car. I was in a hurry to get back here and edit in the new footage I shot tonight; it worked perfectly, too.... Anyway, I may have some ideas for your genealogical research. General background stuff."

"I need all the help I can get."

"So, you, uh, mad about the car thing? Much ado about nothing, right?"

"Forget it. Really. That's not why I'm here. I didn't feel like going to sleep just yet in Daniel Boone's armpit."

"You'd prefer mine, right?" She smiled, challenging him to deny it.

With some difficulty he stopped himself from giving full-throated assent to that idea. "I see you weren't tucked in yet, either." The video equipment gave off a low hum; yellow legal pads with full sheets rolled back lay around the machines. "What do you say we chat until the Moon of Falling Needles sets?"

A slight smile and an eyebrow's elevation told him she didn't miss his use of the traditional Katogoula name for the season. She absently rubbed the rim of her glass across her lower lip before finally taking a sip. Nick felt he'd passed some secret test.

"Sounds like a great idea to me," she said.

They sat down together, each claiming a wobbly arm of a vinyl sofa patched with duct tape. She curled her legs under her, getting cozy in her fleece pullover; he turned toward her, one knee on the sofa, one arm over the back.

"Moon of Falling Needles. Such a poetic heritage. I envy the Katogoula." She parted the curtains right behind them and looked up into the night sky. "We'd say something prosaic and sterile like 'October moon,' or 'full moon,' and go to an almanac to check out the rising and setting times." Her jewel-like eyes focused on him. "American Indians retain that beautiful concept of connectedness, of timelessness. The sky, the earth, the animals and plants, the spirit world, themselves—all interacting!" She crossed her legs Indian style and reached for the bottle on the coffee table before the sofa. "We're all science and money and malls. False things. They've kept an essential beauty in their lives, in spite of all we've done to homogenize them."

She refilled their glasses.

Nick was noticing her own essential beauty, which she wore with unaffected grace. He had known people blessed with great physical or mental gifts, who used their genetic luck to manipulate others, who flaunted it like a big bank account, or who fell into a bog of self-gratification. Holly was not one of these. She considered her quietly stunning looks simply as lagniappe, the thirteenth oyster in that dozen-on-the-half shell of life. And, as she told him a little of her past, Nick discerned a strong personality seeking a cause to build a crusade around, searching for something larger than the merely physical.

"I've been working with the Katogoula for about six months now," she was saying. "At LSU I was an anthropology major—my real minor, by the way, was Spanish, not drinking. I got hooked on the history and culture of Louisiana Indians. I graduated, and then screwed around for another year or so, doing independent study, thinking about getting a master's. No real program. I just knew I loved learning about us"—she patted the soft blue fleece at her breastbone—"mankind. It felt, oh, I don't know, relevant.

"So I did a few archaeological digs with the department, some museum volunteering and a little paid work on my own, started audio and video recording of stories from the old members of various Louisiana tribes…that kind of thing. Usually with graduate students I knew." She gave a worldly laugh. "I also partied a lot."

She took a thoughtful sip from her glass. Nick understood the self-reproach in her eyes. The pleasures of youth had palled early for her, but she'd continued to chase them.

"Eventually my parents laid down the law, in a nice way: 'Get a job,' basically. So then I ended up working at a television station in Armageddon. My parents knew someone who knew someone. You know how it goes. At first as cameraperson, then reporting. The station was small and understaffed, so we pretty much had to do everything. Looking back, it wasn't such an out-of-the-way field for me. As a reporter, I was exploring contemporary culture instead of dead ones."

She shook her head and laughed, as if she were describing a younger, very foolish, sister. "God, when I started, I didn't know a thing about it. But I learned, got pretty good. Won a few AP awards. Television journalism sort of grows on you. Like a wart, we used to say in the newsroom. After five years I'd had enough. I moved back home to Baton Rouge."

"Idealism meets stark reality," Nick said. "I've been there."

"That, and a couple of scuz-wad department managers were forever trying to get in my pants. Unbelievable what schemes those guys tried!" A big sigh of good riddance. "Anyway, I wanted to produce a documentary on the unrecognized tribes of Louisiana. I'd done a story once on the Katogoula; that's what gave me the idea. So, I got a proposal together, and boy was I floored when the Department of Culture, Recreation, and Tourism approved it. LSU's anthropology department is helping me with the research end."

"Government sometimes fouls up and does something right," Nick said.

The strong wine was acting as truth serum for both of them. Nick told her of his youth in Southern California, surfing, toking joints, infuriating his parents; of his discovery of the wonders of language and art; of his college years; of his briefly blissful career as an assistant professor on his way to associate status at Freret University; of his love for New Orleans; and finally, of the fortunate fall that landed him in the business of genealogy.

"My life story sounds more boring each time I tell it," he said. "I'm not the greatest leading man, I guess."

"Maybe you need a leading lady."

His turn to change the subject. Thoughts of commitment made his heartbeat go irregular. "Show me what you've done so far. You mind?"

Holly seemed to enjoy watching him squirm. At last she said, "Love to."

She hopped up eagerly and led the way to the table holding the videotape machines. She moved the room's one chair to the side and sat down; he sat on the end of the appealingly rumpled bed, a little behind her.

"This is newsroom-reject stuff; I'd like to have state-of-the-art equipment, but, you know, it's all I could swing at the moment. I had to change the concept a little when the tribe received recognition. This is just the rough edit. No dissolves or wipes, just straight cuts...that's television-speak for visual transitions. I do the final version with a good post-production house in Baton Rouge. There's no music. I haven't even finished the script yet. I've done my own narration, but later I'll hire a better voice—"

"Are you going to apologize all night or show me?"

"Sorry."

She rolled the tape.

The Sacred Cougar myth was first. Holly's imaginative camera work at sunrise on Lake Katogoula set a nice mystical tone for the introduction. Nick had only read the myth; its true haunting beauty came through in the spoken word and the images of the genuine physical setting. He listened carefully to the myth of the Twins of the Forest, read over footage of the Golden Trace; for this, Holly had held the camera at shoulder level as she walked, giving the sequence a nice immediacy.

A simple graphics unit had allowed her to add some titles. In a section she called "Hidden Heritage," Nick learned that "Shawe," Tommy's surname, meant "raccoon" in Mobilian K, the Katogoula's evolving version of the creolized pidgin language of the Southeastern tribes, Mobilian Jargon, during the period of white settlement.

"Those dark circles under his eyes," she said. "Could be a family physical trait that became formalized in the name."

"Ah, the secrets of surnames. I ought to write a paper on that."

Nick wanted to take notes for his own history of the tribe, but decided to wait until he was clearer headed. Bad scholarly etiquette, anyway, to raid a work in progress; as a teacher, he'd always been wary of that. The bum plagiarism rap had made him an even more conscientious scholar, if a less law-abiding citizen.

Now Holly's narrative was discussing Katogoula art and the tribal museum. Nick was particularly interested in a shot of an intricately designed bowl portraying twin male figures facing each other, over a stylized, repeating pattern of raccoons. Raccoons, he soon learned, sometimes represented a depressed state of being in ancient Katogoula psychodynamics.

"Twins *and* a 'depressed state of being,'" Nick muttered, thinking aloud.

"Tommy, you mean?" Holly paused the machine. "I sure wouldn't want to be in his moccasins. Half the tribe wants to turn the clock back a hundred years, half wants to drive Ferraris. And on top of that, his brother gets shish kebabbed."

Since she'd brought it up, he decided to pursue the subject.

"Carl's death doesn't seem like random or personal violence to me. I think there's a connection with Katogoula ritual and myth. The sheriff thinks so, too."

Her eyes averted, Holly rolled a pencil under her palm on a yellow legal pad. Up, down, up, down…. "Is that what you two were talking about?" Her attempted nonchalant tone hid some pressing worry.

"Mostly," Nick said. "But your name did come up"—the pencil halted below her hand—"as a candidate for driver's ed."

Holly laughed. He'd said the right thing. She could look at him again, sure that the facets of deception in her eyes were still safe.

"The murder's certainly got them rattled," she said. "Are you saying you believe in the tribal myths? You don't strike me as the pious type."

"You go to church, don't you?" he asked.

Her mouth went lopsided with guilt. "Sometimes."

"You're not the pious type either, then, but you'll never shake those deep beliefs. We all have them. Some of us wear our faith on our sleeves. Some of us, like the Katogoula, discover the power of their beliefs in a crisis…. No, I don't believe in the Katogoula myths. Directly, that is. I believe in the facts of human relationships, how rituals and myths can affect what we do, what we do to each other. That's why I need to know everything I can about the traditions of the tribe. The killer knows."

She twisted in her chair to face him. "You really care about the Katogoula, don't you, Nick?"

"Yes."

"Poor Carl," she said. But her tone turned suddenly less sorrowful: "Actually, he was a real shit. He groped me at Three Sisters, once. I socked him one."

She demonstrated with a roundhouse swing that accidentally grazed Nick's jaw. Giggling, she started apologizing and reflexively reached for his face. Their eyes met as her hand lingered. Nick thought he saw an invitation to a kiss. He touched her hand, leaned toward her.

One of the tape machines clunked and whined as gears and belts disengaged. The momentary magnetic longing had been broken; their hands slid reluctantly apart.

"It just went to standby, that's all," Holly said, clearing her throat, straightening up in her chair.

"I'll remember to keep my hands to myself; you're dangerous. Tell me more about Carl—without the pugilistic body language, if you please."

"Well, he did have his good points. He was a storehouse of Katogoula ways. He didn't fully understand that he was, hated to talk about it. I've got a tape here…somewhere…of him tanning a deer hide. He makes it look like ballet. Of course, I wanted to throw up." She shuffled through black plastic tape boxes. "I can't find it right now. But anyway, he had intuitive skills; as a boy he learned things that are lost now. Really remarkable. No wife, no kids, no parents, no friends. Just Tommy, his brother. And they didn't get along. He'd been to jail, I think. Nothing big, though."

"All in all," Nick said, "a guy no one would much miss."

"But his death *will* hurt the tribe in deeper ways. Centuries of tradition died with him."

Holly had hit on a new dimension of Carl's murder. Nick felt a vague sense of its importance, but for now he could only store away her words.

As if feeling a sudden draft, Holly crossed her arms. "I was out there that morning."

"At the lake? The morning Carl was killed?"

She nodded. "The opening segment, the video of the sun coming up, the mist on the lake, the Sacred Cougar myth. I shot it that morning. Sort of a spooky coincidence, huh?"

"Have you told Sheriff Higbee about this?"

"No," she said, a bit too defensively. "Why should I? The landing where I was is on the other side of the lake. You can't even see where Carl was killed. Besides, there wasn't anybody out there because it was just after the early teal season."

"Maybe questioning will bring back a memory you didn't think was significant."

"I have it all on tape," she said, as if speaking to a simpleton. "Watched it, like, a thousand times, editing it. I think I know what's on there by now. I'll show you the raw footage, if you want."

She did. That morning, three weeks before, Holly had arrived in pre-dawn darkness at the concrete parking lot and boat ramp on the shore of Lake Katogoula. During duck-hunting season, dozens of trucks with boat trailers would have filled the area.

The landing indeed seemed deserted as Holly quickly set up the camera on a tripod and experimented with lighting settings, focus, and zoom. She'd recorded sound, too, and Nick could hear her cursing several times, as some piece of equipment pinched her fingers or as she exhorted herself to hurry, because the eerie half-light she wanted would soon be gone. Nick saw her dim athletic figure dash in front of the lens to remove a plastic soda bottle and some beer cans spoiling the view.

At least he knew exactly where she was when Carl was being murdered...if the tape was shot when she said it was.

The stop-and-start shots became smoother and longer as light gradually suffused the scene. Much of what followed made it into the edited version. Slow pans and pullouts captured most of the nine-square-mile dark lake from shore to shore; unused duck blinds and silently pumping oil wells were silhouetted against the faint golden glow. Soon, the sun sent out pink and orange lava flows of daylight.

The sky turned metallic white and the shallow lake came into sharp, prosaic focus. Holly already had what she wanted; she unlatched the camera from the tripod. For a few seconds the tape still recorded, and the image jerked and tilted wildly before going black.

"See, I told you," Holly said, reaching to stop and rewind the tape.

"Wait. Back it up a bit."

She twisted the edit knob on the control panel and the video reversed, breaking up into distorted lines.

"Now forward," Nick said. The image cleared up, but it was the jumpy segment just before the end. "There. What's that?"

"What's what? I didn't see anything." She backed the tape up again and let it run. "Oh. Yeah. Flashes. Could be drop-out—a bad place in the tape."

Holly eased the first frame into view and paused the tape. "No. Doesn't look like a flare on the lens, either. Something's there, all right." The rising sun had caught a reflective object, just inside the dense fringe of pine trees at a curve in the shoreline, about two hundred yards from the camera.

"Could be innocent," she said, clearly interested. "A foil candy wrapper, say, or a fisherman's marker for a honey-hole. A good place to fish," she added, seeing Nick's puzzlement.

"But it moves!" Nick insisted, grasping the knob and moving the video back and forth. "Don't tell me those aren't two different pine trees."

"Okay, Galileo, calm down. I'll get it blown up at the station in Armageddon." Her teeth pressed her bottom lip in mischievous pleasure. "So, does this mean I'm a cub detective? I've heard about your sleuthing exploits."

"Strictly as unpaid volunteer. I have trouble paying the one employee I already have."

"I enlist," she said enthusiastically. "How exciting!"

"Do you know what time you shot this?"

"To the fraction of a second. Time code. See?" She flipped a switch and a black rectangle with numerals appeared in the lower right corner. "Burns in the elapsed tape time. I always keep a shot sheet, so I know exactly when this is." She checked a yellow pad, added the elapsed time in the black rectangle to her logged start time, and said, "We're looking at 6:10 the morning of the murder." Her glass was empty. "How about that second bottle?"

Nick was tired, but he felt it a matter of honor not to be outdrunk by Holly; her boast of superior alcohol tolerance was a challenge he couldn't let pass. Youthful idiocy, that boon companion of bygone days, stood up in the bleachers and egged him on. He uncorked the bottle and poured another round.

"If you want to learn more about Katogoula myths and rituals," she said, "I know just the place to start: the museum. That's where the Twins-Raccoon Bowl is, and lots of other really neat stuff. Grace and Irton Dusong run it. It's over where the Golden Trace enters the state forest. Oh, and there's a fantastic collection of paintings done by a man just after the turn of the century. I'll show you. Just a sec."

She shuffled through a dozen or so tape boxes. "Here it is."

Though his right eye had started to droop from the effects of fatigue and wine, Nick managed to make out what appeared to be an attic in an old but handsome house. On the walls were paintings, watercolors and oils, depicting Katogoula villages, individuals hunting and fishing and playing games, artwork and weapons and tools being made....

"Those are wonderful," Nick said, slurring, to his great mortification. "Who did them? Where are they?" He noticed the second bottle was already half empty. *This woman must have a wooden leg!*

"A historic home near here. Tadbull Hall. Lots of old money, lots of land. They owned the lumber mill that just closed. The man who painted these took hundreds of photos, too, around the turn of the century. The one before this one, I mean. He was the current Mr. Tadbull's grandfather. A Renaissance man, we'd call him today. You know, a dabbler, fascinated by knowledge itself." She rubbed a hand down her face, remembering something. There was a problem. She wrinkled her nose. "But you may have to go there alone. I'm not sure they'll let me in. Anymore.... Why don't you lie down? You look totally trashed."

"Yeah, I think I will," Nick said, wearily slouching over to the couch, trying unsuccessfully to act in complete control of his faculties. "Why wouldn't the Tadbull's let you in? Did you slug someone there, too?"

The last words he remembered were, "Worse. I bet with his chips and lost."

Chapter 16

The Friday morning that greeted Nick outside Holly's room was gray, drizzly, and cool bordering on downright cold. Louisiana fall was a fickle creature, ever promising itself to winter as it dallied with summer.

Tommy had sounded the truck horn a few times before Nick awoke on the couch that backed up to the window of "Annie Oakley." His watch told him he was fifteen minutes late for his eight A.M. appointment. He stumbled outside.

His tongue dry and his head aching, he squinted at the dismal day that seemed to sneer maliciously at him.

"If you're looking for your red-headed gal," Tommy said, a grin of rakish solidarity on his face, "I saw her at Three Sisters Pantry. She looked a lot better than you. And she had a pretty good appetite. Had a big breakfast. No one answered at your room, so I put two and two together."

"Hey, it's not what you think," Nick said in a bullfrog's voice that would have made him an instant radio celebrity. "Really, nothing happened."

"Come on, Nick, don't give me that. You come to the door of her room, looking like yesterday's dog shit? You didn't by any chance spend the night here, did you? And she's all smiley and perky?...Can't fool me. I got a wife, you know. I can tell a happy woman when I see one."

Nick continued to protest. "No, believe me, absolutely nothing—ah, forget it. Give me ten minutes, will you?"

He trudged to Daniel Boone, wishing Tommy had solid reasons to envy him. The cold mist on his grizzled face felt like botched acupuncture. "I'm getting too old for this," he muttered between chattering teeth.

His wet hair and the blood from his hasty shave had almost dried when they reached the Sangfleuve Parish Courthouse in Armageddon. Tommy had tribal business to attend to with lawyers and accountants. Wooty Tadbull, on behalf of his family, had made a generous offer of land for an initial reservation—minus mineral rights, which the family wanted to keep just in case there was oil or gas underground. With this promising development to work on, Tommy seemed in much better spirits than the last time Nick had seen him. He'd dressed up for the occasion in a summer coat that was too small and which must have dated from his high-school days. Within his open shirt collar he wore a silver necklace with a pendant cross that captured the overcast day's stingy light, reflecting—in Nick's symbol-hungry mind, at least—the man's resilient faith and optimism.

This must have been what the sheriff returned to Tommy the night before, Brianne's gift found at the murder scene. He probably would have preferred a new shotgun but would never have said so, Nick thought, succumbing to a twinge of bachelor's snideness in the presence of connubial bliss.

In his own coat of the right season but the wrong decade (this one an academic tweed from a Salvation Army Thrift Store) Nick would have a solid day alone to begin the basic on-site research he so much enjoyed.

The creamy limestone courthouse was a fine example of Louisiana's version of Depression-era Art Deco architecture. Straining with foolish credence in populist lies, it was terrifically ugly and out of context, a cross between a Soviet bureaucratic pile and the state Capitol in Baton

Rouge. But current or personal taste shouldn't be the arbiter of historic value, Nick believed. How much had been lost already to such intellectual arrogance? He was constantly reminding Hawty never to throw anything out of his book- and document-crammed office. Nevertheless, he detested this building and all like it. He would gladly plunge down the handle for the controlled implosion.

He bought breakfast from a blind black man who ran the courthouse snack booth. Nick was surprised to find that the coffee was good, the muffins and biscuits outstanding. As a connoisseur of the amenities of public buildings, Nick never expected much from such places.

Luevenia Silsby, of Three Sisters Pantry, made the goodies every Friday, the snack man informed him, his eyes flitting uselessly about the dark-granite lobby. Miss Luevie had just dropped them off, in fact.

The wild gymnastics of the snack man's eyes made Nick dizzy and edgy. Just what he needed, on top of a hangover, before spending hours studying crabbed script on faded documents and dim, blurry, scratched microfilm.

◻

In Armageddon, the fire had been real; Sangfleuve Parish really was a "burned county." Here, the tale of the conflagration that had destroyed all records—one of the stock excuses used by town-hall clerks to fend off bothersome genealogists—was quite literally the defining moment in the town's life.

The parish clerk of court, Roberta Gridley, was a diminutive woman in her forties, with thinning, frizzy brown hair and the plump, pink features of a cute piglet. In her eyes Nick saw a deep hatred of disorder; she attacked cataloging, indexing, and the collection of fees with zeal. Though their office habits differed considerably, both of them shared a passion for records, which even in their smallest increment added a brushstroke to the portrait of a life.

Nick always made a point to schmooze with courthouse personnel; on-site research was a major undertaking, and a cooperative clerk could make the difference between bridging the impossible gaps in a family history and coming home empty-handed. For decades, the Mormons, with their well-known devotion to genealogy, had been clicking away at the essentials of local genealogical research, around the world—birth, death, and marriage certificates, probate files, tax lists, land records, and other mileposts of life—and these were available on microfilm for research at a distance. But in truth, just a fraction of the holdings of most courthouses and other official repositories made it to microfilm.

Clerks' offices were charged with keeping order in present-day affairs; budgets were too tight and staffs too small to cater to genealogists' insatiable appetite for long-forgotten facts. There were, though, sterling exceptions who could open many hidden doors to the local past, and Nick was instantly convinced that he'd found one in Roberta Gridley. Such a helpful local clerk could guide the visiting genealogist to old records that had not been touched—and perhaps not even catalogued—for a hundred years, through idiosyncratic filing systems and laws, and to more-contemporary records often kept out of the general public's hands. Nick had written and called Roberta Gridley beforehand to explain who he was and what he would be doing for the Katogoula, and he'd even obtained a comprehensive privacy release from Tommy on behalf of tribe members whose family histories he would be investigating.

Now he listened patiently and with genuine interest as Roberta explained what had happened in 1863.

One pre-dawn morning, eight companies of about seven hundred Union soldiers fleeing a rout south of Shreveport floated on makeshift log rafts between the fog-enshrouded banks of the Sangfleuve River. The Federals were hoping to reach the Mississippi and the main Union force fighting its way up the big river under General Butler and Admiral Porter. That fall morning, the water was low at Port Sangfleuve; the rafts snagged on limestone rapids within easy range of a regiment of over a thousand Confederates bivouacking along the town's riverbank.

By the time the Rebels convinced themselves that these shapes in ragged blue were not phantoms, the odds were about even; the Union soldiers, equipped with the new Henry repeating rifles, had not hesitated to exercise their superior firepower. By late in the afternoon, the surviving combatants ceased fire from redoubts on opposite sides of the river, retrieved wounded, and on one of the stranded rafts, they exchanged food, tobacco, and whiskey, and regarded the smoldering town. Before going their separate ways, they agreed the town should thenceforth be called Armageddon, for the battle had been like Judgment Day. The name stuck.

◻

"I'm awfully sorry, Mr. Herald. Hardly anything original before 1863. *The Red Book* and *The Handybook* are right," Roberta said, enthroned at her rigorously ordered desk in her office. A large plate-glass window let her keep tabs on her office staff of three women, who worked in a high-ceilinged room at old oak desks among file cabinets of many sizes, copiers, ever-warbling phones, computers, and massive ledger books. "But we offer an up-to-the-minute computer index of what we do have from the earliest surviving records to today. We run across lost file packets all the time, families bring old documents in for recording, and we've been able to reconstruct some destroyed records based on later property transfers, probate proceedings, civil suits, notarial and attorney papers, and the like.... And since you're interested in Indian genealogy, I ought to tell you—though I'm not supposed to—we have special access to the *Legajos de Luisiana.*"

Surely she'd made a mistake. Could this be true? "Excuse me, Roberta, did you say the *Legajos de Luisiana*?" He struggled to hide his elation.

The *Legajos de Luisiana*, those wonderful, voluminous records of Spain's administration of the territory later known as Louisiana. Part of a larger group of archives known as the *Fondos de las Floridas* (which in turn was part of the famous *Papeles Procedentes de Cuba*), the *Legajos* remained in Cuba after Spain had relinquished its North American colonies. Microfilm of the *Legajos*—a complete set would run to nearly thirty reels—wasn't publicly available as yet, to Nick's knowledge. It had only recently been microfilmed in Cuba, after centuries of obscurity, by the Historic New Orleans Collection. Microfilm sets were expected to cost upwards of twenty thousand dollars. He was still trying to get at THNOC's *Legajos* in New Orleans—not that he wasn't fond of Veronique anyway.

"I keep up with what's happening in genealogy, in addition to archival and preservation issues," Roberta said proudly. "At conferences and what not. You might say I'm sort of a genealogical nut myself. I have some Spanish blood, and I wanted to see what my kin was up to in those days." She leaned forward. "We clerks of court have our little mad-money funds. And then some overdue federal money came our way. Not being one to look a gift-horse in the mouth, and since my department is so routinely efficient, I purchased some state-of-the-art digitizing equipment. In five years, every record in this courthouse will be accessible by computer! The police jury is even talking about making us a regional digitizing center for courthouses around the South."

She went on to say that shortly after receiving the windfall, she met a THNOC scholar at an archival conference. They struck a deal whereby Roberta's office would digitize the *Legajos* with her new system, in exchange for a digital copy of the rare records and the right to make copies for in-house use.

"The State Archives doesn't even have a microfilm set yet. I'm thinking we could put little Armageddon on the map with genealogy buffs. I can just see it now: RVs parked all around the courthouse, affluent retirees researching roots going back to the Spanish period of this area.

Eating at our diners, shopping at our stores, some deciding to even settle here.... Of course, it won't hold a candle to the Katogoula casino."

"You've heard about the tribe's idea, then?" Nick asked.

"Oh, *everybody* knows about *that*. Especially here in the courthouse. People talk."

Roberta then regaled Nick in painstaking detail about the process of transferring records from microfilm to digital form. She rattled on about diazo and silver-halide film, JPEGs and TIFFs, 8-bit grayscale capture, 4-bit GIF previews, lossless compression, encoded text, gigabytes, and metadata.

At last, Roberta handed Nick the sumptuously produced descriptive brochure; THNOC always flew first-class. This would prove invaluable as he trudged through the vast uncharted wilderness of the *Legajos*.

"We have a long way to go before we're finished, so you can't do a complete computer search. Cuban ladies supposedly compiled this guide by hand over many years; they paid particular attention to surnames. Better employment than rolling cigars, don't you think? THNOC provides lots of English to help you along."

In Nick's mind a weird vignette blocked out the present surroundings. Sun-baked elderly Cuban women, smoking cigars and wearing the short pleated skirts and sleeveless lettered tops of the adorable high-school cheerleaders he'd worshipped from afar, pumped out, with preternatural litheness, the silly ditty "Two bits, four bits, six bits, a dollar, all for the *Legajos*, stand up and..."

"Go *Legajos*!" Nick erupted with inappropriate volume. "Well—ahem—this is quite a welcome surprise."

Obviously the lingering effect of too much Gewürztraminer.

Giving him a worried look, Robert said, "We've already digitized the rolls that deal with west Louisiana." She handed him a stack of six jewel CD cases. "There's a computer out there in the reading area. I'm sure, being a professional genealogist, you know your way around a PC?" Nick responded with a lying, but enthusiastic, nod. "Remember our index of holdings; you'll find a link on the start page. Look it over and tell us what strikes your fancy.... I'm sure this won't be your last visit with us, Mr. Herald, but at some point, would you fill out this questionnaire? We give it to all family researchers, so we can see how to improve our service. I'll let you be, now."

In New Orleans, Nick had already mined the available microfilm of Sangfleuve Parish records of the late-nineteenth and early twentieth centuries. There was, as he expected, a lot of crucial information here at the courthouse that he didn't have. Roberta put her staff to work photocopying what he specified. She was not shy about asking for a healthy contribution to the mad-money fund, and Nick cheerfully complied.

He found his way to an appropriately dim corner hemmed in by tall shelves loaded with ledgers and boxes of packets of loose documents; here two old microfilm readers that looked like used launderette equipment seemed to accuse him of disloyalty. As he expected, the machines seemed to be in excellent working order; these old behemoths were nearly indestructible. The public computer was nearby. He turned the chair and the monitor so that his back was to the venerable readers.

The waiting list of researchers in New Orleans for the *Legajos de Luisiana* was almost as long as Canal Street; he'd been dying to take a peek at the immensely important records. Beyond slaking his usual curiosity, he expected to find some mention of the Katogoula—and maybe, just maybe, a long-forgotten fact of tribal history pointing to identity or motive in the murder of Carl Shawe. Yes, it was a fishing expedition; but he had learned to trust his instincts.

What would future genealogists think of the computer-generated dross that passed for public records today? he wondered. The artistry and romance of the world's archives, the continuity with the past through an idiosyncratic flesh-and-blood hand and mind—was all of that doomed to perish in the pure digital flame of the Almighty Gizmo? And here he was, participating in the betrayal of a great and worthy tradition.

Trying his best to appear as if he knew what he was doing, in case anyone was watching, he fumbled with the computer surreptitiously until he found where to insert the CD. Twenty minutes and many warnings and help-dialog boxes later, he was cruising blithely through screen after screen of page-preview GIFs and capsule explanations. He felt fairly cocky.

Nick's Spanish was worse than his French, which was far from perfect; the *Legajos* made use of both. For a while it was like hearing opera without the benefit of seeing the actors on the stage or of having a subtitle box. But he began to pick up clues to meaning in the placement of words and phrases, in the formulaic structures of introduction, elaboration, and conclusion. Soon, he thought he understood the quills' flourishes and curves that were more like the courtly, mysterious realism of Velázquez than the dry proceedings of territorial administration.

Suddenly, a hot-cold zing ran up and down his spine and across his shoulders—his mind's unerring signal that he'd discovered something extremely important. And it was this:

The Spanish had done business with a Kentucky Indian trader. This man's name was not mentioned in the written records; secrecy concerns, no doubt. The trader had sworn allegiance to the Spanish government in 1791, and from then on the Spanish used him to spy on Americans and Indians throughout the upper Gulf of Mexico area. Nick suspected the man might have been a member of General James Wilkinson's entourage.

Wilkinson was a huge enigma of American history. A veteran of the American Revolution, he engaged in Louisiana intrigues in the late eighteenth century and on into the American period. He apparently played on Spain's fears of America's growing power and on her own ambition to grab America's western-most lands east of the Mississippi. Conflicting historical accounts variously portray him as a patriot brilliantly serving his country as a double agent, as a triple agent conspiring with the enemies of the young and vulnerable United States, as a self-serving conspirator deeply involved in, among other things, Aaron Burr's secessionist plot and then in his treason trial, and above all as a crafty operator who always seemed to come out smelling like a rose.

The nameless trader, cut from Wilkinsonian cloth, dutifully reported on the shifting alliances of the tribes in their struggle to understand, befriend, or outmaneuver the Europeans and the Americans, who were interested primarily in military, territorial, and mercantile exploits. He also interspersed his reports with observations that should have put him among the ranks of the great anthropologists of his day.

The trader had heard stories of a long-ago war between the Katogoula and the Quinahoa; his account of it showed neither tribe in a favorable light. Both had been guilty of dirty tricks, but the Katogoula perpetrated the treachery that ultimately proved victorious.

After many years of warfare, the Katogoula, through the supposedly neutral Yaknelousa, offered to parley at an intertribal feast. Both sides were to deposit arms outside the Katogoula central village. Then talks could begin. But as the visiting Quinahoa slept that first night, a Katogoula band hidden in the woods crept into the village and slaughtered many of the defenseless enemy warriors. The war broke out anew with unprecedented ferocity. The Quinahoa avenged themselves first on the weaker Yaknelousa, before finally falling to utter defeat at the hands of the Katogoula.

The Kentucky trader had seen captive Quinahoa survivors, who, though they were very old by the time of his report, were still kept in abject conditions forty years after the event. Even the children of forbidden, but inevitable, pairings between conquerors and conquered were treated little better than dogs.

The year of the trader's *Legajos* account was 1795. If his chronology was correct, the war had been fought in the mid 1750s, before Spanish rule of the area known today as Louisiana. Granted, this account was anecdotal, secondary evidence, falling short of genealogical conclusiveness. But Nick had pushed the timeline slightly further back than

Hawty's date of 1759, with her allegedly authentic journal of the clerk on Mézières diplomatic mission. Still, the clerk and his tribal witnesses were closer in time and experience to the war, a fact which should entitle their account to more credibility according to the standards of genealogical proof.

And then Nick clicked to a page listing names of Katogoula and Yaknelousa warriors, and names of a handful of captive Quinahoa.

"Ha!" he exclaimed, jumping up from the wooden chair he'd occupied for two hours. The office women paused, glanced his way, and tittered to each other before getting back to work. They'd witnessed too many eureka moments, when genealogists strike pay dirt, to be surprised by Nick's outburst.

He'd found *names*, honest-to-God names unknown for two centuries, and which, in all likelihood, were recorded nowhere else—certainly not in the Cuban/THNOC guide. Names from tribes with no surviving written language. Names that could help reconstruct lines of descent to the present day, that could make a crucial difference for an applicant seeking admission into the reborn Katogoula tribe.

Nick sat down again. Genealogists, professional and amateur, live for moments like this. But now was no time to savor his discovery. Every minute in a courthouse was a precious commodity, and public employees seldom shared the family historian's wild-eyed determination to work nonstop until exhaustion—though he sensed that Roberta and her staff were different.

The Kentucky trader of the *Legajos* had the soul of an objective historian. He put down what he saw, without editorial comment, apparently without concern for what the Spanish would make of his fact-filled reports. The names Nick read were Spanish interpretations of an American's version of Indian-language names. What Indian language—Mobilian Jargon?—Nick did not know. And beyond that obvious problem of the accuracy of transmission, Nick wondered whether the Katogoula and Yaknelousa were identified by war names or other public monikers, which would make identification of the families difficult. Had the captive Quinahoa been stripped of their dignity and renamed in some humiliating way?

In spite of the new questions in his mind, he was still grinning as he clicked the print command over and over again, hoping the pages he wanted would slither out of a machine somewhere in the office.

Holly was the expert on Spanish and on local Indian languages and customs. An excellent excuse to see her again.

◙

Sheriff Higbee's office was on the first floor. Nick needed to stretch his crepitating joints.

He entered the cold, damp stairwell from the second-floor landing. An incandescent bulb above the doorway seemed absurdly weak compared with the snow-glare of the fluorescents that blasted most of the clerk-of-court's office. He blinked a few times, and the steps gradually emerged in his field of vision. He leaned a bit over the railing and looked up.

This central part of the building was fifteen stories high, profligate with space in a way modern builders would avoid. The stairwell formed a large square shaft rising to a skylight letting in anemic illumination from the gray day outside. He could see the angled railing turning back on itself like an Escher print, but beyond each floor's railing, nothing. Distant reverberations and the sound of his own breathing echoed off the sweating walls. The smell of cigarette smoke told him this was the refuge of fugitive puffers.

Nick thought he could get used to the slow pace of small-town life. Roberta had informed him that the thirty-thousand person city could boast only about a hundred lawyers; several of those were judges and one was the sheriff. Not at all like New Orleans, where the legal horde made a genealogist's life difficult by insisting that the affairs of the living take precedence over those of the dead.

He descended the moist, slippery stairs, briefly holding on to the wooden railing, black and greasy now from decades of grime. Disgusted, he wiped his hands with a paper napkin he'd kept from breakfast. Pausing at an intermediate landing before a cylindrical trashcan, the top of which was filled with sand and studded with cigarette butts, he ditched the napkin and felt around in his pockets, fishing for odd bits of trash accumulated during his morning's research.

A door opened somewhere above him. Clang! It closed.

From deep within his mind, a warning reached his consciousness. *No footsteps.*

Instinctively he crouched and looked up. A blur of hands on the zigzag of railing, above him in the murky stairwell. Sand and cigarette butts rained on him, blasting his eyes with grit, filling his mouth with foul-tasting ash. He dropped his briefcase and brought his arms up to protect himself. His eyes stung, but he forced them open to mere slits. He had only a fraction of a second to jump back toward the wall, before a dark shape slammed into his right elbow and shoulder. The pain was immediate, sharp, deep. Something felt broken. He lost his balance.

Nick rolled and bounced and ricocheted down the stairs. He imagined the courthouse—which earlier that day had reminded him of a B-movie spaceship—rocketing slowly, weightlessly, into the black void of the cosmos and being swallowed forever.

Chapter 17

Wooty Tadbull spooned thick, steaming, marsh-water brown oyster-crab-duck-and-sausage gumbo into his mouth. Delicious, up there with the best he'd ever eaten—and he considered himself an expert on the subject of Louisiana cuisine. There was an art to making this humble delicacy born of the verve Creoles and the resourcefulness of Cajuns and slaves. He tore off another hunk of a thin-crusted baguette of New Orleans French bread from the basket just beyond his bowl, feeling an emptiness the excellent food could not fill.

The Katogoula, like the Cajuns and the slaves, had suffered a lot of tough luck. Even the closing of the mill didn't break them. They had persevered and triumphed at last. Now he, supposedly their friend and defender, was screwing them. Again.

He'd momentarily blocked out the fact that, across the elegantly set table, state senator Augustus Bayles sat staring impassively at his every move. He began to feel very self-conscious, and the gumbo didn't go down as smoothly as before.

Wooty wondered how much taxpayers' money trickled into this neutral oasis within sight of the Capitol, either as legislators' expenses or as a direct line item hidden deep within the unfathomable business of some committee. Hell, the Legislature wasn't even meeting, and wouldn't again until April. But Wooty knew that politics in Louisiana was a year-round job, thanks to a succession of special sessions and off-the-record meetings like the ones occurring all around him. For so many people to snipe, bite, kick, and scratch for office, it must be rewarding far above the measly salary legislators drew while enduring a few months of boring speeches.

Not his problem. *Laissez les bons temps rouler*, "let the good times roll," the saying goes in boom-and-bust, sin-and-repent Louisiana. He didn't make things the way they were, but he damn sure wasn't going to be left holding the bag. Every man a king, Huey Long had promised; Wooty wouldn't mind being a mere prince. When in Rome...

And Baton Rouge on the Mississippi was the mother wolf suckling more conspiracy, hypocrisy, and delusions of grandeur than even the great city on the Tiber at the height of its doomed glory. The State Capitol stood tall in a long and dishonorable Louisiana tradition as a world-class temple of boondoggling, logrolling, and grandstanding, where cunning glad-handers, anointed with the oil of inside information, became high priests of nepotism, casuistry, and fraud, daily sacrificing their blindfolded constituents on a tax-fueled pyre belching carcinogenic petrochemical incense.

He wanted to jump up and shout, above the intense, discreet conversations at every table, "Stuff those pockets, boys. Let the grand juries sort it out later!" But he was here to make a deal, too. Today, he was playing the game. But not strictly for money. He had more at stake. A lot more.

Wooty's Mexican backers had a long memory and a vindictive temper, but they had tentatively gone along with his plan to salvage their extremely lucrative operations in the area. Lately, they'd shown increasing respect for his intelligence, local knowledge, and initiative; they'd eased up on the vague threats over his stupid mistake. *Her* stupid mistake. Usually with something like that, they held it over you like a guillotine blade, or just got rid of you in pieces too small to fill a McDonald's bag. He was, in fact, enjoying the kind of responsibility he never got from his father, who, in Wooty's opinion, still treated him like a kid. He was sick to death of subservience.

A dangerous responsibility, he'd taken on. But he had a chance now to show everyone, enemies and friends alike, what he was made of; to prove that Wooten Tadbull IV wasn't a pampered playboy from the sticks, a worthless scion of a desiccated genetic tree.

Senator Augustus Bayles had long since finished his shrimp-stuffed artichoke—which had been almost as big as his head—and his heaping platter of chicken fricassee and rice. The senator had a teenager's appetite; and he was a stealthy eater. Wooty hadn't noticed him taking a bite. Bayles even looked like a brainy, fifteen-year-old black kid—in actuality, he was thirty-five. Close-cropped hair. All bones and joints. His off-the-rack black pinstriped suit and starched white shirt engulfed him like an older brother's hand-me-downs. Wooty concluded from the rising politician's eating habits that Augustus Bayles was indeed devious, insatiable, and merciless, as people said; and from his clothes, that the immediate perks of malfeasance meant less to him than the delayed attainment of ever greater power.

Augustus Bayles stared at Wooty. A humorless, unreadable, almost unblinking gaze. *As if he expects me to steal something of his*, Wooty was thinking. *Paranoia must be reasonable defensive behavior around here. This guy doesn't trust anyone. And why should he?* Wooty took in a quick panorama of the room filled with the snakes and alligators who ran the Bayou State behind the scenes.

How could a guy eat under such scrutiny? Everybody was slyly watching everybody else. He put down his spoon and wiped his mouth on the sky blue linen napkin, then drank some of his iced tea.

This was the Blue House. Just about everything in the damn place was some shade of blue. Royal blue paisley wallpaper, teal-blue patterned carpeting, navy blue uniforms for the stolid black waiters, who served the lobbyists and legislators without registering the slightest hint of apparent interest in the overheard conversations. Conversations that determined what legislation passed, and who got paid for it.

"Well, I guess we better get to the matter at hand, Senator Bayles—"

"No names, if you don't mind."

"Yeah, sure." *Probably thinks I'm wired.* "Look, my associates believe you can help us out. Seems they've dealt with you before."

Wooty waited for a confirming response. But Bayles merely stared at him with those unblinking eyes. *Man, this guy is good! He'll be governor, one day.*

Wooty continued: "We understand there's talk of the legislature moving to ban gambling—with some exceptions that don't include us." State Representative Rufus Girn's plan, he knew only too well. Fortunately, he didn't have to worry about Rufus showing up at the Blue House today: he and Mr. Tadbull were in the coastal marsh of south Louisiana getting drunk and fondling loose women at an oil company's posh duck-hunting camp. "My associates have a substantial investment in video poker. They're interested in protecting their investment. I'm authorized to offer you the take from ten machines, anywhere in the state, if you work against the anti-gambling forces."

The Mexican cartel Wooty worked for had begun to diversify. One of the most successful new enterprises was video poker, very profitable in its own right—a good location could produce $8,000 gross per machine a month—and even more valuable as a vehicle for money laundering. Since Louisiana had legalized "gaming," organized crime had declared open season on the state, as in past outbreaks of corruption, the first Louisiana lottery of the late nineteenth century being the outstanding example. The cartel had formed an uneasy alliance with the New Orleans Mob, which had its long tentacles into other coin-generating enterprises such as pinball arcades, vending machines, and magazine wholesaling. Wooty himself, as titular head of one front company, had been granted the take from five poorly placed machines.

"That won't do," Bayles said, without hesitation. He leaned forward, his long fingers almost touching Wooty's hands, an uncomfortable proximity.

Wooty didn't want to insult the man by drawing back, so he kept his hands where they were. Maybe it was a test of some sort, or a subtle negotiating tactic to distract him. It worked.

"Why did you and your associates choose one of the few African American legislators as your potential ally? I'll tell you," Bayles continued, not waiting for an answer. "I'm the cheap Negro. Naive, hungry, cap-in-hand grateful for the chance to rise above marginality and sit at the kitchen table in the big house with the white folk. You'll have to do better. Much better. I don't work for minimum wage anymore. Thirty machines, and we can begin serious discussion."

"Thirty!" Wooty exclaimed. Three million gross yearly!

"Please keep your voice down," Bayles said calmly, his eyes moving smoothly right to left and then back to center. "There are certain rules here. I am taking a chance by even talking to you. You see, I know your associates, as you call them. They are dangerous men bringing drugs into this state, rending the social fabric with all manner of associated evils, primarily affecting my African American constituents. The risk premium is necessarily very high for such arrangements."

Wooty started to deny it, but he saw certainty in Bayles's eyes.

"You run Mexican marijuana through the pipeline of your daddy's property," Bayles went on, as if he were discussing a third person. "You aren't a big fish, but you seem smart beyond your station. And you don't deal in the deadly stuff—crack, crank, heroin. My sources say you're not a user—at this time. You're just a medium link in the food chain. The video poker machines are important to your friends because they make a huge profit, and because they allow even larger quantities of dirty, untraceable money to enter the system. Money my people, African Americans, sweat blood to make in order to pay you for your destructive product."

A waiter took Wooty's plate away, and a moment later, Bayles, not even consulting his dining companion, imperceptibly rejected the dessert cart. Soon coffee appeared. Bayles carefully prepared his cup.

Wooty watched the graceful fingers, fascinated by the ritual. He knew a little of the senator's background, and tried to imagine the impoverished upbringing that had led to such odd eating habits: wolfing food, denying extravagant indulgence, and savoring to the point of idolatry a small delight like a good cup of coffee. Somewhere along the line Bayles had also acquired his irritating pretentiousness of speech. Wooty could tell he was very proud of his education, and with good reason. The young legislator had attended prestigious Freret Law School, on a well-deserved scholarship, about the time Wooty himself had been partying his way through business school, a beneficiary of good old-fashioned plutocratic influence.

"I guess you got my number," said Wooty, draining his coffee, pushing back in his chair as if to leave. "Your feelings on the matter are pretty clear. Sorry for taking up your time. Thanks for the gumbo." It was partly a bluff, to see how the guy handled pressure, but Wooty wouldn't mind forgetting the whole thing. The senator's words had taken him down a peg.

"Thank the good people of Louisiana," Bayles said, signaling their waiter for a refill of Wooty's cup. "Please stay. We've just begun. Even though you and your partners are enemies of my people, poisoners of society in general, we've learned new tactics. We're interested in strategic alliances that serve our long-term interests. Realpolitik, the Russians used to say, when they had to do something unpleasant. We've grown out of quotas and equal opportunity, passive remedies. We don't come to the kitchen door, we don't need your handouts anymore. We've learned a lot from our history, and from yours. Now we take what we want, just like everyone else."

"You're preaching to the choir, here," Wooty said. "Seems to me we can come to an understanding and leave off all the propaganda. I'm a progressive kind of a guy. I got black friends, white friends, Indian friends." The last two words were out before he could stop them. But now was no time for guilt or weakness, not with this guy. "So what do you say, can we do a deal? The number you mentioned probably isn't a problem. Hell, they don't even know how many machines they got now. The bottom line is, how do we save video poker, and my little piece of the action, from a general gambling prohibition?"

Bayles took a long, ruminative sip of his coffee. "*Our* piece of the action. It's quite simple, really: local option. Each parish votes on the gambling it wants to keep. The constitutional machinery has been in place since 1996, the last time there was a groundswell for gambling prohibition; the language is vague and open-ended, to allow us periodically, when necessity dictates, to make subtle changes here and there. Local option, with its illusion of self-determination, appeals to the voters' sense of fair play; it is a good alternative to legislative fiat. Louisiana voters hate change, and hate being told what to do even more."

"And what they don't know won't hurt them, right?" Wooty said.

Bayles inclined his head slightly in apparent agreement. "In Louisiana, a law is only as good as its loophole. My bill calling for new local-option elections will provide that a two-thirds supermajority of parish voters will be required to kill each form of gambling. The anti-gambling faction—in general, amateurs—can never muster those numbers, or educate the public on the complex issues and ballots. A negatively phrased ballot issue is always hard for the ordinary voter to fathom; many befuddled citizens who vote 'no,' thinking they're helping to eliminate gambling, will actually be voting for its continuance. Breaking down the various types of gaming into numerous separate issues will further confuse the electorate. The intimidating nature of a long ballot full of fine print is enough to drastically reduce turnout.

"Moreover, state workers, teachers, city and parish leaders, chambers of commerce, all know gambling is a free ride that keeps their paychecks, raises, and profits coming. One winner's splurge can make a local retailer's month, whereas a problem gambler probably has been a bad credit risk even before he started losing. Gambling is an invisible, voluntary tax. Ideal. They complain loudly on the six o'clock news about gambling's deleterious effect on morals, but in the sanctity of the voting booth, a sufficient number will vote their pocketbooks. These people will know which lever to pull."

Wooty was impressed by the senator's grasp of human nature. "'Don't tax me, tax the man behind that tree,' right?"

"Yes, that is our anthem here in the Gret Stet," Bayles said, a flicker of a smile coming into his melancholy eyes. "Where an outcome is in doubt, we buy the votes, as we do with elective office. We'll procure school buses, pay voters five or ten dollars, and bus them to the polling places. In the unlikely event of a defeat in a parish, we'll simply bring it back for another and another vote, until we wear our opponents down and they have to return to their everyday business."

"You could always add a rider," Wooty said. "Dedicate tax money to something socially irresistible. Like boll weevil eradication or a school for the blind." He winked, knowing that some years back this ploy had secured voters' approval of slot machines at several Louisiana racetracks that claimed video poker competition was affecting their profits.

"Ah," said Augustus Bayles, "you are indeed a keen observer of our political process. My compliments. Democracy, as you clearly realize, is grounded in self-interest. As there was in the big 1996 gambling vote, there will again be widespread relief that all-or-nothing, statewide prohibition is not the only choice. Public debate on local option will have a cathartic effect, satisfying to both the pro and anti forces; they will feel empowered, in control of their destiny. If we wished, we could add dog racing and jai alai to the ballot—about the only kinds of gambling we don't presently have—and these also would pass."

"Is all this...well, constitutional?" Wooty asked.

"It is if we legislate it so and persuade the people to agree," Bayles replied with regal confidence. "Should some group decide to undertake an expensive challenge in court, so be it. Louisiana judges and editorial writers have mortgages, children in school, and desires beyond their means, like most people. With the right encouragement, such allies will make sure we carry the day."

"So, let me get this straight: you're certain you can get a major local-option election tied to any anti-gambling constitutional amendment that may come out of the legislature? I hear it's an unpredictable process. You know what they say about watching sausage and laws being made: best for the uninitiated not to witness it."

"Yes, your parish *will* retain video poker. I make it a practice to maintain a large stack of IOUs," said Bayles. "And the gambling industry will open its coffers even wider than normal. In the recent past, one out of five state campaign dollars has come from that source. Millions, perhaps fifteen or twenty, will be spent on pro-gambling advertising. With that sort of financial muscle, be assured that video poker is here to stay."

Wooty knew that Bayles was a partner in a minority-controlled company that owned several radio and television stations in Louisiana, Texas, and Mississippi. The company would rake in piles of cash from the advertising campaign to convince voters to keep gambling legal. What a brilliant set-up, Wooty thought. The guy makes money no matter which way the coin falls!

"Good deal," said Wooty. "Speaking of casinos, we'd like a little less competition. I'm talking about Indian gambling?"

"That's a tougher problem. Federal law, as now interpreted, allows it as long as the state has analogous forms of gambling. The Katogoula, I understand, are planning a casino in your vicinity." He paused, seemingly waiting for Wooty to respond.

Is there anything this guy doesn't know? "As a matter of fact, my father and Representative…um, I mean, some business friends of mine are trying to get the casino management contract, and I'm supposed to be convincing the tribe to bite at our offer. My original associates would just as soon not have all that activity in the area. Would kind of mess up our quiet little pond, the way we do things."

"Yes, I'm informed that there isn't a better corridor between I-10 and I-49 anywhere in the state. Your property is indeed uniquely situated for your associates' purposes." Another slow sip of coffee. "A former legislative colleague needs an emergency infusion of cash. Legal expenses. He had the bad taste to get himself videotaped and indicted. He owns a large tract of land not far from your family's property—but far enough, I submit, to be less of a drag on the video poker business and certain other enterprises you may or may not have an interest in. Land eminently suitable for an Indian reservation, in my opinion. I'll acquire it at a fire-sale price and make the tribe a counteroffer that is even more attractive than the one your casino friends have made."

"You got your work cut out for you," Wooty said. "The tribe's a real indecisive bunch. Internal politics, you know?" *Of course he knows.* "One day they're for a casino, the next day they're not. You'll need someone who understands them, where they're coming from, where they want to go. Not some slick lobbyist." He pointed with his thumb around the room, indicating the men huddled in conversation at every table. "That just turns them off, big time."

"Duplicity comes naturally to you," the senator said. "From me, that is high praise." Bayles smiled. An engaging smile that helped Wooty understand why so many people believed in and trusted this man. "Tell your Mexican associates this: I will trade my assistance and my compensation of the video poker machines for you."

"For *me*? What—what do you mean?"

"Consider our discussion a job interview. You're hired. Baton Rouge is not my final destination; I need people like you beside me on the difficult road to Washington. You also have a unique rapport with the Katogoula. Therefore, make it clear to your associates: you, or no deal."

The frigging nerve of this guy! What if I'm not interested? But he was, and the fact that Bayles had somehow read him like a book fascinated him.

"From a financial standpoint," Bayles added, "you will be rewarded. Handsomely and soon. In the near term, you will take on significant duties in my media division. When the casino becomes a reality, you will be a ten percent partner."

Perfect. This was turning out better than Wooty could have hoped. He was protecting the turf for the Mexican cartel; maybe relations would improve between them, the threats cease. The Katogoula would have another, perhaps better, opportunity to open a casino. And financially, his bases were covered: his video poker machines, provided he could keep them if he left the active employ of the cartel, were out of danger; if the tribal casino happened on Tadbull land after all, he would inherit the deal and the profits eventually; and if he could pull off what Bayles planned, he'd get ten percent of that casino!

"This is all sort of sudden...." Wooty cleared his throat, shifted in his chair. "But yeah—*hell yeah*, I'd like to be on your team. Tell you what: I'll leave the sausage making to you, and I'll do my best to bring home the bacon."

Senator Bayles spoke quietly in his overly cultivated voice about his far-flung enterprises, his grand battle plan for storming the heights of power. The Blue House had emptied of diners by the time he finished. Bayles never asked why Wooty was double-crossing his own father. He didn't need to, Wooty figured. The young, sad eyes seemed possessed of a knowledge of human contradictions beyond their years. As a black man in Louisiana politics, Augustus Bayles surely understood suppressed ambition and the impatience of a son kept at arm's length from wealth and power.

At last, the senator carefully folded his napkin the way he'd found it. The two men stood and shook hands, new friends with a common purpose.

Wooty felt he'd moved up the food chain one very important level.

Chapter 18

Saturday morning, Nick's bruised right shoulder and sprained, possibly fractured, elbow hurt worse than they had the afternoon before, when an emergency-room doctor prodded and poked him and finally decided that he would live. His right arm was encased in a padded nylon tube affair, resting in a sling. The doctor had determined there was no concussion, but it was a close call. Holly occasionally cast glances of empathetic pain his way.

"If we have to move," Irton Dusong was saying, "we'll sure enough do it. I'd just as soon give up this place and be on our own reservation. We don't even have a sprinkler system."

"We sure could use a new facility," Grace Dusong confirmed, "and a bigger operating budget. We could advertise. No one knows where we're at. Hardly ever more than a dozen visitors on a weekend."

The Katogoula Museum was a Spanish-style stucco building just within the boundaries of Tchekalaya State Forest. Nick, Holly, and the husband-and-wife caretakers stood in the brick courtyard.

Irton had apparently forgotten to comb his silver hair or shave for several days. Once a tall man, he now leaned forward at an unnatural angle, the result of an accident years before at Tadbull Mill. Grace, his wife, was a round woman with the stiff joints and gnarled hands of advanced rheumatoid arthritis. A cheery yellow floral bandeau secured her long charcoal-streaked ashen hair. They'd gained unwanted notoriety, and the animosity of certain other tribe members, by favoring at the last moment a tribal casino.

"I'm always patching something or other together, as 'tis," Irton said, drawing out a screwdriver and pliers from his overalls chest pocket. "Maybe we'll set us up some of them video poker machines in the new museum. That ought to help out the budget some!" He burst into laughter.

Nick, as he listened to the couple discussing the pros and cons of moving, unobtrusively probed the tender, throbbing bumps distributed randomly around his head.

A deputy had found him, half-conscious, at the bottom of the courthouse stairwell. The culprit had escaped, and Sheriff Higbee had no suspects. Nothing had been taken from Nick's briefcase—a fact which didn't surprise him: he was carrying easily replaceable copies of genealogical documents. Had his mysterious assailant, fearing future connections Nick might discover, tried to erase what was in his head, forever? Was this attack on him connected to Carl Shawe's death, another warning, perhaps, intended to persuade the tribe to change directions? Or was the motive to hurt or kill him rooted in his own experience?

He felt lucky to be alive. More than once in the last eighteen hours he'd been tempted to throw in the towel and hightail it back to New Orleans, where at least the rampant street violence was nothing personal.

Grace Dusong was explaining that the small yearly allowance from the legislature was one of the few benefits of state tribal recognition. The museum dated from the 1950s, the end result of a controversy involving Katogoula relics that had been dug up during highway construction in the thirties.

Holly declined Grace's offer of a guided tour.

"I've been here once or twice," Holly said, smiling in a friendly, familiar way at the older woman's solicitousness. "Well, maybe a hundred times. Let me show off a little. You could take this off my hands, though, Grace. Thanks." She squirmed out of her backpack, which was stuffed with the picnic lunch she and Nick were to eat later, at a "special place," Holly had promised.

She was a much better guide than Grace would have been, Nick was thinking, as he followed the beautiful red-haired woman. With great difficulty he managed to pay attention to her commentary on the dioramas and hangings and other dusty displays. What was it about her?...The delightfully sensual way her lips and tongue danced across her white teeth? Her expressive green eyes? The lovely curves below her supple jeans and snug sage pullover sweater?

Twelve hundred years ago, Holly was saying, the prehistoric Indians of the area made coiled clay pottery, hurled their spears with atlatls, used boiling stones in cooking, and kept dogs as pets. Only a few incomplete pots and isolated bones remained of this early period, and much of that evidence was enclosed in the cases before them. A replica of an atlatl caught Nick's attention.

It was a foot-and-a-half-long sturdy stick, with one end curved slightly upward and notched to hold the feathered tail of a yard-long spear, the other end wrapped in hide as a grip. A sketch showed how it was used: as if pitching a fastball, the thrower catapulted the loaded atlatl at the prey or enemy, sending the spear—referred to as a dart by modern aficionados—flying with the velocity of a bullet; the atlatl remained in the hand, a good close-combat weapon. Depending on the tribe and time, spear tips might have featured fire-hardened, pointed ends, or stone chipped to incredible thinness and sharpness, or scavenged, shaped metal.

Indians of this archaic period didn't ventured far from the many lakes and rivers, and their shoreline villages were built on middens, communal dumps formed from clam and mussel shells and other refuse.

By 800, a cultural transformation had occurred. New knowledge came from the west, probably originating in Mexico. Farming and the sacred corn arrived, along with a new religion that emphasized elaborate burial rituals and mound building. Tobacco smoking, head flattening, extensive regional trading, and the building of fortified villages were other characteristics of the new order.

"The favored theory is that these prehistoric tribes vanished," Holly said. "I don't think so. Entire cultures don't disappear, not without a trace, anyway. You know that from your genealogical studies."

"True," Nick said. "We all leave tracks in the mud of the past. In your lifetime, you'll generate a trail of documentation seven miles long."

"Really. That's amazing...a little sad. Genealogists must love to hear that statistic."

"If these nameless ancient tribes are still around, where are they? They ought to be clamoring for recognition and their own casino."

"I don't mean they're here in a physical sense. They're hidden below layers of genetic and cultural mixing. Oh, we aren't going to have the kind of definitive written evidence you work with all the time. But elements of customs, languages, and myths survived. The fun part about studying the Katogoula is tracing one of those cultural strands back to its origin. Take a look at this."

She led Nick to a modern mural of an ancient scene. Black-robed Indians ministered to a body that had been removed from a sort of scaffold. The attendants were frightening figures enveloped in smoke, nightmarish, unkempt, their long hair concealing their faces and even their gender. Their fingernails were extraordinarily long.

"Looks like something from Goya's late paintings," Nick said.

"The Vulture Cult." Holly stared at the illustration with the rapt excitement of the true student of history. "They were sort of combination undertaker and estate lawyer. There were male and female divisions. Each gender took care of its own, even down to acting as what we'd call a probate officer today. They let the body smoke for a few days, then they picked the flesh off with"—her face puckered in revulsion—"their long fingernails. Ewwwwww! A hereditary job. And they got a stipend, too."

"Lawyers as vultures? Say it ain't so!"

She laughed. "The tribe actually held them in great reverence, and it was an honor to marry into the cult families. At other times, they were unclean, outcasts. Couldn't be around food or participate in war councils. They were also the preeminent artisans of the tribe; used their fingernails to do paintings, make pottery.

"Primitive peoples have a way of handling the contradictions of existence. For instance: water is life giving, but it can also drown you; the sun makes the corn grow, but it can also scorch; large predators are beautiful to watch, from a distance. Gods help out mortals, but they also trick them, kill them, cause disasters to come down on them. Everything has two sides, a healthy side and a deadly one. It was like that with the Vulture Cult."

"Reminds me of the Jewish burial societies," Nick said. "The body, as the former and future home of the soul, was entitled to great reverence. The parting ceremonies also helped the living, by getting the corpse away quickly. What happened to the Vulture Cult? Have you found any remnants, symbolic or behavioral?"

Holly shook her head. "Christianity and exposure to other Western ways did it in. There's still some vague memory of the cult, as far as I can make out from a few of my interviews. I think it was active as late as the 1700s. What I find really interesting is where it came from. These elaborate burial practices weren't originally Katogoula, from everything I know of their earlier history in Mississippi and Alabama. They picked this up during their wandering or from tribes already here. That's what I was saying about a people disappearing. Tribal identities get buried, just like archaeological artifacts. But they're never truly lost."

"Until we stop looking for them," Nick said.

He regarded the painted scene; something about it held his attention.

Hands. Beautiful hands, somehow connected with death. The hands of the Vulture Cult...picking bruised flesh from my battered bones!

He'd seen a brief flash of such hands on the stairwell the day before, when he looked up to see the trashcan hurtling toward him.

Where else, where else have I seen them?...

His fall and the medication he was taking clouded his memory. Maybe the vivid image of hands was just a hallucination.

"Are you all right?" Holly touched the fingers of his free hand.

"Yeah, I'm...I'm fine. Just daydreaming, that's all."

She walked slowly beside him. He felt her worried scrutiny, but pretended he didn't. *Being an invalid isn't all bad.*

"Take a look at this Bible," she said, leaning over a display case, stashing her hair behind her ears. "It's in French. Probably given to a Katogoula by a missionary, but some front and back pages are missing so we can't be sure about the date or the owner. Isn't it remarkable?"

Nick saw a small Bible, about the size of an adult palm, held open to reveal two pages of Lamentations. The cover was frayed, once of lustrous blue velvet. Too bad about the missing leaves, he thought. Families usually recorded crucial birth, baptismal, marriage, and death information in their Bibles.

"In ancient times," Holly said, "the Vulture priests and priestesses created their own ritual art and implements. When Christianity came and made them pretty much unemployed, they dedicated their artistry to the new religion. See the fore-edge painting on the ends of the Bible pages. A Vulture Cult specialty. You have to look at it just right." She stooped down, demonstrating the angle for viewing the intricate, hidden painting, which looked to Nick like a primitive rendering of Lake Katogoula.

He followed her example, until new aches made him stop. "Nice to have a hobby to take your mind off picking flesh," he said, straightening up, wondering if Grace Dusong, with her arthritis, felt this way all the time.

They strolled through the museum, examining other artifacts of more recent vintage. An apparently ancient, perfectly preserved pirogue sat in the middle of the walkway, amid cypress knees and lake reeds; the late Carl Shawe had crafted it twenty years ago, using only traditional methods and tools.

The Katogoula had always excelled at beadwork and basketry. Nick marveled at the examples on display. The pine-needle baskets were so tightly woven they could carry water, the wall texts informed him.

An hour later they'd made a full circuit of the museum and ended up in front of the Vulture Cult mural.

"Something I forgot to mention," Holly said. "There *was* one ritual artifact that outlived the cult's function. I've seen photos from the 1880s of Katogoula with these long nails." She held up her hands, measuring out phantom foot-long nails. "They became an upper-class fashion statement, exaggerated to impractical lengths, completely divorced from the religious and ceremonial aspect."

"Photos at the Tadbulls', right?" Nick asked. She nodded. "You're still persona non grata over there. If I keep hanging around with you, I'll never get to see this renowned collection."

"Oh, that. It was a couple of years ago. Wooty—that's the guy I dated—he can't possibly still be angry." She didn't seem convinced. "Besides, it wasn't all my fault. It was…oh, you don't want to know."

"Only if you want to tell me."

"Let's just drop it, okay." Her voice had the rough edge of emotions still healing. When she spoke again, her chagrin seemed gone: "Look, I promise, I'll bite the bullet and take you one day. It's really something to see. The collection really ought to be here, in the museum. Grace and Irton and I've talked about it a lot. That'll be my excuse for visiting, to ask them to donate some photos and paintings. I think most of them are in storage, anyway. Oh, look! We walked right past the Twins-Raccoon Bowl you saw on tape. Isn't it fantastic?"

"I'd like it much better if it had lunch inside."

◳

It was a beautiful fall day, not overly cool, and the tall pine trees swayed and soughed with the wind that filled the upper branches. Sunlight softened by countless pine needles danced on the forest floor. Holding hands, they strolled along the Golden Trace, toward their picnic spot.

Nick felt like a boy with his first crush. But he came back down to earth, realizing he couldn't recall even the name of the girl he'd given his ID bracelet to, almost thirty years before.

Holly told Nick the story of the Golden Trace Treasure, and the circuitous journey it had made.

When the first highway was being constructed though this nearly impenetrable rural area, during the Depression, work crews leveled any Indian mounds in the way. One day, a crew hacked into a mound and uncovered a fabulous hoard of artifacts. The foreman took possession of the priceless items, later selling them. The artifacts passed through the ownership of private collectors, and then the archaeology departments of several colleges, before ending up at the Smithsonian. After a long court battle, the Katogoula finally brought the treasure back to Louisiana, where a vote-currying governor built the museum Nick and Holly had just visited.

◳

Lookout Point commanded a striking view of the rolling, red Tchekalaya Hills of central Louisiana. Holly had brought a simple but ample lunch of sandwiches and salads.

"You can see for miles from up here," Nick said. "Doesn't look like the Louisiana I know. In the French Quarter, you're below sea level. You glance down a street toward the river, and you see these huge ocean-going ships towering over you. They seem to ride along on top of the levee, like Mardi Gras floats. It's eerie."

"This is the highest point in the state," Holly said, between bites of her sandwich. "Something like four hundred feet."

"A regular Mount Everest."

"I don't think we'll see many ships," she said, "but the Gulf did cover this area millions of years ago. We're sitting on the sediment left by that inundation. Erosion from the runoff and rivers changing course carved these hills. Once, on a dig just over there"—she pointed to a thickly forested hill below them—"we found a Zeuglodon, an ancient whale.... God, I'm still starving! I could eat that whale. Where are the cookies?"

She rummaged through her backpack and found their dessert.

"What's that?" Nick asked, pointing with his good arm to a man-made structure peeking over the tree line, about half a mile away.

"It's an old fire tower. Nooj Chenerie lives there, believe it or not."

"The Wildlife and Fisheries enforcement agent? Yeah, I believe it."

"Um-hmm," she responded, swallowing some of her cookie. "The Agriculture and Forestry Department relies on aircraft and satellites mostly now. Nooj is a loner, doesn't like people very much, white or Indian. Perfect guy to keep vandals out of an unused tower and keep watch on the forest, too. Louisiana government's really a big game show of brother-in-law deals."

"He and Carl sound a lot alike," Nick said.

"Carl I could take. Usually." She looked at the tower as if it were going to stride over the trees and crush them. "Nooj gives me the creeps. He's always showing up where you don't expect him, quiet as a cat." She shrugged and nibbled more cookie. "But who am I to criticize? He's devoted to the tribe. Volunteers a lot of his time for tours and fairs where the Katogoula have a booth. I don't think he's wild about the casino idea, but he'll have to learn to like it, I suppose."

Nick was sitting against a pine trunk. She scooted over to him and leaned against his chest, careful not to press too hard against his injuries.

"You be Cary Grant and I'll be Grace Kelly," she said, "in that scene from *To Catch a Thief*, the picnic on the Riviera. I love that."

"I'm driving back, then. Remember the car chase before the picnic?"

"Very funny. You're helpless with just one arm."

"Oh, yeah?" He kissed her.

She dropped her cookie, reached back and caressed his head.

With his good arm just under her breasts, he gathered her to him with an urgency he hadn't felt in a long time.

They didn't notice the momentary flash of reflected sunlight from the dark eyes of the fire tower.

Chapter 19

"Look! I'm big chief of the mountain!" shouted eleven-year-old Matt Shawe with triumphant glee.

He'd ridden his horse to the top of a burial mound, one of six fifteen-foot-high grassy hillocks dotted with struggling dogwood, persimmon, redbud, and the odd lightning-blasted oak.

Sam, Matt's twin brother, and his horse had lagged behind in the race through the grassy meadow, and now they arrived, both considerably winded, at the foot of the mound.

"Matt, you better come down from there."

"Why? You afraid of ghosts!?" In a defiant challenge to any invisible beings, Matt made his horse strut around the relatively flat top of the mound. "It's daytime, stupid. Ghosts don't come out in the light."

"Dad said it's like church, remember. Sacred, sort of like. Come on down. You're gonna get us in trouble."

"Oh, okay, chicken. Baaawk, bawk, bawk, bawk!" Flapping his elbows in added derision of his brother, Matt urged his horse down the mound, impatient with her careful steps. "Baaawk, bawk, bawk, bawk!"

These were Mr. Tadbull's fine horses. The old man got a kick out of letting the boys do some easy chores on the weekends and go out for a ride.

A tributary bayou of larger Bayou Fostine ran through the thick forest at the western boundary of the meadow, where hardwood trees were more prevalent than pine. The twins headed there to give the horses a drink and to enjoy the snacks their mother, Brianne, had packed for them.

As the boys entered the dense stand of trees, the muffled thud of hooves gave way to the din of leaves and other forest litter being crushed. Their mounts seemed nervous.

"What's with these stupid horses?" Matt complained aloud, ducking for a low limb.

With the motiveless cruelty of adolescence, he kicked his horse too harshly. But the more he kicked, the more his horse balked, tossed her head, and stamped her feet.

"Maybe they're not thirsty," Sam said from behind. He took a piece of apple from his pocket and reached around to offer it to his horse. She refused it.

"Horses are always thirsty, buttface," Matt sneered.

Sam's mount saw the cougar first, as it jumped from a tree between the two horses. Before Sam could shout a warning, she reared up and threw him to the leaf-carpeted forest floor.

Matt's horse turned her head, got a glimpse of the crouching cat, wheeled, and then bolted off at full, wide-eyed gallop toward the closest curve of the meadow. "Whoa!" Matt shouted over and over again, but it didn't do any good. He clung for his life to her neck, his feet slapping the horse's sides. Saplings lashed his face as he desperately searched for the stirrups, looking down perilously on one side and then on the other of his panicked mount, but he kept missing the flailing foot supports.

Sam had landed with one leg underneath him. His ankle was badly twisted. He got to his feet, limped to a nearby tree, and watched, horrified, as Matt and his horse, now fifty yards away, moving much too quickly for safety, weaved through the trees and sailed over fallen trunks and overgrown stumps. Just a few more yards and they would make the clearing. And then Matt could come back and together they'd go round up Sam's spooked horse. Sam, aware now of building pain, knew he'd have to go to a doctor, have his ankle examined.

He was thinking of big needles and hanging bags in an emergency room, when he focused on his brother again. It was, Sam thought, as if someone had a rope attached to Matt and suddenly yanked it taut. Sam knew that what had really happened was that the horse had ducked, but that a low magnolia limb had caught Matt, stopping him instantly in midair.

The collision had happened so quickly it seemed to take Sam's mind an eternity to catch up with it.

Matt hung on the limb for a moment longer before falling limply to the ground.

Sam tried to run, but it hurt too much. He skipped from tree to tree, until finally he reached his brother. Matt was curled up and didn't seem to be breathing. His face and neck on one side were bloody; fragments of teeth and more blood littered his split lips.

"Matt! Matt! Don't be dead, Matt!"

On his knees beside his brother, Sam put an ear to Matt's chest. At that moment, Matt gasped, his wind back; he started to moan.

Sam was crying with joy now, for this was a good sign. His brother was alive!

"Don't move, Matt. Stay there. I'll catch a horse. Just don't move, all right. You might have something broken. I'm going for help!"

Sam stood up and wiped the tears from his downy cheeks. He spotted the horses in the meadow, grazing in tandem, muscles quivering and tails wildly thrashing, the reins hanging loose. They occasionally raised their heads to sniff for danger.

Only now did he think about the big cougar, and his fear returned. The rumors of angry spirits walking the forest were true! If it was an animal, it could be defeated or killed. But this…this was the Sacred Cougar! He trembled at the memory of its awesome size and speed, its ability to appear and disappear at will; and with each moment the supernatural beast grew more fearsome in his youthful imagination.

From the Sacred Cougar, there was no escape. The tribe would suffer until it was appeased. He no longer doubted the truth of the stories his grandfather and father had told him and Matt.

Sam had to get help, and he had to warn his father. The tribe was doing something wrong, the way he and Matt had desecrated the old mounds. He'd been only vaguely interested in the big controversy swirling around the casino question, but he knew now with an inexplicable certainty that this is what had awakened the angry spirits of the forest, which had killed his Uncle Carl.

In religion class at the Catholic church serving the tribe—CCD, the class was called, Confraternity of Christian Doctrine—Sam had heard the stories about children who'd seen visions of Mother Mary or Christ. He'd never paid much attention to those legends, or, for that matter, to the words and actions of adults in general; it all seemed designed just to trick you, to get you to do what the adults wanted. But from today on, he understood so much more. In an instant he'd become a man, and he'd been given a glimpse of ultimate truth.

Isaiah's prophecy "And a little child shall lead them" rang in his ears, filling him with a strength he didn't know he had. Was he now a divine messenger? Would they teach the story of *his* epiphany in CCD one day?

Sam hopped and limped into the clearing, holding out a piece of apple for his horse and softly calling her name.

Chapter 20

Flames clawed through the flat roof of the Katogoula Museum. History went up in smoke, billowing into the soft blue sky framed by towering pines.

"Grace! Irton!" Holly shouted through cupped hands over the crackling tumult of the fire. "Where are they?!"

"Not in there, I hope!" Nick shouted back.

Power lines had melted and fallen away; a transformer bellowed warnings through the forest that a vital circuit was forever broken, and that one wrong step would bring instant death.

As soon as Nick and Holly had seen the thick smoke from Lookout Point, they hopped back into the clothes they had already taken off, halfway through the process of seducing each other. Seconds later, they were running down the Golden Trace, back to the burning museum, Holly in front, and behind her a suffering Nick, holding his bad right arm close to his chest.

"The office!" Holly sprinted past the front entrance. Panes of window glass exploded in her path. She hit the ground on her knees, her hands over her face.

Instantly, Nick crouched down with her. "How bad?"

Pinpricks of blood appeared on her cheek where the glass had sprayed her.

"I'm okay. I think." She touched her face to check out the damage. "Yeah, I'm okay. Had my eyes closed in time. Come on!" Now she was up, running again toward the office, blood from her knees beginning to stain the rips in her jeans.

They reached the side room that served as Grace and Irton's office. The windows were still intact, closed and securely locked.

Holly put her face against the window and then shielded her brows with her hands to lessen the outside glare.

"I see them, on the floor!" Her cheeks left bloody smears on the smoke-blackened glass, which now was more mirror than window.

"If we break it, the fire could spread," Nick warned.

"We don't have a choice. Find a rock, anything!"

Nick found a baseball-size rock and with his left arm hurled it hard through the window. He winced and groaned involuntarily. His rapid movements had set off waves of deep, gnawing anguish in his right shoulder and elbow.

Brown smoke the consistency of liquid chalk poured from the broken window and rose, in seeming defiance of gravity, to join the dense cloud above the building. Heat had denuded the branches of surrounding pines to a level of seventy feet.

Holly, in a black tank T-shirt, used her sweater wrapped around a hand to knock out remaining shards of glass. "I'm going in. No!—don't argue! No time. You can't lift them with that shoulder. Can you pull them out if I get them in the window?"

Nick gave an brisk nod, not sure if he could, and began unbuttoning his shirt. "Use this."

She quickly helped him out of it, and Nick tied the sleeves around her mouth and nose. Then he squatted down, offering the shelf of his thigh as her foothold. He was careful to keep his distance from a group of sharp yucca behind him.

"Watch the spears," he said.

"I hate those things." Holly confidently stepped up on Nick's leg and then catapulted herself into the smoke-dense room.

He hadn't known he loved her, had thought the fresh bud of infatuation was reserved for the young; the sudden realization now came as a shock, obliterating even his fear for her safety, his anxiety over the condition of Grace and Irton, and his sorrow for the loss of irreplaceable objects that would never again provide a dim pathway to the past.

"Holly?!" he cried out. "Holly!"

No reply from inside. It had been only seconds, but to Nick it seemed like eons.

He heard muffled coughing, and then Holly shouting, "I have them!"

A limp, gnarled hand, and then two, appeared at the window. The rest of Grace Dusong followed. Nick got under her heavy, inert body, propping her on his good shoulder. Bayonets of yucca gored him in the buttocks and bare back. He jumped away in startled pain and his knees buckled. Grace fell on top of him.

Nick rolled her over. The smoke had blackened her. He scarcely recognized the pleasant woman; most of her brindled tresses had been singed away, and her bright hair band was now merely a shriveled black rubber band. He searched for a pulse, but didn't find one. He tried mouth-to-mouth resuscitation. After a dizzying minute he stopped; he didn't really know what he was doing. He spat out the foul taste of smoke and burned flesh and hair he'd picked up from Grace's hot, lifeless lips.

"Nick! Help!" was all Holly could say, before a racking, uncontrollable cough gripped her. She stood at the window, gasping for fresh air, but her lungs demanded to expel what they had breathed of the conflagration. Still coughing violently, she pushed Irton through the window, and he fell the four feet to the ground. One of his sneakers caught on the yucca; he appeared to be walking up an invisible wall.

Nick helped Holly from the burning building. As she bent over, hands on bloody knees, continuing to retch and cough, he clumsily dragged Irton over to his wife.

Maybe they would walk together in another world, but not in this one, Nick thought, looking down at the Dusongs.

Nick led Holly past the two bodies. Leaning heavily on him, she stared at them but didn't seem to understand. Her face was covered with soot, except for the relatively clear band where his shirt had been. Black trails below her nostrils gave evidence of the noxious fumes she'd inhaled, in spite of the shirt. She looked like a raccoon; at another time he would have laughed.

Her singed hair bristled out in every direction. She grabbed a hank and smelled it. "Yeccchh! Gross. I'll have to cut all this off." Her voice betrayed the dissociation of the traumatized. Then she threw up.

Nick maneuvered her to a park bench. "Lie down. I'll be right back."

"Where are you going?" But she didn't press him for an answer; she had lapsed into exhausted semi-consciousness.

The office ignited with a great inrush of air. Flames shot out of the window like rocket exhaust. Sirens wailed in the distance.

Nick touched Holly's blackened, bloodied cheek. She had imperiled herself for these two lives; he would take a risk, too, for the life of a people. He knew she would do it, if she could.

He ran around the other side of the crumbling stucco building. He made a quick determination of where the Twins-Raccoon Bowl would be, moved to the right, and then started kicking the wall with his remaining strength. After a few tries that cracked away the stucco, he sat down, put his hip behind a kick, and drove the crepe sole of one of his already beat-up leather chukkas through. He heard a display case crash inside and hoped it wasn't the one he wanted.

Working stucco, boards, and old insulation loose, he managed to widen the hole he'd made. The fire inside seemed to have started in the back of the building, and that area was completely engulfed in red-and-yellow chaos. This side of the interior was still relatively intact, though Nick could feel intense heat. The big pirogue a few feet closer to the back of the building was an elongated bowl of flame. How long before an explosive outbreak, triggered by the oxygen he'd just let in?

Shaking off his fear, he crawled inside. His whole right side from waist to shoulder was killing him; he scarcely noticed the rusty nails scraping his bare torso. But he'd guessed correctly: the bowl was waiting, almost within reach. The heat was beginning to barbecue his skin. He picked up a piece of smoldering lumber, and broke the glass on the display case. The bowl was his. He stowed it in his sling, where his arm should have been, and wriggled again through the hole in the wall.

Only his feet and calves were inside when that section of the interior exploded.

He crawled quickly in tripod fashion away from the building. The hair on his legs from his knees to his socks was mere foul-smelling stubble. He scraped up handfuls of dirt and smothered the spreading sparks eating away at the fabric of his khakis and shoelaces.

He was lucky—he'd saved the bowl. Without it, what myth of contrarieties would the tribe lean on in this tragic hour?

The enigmatic Katogoula twins of good and evil danced with moody raccoons in a timeless circle, offering no easy answers to mortals' questions.

Nick lolled back on a gentle upward slope of cool grass and stared at the expanding cloud of smoke. He was only vaguely aware of the diesel growl of emergency vehicles swarming into the parking lot.

Chapter 21

The crew from the parish coroner's office loaded body bags containing the remains of Grace and Irton Dusong into a white van dwarfed by fire trucks. Deflated hoses snaked from the small parking lot to the dripping, reeking, charred shell of the Katogoula Museum. As usual with suspicious deaths occurring in this rural part of Louisiana, the autopsies would be performed in Bossier City, adjacent to Shreveport, two hours north.

Watching the van drive slowly away, Nick was sorry the Vulture Cult no longer existed, to give the innocent couple a dignified, if by modern standards grotesque, ritual burial, instead of the further violation of a cold steel table and the prying hands of strangers.

It was late afternoon, three hours after the firemen had extinguished the last flames. Sheriff Higbee and his detectives were certain that the fire had been deliberately set.

"Spalling," Big John had said to Nick earlier, as he pointed out the pockmarking on the concrete in the utility area behind the museum. "And up here on the wood, we got what they call alligatoring—see these rolling blisters. This kind of char pattern pretty well shouts out somebody used an accelerant. It got mighty hot, mighty fast, before the fire took its normal course. Now who would want to do that, I wonder? It was just poor old Grace and Irton. They never hurt anybody in their lives." He let out a gargantuan sigh. "Tell me again what color the smoke was you saw."

Nick told him that he'd noticed black smoke at first, and later, when he and Holly got nearer, gray and brown smoke.

Higbee nodded his big head. "Gasoline or kerosene, like I said. 'Course gasoline's common as dirt, and around here lots of folks use kerosene for heating; foresters use it for prescribed burns. Shoot, you can get all you want at Miss Luevie's store anytime."

"Doesn't exactly narrow down our suspects."

"No, it doesn't," Big John agreed. "Well, I best be talking to a few people, and trying to keep my chief of detectives from making any LAPD mistakes. All he did at that Miami forensics seminar was sit on the beach and drink beer and try to get him some fur, if you know what I mean. Nice sweater, by the way."

Nick had found a sweater in Holly's van, a pink cardigan that would have been too small even without the new elastic wrapping that held his right arm immobilized across his stomach.

Now Big John worked with his uniformed deputies and plainclothes detectives, who were methodically scooping samples into evidence bags, taking photos, and dusting for prints. Sooty firemen from Armageddon and every nearby rural volunteer station collected their gear. A utility-company fire investigation team of two men and a woman hovered around the gas meter, hoping, Nick supposed, that the fire wasn't their company's fault. A man from the Louisiana State Police Crime Laboratory in Baton Rouge removed duffel bags from his Explorer.

Would all this forensic firepower be enough to stop angry tribal spirits?

That question, Nick was certain, haunted the minds of the assembled Katogoula. Faces grim, they listening intently to Luevenia Silsby. There seemed to be much somber agreement with what Luevenia was saying; her voice didn't carry to Nick's ears. More tribe members drove up each minute.

Nick walked to one of the ambulances in the parking lot, beside a car from the state Fire Marshal's Office. The paramedics had determined that Holly was okay. He'd aggravated his injuries in the rescue attempt; the preliminary word was that he would be fitted with even more restrictive implements of medical torture at the hospital.

Holly was sitting up on a bed inside the cluttered treatment compartment of the ambulance, a blanket draped over her shoulders, her legs dangling over the side. She swatted away an EMT's hands when he tried to put the oxygen mask back on her. She continued cutting her hair with surgical scissors, using a mirror mounted on the opposite wall. Her singed hair fell on white bedding paper spread on the floor. Not as much as Nick had feared would be necessary.

Even with brown antiseptic painted on her cheeks, she made something flutter in his solar plexus. A cork seemed to have come off the bottle of his emotions. Probably the tragedy, he thought. He wished he could put the cork back in. Caring this much for someone distressed him.

"It was murder," Holly said, snipping too much from one side of her new shorter hairdo. Suppressed fury made her hands shake as she corrected her error and handed the scissors to the EMT. He smiled and winked reassuringly at Nick. "Jason here heard the investigators talking. The office door was tied shut with rope, probably from one of the exhibits. Grace and Irton didn't have time to..."—tears slid down the brown antiseptic—"Nick, they were my friends."

Jason the EMT offered a box of tissues and climbed down from the truck.

Nick sat on the ledge of the compartment. "I'm really sorry, kid. We almost didn't make it ourselves."

"Who's doing this? What a *monster!*"

Nick hoped that only her emotions were speaking, and not a crisis-born clairvoyance.

Holly wiped away the last vestiges of outward sorrow. "Why them and not us? We were an easy target all day—especially at a certain moment." She managed a naughty half-smile.

Nick was relieved to see anger and humor returning. "The killer wasn't after us," he said. *Not today, at any rate.* "Carl was a unique repository of tribal knowledge. Now the museum's gone, too. Do you see an MO emerging?"

"Yeah, it's like the killer's chipping away at the history and spirit of the tribe, one bit at a time. Why are you still alive?"

"You sound disappointed," Nick said, sulking for effect.

"Oh, give me a break." She kissed him.

It hurt to turn his head, but he didn't mind. Her warm, vital mouth was an antidote to the taste of death on Grace's lips.

"That's not what I mean," she said. "Did the killer screw up, or don't you fit the pattern?"

"This killer doesn't make mistakes, I'm afraid. The events leading up to the murders were perfectly stage-managed. And the victims were all Katogoula. That's the common element. I'm just the schmo helping them get their family trees organized."

"Schmoes have to be careful, too."

He reached for her hand. "The attack on me meant something, I just don't know what. But we're both still in danger, that I do know. The killer may decide to expand the menu."

"So, if someone's hunting tribe members, does that rule out the Katogoula as suspects?"

Nick studied the Katogoula gathered near the museum, still listening to Luevenia holding forth. "Otherwise it's a strange form of suicide."

"'Strange' is right." Doors slammed and Holly looked beyond Nick to a newly arrived car. "There's the Channel 6 news crew from Armageddon. The reporter's one of my old newsroom buddies. He's handling the tape I dropped off."

The tape showing the suspicious flashing on the shore of Lake Katogoula the morning of Carl Shawe's murder.

She hopped out of the ambulance. "I'll go see if there's any progress." She jogged over to the Channel 6 car.

Nick didn't try to stop her. She wouldn't listen, wouldn't rest. He shared her sense of urgency. Someone was systematically attacking the body and the soul of the tribe. Holly's work of chronicling Katogoula cultural identity and his own efforts to establish the genealogical record were more important than ever now. He had saved the Twins-Raccoon Bowl from the fire; now the two of them had a new, vitally important responsibility: building a new museum of memories before a stealthy, rampant malice targeted more of their raw material, and perhaps them.

回

Sheriff Higbee couldn't have chosen a better time to conduct interviews among the Katogoula. Almost everyone was here, to mourn the loss of two friends and of so much tangible history. Nick made special note of a few faces he hadn't seen at the Three Sisters Pantry meeting. He'd always heard that some killers needed to feast on the pain they created, to reinforce their sense of power by silently taunting law enforcement and victims. Nick had a feeling that the sheriff would be similarly observant.

The assembled Katogoula stood in a tight circle around the bowl Nick had rescued; a few other shattered relics had been thrown out in the fire-fighting action, and they too had been reverently placed within the tribal circle. Tommy and Brianne were absent; the news that the twins had been injured—one seriously—cast a further pall on the mood of the gathering.

Nooj Chenerie wasn't there, either; he'd driven the twins to the hospital in Armageddon. After Sam had captured his horse, he rode to Nooj's fire tower, broke a window to get in, and used a recharging two-way radio to summon the absent game warden for help.

The sheriff wouldn't let anyone venture into the still-smoldering museum, but Nick understood from the hushed talk and anxious expressions that there was an ardent desire to collect what was left. And something else was going on, too.

Holly joined him. She held up two black tape cases: the original tape and the digital enhancement. "There's someone walking in the woods, all right," she said in a lowered voice. "But you can't tell who it is. Just a gray human form. Looks human, anyway. The flash comes from the chest area."

"Male or female?"

"Can't tell," she answered. "They showed me the enhanced section in the car. Not much to go on, I'm afraid. You want some coffee?"

Indeed he did. She went off in search of some, as he moved closer to the Katogoula.

In the parking lot beyond the emergency vehicles, Nooj Chenerie got out of his official green GMC pickup and strode to the ruins of the museum. He spoke briefly with the sheriff and the chief detective, and soon walked over to stand slightly apart from the circle of fellow tribe members. All heads turned toward him.

"The twins'll be fine," he said.

Relief rippled through the group.

"Sam believes he saw something. Swears up and down the Sacred Cougar attacked them."

The Katogoula let out a collective murmur of shock.

"Now hold on," Nooj said. "He's just a scared boy, so it's hard to say what really happened. But one thing's for sure: them two Tadbull mares been gentle all their lives. Must have been something bad to spook 'em like that."

Holly returned and handed Nick a plastic cup of steaming black coffee. He wanted to hug her in thanks for that gift to his nervous system.

With head held high, Luevenia Silsby marched the few feet over to Nick and Holly. The little woman had just won some sort of victory. Nick could see confirmed in her dark eyes the truth of his belief that strength of personality is often inversely related to physical size.

She thrust up a thick stack of small-denomination bills at him. "Two thousand dollars. Count it if you want. Now go. You, too, Holly. We don't owe you nothing. Just go and let us alone."

"Shouldn't you discuss this with Tommy first?" Nick said. "After all, you elected him tribal leader."

"He's just been un-elected. I'm in charge now."

"Let me talk to them," Holly said. "They've known me for a long time." She waded into the assembly of tribe members, trying to engage several in conversation; they shied away from her as if they were of different polarity.

"Take the money, Nick," Luevenia insisted. "We don't need a genealogist to tell us what we already know: we are the tribe. The spirits of our ancestors have always been with us; now we're straying and they're sending us a sign. The gambling and the casino and that shopping mall and stuff are all wrong. We don't want new members or outsiders here. Been some hard times for my people; we made it through those, with no help. We got to do what we believe in, stick together, just like we always done, or we won't make it through this." She directed a stern gaze at the wildlife agent, who still remained a few feet from the main tribal body. "Well, Nooj?"

He took a deep breath that inflated his wrestler's chest; then he stepped over to stand with the others.

Luevenia closed her eyes behind her steel glasses in triumph.

Nick had seen this happen before in other genealogical projects where a lot was at stake, financially or psychologically or both. The unknown can ambush the known, and vanquish it. The past, newly discovered, exerts a shaping influence on those who rarely gave it serious thought. The Katogoula were undergoing such a dangerous metamorphosis. Now they were more Indian than they'd ever been able to claim; and suddenly they were emerging from a Westernized cocoon, believing in and acting on their ancient traditions as never before.

Nick had a feeling the Catholic bishop of the area wasn't going to be a happy man when he heard about the new spiritual competition manifesting itself among his Katogoula flock.

"I didn't cause any of these tragedies," Nick said. "I'm on your side."

Luevenia Silsby eyed him, weighing his words, interested but unconvinced. "Well then, how come they all started about the time you showed up?"

"I'd like to answer a lot of questions, but I can't yet. We all need to help the sheriff. With your knowledge of Katogoula ways…"

Still grasping the money like a cross before her to ward off a vampire, she held up her empty left hand to silence Nick.

Those beautiful hands! The courthouse stairwell. Remarkable hands on the railing, seconds before the garbage can came hurtling at me!…Maybe this image wasn't just a phantom in the mist of his memory. Could this plucky little woman have attacked him? Was she the murderer?

Luevenia must have noticed his distracted attention. The hands crept stealthily behind her. "Since you got involved with us," she said venomously, "all these bad things been happening in twos, or they got something to do with the twins of the tribe. First there was Carl Shawe, then there was Grace and Irton, and now Tommy's twins been hurt. There's talk of a big cat that don't act like any regular animal. The Sacred Cougar—that's what we all think." Caught up in the ardor of her sermon, she nodded vigorously. "The Sacred Cougar is trying to purge the evil from us! But like in the Story of the Twins of the Forest, the evil one's tricky. Oh, yes, he is! Could even be you."

The tribe members mumbled ominously. Nick had been accused of being a plagiarist before—perhaps slightly worse things, as well—but never a witch. Seventeenth-century New England suddenly seemed alive and kicking in the piney woods of twentieth-first century Louisiana.

"Hey," he said in his defense, "aren't you forgetting that somebody tried to kill *me*?"

"That's what you say," Luevenia countered. "What if you're the bringer of evil disguised as a man. You might have done that to yourself, so maybe you could trick us into letting you stay around here and do more evil. Who walks out of the fire with the Twins-Raccoon Bowl? That's no human thing to do."

The crowd grumbled assent.

Luevenia now spoke with stony control, like a judge issuing a death sentence: "The evil raccoon can even trick the gods, make them strike at the innocent. And then, the tribe and the chief must strike back."

"You don't really believe I'm an evil spirit, do you?" he wanted to mention the pink sweater as exculpatory evidence, but decided against it.

"She's right," Nooj said, taking up the case against Nick. "This all started when your name first came up. Tommy went to talk to Chief Claude at the Chitiko-Tiloasha casino, and we ain't had a day's peace since then."

"Look, Miss Luevie," Nick said, rubbing his throat where he felt a phantom constriction, "I respect the Katogoula traditions. You can't be a genealogist for long by not taking a client's beliefs seriously. But I work with facts, with evidence, in many ways just like the police. The old stories may be involved in these tragedies, but I think the actors are human beings. That's where the answers are, in human motivations. With our help, the sheriff is going to figure it all out."

She wavered a moment. Her eyes flicked away. But her resolution returned, and again she thrust her right hand at him with the stack of bills.

"We want the wasps back in their nest. Go home to New Orleans, while you still can."

A tidy sum, Nick was thinking, his gaze drawn to the cash. *Take it. They don't want you here; and you can't make much progress without their cooperation. Hawty would certainly like to see a bit of cash flow her way.*

"Sorry," he said, finally. "Can't do that."

Her tensed lips and chin showed her quaking anger. She turned her back on him without a word. Then she motioned to the other tribe members. They again encircled her and the Twins-Raccoon Bowl, where Luevenia had placed the money she'd offered to Nick. Each contributor retrieved the appropriate amount, as if dipping for sacred water from an ancient well.

Nick felt Holly tugging on his sweater sleeve. "Look!" she whispered in his ear. "His badge!"

Nick didn't understand at first, but then realized she meant Nooj Chenerie. He attempted a nonchalant glance at the state-shaped LDWF badge on Nooj's chest; it winked brightly in the sunlight. Then he moved his gaze up to Nooj's eyes, which stared directly back at him. Nick waved affably at the unsmiling man.

Chapter 22

The Greensheaves Court Motel was as depressing as ever.

After several rings, Nick answered Daniel Boone's obsolete phone.

"I have something interesting," Hawty said over the line from New Orleans.

After a day that had included a tragic fire, two murders, a nearly fatal assault on the Shawe twins, and the loss of a golden opportunity to have sex with Holly, whatever it was had better be *very* interesting to justify invading his peace and quiet.

"Why didn't you answer your cell phone?" Hawty said, not allowing him a chance to defend himself. "You let the battery run down again, didn't you?"

Nick was afraid to tell her that he wasn't sure where the phone was, and didn't really give a damn. He hated it as part of the giant tech-wing conspiracy, as the most visible incarnation of the Almighty Gizmo, the god of the technological religion that was making us less and less human every day, turning each of us into a mere marionette twitching on digital strings. It was in his glove compartment, or maybe his briefcase.

"Remember that journal of the clerk in Mézières' diplomatic mission?" Hawty asked with ill-disguised excitement.

"Seventeen sixty-eight," Nick grumbled. He drew in a deep breath and massaged his pillow-creased face. The telephone had ended a wonderful nap. *But that's no excuse for being a jerk to Hawty. She counts on you to be her mentor—as they say in business-speak. Teach her to doubt and examine, herself and others; prepare her for all the dragons of deception that will assail her with flaming lies; arm her with a sword of skepticism to thrust at her own untested hypotheses and to shred the fallacies of others.* "If this journal even existed," he added, goading her. "I also remember a certain young female student during the Roaring Twenties—"

"From California, who was in Professor Bolton's class and who wrote a thesis citing the journal wherein the clerk mentions the big intertribal war—"

"Between the allied Katogoula and Yaknelousa tribes, and the Quinahoa. Yeah, we're on the same page now, Hawty. Is this an exam or what?" Nick imagined Hawty flipping him the bird two hundred miles away.

"Hush up!" she commanded irritably. "I found her. She's a hundred and three now, in a nursing home in sunny Southern California."

Hawty's dogged investigative instincts would put any PI to shame, and her unflagging fascination with knowledge would one day gain her star status at some college or business—a business other than his, he realized at self-pitying moments like this. "A hundred and three? That's incredible. Does she remember anything about it?"

"Sure does," Hawty said. "She has her wits about her still; a remarkable memory, in fact. Unfortunately, she's pretty much blind, but that doesn't affect our project. Lovely lady. She has a taste for real French Market pralines, so I'm sending her some from Aunt Sally's. Nick, she didn't make it up. She really did work with the clerk's journal. She told me it ended up at a place called the Karpeles Manuscript Library in Santa Barbara."

"The Karpeles, huh?" said Nick. Documents that changed history and altered human thinking forever, manuscripts from the hands of poets, philosophers, composers, scientists, and statesmen, unexplored sources rich with genealogical booty...very, *very* interesting!

David Karpeles, a phenomenally successful mathematician and real estate entrepreneur, began assembling his renowned rare manuscript and document collection in the late nineteen seventies. Today the Karpeles owned a million or so pages of priceless handwritten and printed treasures. The thought of possessing such a historic, precious hoard made Nick giddy, and by comparison his own growing collection of scavenged and "borrowed" letters, diaries, books, and other assorted artifacts of genealogical interest seemed pitifully insignificant.

But every great bibliomaniac was a middling collector once, and for Nick the starting point was Jacques Vulpine—an early Jewish immigrant to newly American New Orleans, a protean figure of many talents in a fascinating time, who was variously during the early and mid nineteenth century a notary, a historian and man of letters, a bon-vivant, a prosperous merchant and investor, a bankrupt speculator, and an amateur detective. Nick already owned some of Vulpine's correspondence and rare editions of his poetry and prose; he was ever on the prowl for more.

"And?" he prodded, knowing Hawty was eager to continue.

"And...I had them e-mail the journal to me," Hawty said. "Fabulous place. They have an aggressive digitizing program and are very nice about sharing their material. The journal is full of names, but it's in French so I'm not sure what else it says. I'd fax the most important pages to you but your yokel motel doesn't even have a fax, much less a computer. You'll just have to go to the Armageddon library or courthouse or Kinko's and use one of theirs. If all else fails, I can overnight—"

"Ah, my resourceful little cyber-princess, I do have a computer."

"Uh-huh," was her skeptical reply. "Where'd you get one? Steal it? You wouldn't know how to work it even if you weren't lying. Now, I didn't call you at 9 P.M. to have you messing with me. I'm tired from juggling our other clients—all three of them. They want to know what's taking so long with their projects."

"Well, finish them up and make the presentations. Sign my name; you've done it enough already. Aren't you a card-carrying Certified Genealogical Record Specialist? You're always pushing for more responsibility."

"Responsibility *with commensurate pay!* Don't worry, I'm actually getting more work done with you out of town. The presentations'll be ready when you get back, so you can have all the glory."

Then he recounted the day's events, making sure to highlight his heroics. "My local doctor is a paranoid chap worried about a malpractice suit, so he's setting up an appointment at Freret University Medical Center for tests."

"I hope someone else is paying," Hawty said, informing him that his health insurance company was threatening to cancel him for nonpayment. She'd mailed a hot company check to buy some more time. "What kind of computer do you have, PC or Apple, *if* you really have one?" He told her the brand name. "A notebook or a desktop? What programs are you running? How much RAM have you got? What's the frontside bus speed? How much cache do you have? Is there a PCMCIA-card slot? Because I'm not even going to try to get you on the Web through that motel's antiquated phone system. Probably still has four-prong wall plugs."

So much for commiseration. "Hey, Hawty, all I'm saying is I have access to a computer. I didn't say I somehow turned into Bill Gates. And as far as my cash situation goes…well—"

"That's with *c-h-e*, not *s-h*. You don't have to tell me about your cash situation. I handle your bookkeeping, and you're definitely no Bill Gates. Whose computer?"

"Well, she's a, uh, colleague, of sorts."

"Uh-huh?"

"And in certain respects our work has points of contiguousness."

"That pretty, is she? Never mind. None of my business. I don't want to know any more about your personal life than I have to. I'd need to go to church twice as much as I do. Tell her to call me. I'm at home. We'll figure something out."

"I'm writing this down. 'PCM-' what?"

"Just tell her to call! Don't make it too late, either. I've got to teach an eight o'clock 'Genealogy on the Web' class in the morning at the library. Mostly grandmothers. Did I tell you I was doing that?...Look in your briefcase, the small pocket with the snap, where your cell phone should be. You'll find a thin plug-in PC card there, too. Have that and your charging cell phone in your hands when you call. And quit hurting that scrawny body of yours. You can't even load a microfilm reel, in the state you're in now. What a fine team we make: I'm in a wheelchair, and you've got one good arm!"

◻

After his conversation with Hawty, Nick rushed over to Annie Oakley, Holly's room. On the land line, the two women prattled about girlish things, Nick assumed, and they shared quite a few chuckles, apparently at his expense, before getting down to the nuts-and-bolts technical issues. Nick was bored until Holly mentioned "zipping" and "unzipping," which drew his gaze to her jeans and turned his mind down carnal byroads having nothing to do with the ultimate genealogical destination. She caught him staring; both of them blushed and pretended it didn't happen.

It proved difficult to get a good cell signal—Hawty theorized that there weren't many towers in the rural area—but eventually the data streamed miraculously through his cell phone and into Holly's notebook computer.

Nick had escaped the sentence of a hard cast. Instead, his doctor had fitted him with a semi-flexible one strapped to his torso with an itchy arrangement of plastic, Velcro, and textiles he'd never seen before and wished he never had. The contraption was extremely uncomfortable, especially after a couple of hours in a chair, reading the screen of Holly's computer, which sat amid her video equipment.

"How do I get back to page three?" Nick asked.

"Roll that ball at the bottom of the keyboard, and then click the menu down…"

"Yeah?"

"Click on the 'Go To' command…"

"'Go to, go to'? Sounds downright Elizabethan. Ah-ha! Got it."

"Great. Now be quiet while I try to crack *my* names."

That made the second woman in one night to tell him to shut up. Maybe he should try being the strong-and-silent type. Trouble was, he wasn't particularly strong, either.

Holly was much better at Spanish than he was. She worked patiently by the room's inadequate lamp light on the copied pages containing the names he'd found in the *Legajos de Luisiana* at the Sangfleuve Parish Courthouse—a goodly number of Katogoula and Yaknelousa names, but also those of Quinahoa slave families the Kentucky trader had seen among the Katogoula, forty years after the epic battle. Holly's sagging, squeaky queen-size bed was littered with legal pads, a well-thumbed Spanish dictionary, and guides to Choctaw, Chickasaw, and Mobilian Jargon.

Nick, for his part, pored over the French of the journal pages Hawty had zapped across cyberspace. Within the gracefully written sentences of the accomplished penman were other names of Katogoula from 1768, or what the clerk determined these names, strange to him, sounded like in his native tongue. Chiefs, great warriors, female leaders of the matrilineal clans…. And—he grinned—a detailed description of the Vulture Cult!

He read slowly at first; but his speed and excitement increased as he became familiar with the clerk's style. Soon he hardly needed to touch the pocketsize French dictionary at his hand. This, to him, was the pay-off, the beauty, the thrilling secret allure of genealogy: reawakening an eye-witness reporter from the past, sitting with him in an imaginary tavern at a rough-hewn table over flagons of ale, seeing through his eyes, hearing through his ears, with incomparable immediacy, times, places, and ideas lost to those of us imprisoned in the now.

Luevenia Silsby's accusation still rang in his mind. Was he responsible for the plague of misfortune that had struck the Katogoula? He did feel guilty…but not for the reasons she'd put forward. He could feel the proximity of the killer in the chill down his spine, the same chill he felt at the imminence of an intuitive leap that suddenly, irrefutably, joined distant generations of a family. The killer's identity lay somewhere in the genealogical record, and he was missing it! He needed more than a flash of a badge on Nooj's chest, or the recollected image of—perhaps—Miss Luevie's hands, more than just coincidences that probably in the end meant nothing. He needed to hold up the lantern of Cartesian Doubt, illuminating seemingly insignificant facts, testing them against his knowledge and experience, finally discovering the truth…perhaps, in a 1768 journal.

The French clerk revealed his mingled fascination and revulsion when writing about the ancient tribal undertakers, the Vulture Cult. Yet, like so many of those adventurous men of that age of discovery, titled and humble ones alike, who saw people and practices no other European could have dreamed of, the clerk knew he was writing for posterity.

Sometime around midnight Nick realized that for some minutes he'd been staring at the screen without comprehending anything at all.

"Enough!" he declared. "I can't take any more written words—in any language." He'd compiled a list of fifty-three names, translated into his best guess of the English equivalent.

He trudged over to Holly's bed and cleared a place to sit among the books and legal pads.

"Same here," she moaned. "This is about to drive me batty." She slapped down a dog-eared pamphlet and slowly rolled her head and flexed her shoulders. "The Kentucky trader mentions a language used by Katogoula and Yaknelousa masters and their Quinahoa slaves or servants, but I'm not sure if he means Mobilian Jargon or an entirely different slave language. Mobilian Jargon—or a variant of it—did serve as a master/slave language, but they called it"—she yawned—"*yoka anompa*, I'm pretty sure."

"*Yoka anompa* to you, too."

"Maybe you need to copy some more pages of the *Legajos* for me to work with.... How do you feel?"

He leaned back on two pillows she'd propped for him against the headboard. "Almost as bad as I probably look. Does your face hurt?"

She shook her head. "Not really. Wonder if it'll scar." She'd managed to wash off the brown antiseptic.

He gently touched her speckled cheeks, which had begun a scabby healing process. She didn't wince much. Tough girl.

"Did you find anything?"

"Great stuff," he said after a satisfying yawn. "You were right about the Vulture Cult as an immigrant practice. For years a Yaknelousa religious aristocracy held the sacerdotal reins. They'd been both chiefs and shamans in their own independent tribe, but gave up political power when the two tribes merged and the Katogoula adopted major aspects of their religion. My reporter, the clerk, thinks this merger happened in the late seventeenth century, just as the Europeans started to upset the balance of tribal power."

"Hmm." Holly scribbled on a yellow pad and bit the eraser, thinking. "I need to work that into my documentary script. That's important."

"I also found lots of names that so far don't mean much to me. Big Owl, Fast Snake, Thirsty Beaver, Long Black Feather...those are the ones I remember at the moment. My brain feels like cold grits. I think Long Black Feather was a leader of the Vulture Cult for decades."

"Clan totems, I bet," Holly said. "Southeastern Indians organized themselves by clans below the tribal level. If you belonged to the Owl or

Snake or Wind clan, that's where your loyalties were, as much as with your flesh and blood, maybe more so."

"Matrilineal, right?"

"Oh, a smarty-pants, eh?" Holly wisecracked. "Yes, most were matrilineal before the white man came; the husband joined the wife's clan and allegiance passed from mother to child. What do you do with the names now?"

"I'll check to see if anyone in the present-day core families mentions them in family lore. It would be nice to find them on federal Indian rolls, especially the transitional ones that record when a Katogoula family began using English surnames. Then we'll know where this family was living, what localities and sources to check for more family data. These names will become reference points for future membership, targets to trace back to."

"The government didn't consider the Katogoula a real tribe," Holly said. "I didn't think they were enumerated separately."

"They weren't. On and off for a couple of centuries they lived among the Choctaw, Chickasaw, and Chitiko-Tiloasha. The rolls and associated case files of those tribes can sometimes hold good Katogoula info. Let's say Tall Worm—"

"'Tall Worm'!?" She laughed, making the rickety bed squeak. "You wouldn't catch me in that clan."

"Whatever," he said, trying to suppress his own mirth. "I made him up. Let's say we found Tall Worm in our clerk's journal of 1768. On an 1858 Mississippi Choctaw removal roll a mixed-blood Choctaw testifies that Tall Worm, of unknown heritage, was his grandfather."

She nodded. "I'm with you so far."

"The grail in American Indian research is finding the full-blooded tribal ancestor—and in 1768, Tall Worm was probably full-blooded. Now we have a historical Katogoula linked to a line possibly surviving into modern times. With that information, we can figure out the exact Katogoula blood quantum of later descendants—if and when they get interested in their ancestry. The federal records are massive, but sometimes an odd source like this clerk's journal is better than a ton of National Archives paper."

"So what would he be, our 1858 man?" Holly asked. "I wonder how Tall Worm and his wife—"

"Mrs. Worm?"

"Yes, Mrs. Worm." She playfully threw a wadded sheet of paper at him. "I wonder how they would have felt about the future of their line. There was already intermarriage with bigger tribes, and in their generation or the next, maybe with whites. Did they feel that their Katogoula heritage was dying? What did they teach their children? What would their descendants call themselves today: Katogoula, Choctaw, white?"

"All three. None of the above. The soul doesn't follow rules of genealogical evidence." Nick leaned back, sighing from fatigue. "And take it from me, sometimes the soul doesn't want to know. I need to get back to New Orleans, sift through a few hundred of my favorite microfilms.... Well, a few dozen, at least. *After* a good night's sleep."

"But you've been fired, haven't you?" Holly said. "They can't fire *me*; I'm not working for the tribe. Anyway, I have almost enough footage to finish the documentary. Now all I need is some historic filler. The photos and paintings at Tadbull Hall would be just perfect.... Oh, I'm sorry. Were you asleep?"

"Holly, Holly, give it a rest, okay. You're tired, I'm tired. We've been working for hours, non-stop. It's been a hell of a day. This isn't the time to start again with that documentary of yours." The pain medicine was about to pull him under the calm surface of sleep. "Shhh. Try to relax, so I can." He scrunched deeper into the pillows.

Finally, he'd been able to shush a woman for a change. He began to drift off, relishing this small victory, not concerned in the least that he was a trespasser in this bed. The overpowering desire to sleep made all counter-arguments irrelevant.

"Why are you so interested? In the Katogoula, I mean. Why do all this work when they want you out of here?"

"Because I'm such a nice guy," Nick said, his undamaged arm slung over the bridge of his nose.

"Are you?" she asked in his ear.

No use. He gave up any idea of a blissful catnap.

"When you know me better, you tell me.... I'm curious, for one thing. Curious by nature, I guess. For another, Tommy will probably get control again and rehire me; he's a fighter, below his laid-back exterior. And then, there's that nagging small question of who tried to nail me with a trashcan. I'm a little ticked off about that.

"Those are the selfish reasons," he said, now staring at the water-stained ceiling. "I'd like to believe I'm still here because I take genealogy seriously. When someone asks me to explore his family history, I become a surgeon who opens up a patient to see what's in there, what malignant misconceptions and blockages of ignorance and fear need to be treated with truth. I can't just walk away, leave the patient on the table. Sometimes I swear I'm holding a family's heart in my hands, feeling it beat with an ageless, stubborn vigor.... Chief Claude of the Chitiko-Tiloasha calls me the Midwife-of-Yesterday Man."

A sure sexual turnoff, that title! But when he looked over at Holly, propped on an elbow, he saw that the jade jewels of her eyes swam in crystalline pools of tears.

"How sweet," she managed to whisper in a voice choked with feeling. "I'm glad you survived to be ticked off. Especially now that we're getting to be such good friends." She leaned over and kissed him. Her hair dusting his face was a warm, glittering, coppery avalanche of fragrant flowers, with just a hint of smoke. "You can stay—not on the sofa this time. If you want."

"Oh yeah, I want," Nick answered, drawing her down to him again, kissing her between words. "I want, I want, I want..."

Chapter 23

Val watched Joel Shosterman lick the tip of his right middle finger and bring it down to polish the inch-square surface of the gold ring on the fourth finger of his left hand. The incised logo of Luck o' the Draw International, she noted, was already spotless and gleaming. Shosterman moved the ring a fraction of an inch. At last, it pleased him.

Val knew he was a meticulous and dangerous man, but sometimes he really cracked her up. *That's why he's in charge of a few billion in casino cash flow*, she supposed. It was more difficult to belittle him—if only in the privacy of her own thoughts—in view of that. Even a toad like Joel, dressed in all those zeroes, began to resemble a prince. Sometimes, in the right mood, just thinking about that kind of wealth almost made her come in her stretch jodhpurs.

She recalled the twenty or so times they'd screwed, twice or three times right in this luxurious bus. Sex with Joel was always strictly business for Val, a career boost, a résumé enhancer. But fun? Forget about it. Like getting it on with a calculator. A pocket one, at that.

Val suppressed a smile at her interior witticism.

Fortunately, on her frequent trips back to Vegas, she rarely had to put out for Joel anymore. He'd acquired other squeezes in his new territory who kept him busy, now that he was Vice President for Development—South-Central Division. Joel wouldn't fly. Didn't like the odds, he said. So he used this ritzy motor coach; consequently, his perfect toupee, his artificial tan, and his hand-made English suits were no longer fixtures at the home office.

But several times a year, Joel showed up at Bayou Luck Casino, ostensibly to confer with Chief Claude, but in reality to interview the non-Indian employees in this big RV. Seventy-five percent of the Bayou Luck staff was Indian, and Joel had no direct control over these workers. That was the contractual minimum Indian-employment ratio. The other quarter, though, to a man and woman, followed elaborate procedures to siphon money from the unsuspecting Chitiko-Tiloasha Tribe. There was so much cash being dumped at Bayou Luck Casino that the Indians were still stunned and overwhelmed; the naive fools didn't miss the individually insignificant amounts sneaked out, for example, in charges for phantom corporate advertising or for overpriced work done by company-owned contractors. Val was in charge of this continuing, and very successful, covert operation. Of course, she had other duties, too.

Val was not stupid, although she'd come a long way by appearing so. She'd honed her skill at reading men during nine years as a Vegas dealer. She knew that most men could be reduced to blithering imbecility with a vague promise of big money, free booze, and easy pussy. God, did she hate all those rutting conventioneers, away from their wives and kids, making whoopee on expense accounts! For all the ham-handed groping and disgusting propositions she'd had to endure, for his refusal to fall whimpering at her boots as so many conventioneers had, she wanted to see Nick Herald grovel.

Joel, too, was basically immune to her over-the-top sensuality. Her dumb-blonde routine no longer worked on him. He treated her with a certain wariness, as if she were a specimen of an unidentified species that could slip inside his polished surface and deliver a deadly bite. She would love to do just that, but Joel was too powerful to cross.

The corporate meeting room on wheels featured bolt-down furniture that could be arranged in a variety of configurations. Today, the plush chairs faced one another along the length of the bus. Joel and Val sat in a partitioned area at the rear. They were alone. The padded quietness of the interior made Val edgy; her preferred habitat was the chilled dimness of the casino, where the unceasing noise befuddled the suckers' minds and allowed her to work her magic.

"The news is good on our potential neighbors to the north," Val said. They had already spent an hour and a half poring over reams of computer printouts.

"W. P. is pleased," Joel said, in his arid tone. "Fill me in."

W. P. was the dreaded CEO of Luck o' the Draw International, a man of well-known wholesomeness and religiosity who didn't drink, womanize, or gamble for his own account, who loudly, repeatedly told the Mafia to shove it. W. P. nevertheless was not above breaking the fingers, killing the pets, or worse, of dealers and pit bosses whose loss figures were too high. He was outstandingly ruthless in a ruthless business.

"The Katogoula are scared shit-less, Joel. I would be, too, probably, if a few of my near-and-dear ones turned up dead the way theirs have. They even had a fire at their museum. Whole damn thing burned down. We have anything to do with any of that?"

Joel smoothed his toupee where it met his nearly matching hair. "Not to my knowledge. But you know W. P. Some things are, let's just say, off the books."

"Boy, do I ever know. You remember that pit boss who was skimming from the roulette tables? They didn't find him till a month later. Out in the Arizona desert. The poor bastard had been—"

"We're not here to tell tales around the campfire about W. P.," Joel interrupted. Val noticed an outbreak of sweat at his forehead, under his rug. Was he skimming a little cream for himself?

"When's that old S.O.B. going to retire? Ever notice the assholes of the world live longer than the rest of us?"

"The Katogoula casino?" Joel said, impatiently.

"In limbo. They've dethroned their pro-casino chief and there's even talk now of closing membership permanently. Chief Claude confides in me." She noticed Joel's leer. "Sorry, Joel. The chief isn't that kind of guy."

"What can we do to make sure they don't get ambitious again?"

"I have a few ideas. One thing's that genealogist I told you about. He's still a pest, getting the natives all worked up. Gung-ho about growing the tribe, helping them be self-sufficient, all that do-gooder crap." She hadn't heard this exact spin from Chief Claude, but she knew what Joel needed to hear. "Sure would be simpler if he sort of dropped out of the picture."

"Yes, wouldn't it," Joel said. "Handle that. Use the discretionary fund for any necessary expenditures. I emphasize *necessary*." He took a small black memo book from his inside coat pocket. "Memorize this number."

Val did. 504 area code. Probably a New Orleans number. At the company's *Crescent Luck* riverboat, docked in downtown New Orleans, she'd seen card counters who'd won too much escorted away and reportedly beaten to a pulp by big, mean-looking men she didn't know until they flashed company ID cards. Never the same bruisers, and needless to say, card counters and less sophisticated troublemakers didn't return either.

"If you need to take stronger action, they'll know what to do. No communication with the home office on this. Got it?"

Val nodded. So if anything goes wrong, she takes the fall. Tidy.

"I'll expect you tonight," Joel said. "The Leprechaun Suite."

She could answer only one way, though the thought of having to spend another night with him, even in the luxurious confines of the Chitiko-Tiloasha's fabulous hotel, made her boiling mad. Her boyfriend, a guard on the *Crescent Luck*, would flip out if he heard.

"Oh, sure, Joel," she said, her practiced smile generating the dimples that drove some men wild. "Looking forward to it."

Chapter 24

Luevenia Silsby caressed the Bible in the palm of her hand. It had seemed so large and important to her, as a child. Now she could read the tiny words only with a strong magnifying glass.

Tadbull Hall, though, was just as she remembered it. Every detail was burned into her memory. Details of the house and the landing on Bayou Fostine, where, almost forty years ago, she finally let him, where they…

Time was a funny thing. How it could transform pain into joy, tragedy into blessing, disgrace into pride.

So long ago…she had been a pretty girl in the early bloom of womanhood, innocent and trusting, slightly rebellious, seeking a thrill. It would have been better, she thought now, if she'd paid more attention to her little Bible and its eternal lessons writ large.

Her great-grandmother had given it to her. Luevenia was only six at the time, and Gray Wing was over a hundred and ten, people said. She was a formidable woman even then, not long before her death. Very few used her Katogoula name, but something of it survived in what almost everyone called her: Birdie.

The Bible was in French, and in other respects it was a lot like the anonymous one that had recently been destroyed in the Katogoula Museum; there used to be lots of them around, but as the old ones died, the Bibles seemed to leave the earth with their spirits. Birdie's even had an intricate little scene painted on the ends of the pages, which could be detected only when you held the book at a certain angle, the pages curled just so. Otherwise, gold leafing shone, obscuring the scene, which held mystic secrets: a cornfield in full ear, growing before burial mounds topped by temples.

Temples of the Vulture Cult, Luevenia learned from her great-grandmother.

Birdie had made her promise to keep the book and its secrets hidden from her parents, who would not understand. Luevenia came to know the truth of the old woman's words. Her mother, the old woman's granddaughter, always changed the subject when Luevenia asked her about the cult; but she caught snatches of whispered conversations between her mother and father. Her questions upset them; from what Luevenia overheard, there was something ugly and unclean in her ancestry.

And when one day her mother caught her picking the flesh from a dead squirrel, as Birdie had said the Holy Ones of the Vulture Cult did to dead human beings, her horrified, enraged mother administered a whipping she never forgot. Some line had been crossed; Birdie was not so talkative after that, and less than a month later she died.

Luevenia's mother was a traiteuse, as the Cajuns and African American Creoles referred to a female "treater" or "healer." With common sense, sympathy, often bizarre treatments, superstition, and Catholic doctrine, the traiteuse and traiteur (male) once filled the gap in bayou-country lives left by the busy priest and the rarely seen doctor. Many of Luevenia's ancestors in the female line had been healers with family ties to the Chitiko-Tiloasha inhabiting the southwestern prairie marshes; Birdie was one of these, and she'd passed her knowledge on to her daughter, who passed it on to Luevenia's mother. Some years later, in the heat of teenage rage at some petty quarrel that didn't go her way, Luevenia wondered if her mother had cured Birdie of living, for the crime of revealing the past.

Luevenia walked around the back of Tadbull Hall, to the kitchen door. She used to do this more than three decades before this day, when she was young and pretty. Mr. Wooten Tadbull II liked to have pedicures and manicures; he especially liked soaking his feet in an herbal bath Luevenia prepared from forest plants she and her mother gathered. Young Wooten—the present Mr. Tadbull III—had Luevenia do his nails, too. But for other reasons.

Her maternal line had always been good at tasks requiring dexterity and delicacy. Like her mother, Luevenia acquired early on a reputation as a healer, a masseuse, a superb cook, and a champion basket maker. She believed that this knowledge had passed to her in her blood—the fading heritage of the Vulture Cult, no longer put to proper use. But as she grew older she began to understand that her heritage must remain concealed. She never did become a practicing traiteuse, and she was not surprised that her mother was not disappointed.

No one remembered which families belonged to the Vulture Cult; at least no one talked of it now. This knowledge had been yet another part of the slowly eroding Katogoula ways, one more irrelevance the past held for a people who were more concerned with putting food on the table in a society that despised them, or pretended to ignore them, at best. And though the long fingernails were things of the distant past—but not as distant as some might think—Luevenia now felt in her heart that the revelation of such a "disgusting" heritage would be a disgrace that would cling to her family, and even her husband's family, like the smell of death.

The Vulture Cult was fine with her, while it remained safely distant and impersonal in a museum. She vividly remembered how children used to point at Birdie and shout "witch"; Luevenia would never subject her family to that, or even to whispers behind hands in church, to the subtle shunning the healthy give to the diseased. Her mother had been wise to caution her about Birdie's rash confidences. Now, in hindsight, she didn't blame her if she'd actually hastened the old woman's departure.

As a mother, Luevenia, too, must act in the interest of her family.

Yet...her feelings about her heritage had always been ambivalent: she could not reject it outright, even today.

Now she waited in the Tadbull kitchen and watched Verla, the maid, cooking up a storm. Mr. Tadbull was having his afternoon siesta. He had not proved worthy of the gift of her virginity; Luevenia had ceased to waste regret on him. Wooty would be with her soon, Verla had said. Through fragrant clouds filling the spacious, old-fashioned, high-ceilinged kitchen, Luevenia tried to listen to the black woman's proud recitation of her children's college successes. But her mind insisted on traveling back thirty years and more, to this same yellow-tile counter.

She saw herself holding a younger Mr. Tadbull's hand in hers as she dipped and filed and polished his nails...his other hand under the counter, inside her dress, between her legs.

◻

Luevenia's great-grandmother had explained the scene she herself had painted on the Bible's page edges. It was heavy with symbolism. One day, Birdie said, Luevenia would understand the meaning of many things behind the painted surface of life.

The old woman liked to be out in the woods when the weather permitted, and sometimes even when it didn't. Luevenia learned more from this hobbling, muttering woman than from anyone else, before or since. They would walk slowly to the ancient burial mounds on Tadbull property, to the old graveyard in Tchekalaya Forest, sometimes farther along the Golden Trace, all the way to sacred Lake Katogoula itself. She was a strong woman, who saw her great-granddaughter as the torchbearer for another generation.

Birdie always carried the little Bible with her; and when they rested in the shade of tall pine trees, the old woman would take it out and hold it in her beautiful hands, with those long nails of hers. For hours she would explain the many truths of the lives of Christ and the saints and the martyrs; truths that the Katogoula oral stories told in different, but not inferior, ways. In the unwritten Katogoula Bible, forest, lake, and sky were the settings, and God, the Great Spirit, gave life to demigods in the guises of human beings, animals, plants and the elemental forces of nature.

The luxuriant corn of the fore-edge painting symbolized life and fertility, Birdie said. The burial mounds, pregnant with death, stood for the necessary power that cut down the corn, according to the preordained plan of all existence, in a harvest that fed the living. The temples atop the mounds represented the Holy Ones of the Vulture Cult, who once administered the rituals of death and lived in the temples, even as the chiefs lived in their own houses atop different mounds. The smoke rising from the fires were the souls of the dead, freed from entombment in their earthly bodies.

The Bible hid much more than it revealed. It had become for Luevenia the embodiment of her complex heritage, a reminder of her high status as a daughter of the Vulture Cult, as a descendant of the ancient Yaknelousa who, caught amid the European power struggles, had been absorbed by their ally, the Katogoula. But she was also a descendant of Europeans, whose alien culture, more than any war, destroyed the world of her great-grandmother and turned the sacred stories transmitted from generation to generation into mere primitive and cartoonish myths.

Her husband, Royce, had seen the Bible daily; she'd kept it on her dresser; but he didn't know what it meant to Luevenia. Nor did he know what the inscription meant; Birdie had always said it was Yaknelousa, the lost language of her ancestors. It was actually Cajun French, which Royce, fortunately, could not read or speak. What else had the old woman made up or garbled in her dotage? Luevenia never decided satisfactorily on that question. Birdie had loved her; that was enough to trust.

She didn't need to read the lines of the inscription now. The old woman had told her from her own lips what the inscription meant, and she would remember it to her dying moment:

> To my Little Wing, from her great-grandmother, Gray Wing, granddaughter of Black Wing, daughter of Long Black Feather, High Priest of Vultures. Grow like Corn, be strong as Death, like smoke rise to Heaven.

She had come here to Tadbull Hall today because she could not destroy the little book. This genealogist was stubborn and clever, more so than the others who had preceded him. He would not stop digging up the past, he would not go away, in spite of the harsh words she'd said to him in front of the smoldering museum, words she did not fully believe herself.

Death. Death had been on her mind a lot lately. Was his death the only way to stop his snooping, to end her torment? And what if she died, what if the Sacred Cougar came for her this time? Someone would go through her things, find out the secrets she had kept even from her husband! Death would not be enough. She had to get her affairs in order, in case, in case...the worst happened.

Over the past few days, she had secretly burned in the trash barrel behind Three Sisters Pantry everything else she treasured. The photos of her great-grandmother in her rocker, weaving a basket of pine needles. Her grandmother's big English Bible that recorded the births, marriages, and deaths of generations unaware that they were Vulture Cult descendants. Letters, postcards, clothing, quilts...whatever had been passed down to her mother, whatever might give this prying Nick Herald a clue, whatever might taint others with her awe-inspiring, horrible ancestry. Watching the smoke from the barrel drift heavenward, she had realized with a start that she was performing the ancient rituals of death on her own life.

She feared this Nick Herald. His brown eyes were always thinking, working things out. Whenever she lied to him, his brows contracted into one, and she could feel his doubt touch her, like hands probing a sick place on her body. He saw with all his senses, like a traiteur. Was he a healer of the family soul, or a wicked spear-thrower of evil knowledge?

Exposure would be unbearable, but still she could not destroy everything, not her great-grandmother's special gift, this little French Bible, as damning as it might be. Those forest days spent with Birdie had stuck with her, as had the stories of the great honor bestowed on the families that constituted the Vulture Cult. Today, people would not understand; they would turn on her, say things behind their hymnals, refuse to eat the good food at her store...but the heritage should not die. Her own child should have the Bible, even if he did not know what it signified, even if he did not know he was her child.

回

This was why she had called Wooty that morning, why now she followed him up to the attic, to Old Man Tadbull's collection of Katogoula artifacts and images. She and Wooty had always been like aunt and nephew.

"Now that our museum's gone," she said to Wooty, "had an idea maybe you'd put this old Bible in amongst the other Katogoula stuff up here. Cleaned out some old closets and found it. I was going to try and sell it at the store, but it's such a pretty little thing. I wanted it to have a good home."

Such a beautiful baby he had been. How he had grown into this fine man, future master of this wealthy place.

He hesitated and then extended one of his handsome hands to take the book, no bigger than a deck of cards. *Her* hands...his were so like her hands. For a moment, she thought she might cry, tell him the whole story so elaborately hushed up, the sad tale that not even Royce knew. She would have gladly died just to embrace him.

No, she was all right now. "You'll take it, won't you, Wooty?"

Chapter 25

Tuesday morning, three days after the fatal museum fire and a day after Luevenia Silsby's visit, Nick, Holly, and Wooty followed Mr. Tadbull up the central spiral stair tower toward the attic of Tadbull Hall.

"Great-granddaddy, Wooten the First," Mr. Tadbull said proudly through wheezes, "fought for the Confederacy under Pike, Cooper, and Stand Watie—you know, that Cherokee from Georgia—in the Trans-Mississippi Department. 'Course Great-granddaddy, he already knew lots about Indians before he went to Indian Territory, you understand. The man damn near spent his whole life amongst 'em here."

Wooty brought up the rear, hanging back several steps, hands in pockets, tight-lipped, preoccupied. Nick could see Holly wasn't comfortable with this meeting, either; there was still bad blood between them, and her phone call setting up this private showing hadn't helped matters. Unusually reserved, she tried, not quite successfully, to ignore Wooty; now and then she glanced up at Nick, as if searching his face for a sign he was ready to leave. But he wasn't.

Nick could smell the past exuding its musty, alluring pheromone from every crevice of the solid old house, hear it call his name softly like a dream-lover in the night. America, for most of its life, had cannibalized its physical past to feed its revolutionary appetite for unfettered progress. As if fulfilling some mythic destiny, this modern giant heedlessly ate its parents. But the old could nourish the new as more than just fuel, and Nick was glad that this appropriately radical idea had taken hold in America's continuously maturing ethos. Landmark structures like Tadbull Hall served a crucial purpose in preserving the history of America, just as monasteries and manor houses in medieval Europe salvaged remnants of their times.

The original resident families were influential and wealthy, their houses centers of economic, political, and social life when local government and associated record keeping had yet to be established. And it was odd characters like Mr. Tadbull's great-grandfather and grandfather who snatched bones of the past from the rapacious, dumb jaws of unchecked expansion.

The houses themselves were archaeological treasures, holding vital clues in their very construction to contemporary thinking and social organization. Tadbull Hall featured many of the architectural strategies of the time to lessen the effects of the brutal Louisiana summer heat. The plenum, as it was called, the column of open space around which the stairs circled, was one such innovation; it took advantage of natural convection to move hot air up and out of the house, and to bring cool air up from the brick basement. Nick had also noted the central hallways, with doors and windows placed for maximum cross-ventilation. The sun-blocking large adjustable shutters and latticework made him homesick for Creole New Orleans.

No, Nick was not ready to leave. Not by a long shot.

"Spent lots of time in Indian Territory, Great-granddaddy did," Mr. Tadbull continued, considerably winded from hauling his belly up the steep stairs. "Helped get some of those tribes out there to go with the Confederacy. Later on, he took a minié ball in the butt at Prairie Grove, Arkansas. Gotdamn, that must'a hurt like hell! Damn thing's downstairs in my study. Yep, Great-granddaddy organized a company of these here local Indians when the war started. Not many of 'em came back, though. Most of the surviving ones went on to Indian Territory, called for their families to join 'em. A few stayed in the forest and hereabouts. Good thing, too. Got 'em recognized, didn't it?"

They entered a narrow room that stretched across the width of the house and meandered to the rear, in an eccentric way—which seemed the common thread in everything associated with the Tadbulls. Nick determined that the open space didn't occupy the entire area of this floor. Several generations of Tadbull women had been unwilling to cede all of their attic storage space to this family art gallery and local-history museum.

"There's closets and storage rooms up here you couldn't find with a gotdamn Katogoula hunting hound," Mr. Tadbull declared, referring to the famous local breed of big shorthaired, hog-chasing dogs with strange dissimilar eyes of bright blue, gray, or yellow. "Who knows what all's in 'em. I sure don't."

Crammed storage rooms, hidden closets, padlocked chests...holding, perhaps, a faded list of unknown significance, a diary, an album of stained photos, or a rodent-nibbled batch of letters. Nick let his mind wander among such imagined genealogical riches; he missed some of Mr. Tadbull's subsequent narration.

"His son, your grandfather, painted these watercolors?" Nick asked finally, hoping he wasn't betraying his raging curiosity enough to set off any warning bells in the man's head. It was the same in genealogy as in antique- or stamp-collecting: the owners of treasures often clammed up when they realized the immense value, monetary or otherwise, of what they had.

"That's right," said Mr. Tadbull, still without any telltale suspicion. "My granddaddy was like that, you know. Sorta strange. An artist, and all. After the War Between the States, Great-granddaddy used to go off for weeks at a time with the Katogoula men, hunting and fishing, living with the damn tribe. Took my granddaddy with him. That's how he got to know so much about 'em, and put down what he saw in these here paintings. Wooty kinda followed in my granddaddy's footsteps, you might say. We couldn't hardly keep him inside, but he was always running off to play with the Katogoula children."

Still no reply from Wooty.

Far from the clatter of family life downstairs, these attic quarters had served as a restful enclave for the Civil War veteran and then for his son, the artist. Bleached-pine floor, white plaster walls, cantilevered ceiling altered to accommodate modern air ducts. Watercolors, oils, and black-and-white photographs of local Indians covered almost every inch of wall space. Mr. Tadbull explained that Katogoula women, a hundred years ago, had made the unpainted wicker furniture, using local vines and twigs. The day bed, rocker, and tables were all still in place, just as his grandfather had left it, ready for another century of use.

Close to a window stood a tall easel with a nearly finished oil painting of a moonlit bayou scene, pencil lines indicating where the paint would have gone.

"He went a little soft in the brain, at the end," Mr. Tadbull said. "Started seeing things in the moss and the fog." He chuckled, shaking his head. "Bascove Tadbull. The Indians just called him Old Man Tadbull."

Holly said, "If you look closely at the trees, you'll see the limbs are the hair of a malevolent female creature of the swamp."

The woman had the soul of a teacher: she couldn't keep a good lesson down. Holly retreated into sullen silence when she saw Nick's smirk. He thought the work showed the influence of Caspar David Friedrich, the influential nineteenth-century German painter, but kept quiet, not wanting to sound pedantic himself.

Nick moved so that the window was behind him and squinted his eyes. "Yeah, I see it now. It would have been his masterpiece, I'd say."

"Gothic Romanticism," Holly said, caught up in the dank spookiness of the painting. "Caspar David Friedrich."

"I don't know who y'all talkin' about there," Mr. Tadbull admitted, "but I'll take your word for it. Anyhow, we keep the attic this a way for folks visiting us, show 'em *somebody* in the family had a little culture. Right, son?"

"Whatever, Pop." Wooty would not share his father's good-natured self-depreciation.

Mr. Tadbull went on, showing no awareness of his son's silent brooding.

"They say when Great-granddaddy Tadbull came back from the war, an old Katogoula healer-woman told him he'd die one night soon in this house, while he was sleeping. So you know what he did? Gotdamn if he didn't never spend another night here as long as he lived! Had him a tent out there under that old oak, and he used to sit with his Indian friends—the ones that were left. They'd smoke and watch the fire till dawn. They say he slept up here during the day a lot. Guess he out-foxed old Death, 'cause he lived to his nineties. Died two...no, no, wait, three years, wasn't it Wooty?—sure was, three years before I was born."

Nick had turned his attention to the paintings and photographs—windows of art, allowing glimpses of Katogoula ways during the nineteenth and early-twentieth centuries. Grandfather Tadbull clearly loved the subjects of his works, the Indians who had been his companions since childhood. He'd shared much of his father's superstitious nature, judging from his selection of subjects and cryptic style.

The modern Tadbulls seemed unconcerned with anything remotely spiritual. Still, there must be something to Wooty. Nick couldn't see Holly falling for a clod.

"Mr. Tadbull," Nick said, "these should be put on wider display. Scholars would love to get their hands on these pictures. They could answer a lot of questions about how the Katogoula lived in those days."

"Well, now," Mr. Tadbull said, rubbing his chin, "I never thought they were that important. Or that valuable, either. But the fact of it is, I'm of a mind with my daddy. He wanted to burn 'em all, turn the attic into a billiards room. Say, did I tell you there's descriptions and such on the back of some of 'em?"

This was new to Holly. Nick could see the explorer's lust awaken in her green eyes.

Mr. Tadbull stopped before a watercolor showing men and boys wading in a sluggish bayou, casting a white powder on the water. The painting dated from the twenties or thirties, Nick guessed. The Indian fishermen wore shirts, trousers, and hats that would have looked natural on Main Street, though it was odd that they were fully dressed and half-submerged. Had Christianity made them ashamed of their traditional, natural nakedness? Nick saw the scene as a clash of ancient and modern ways.

"I always 'specially liked this one," said Mr. Tadbull, removing the watercolor from the wall. "Let's see what Granddaddy says is going on right here. I do believe some of those descriptions fell off over the years and got swept up in the trash."

"That's too bad," Nick said, as blandly as he could manage. *Good God, what irreplaceable genealogical information had been lost already?!*

On the torn, brittle paper backing, only a portion of the pasted-on descriptive label remained: a scrap of flowing words, in the elegant style of the day, by a hand used to transforming inner visions into art.

> Vince...grandnephew of Luke.... and their clan...
> A meth...ng used by the Katog...
> On the Bayou Fostine, August...
> They take the poison, devil's shoest...
> Many fish thus are...

Grandfather Tadbull had meant this inscription to be the finishing brush stroke of the painting, an integral part of the whole work of art. Nick was sure the old man would have gritted his teeth to know what a dolt his grandson had grown up to be. Maybe Wooty was right to have such a low opinion of his father.

Nick imagined himself running away from Tadbull Hall, carrying half a dozen pictures, stealing them to save them from further sad deterioration at the hands of the present master of Tadbull Hall. What a crime to allow this precious heritage to fall victim to further neglect! He'd done worse for baser motives.

He squirmed in the cast. The arm and shoulder felt much improved, but probably not up to his over-eager ideas for honorable larceny.

As he handed the picture back to Mr. Tadbull, he spotted a small Bible on a shelf of one of the wicker tables, haphazardly resting amid other old books. He knew instantly that it was almost a twin of the one lost in the museum fire. *Twins again. Has to be a sign.* He could be superstitious himself, when it suited his purposes.

This Bible, at least, was something he could save. Wouldn't even strain his arm. It was his duty, right? He tried not to look at it, but his mind whirred away with elaborate rationalization.

From downstairs the maid shouted that Wooty had a telephone call. He curtly excused himself and left.

Mr. Tadbull hurried to the plenum. "Wooty, you going out, son? You let me know if you do, 'cause I need me a pree-scription from the Wal-Mart."

Even at the distance of two floors, Wooty's exasperation came through in an unintelligible, snarling retort.

"Excuse me," Holly said. "I'm going to the, uh..."

"Oh, well, sure, sweet thing," Mr. Tadbull said. "You know where it is. You bring your cameras over here anytime, you hear?" And then, after Holly had descended the stairs, he said, "I sure do like that gal. Liked her hair long, though. Can't understand why my *got*damn bull-headed son don't sling her over his shoulder and carry her down the aisle.... Now, look at this one, here, Nick."

His back to Nick, Mr. Tadbull now faced another painting, which portrayed a nighttime powwow, with the Katogoula participants in full ceremonial regalia, masks and feathers and animal skins and weapons abounding. Nick quickly walked to the wicker table and slipped the Bible in a side pocket of his coat.

◫

Mr. Tadbull showed Nick to the door, after a quick tour of the study stuffed with historical oddities dug up or collected by several generations of the family. Nick had expressed appropriate wonder at Great-granddaddy Tadbull's minié ball.

He took the opportunity to visit the Tadbull family cemetery, a short walk behind the house—a pretty little graveyard overhung by serpentine oak limbs dripping moss. A few minutes later, he dawdled on the white shell drive, waiting for Holly. She'd been gone half an hour or so, but he knew she could take care of herself. He wasn't worried. Probably some unfinished romantic business with Wooty. He began to face the possibility that their recent intimacy had been a fluke.

Gargantuan fatsia partly obscured her VW van in a three-car parking area to the right of the porch. Daydreaming, Nick thought the fatsia looked like dark green hands reaching for the overcast fall sky. Then he noticed them: Holly and Wooty standing between her van and his muscular, feline, black Porsche. Through the van windows, Nick could clearly see that Wooty was angry, Holly worried and angry. He spoke fast, each word an accusation; he whipped an index finger repeatedly in the air before Holly's face.

Holly slapped him, hard. That shut him up. He glowered at her, moved a few inches closer. For a second Nick was afraid he was going to hit her back, and he considered what he would have to do to break it up. Instead, Wooty turned quickly away and stalked off on a strip of lawn between a vegetable garden and a rose bed, toward the back of the house.

◫

Holly drove her van away from Tadbull Hall. Nick had some more work to do in the Armageddon courthouse, and then he was heading to

New Orleans. He'd convinced himself he could drive, in spite of his injuries. Holly was dropping him at the motel to collect his stuff.

He'd rather skip the appointment with a famous orthopedist, but since Sangfleuve Parish was footing the bill, hey, why not? Hawty had insisted he report to the office to handle a client problem—"You don't pay me enough to argue with bigoted white women who don't like the ancestors I've found!" And Val, the vixen from Bayou Luck Casino, had called him at the Greensheaves. She had information on the Katogoula murders. Couldn't say on the phone. Had to meet him at her company's riverboat casino, the *Crescent Luck*, the next night, Wednesday.

"You were right about that Tadbulls' collection," Nick said. "Fantastic." Holly had not spoken since they left the house. "I know you probably won't approve, but I felt it was my scholarly duty to liberate one of the prisoners." He held up the small Bible.

She barely glanced his way before again staring down the rural, rutted two-lane highway, running the gears to the limit and then shifting ferociously, so that the boxy van seemed to be riding a rough sea.

"It's my fault," she said.

"That you slapped him?"

"He deserved that. It's my fault we're in deep doo-doo. I guess it's time you know. Here goes: Wooty runs pot through Tchekalaya Forest. When we were going together, I was his mule, they call it, a few times, maybe seven or eight trips. I used my van to take some small loads to an airstrip near St. Francisville. He had a Cajun buddy of his weld a false muffler section or something underneath."

Nick didn't interrupt her; he could tell a free-flowing confession when he heard one. The fever must run its course, he believed; you'll feel better afterward.

"At first I thought it was an adventure, you know, a blow against stodgy old Southern society. Then I realized how stupid, how incredibly un-idealistic, uncool, unsafe it all was. This was dirty, bloody business, that destroys lives. These people have no conscience, don't care who they hurt."

She sped past a slow-moving logging rig overloaded with pine tree trunks.

"I know, sounds hypocritical. Sure, we both smoked our share of pot in those days. The danger was a rush; real cloak-and-dagger. And the money was good. But now…he tells me he can't quit. I don't mean he's addicted or anything; his suppliers are being assholes. And it's my fault."

She told Nick about their first years together. Holly and Wooty had met in college; she was going to LSU, and he was at Freret in New Orleans. "I spent more time on I-10 and in bed with him than I did in class," she quipped.

Wooty was different then. A fiery rakehell of Shakespearean proportions, afraid of no one and nothing, always seeming to land on his feet, and get passing grades, even though he rarely attended classes.

His muscles and his hormones seemed to do his thinking for him. The aura of the jock superstar hung about him, even though he'd made only third-string, and in his freshman year quit the football team, which at Freret was pretty much of a joke anyway, Holly related.

But he had money—at least, more than anyone else in their circle—great looks, fine cars, lots of fraternity and sorority friends, and a contagious need for excitement. It was a kick just to be around him. In an undeclared competition, testing their newly fledged adult bodies, they tried to outdo each other in wildness. Who could fly closer to the sun?

"Sex, drugs, and rock-and-roll," Holly said. "Wooty finished business school and came home, so after school and some traveling, I moved up here for my job at the television station in Armageddon. Still a wild child. And following him, I guess. About two-and-a-half years ago I decided I was smarter than those Mexican guys, that we could have our cake and smoke it, too. Oh, I was in the *media*; I knew it all! Guess I was still trying to impress him, just like in college. On my last trip, I pretended the van was burgled, and the grass stolen. Instead, I sold it to some guys I know in New Orleans. He didn't know anything about it, I swear, until afterward. I thought the creeps would just write it off, or at worst stop using us. What do they care about one load of dope, anyway?"

"That's where the money for your documentaries came from, right?" Nick said.

She nodded contritely. "Most of it."

"Was there ever a grant from the state?"

"A small one. But I went through that in no time. I'm sort of a perfectionist, so I never could meet their damn deadlines for funding. Anyway, the suppliers checked out my story. They didn't believe us. Told Wooty he owed them a *hundred thousand dollars* for the lost shipment! Which is crapola, because I only got forty-five. And he didn't even keep any of the money; he wanted me to have it. Said I'd taken the risk for it. So for over two years, they've deducted that much and then some. How do you argue with assholes waving Uzis or whatever around?

"Now something big's come up. Wooty's talked to a Louisiana legislator named Augustus Bayles about a dream job, and he wants to take it, just get out of here, go somewhere and start fresh. I interviewed Bayles a couple of times—I'm not sure who's scarier, him or the druggies. But you can't simply walk away from these creeps. Now they're saying it'll cost *another* hundred grand as an exit fee, and a hundred thousand every week he hasn't paid! That was the phone call he got. They want the money, like, yesterday. It's some honor bullshit. I mean, what's money to them?...God must have been in a real sadistic mood when he invented men!"

"Can't they just take it out of his earnings on his last few runs?"

She shook her head. "Telling them he was through was the last straw. They haven't trusted him, really, since my screw-up; right after that they started these elaborate routines, never the same thing twice. It's so James Bond-y. Now they've decided not to use him or Tadbull land anymore, period, no matter what happens with the Bayles deal. And if he doesn't come up with the money, they say I'll get hurt. Or worse. *Christ! how could I be such an idiot!?*" She hit the steering wheel with her palm, and the van swerved across the centerline and back. "It *is* all my fault. What do I do?"

"Know a good plastic surgeon?" Nick said, easing up on his deathgrip of the armrest.

"Oh, that's a big help!"

"Just kidding. Where's all the Tadbull money? Can't Wooty use that to get off the hook?"

"No. He draws a pretty good income from a trust fund, but can't get at the principal until his father dies. His father...well, in case you haven't noticed, he can't stand him. I can take him, usually; he's just, oh, I don't know, shallow. The casino, if it ever happens—which looks doubtful—will take a while to build; and, from what Wooty's told me, Mr. Tadbull will control that, too. He won't ask Bayles for the money, though he says he'll eventually make a potful.

"Every cent Wooty has is tied up in all kinds of illiquid projects— wildcat oil in Paraguay, a construction company in Russia, Canadian diamond mining, American fast food in China, speculative real estate partnerships...God, every time I see him there's some new screwball scheme. Of course they're all bleeding money. And now here's this Bayles thing. Wooty's not your ordinary good ole boy, Nick. He's trying to be someone, he really is. And if he's a loser so far, at least he's a heroic one. He's more like the pioneers, warriors, and artists of his family, than his father."

"Don't forget the crooks," Nick said.

"Oh, you're one to talk! That Bible you lifted, I've never seen it up there; wonder where it came from." But Wooty's troubles soon put her curiosity to flight. "Anyway, he wants to do something major, something he can call his own. It's a dangerous obsession, I guess. Could get somebody killed. Like me."

"We all have our obsessions. If we're lucky. Only one thing to do, then: raise the cash."

Holly turned to him. The van drifted. "Didn't you hear what I—"

"Watch the road, please. I have a plan. Maybe not a great one, but it's something." He waited half a mile before he asked, "He still cares about you?"

"Yes. But we haven't been...close for about a year. Really, since I pulled my dumb stunt, it's been nothing but one long argument."

"You love him?"

She thought for a minute, jerked the van back to the right side, and then nodded.

"Why'd you slap him?"

"He said I wasn't a two hundred thousand-dollar piece of ass. But he didn't really mean that. He just feels boxed in. I'm sorry I hit him."

He was a fool if he did mean it, Nick thought. The love of a woman like Holly was more valuable than mere sex, worth a man's last possession, worth the planet's weight in diamonds, worth everything.

Chapter 26

"That money's for education and health care," Tommy complained. "I just don't seem right."

"But this *is* education," Nick said, "*and* the health of the tribe's history. Besides, it's only a loan."

The two men sat drinking strong coffee at a sturdy old homemade table in Brianne's kitchen. Tommy was now tribal treasurer; for Nick's purposes, this demotion was perfect.

Brianne had left the room earlier to bathe her little girl. Distant splashing and the indistinct, soothing words of the mother's monologue flowed into the kitchen. Matt, the more seriously injured twin, was mending well and milking his temporary invalidism for all it was worth. Nick heard Sam outside in the blustery afternoon shooting a BB gun at an already well-perforated jack-o'-lantern, trying to amuse his brother.

"We're saving up to fund a tribal center, too," said Tommy, stirring his coffee. "Maybe we can at least have public bingo there since it looks like my casino idea's pretty much dead. I sort of wish I'd never brought it up, what with all that's happened…but it's still a good idea and I'm not ashamed of it." He placed the spoon back in the saucer, with a resolute clang; no more self-pity, apparently. "I can see Wooty being hard up for cash, if he was counting on our casino deal coming through soon."

Tommy had told Nick of his worry over the increasing dissension within the tribe. A pro-development faction opposed the no-development faction led by Luevenia Silsby. Minor family jealousies and old petty quarrels had broken out like a virus with a long incubation period. At Three Sisters Pantry, fingers were pointed, bitter words shouted. Some even spoke of splitting off to form separate tribes, of allegedly purer descent than the main tribe. The casino companies which had been so eager to sign up the Katogoula were losing patience.

The Katogoula were all capable of murder now, Tommy believed, and he was finding it more difficult every day to look his old friends in the eyes.

"But Jesus, a hundred thousand dollars, Nick! I've already disbursed some of the money on 'emergencies' everybody's got all of a sudden. I'm not supposed to decide on an expenditure of this size. Miss Luevie's the new chief, you know. And she's not real big on doing anything to bring more attention to the tribe. That's why she fired you. Says the tribe's got enough problems without inviting in more outsiders for a free ride on our BIA money."

Nick gave another shot at pressing his case. "Tommy, we're talking about a priceless collection documenting Katogoula history. Have you ever seen it?"

"Maybe twenty years ago, when Wooty and me played together up in their attic. But I never paid it much mind. Just some old pictures."

"Take my word for it: incredible! Hundreds of unique, very valuable pieces. After the loss of the museum, how can you pass this up? Everything owned by the Tadbulls relating to Katogoula history will come to the tribe when the new center is ready."

"Wooty'll pay back the money *and* give us the collection?" Tommy asked skeptically. "His daddy agrees to all this?"

"Says so right here." Nick held up Wooty's promissory note. "The tribal center will become a major attraction, a place of scholarly pilgrimage, with or without a casino. Hey, trust me. I'm the guy who risked his life for the Twins-Raccoon Bowl, remember?"

Earlier that hectic afternoon, while Nick did his courthouse research, Holly and Wooty put Nick's plan on paper; Mr. Tadbull, in fact, knew nothing of the scheme. Nick realized his plan would make the lovers' reconciliation easier. He consoled himself by recalling Chief Claude's epithet: a "midwife" brings new life to love, with no envy of others' happiness.

"Oh, I trust *you*," Tommy said. "It's Wooty I ain't too sure about. He's into some shady stuff I don't want to get involved in." Tommy got up to put his cup in the sink, thinking, looking out at his sons in the yard. He turned around to face Nick. "Wooty's always played fair with us Katogoula, helped us out of some tough spots when he ran the mill. But it sure is a lot of money."

"A refundable deposit on your future, my friend." Nick joined him at the sink and slapped him on the back for positive emphasis. He felt like a used-car salesman inches away from closing a sale. "When's the next tribal meeting?"

"First of the year, probably. Most everyone's going to a big intertribal powwow on the Chitiko-Tiloasha reservation for Thanksgiving. Crash course in being real Louisiana Indians." Tommy grinned. "Feathers and drums and dancing and all. Even a turkey shoot with atlatls..."

His words trailed off as, Nick presumed, he remembered the manner of his brother's death.

"Great," Nick said, covering the awkward moment. "You won't have to explain the expenditure for a while. Holly's documentary is almost finished. I've convinced her to donate half ownership of the program rights to the tribe. I just happen to have a signed statement from her, too." He showed Holly's agreement to Tommy.

"You sure been busy."

"All part of the service.... So, by the end of the year, you'll have your money back. When the tribal center goes up, you'll receive the Tadbull collection. And to top it off, you'll own half of a program that's undoubtedly going national."

"More white man's promises." Tommy crossed his arms and stared at the vinyl floor covering; a smile gave away his decision. "Okay, okay. You win. The deal don't sound half-bad, the way you're putting it. I got the checkbook for the tribal account yesterday. It's in the den. I've been meaning to show you the BIA presentation, anyway. Come on."

In the den, Tommy proudly pointed to a framed 8-by-10 glossy on the wall. The photo had been taken in Three Sisters Pantry a week ago, before Nick's arrival, the museum fire, and the late schism in the tribe. Tommy—as the chief at that time, and as a descendant of the family that had pushed so hard for recognition for decades—and Miss Luevie received an oversized check handed over by a grinning fellow from the acknowledgment branch of the BIA. Squeezing into the shot behind those three were two of the district's congressman, angling for Indian support, a new power in Louisiana politics.

Two hundred and eighty-five thousand dollars, made out to the Katogoula Indian Tribe of Cutpine, Louisiana. Tommy wore a nervous grin below his darkly circled eyes; Miss Luevie was even more ill at ease, looking away from the camera, her head slightly lowered, as if trying to hide her innermost thoughts from the prying eyes of the outside world.

Tommy took a seat before the fold-down secretary desk where Brianne paid the household bills.

"We want to keep this quiet, of course," Nick said. "Wooty mentioned that he'll call you soon. Something about a new development on the casino front." Nick shrugged. "Don't ask me. Just delivering a message."

"This could land me in some serious trouble, you know. I'd feel better if I went to Miss Luevie and the council for approval."

"They'll thank you for this, one day. Don't worry, you're doing a good thing, Tommy." *If he only knew how good—saving the lives of two people.* "Make out two checks, will you? One for $100,000 to Wooten Tadbull IV, and one to me for $500."

Tommy held the pen poised in the air, a wavering needle on the gauge of his resolve. "What's the five hundred for?"

"Your re-election campaign fund."

Still reluctant, Tommy shook his head but continued writing. "I hope you know what you're doing."

Nick slowly let out a quiet breath of relief and uncrossed his fingers behind his back.

◻

Late that afternoon in the intriguing study of Tadbull Hall, Nick handed the check to a surprised Holly. So grateful, can't believe it, you're wonderful Nick.... She hugged him a long time. His heart thumped up into his throat. But it was a different kind of embrace for both of them.

In countless nature shows he'd seen on television, males of the wild know that when the antler-tangling contest is over, when the female has made her choice, the loser must limp away. Why couldn't he, too, accept the judgment of selfish genes looking out for themselves, bow to the inscrutable dictates of DNA drawing us to one and not another? Hope, love, poetry, philosophy...mere distracting byproducts of the double helix's indomitable instinct to survive. Free will? What a laugh. A biological microchip rules our lives, Nick was thinking as Wooty thanked him with real warmth; no sense losing your cool over it.

Wooty urged him to look through the attic closets now and anytime, as long as he liked. Mr. Tadbull had departed for another duck hunt on the coastal marsh. Nick would be undisturbed.

◻

The cedar closets upstairs were dry and nearly dustless from decades of unmolested slumber. There were four main ones, two framing the plenum, and two at the front of the house. Nick first tried the closets nearest the stairs.

He could see no evidence of rodent damage. It was as perfect a storage area as he had ever come across in his genealogical excursions.

These closets were the size of some of the rooms downstairs, each one big enough for a glittering dinner party. There had been lots of those in Tadbull Hall, Nick could see, judging from the many china sets in zippered cases and silver tea and coffee services under plastic that had been banished to the attic as each new Queen Tadbull began her reign, with her own proclamations of taste.

Nick walked through a century and more of Tadbull clothing, furniture, appliances, toys, photographs, and books. Shelves from floor to ceiling were jammed with everyday things that, in their contexts, probably were ignored. Separated from their times and uses, even the smallest personal article had an elegiac air, an allegory of impermanence to impart to the attentive explorer.

He let his hand run across objects once held or kissed or cried upon by Tadbulls long since moldered to dust. True, he learned essential genealogical facts from the written record, but a shared touch, even separated by many decades, filled him at once with awe, reverence, and a rising rage. For contemplating mortality, knowing that in a blink of geologic time the human race itself would be gone, was enough to knock out the underpinnings of the most determined agnostic or believer alike, and send him off naked into the storm, shaking fists at the sky like a King Lear who has seen the futility of the bubble we call living.

Forty-five minutes later he'd moved through the second closet, and had rummaged around in six large cupboards concealed behind panels of the attic walls. There was so much here to sift through, and with only one arm in good shape! His uninjured arm and shoulder already ached from overuse.

He pressed on to the third closet, where he sat down on a trunk, his penchant for metaphor working at full tilt. The genealogist's classic dilemma: an astounding mass of raw material, the handicaps of time and stamina, the certainty that an incredible treasure of information hid among the commonplace, just out of sight.

He noticed a tall chest in a cluttered corner. Twenty or so drawers, wide and shallow, seemed ideal for holding documents or papers of some sort.

He cleared away three table lamps, a tuba, five odd stringed instruments from various continents, two heavy standing fans, and four boxes straining with smaller junk.

The drawers held dozens and dozens of preliminary sketches and more fully developed partial works done by Grandfather Bascove Tadbull, most of them studies of Katogoula Indians and how they lived during his artistically prolific years.

Tommy Shawe and the present-day Katogoula were going to get their money's worth for the hundred thousand-dollar loan! Bascove Tadbull's collection would be highly desirable to any large museum or private collector.

The artist had also written descriptions of his subjects, sometimes just a name and date, at other times paragraphs explaining what he had drawn or painted. As he examined the loose canvases and sheets, Nick took detailed notes.

He came to a sheet with charcoal sketches of a remarkable pair of hands, in various poses. The fingernails were unusually long. On the back of the sheet, Grandfather Tadbull had written:

> The hands of the Katogoula woman, Birdie [ ]x, sometimes called Gray Wing. She is a healer with plants and potions, of that I can attest. Many believe she talks with spirits. I think she has a streak of madness in her.
>
> Jan. 10–12, 1893.

Birdie what?! A roach had chosen this crucial spot to die upon, years before; a brown stain obscured the surname. He brushed away gossamer bits of legs and wings, and held the sheet up to the light bulb. No good. A short name, ending in *x*, but he couldn't quite make it out. Who among the living Katogoula was related to Birdie, if anyone was at all?

The surname felt familiar; but he couldn't quite visualize the other frazzled rope end that might form a knot of family connection. That would have to wait until he could review his research notes, most of which were in his car downstairs or with Hawty, who, as a healer in her own right, was exercising her collating touch on them.

The name Gray Wing did strike a familiar chord, though. From his pocket he removed the Bible he'd pinched earlier. *Yes!* The dedication, in what he thought must be Cajun French. He found that he could tease probable meaning from it:

> To my Little Wing, from her great-grandmother, Gray Wing,
> granddaughter of Black Wing, daughter of Long Black Feather,
> High Priest of Vultures. Grow like Corn,
> be strong as Death, like smoke rise to Heaven.

Birdie-Gray Wing at some point had given this little Bible to her great-granddaughter, Little Wing. If his translation was correct, Nick realized that the dedication was a major find, outlining a lineage extending back at least to the eighteenth century. But whose? In a somewhat confusing way, Birdie had recorded that she was the great-granddaughter of Long Black Feather, a big man in his day. Nick had run across this name in the journal of the French clerk, who had written at some length about the Vulture Cult.

Nick's chance discoveries today in the attic had connected several sources of genealogical information and had provided a tantalizing link between the living tribe and the ancient mysteries of the Vulture Cult.

Descendants of Birdie would be fascinated to discover their Vulture Cult heritage. *Or would they?*

More questions rushed into his mind as he replaced sheets in drawers and moved on to others.

If this obviously beloved Bible had belonged to Birdie, whose hands Grandfather Tadbull had portrayed in his sketches, why was it here? And who was Little Wing, the woman's great-granddaughter? Was she still alive? Did she know she sprang from the Vulture Cult line? And if, as Grandfather Tadbull hinted, the old woman Gray Wing was a little crazy, could Nick even trust the genealogical information she'd apparently inscribed in this book with her own bizarre hands? Corroborating evidence gleaned from other sources would be vital.

He found nothing of great relevance in the next four drawers. But in the last drawer of the chest he came across a series of details for the watercolor Mr. Tadbull had shown him earlier in the day. Fisherman wading in Bayou Fostine.

The artist had rapidly caught the action as it happened: the bend of an arm, the tilt of a hat, a face in profile, the paralyzing fishing powder on the water's surface.... Grandfather Tadbull must have used these studies to give his painting life, later, here, in the tranquility of his attic studio.

One sketch showed the face of a man in three-quarters aspect. The resemblance was unmistakable, astonishing: it was as if Nooj Chenerie were there in the water on that day. This had to be one of Nooj's relatives, Nick thought, maybe a direct ancestor. On the back of the sketch he read the artist's notes, which had served as the basis for his briefer, now-crumbling description on the framed painting hanging on the attic wall:

> Vince Madeul, grandnephew of old Luke Chenerie. On the Bayou Fostine. Their clan here uses a method of fishing very old among the Katogoula. They take the poison dust, which is from devil's

shoestring (the forest herb *Tephrosia virginiana*), and scatter it upon the waters. Their clothing protects them. Many fish come up to the surface, not dead, but drunk. The damnedest way to fish I ever did see. Not much sport, but good eating. The men laugh and joke, happy to be in the water, because it was exceedingly hot this August 23rd, 1912.

回

"You're doing me a favor by scrounging up this money—a big favor," Wooty said, on the porch of the house. "So I guess I ought to do something for you." He looked at Holly, who clung to his arm as if she would never let go again.

"He's our friend," she said. "Tell him, Wooty. He may see something in it we don't."

Wooty nodded. "Just to set things straight, I wouldn't do anything to hurt the Katogoula. You can take me out of the line-up. But I...but I was out there in the woods the night Carl was murdered."

"You haven't mentioned this to Sheriff Higbee?"

"Hell, no! I was out running marijuana. You know that already, of course. Not something you'd confide to the cops, is it?"

"What exactly did you witness that might interest me?" Nick asked.

"Early that morning—it was still dark—I saw what looked like a big buck. One of the biggest racks I've ever seen around here, and I've been hunting all my life, since I could walk, just about."

"I go to the Audubon Zoo now and then, but I'm a genealogist, not a zoologist. What was so important about this deer?"

"It wasn't the deer so much as what was following it. At least, what I think was: a cougar. The moon was just going down, so I couldn't see a lot of details. Like looking at something under a black light, you know? So the cougar was stalking this deer, okay, but then it stopped, looked right at me. I was a good distance away but I'm sure it saw me. And then a weird thing happened. It rose up a few feet off the ground and"—he glanced down at Holly for reinforcement; irritated at his hesitation she yanked his arm—"well, *floated* real fast into the woods." Wooty illustrated the cougar's trajectory with his hands. "I know it sounds crazy."

"Were you alone?" Nick asked.

"No—well, yes."

"I'll take that as a maybe," Nick said.

Nick wasn't going to get the whole story, but Wooty's testimony might be useful later, combined with other data. In genealogy this research method was called a cluster search: pay attention to everything, no matter how seemingly irrelevant at the moment, no matter how little faith you put in the source.

"Look," Wooty said, "that's all I can say about my situation that night. But I did tell Nooj about the cougar the next day. We have sort of an understanding. He looked rattled when I mentioned the cougar, like he'd seen a—"

"Ghost?" Nick asked. *Ah, an "understanding"...so Nooj is on the take, despite his sanctimonious airs.*

"Yeah, a ghost. He told me about Carl's murder and the claw marks on the cypress knees. That really perked up my ears, made me wonder about that old myth of theirs, the Sacred Cougar carrying the dead deer, walking on the lake."

"So this understanding between you and Nooj...would he have known that you were in the forest about the time Carl was killed?" Nick asked.

"He knows everything going on out there. Hell, he might have been tracking that damn cougar himself," Wooty said in an offhand way; but his speckled blue eyes grew thoughtful. "Anyway, cougars are so rare around here, I thought he'd want to know for, you know, official game-tracking reasons."

Now that's odd, Nick was thinking. Nooj Chenerie might have known that Wooty, a possible witness or suspect, was in the forest that fatal night and morning transshipping marijuana, and yet he didn't report it. And even if Nooj hadn't been aware of Wooty's activities that night, Wooty most definitely told him the next day. That was vital information the sheriff should have received, especially from a sworn law-enforcement officer, something that might have made Tommy Shawe's questioning less of an ordeal. Maybe the "understanding" made doing his duty a bit of a dilemma.

"Was it a real cougar?" Holly asked. "I'm not getting a consensus here."

"Nooj must not have thought so," Nick said. "Word spread like wildfire that the Sacred Cougar was on the prowl when Carl was murdered. The news and the supernatural spin must have come from him." To Wooty: "He was the only one you told?"

Wooty nodded. "I knew I could trust him to keep my name out it. And he did. He said some campers saw…whatever it was."

"The whole tribe's been terrified since," Holly said. "That sighting set a dark tone for everything else that's happened. I don't think any of the Katogoula have been thinking straight from that moment on."

Wooty gave a world-weary chortle. "I had my doubts that night about it being a real one, too. Foolish, I know, for a grown man, but I was thinking, did the Sacred Cougar give me a message I was supposed to carry back to the tribe? That's the talk about what happened to the Shawe twins. Guess I didn't do a very good job of it." A shadow had crept into his usual self-confidence. "I tell you, for those few minutes, this country white boy believed, *really* believed."

回

As Nick drove away from Tadbull Hall, Holly and Wooty held hands and walked slowly down the long white-shell drive toward the landing on Bayou Fostine.

Through dusk and into night, on the long trip to New Orleans, Holly's question repeated itself: *Was it a real cougar?* Long-nailed hands crisscrossed like a curtain just beyond the MG's windshield, and with each pass Nick saw above the highway reflectors the faces of Luevenia Silsby, Nooj Chenerie, other Katogoula present and past, the Tadbulls of many generations, lovely Holly, and the Sacred Cougar, merging into ever-new forms.

Chapter 27

Hawty Latimer read aloud from the screen of her wheelchair's wirelessly connected tablet computer: "*American State Papers*, Hill index of the Cuban Papers, Santo Domingo Papers, *Fondos Floridas*, Draper Manuscript Collection, Mississippi Provincial Archives, Vaudreuil Papers, Father Hebert's Catholic records, University of Louisiana at Lafayette's Center for Louisiana Studies—"

"The Panton, Leslie Papers?" Nick asked, leaning back in his unsteady banker's chair on the other side of his 1920s corporate titan's kneehole desk. A delivery truck rumbled down the little-traveled street below; heaps of folders, papers, and books rearranged themselves in small avalanches.

"Yes, yes, hold your horses," Hawty said, eyeing Nick's disorderly desktop with disdain. "I was getting to that and a lot more, too."

He was silently pleased. She'd done an excellent job of plugging most of the holes in the genealogies of the six core Katogoula families. Which meant that he'd done an excellent job of instructing her in the past few years. True, he'd lost some minor scholarly perquisites at Freret U. as a result of the bogus plagiarism rap, but no one could steal his gift for teaching.

He'd taught Hawty that local research, as crucial as it was, had its limitations; records might have been damaged, destroyed, stolen, or falsified. But other important genealogical information might very well be scattered across the country and the world; sometimes the most distant source held the most objective facts.

Like the French clerk's journal, these better-known but often-ignored sources Hawty had searched were gold mines for Southeastern Indian genealogical information—official reports of alliances, conflicts, trade agreements, grievances, land transfers, mixed-blood unions...compiled by soldiers, bureaucrats, and merchants who'd spent time among Indians still living according to their ancient ways. And usually, somewhere along the way to modern times, patient volunteers had run their fingers along each line, indexing names and places and subjects.

"Oh, another thing," Hawty said, "you were right: the priest at the Katogoula's church was terrific. Loves to talk about the church's extant sacramental records. He's a young guy from Belgium, interested in his own genealogy, wants to hire us to...*what* are you staring at? My hair?"

"Your hair's...fine." He noticed it now for the first time this Wednesday morning: a mass of jet black, shining streamers. "Actually, I'm staring at him," Nick said, pointing to the bust of Descartes presiding over jam-packed, dark-wood bookshelves in the narrow room he called his office. "Our patron philosopher of Genealogical Doubt."

Boxes of orphaned records he'd rescued from destruction slumped against one another across from the bookshelves, on the other long wall below tall windows, few of which actually functioned. Paint peeled, pipes clanked and leaked, and the wiring dated from Prohibition years.

This was the Central Business District, where nineteenth-century Americans practiced their brash capitalism to the jeers of the Creoles across Canal Street. "The past is dead, things are going to change. It's a new era!" successive generations of go-getters had declared here, with architectural hubris. Such naive aspirations inevitably die young in New Orleans, and in the corrupting heat of the next rising sun, every gaudy bloom turns brown.

Nick's frowzy, unassertive building squatted in the shadows of downtown's few incongruous pre-oil-bust skyscrapers, seeking companionship among other battle-scarred veterans of futile local enterprise: abandoned cotton and sugar and coffee warehouses, boarded-up Reconstruction banks, hotels morphed into shelters, and bloated federal buildings hunkered down behind black wrought-iron fences and civil-service protectionism.

The fourth-floor view from Nick's windows took in the wide Mississippi giving a fatherly elbow nudge to the French Quarter, soul of the Crescent City, a wayward daughter too drunk on pleasure, anarchy, and ennui to rise above her eighteenth-century dreams of grandeur or to heed any lessons the wise old river would impart. Looming over the levee and the Quarter, massive ships glided on the river's surface like giant snails, threading through stout tugs and low-riding barges, all coming perilously close to the sightseeing boats and casino paddlewheelers and the hundreds of shops, restaurants, and bars nearby that, twenty-four hours a day, urged tourists to forget everything but their stomachs and crotches.

Hawty's domain was an anteroom that she'd meticulously arranged for maximum efficiency and wheelchair mobility, but Nick's personal collection of documents, while not on the priceless level of the Karpeles or Huntington libraries, was off-limits to Hawty's mania for order. She claimed that his mind was stuffed with similarly useless junk, fragmented bytes that would never add up to anything of genealogical value.

Hawty twisted around to look at the patinated plaster head and shoulders of the great seventeenth-century French philosopher, and then she faced Nick again. "Doubt everything, and what's left must be the truth, right? Are you going to tell me what's bothering you, or do I have to take stronger measures?" She held up a formidable fist.

"Nugent Chenerie and Luevenia Silsby," Nick said, forcing his attention back from the crepuscular world of lies and death he'd left the day before. He cautiously leaned forward in his chair; a good idea, because it lurched wildly left, then right, before dropping to level. "My mental lie detector goes off every time I talk to them. I get that funny feeling."

"Your funny feeling is hardly ever wrong *or* funny. You think Nooj and Miss Luevie are hiding something? Something bearing on these murders?"

"Afraid so," Nick replied, "according to the Theory of Inverse Interest, and a few other stray intuitions."

Formulated early in his career as a professional genealogist, the Theory of Inverse Interest postulated that the more eager a person was to sift through his family history, the less likely that some embarrassing—or deadly—skeleton hung in the family closet; the opposite also held.

"Nooj is evasive about his ancestry," Nick said. "Talks in circles. I hit a brick wall after his paternal grandfather. He says his people on that side avoided every species of prying government official, moved around a lot."

"Those Cheneries were awfully good at laying low," Hawty said. "Even for Indians, who are hard to trace under the best of circumstances. You'd expect local records to be scarce, since the original Sangfleuve Parish courthouse burned during the Civil War. But we should find *something* between then and the few records his parents and he have generated in the last thirty years or so. Nobody's invisible. I had good luck with his maternal line, the Bellarmines, and the other five core families. Took me awhile to figure out that Indians in the 1900 and 1910 censuses are enumerated separately; they put them at the end of city wards and enumeration districts. Paper reservations, you could say."

"I meant to tell you about that. Sorry." He wasn't really. Some things can't be taught. The Zen of genealogy: skill and perseverance grow from within, after many mistakes, frustrations, and losses. "Nooj did mention a family oral tradition that sounded plausible; it could help explain the scarcity of Chenerie genealogical records. His grandfather's father might have been a white man who raped or had an unapproved affair with a Chenerie girl. The family drove him off. No one knows exactly what happened.

"This would be an opportune moment for me to say a few words about—"

"Uh-oh," Hawty said, "I feel a lecture coming on."

"A few words about censuses and undercounting on Indian reservations."

Nick explained to Hawty—who surreptitiously tapped icons on her screen as she listened—that most reservations were large and remote, and that census canvassers were always too thin on the ground. Over the course of two centuries and even today, these canvassers routinely faced daunting physical conditions and deadlines, language and cultural quandaries, and sometimes hostility and obfuscation. Living conditions were often overcrowded on reservations, with many individuals from several families staying, perhaps only temporarily, in one domicile. Census takers had to decide on the spot who was Indian and who wasn't, and who was related to whom, based on what they saw and heard in the household. There was a lot of room for error. Contemporary Indians are acutely aware that federal grant money is at stake, and they are challenging census results and winning re-counts.

"You know what I think?" Hawty asked, purely rhetorically. "The Cheneries aren't missing from the records because of canvasser error. I think this Chenerie grandfather misinterpreted the lack of family information. There wasn't any scandal, any rape; it was a taboo he didn't understand, simple as that. And it went way beyond his grandfather's time."

She'd been reading the work of John Swanton, a preeminent anthropologist and student of American Indian cultures. His groundbreaking research, notably *Indians of the Southeastern United States*, was still used today, over half a century later.

Hawty said, "Nooj told you his Chenerie kin lived with the Choctaw, didn't he? Well, let me tell you what Swanton wrote about a Choctaw taboo—"

"No one was to speak the name of the dead and wives weren't to utter the names of their husbands—makes you wonder what they *did* call them."

"Oh. You already know that." Hawty recovered quickly. She never gave up trying to spring something new on him. "Even into the mid-nineteenth century, government Indian agents saw families line up and place sticks on the ground to show the relationships of dead relatives. Cool, huh? What if Nooj's ancestors picked up that taboo or observed it to fit in with their Choctaw neighbors?"

"And the old taboo became part of family practice, even though they were Katogoula, long after anyone knew what it meant?"

"Sure. Why not? Lots of weird things make it into family belief systems. You ought to hear some of my mama's hang-ups from way back." A broad smile briefly lit up her full brown face. "Chenerie kids, seeing their parents' reluctance to talk about the dead, think there's something ugly in the family's history. Kids are smart, pick up on things fast. Eventually, the family memory is truly lost, because nobody will talk about it."

"Possibly." Nick rubbed a finger over the cleft of his chin. "If he's not in fact hiding anything, if that's just the nature of his family personality, that would tend to make Nooj less of a suspect. All right. What about Miss Luevie? She should be gung-ho for establishing a good genealogical foundation for the tribe, but instead she orders me to stop my research."

"She fired your butt," Hawty said, "not to put too fine a point on it. Boy, you really have a way with some clients. My theory about her? She's a private, practical woman upset that her friends are falling into mass hysteria over money. I think they're both innocent. The casino and the drug angle, all those shady characters from Las Vegas and Baton Rouge and Mexico, that's where they ought to look. *Cherchez la femme*, the French say. In Louisiana, honey"—she rubbed her fingers together—"*cherchez la moola*."

"I'll tell Sheriff Higbee that when I see him again."

"What! You're going back? I thought we didn't work on spec. Who's going to pay us? You better stick to genealogy and leave detection to the detectives. We have paying jobs to do, and you're gallivanting around romancing drug hussies and playing Hercule Poirot! You've been reading entirely too much Tony Hillerman."

"Does the given name or nickname Birdie ring a bell?"

Hawty calmed herself enough to think about it. "No. Who is he?"

"She. That's what you need to find out. And four- or five-letter Katogoula surnames ending in *x*. Fairly common with French heritage, I know, but check it out, will you?"

"*Those* are your stray intuitions? Doesn't sound like much to me."

Nick told her about his fortuitous linkage of the diminutive Bible from the attic of Tadbull Hall, Grandfather Tadbull's drawing of Birdie's hands, and Birdie-Gray Wing's Vulture Cult lineage. He told her about the strange recurring image of the hands, from the present and the past; of the inexplicable flashing in Holly's video, the very morning of Carl's murder, of the shiny badge on Nooj's LDWF uniform.

"Oh, so you *have* done something constructive. Birdie, Birdie.... Give me a minute." Her fingers darted around a keyboard of ruby light that had mysteriously appeared on the retractable work shelf of her chariot. "I've flagged personal names in our reports so we can call them up in a relational database..."; her explanation petered out as she worked.

"No Birdie, so far," she said after two minutes. "But I still have some of your notes to enter. And, of course, *this* mess." She gave her chariot wheels two precise pumps, picked up Nick's new paper pile, and placed it on her shelf. Her chariot had sophisticated servomotors and other cutting-edge technology fresh from the labs of her engineering and computer friends at Freret University, but around the office she preferred to propel herself. Good exercise, she maintained. "If only it could have been your left arm. Your handwriting may be better with your right. What did the orthopedist say?"

"'Thank you.' I made him a wad of insurance money." Nick moved his newly free arm around in the lightweight sling; it felt great. "Seriously, he had a few choice words for the other doctors. Accused them of overreacting. The sheriff must have leaned on them, so I wouldn't sue the parish."

On her way out, Hawty pivoted her chariot. "By the way, the Vaudreuil Papers had a few tasty details about the Quinahoa."

"Really? I'm shocked: there *is* actually something I don't know. Enlighten me."

She warmed to the subject, eager to teach her teacher. A French missionary priest saving souls in the dense swampy forests of eighteenth-century Louisiana had heard tales of the Quinahoa, reputed to be extinct by then. The priest reported that the Quinahoa had been a buffer tribe between the Caddo and Choctaw confederacies. Now hostilities flared, making his job perilous. He demanded soldiers for protection as he sought to spread the Gospel.

"The Quinahoa shared some customs with both," Hawty said. "Part Plains Indians, part Southeastern. They were nomadic hunters and traders, but seasonal farmers, too. I bet you didn't know there were buffalo around here once? And—isn't this a coincidence?—the priest was told they didn't talk about their dead, just like the Choctaw.... I swear, I'm getting more like you every day, stuffing my brain with nonsense that doesn't have a thing to with the price of eggs. Pitiful. Downright pitiful.... *Now* what's wrong? What did I say?"

Nick offered no answer, didn't seem aware of Hawty at all. He was transfixed, deaf and blind to outside stimulation. He merely stared at Descartes, hardly blinking, his eyes narrowed as if he'd suddenly perceived in the far distance a scout returning from the uncharted frontier of time.

Hawty, shaking her head and grumbling that she didn't expect any more work out of *him* this morning, wheeled herself with unnecessary vigor into her room.

Chapter 28

New Orleans was patting itself on the back: homicides were on track to dip below four hundred a year. Only gala-going do-gooders with private security, fresh-faced reporters fond of free lunches, and relentlessly effervescent city boosters with secret contracts allowed themselves to fall for these official statistics. The governmental in-crowd of future indictees and featherbedded relatives bragged in frequent press conferences about innovative policing and wildly successful grass-roots neighborhood initiatives that had cost billions, most of which had fed the obese, insatiable god of corruption that in actuality ran the city from administration to administration.

Realists—that is, everyone not making millions through such institutionalized dishonesty—knew that robbers, rapists, murderers, flimflam artists, and dealers had merely turned on each other sufficiently to reduce their ranks temporarily. Relative sanity didn't last long in New Orleans; the mood would swing down again in this manic-depressive city when the thugs regrouped or a new crop attained gang age, when the arms parity on the streets reached imbalance, or when the ad hoc state economy began to sink below the waves again, like the state's coast, both propped up by oratorical gimmicks, pocket-lining arrogance, underhanded pique, and blinkered stewardship, the earmarks of Louisiana's fiasco politics.

New Orleans will always be a package tour of sin and danger; you can't see the show without sometimes paying an unexpectedly onerous cover charge.

Wednesday at dusk, meditating on this pearl of wisdom, Nick walked with a wary eye from his apartment on Dauphine down St. Peter, taking in the sights and sounds and smells the French Quarter offers to her lover, who, bedazzled by her red hourglass of carnality, might very well end up as her post-coital snack.

Crumbling pastel stucco façades hug the street. Footsteps on flagstones. A portcullis clangs shut. Cloistered purling of a tropical patio fountain. Intimate quietness, deceptive solitude, masking a siege of centuries: secrets living in the cool, musty darkness just beyond solid doors four steps up a glossy green stoop, behind peeling louvered shutters, imprisoned by studded gates, or up there, on the balcony veiled by fanciful iron railings and trailing fern.

The outsider can only yearn and wonder.

Nick bought a big cold beer in a plastic cup; his arm in the sling was a perfect cup rest. He cruised the relatively safe streets of Bourbon, Royal, and Chartres. The Vieux Carré never failed to put him in a Beat poet mood. What a place!

Singing, swaying, swigging, groping; yells and laughter; sirens' song of croaking barkers proffering a red flash of sequined flesh on a pole, plastic-speaker jazz, bump-and-grind/rap/rock from swinging padded doors; black kids heel-and-toeing the bricks; guided groups open-mouthed in wonder; turbaned taxi drivers; blue cops at barricades. Lights, lights, lights! Bread and burned sugar in the air, wet raw oysters in hot sauce on marble bars, burlap bags of reeking shells, shrimp heads in garbage cans, trampled muffuletta spilling olives and salami, alleys leaking dumpster sludge, steaming Lucky Dogs, sizzling fat and onions and garlic and red pepper from kitchen fans, beer slosh, fruit and rum, vomit, urine, police-horse and carriage-mule droppings, fishy river rot on the cool breeze, diesel, affluent perfume ducking into limos, foreign words before expensive

Marie Antoinette windows, smoke from cigarettes, joints, and after-sumptuous-dinner cigars....

◙

"Watch where you're going, man," a muscular, dark-brown fellow warned as he gently rammed Nick on the observation deck of the *Crescent Luck*. Nick looked up, and up, until his gaze reached the shaved head of Shelvin Balzar, NOPD. In plain clothes, just a tourist throwing away a few bucks. Nick understood instantly: they were supposed to be strangers. Shelvin was working.

And Nick was having a blast, getting pleasantly drunk and gambling disastrously at slot machines, on the house. He'd needed a break. A Luck o' the Draw underling had found him on the gambling floor soon after his arrival. Val would not be available until midnight; her apologies. Until then, he had credit wherever he wanted it; the young man gave him a plastic card that apparently had a stratospheric limit encoded in its invisible microchip. "Service Included," the card read. *Yeah!*

Nick rapidly made the acquaintance of the counter staff at the four Mark Twain-themed bars placed strategically around the gambling deck, and for hours now he'd been slowly working his way down the California coast on a highway of superb wine.

◙

"The Prince and the Pauper" had a marvelous view of the toy-like Quarter from a balcony above the observation deck of the *Crescent Luck*, a casino boat that so far had never once paddled out into the river, as was once "required" by state law.

No minnows allowed here. This secluded and luxurious cabin was reserved for "whales" only: lots of green baize for the elite class of gamblers, the few thousand individuals on the planet with millions to bet in a night at blackjack, baccarat, poker, craps, and roulette. As they pitted fortunes against inescapable probability—a Passion play of their corporate or criminal lives—whales disliked rubbing flippers with penny-pinching tourists. Casinos sent jets to fetch these high rollers and spent lavishly to assure their comfort. A whale basically owned the place as long as he continued to put down thousands with each wager.

A butler had led Nick up private stairs. Chef, bartender, waitresses, valet, female "companions," princely penthouse in the casino's nearby hotel…all this and anything, the butler explained before departing, awaited his slightest intimation of a wish.

Nick strolled around the suite of three compact, first-class rooms—gambling parlor, den, kitchen/dining. Jim West's private train car in *The Wild, Wild, West*, with modern updates, came to mind. In the den, six recessed, muted televisions showed programming of as many countries. Computers, fax machines, gizmos he couldn't figure out. Enormous flower arrangements scented the rooms.

A whale for a night, a prince, for a change, instead of a pauper. Ignoring the thin, small warning voice in his head, he sank into a leather couch and took up the bubbling glass of champagne the butler had poured. *Ah, an excellent year!*

He somehow punched the right buttons of a disc player on an end table, and Sinatra's "Luck Be a Lady" flooded from invisible speakers with such lifelike fidelity Nick closed his eyes and saw the incomparable Chairman of the Board in the spotlight singing for him alone.

◙

The third time Butch hit Nick in the stomach was not as painful as the previous two. Or was he numb, dying even, after the hammering elbow to his jaw that still had him seeing explosions of starry whiteness?

Val said, an animal gleam refracting through her fake tears, "Butch, oh, Butch, he tried to"—her voice broke admirably on the accusation—"he tried to make me have...have *sex* with him."

Butch paused to admire his handiwork, watching Nick not breathing, doubled over, wanting to explain that, no way, that's not even remotely how it happened. Sobbing on one of Butch's massive shoulders—*a pit bull on steroids, this guy*—Val primly adjusted her foxhunt outfit, tucked and buttoned her ripped frilly shirt.

Really quite professional sobbing, convincing, Nick thought, marveling at the detachment he could muster through the throbbing, whirling pain. He had to hand it to her, she was a great liar.

Butch moved in on him again. Small black eyes burning with hatred, an off-kilter face that reminded Nick of a red bell pepper, fists like pumping pistons in a Futurist painting, buzz-cut dark hair like a thousand nail points Nick was being dragged over at the moment the cabin door burst open and Shelvin, brandishing his NOPD badge, sent Butch stumbling across the room with a remarkably smooth and quick motion of one arm and hand, thanked him for capturing an international criminal, handcuffed Nick, and took him away, far away, thank God, from Butch.

▣

"I compromised our investigation over you, Herald."

Nick felt like a *beaten* poet now. He lay tensed with pain in the back seat of Shelvin's unmarked police cruiser, seat-belt buckles gouging his back. The radio squawked, and Shelvin, in the driver's seat, said something into the microphone. He turned his head to check on Nick.

"You want to go to the hospital?"

"Nah. Just got out of one. Give me a minute...or two."

Shelvin spoke in his deep, forbidding monotone, staring out the windshield at the big wedding-cake casino boat, a few blocks away.

NOPD was assisting in a State Police undercover operation to slow underage gambling, he said. Law enforcement and politicians knew it couldn't be stopped.

Though twenty-one had always been the minimum age for riverboat- and Indian-casino gambling (riverboats that no longer had to sail, of course), Louisiana until fairly recently had allowed eighteen-year-olds to play the lottery and land-based video poker. A new law in the mid-nineties had also upped the drinking age to twenty-one. Was the state turning prudish? Not by a long shot. Through clever legislative bill writing, entrance to a bar or lounge was still legal for eighteen, nineteen-, and twenty-year-olds, so long as they didn't gamble or drink—fat chance.

Louisiana acted on such matters only on pain of losing federal highway funds or of some similar dire consequence that would jeopardize the pork-barrel projects public servants lavishly distributed to ensure their reelection. The altruistic claim from legislators and lobbyists that they were protecting individual and states' rights was a classic Louisiana exercise in demagoguery. Meanwhile, the cash-stuffed envelopes continued to change hands and the cases of beer and liquor still appeared like clockwork under bureaucrats' Christmas trees. Statutory wiggle room and procedural cards up the sleeve always saved the day for graft, greed, and other assorted corruption.

Logic and consistency were alien to Louisiana bureaucrats, who hid their real agenda—power and money—within constantly shifting law; constitutional amendments, it seemed, created a different set of regulations for each week. No one could keep up, few bothered. And the lobbyist with the biggest stack of hundreds always got exactly what his client wanted.

It was the Louisiana way, a time-honored tradition that worked miracles for those in the know, Orwell's *Animal Farm* on the bayou.

And so it shouldn't be surprising that, despite the admittedly leaky laws on the books and the promises of the owners, underage "adults," some in their high-school uniforms, routinely gambled and drank at Louisiana's casinos and gussied-up betting parlors. Pari-mutuel betting and charitable bingo and raffles got the official wink and nod, as well, for the young set.

French Quarter restaurateurs and hotel owners—big political contributors—hated electronic gambling and the riverboat casinos and the new, huge one reeling in the suckers on Canal by the river, all of which competed for tourist dollars. Politicians, for their part, needed a grand gesture of enforcement to show that the funding of ballooning government and their ever-increasing salaries and kickbacks through gambling vexed their consciences. Casino operators understood these periodic outbreaks of goodness; the money flow was so phenomenal, the laxer ones were content to take the odd slap on the wrist as symbolic penance, and in time go back to catering to everyone not actually in a stroller.

Even through his pain, Nick was impressed by Shelvin's penetrating analysis of Louisiana's political burlesque show.

Shelvin had moved up to the Special Investigations Division. "Mostly vice, dope, and fugitives." The department's new brass had noted that Shelvin was tough, smart, and, by all accounts, incorruptible. After a ballyhooed departmental cleansing, he'd been promised the fast track to the homicide section. "It ain't fast enough," he noted.

Nick recalled the first time they met. Shelvin was an angry young man from Natchitoches, the historic colonial town in north Louisiana. He was a Gulf War Veteran and an Army reservist, but still his frustration over a lifetime of prejudice and lack of opportunity was, at that time, about to boil over into something that would have sent him to Angola penitentiary or to the graveyard.

In the course of a complex and deadly genealogical case, Nick discovered that one of Shelvin's ancestors had been cheated out of a considerable inheritance, over a century before. Nick's resolution of the sordid tale of sibling jealousy, racial and religious intolerance, and twisted guilt brought a fortune to the Balzar family, but also tragedy: Shelvin's younger brother was murdered, and Shelvin was stabbed, almost fatally.

Nick sensed this was a wiser, calmer, more seasoned man than the simmering volcano he'd known in Natchitoches.

He gingerly probed his midsection for unfamiliar protuberances and unusual movement of bone. "What do broken ribs feel like?"

"You'd wouldn't need a second opinion if you had some. They're probably just bruised. You'll be all right in a few weeks. Unless it's your liver or spleen."

"Oh, thanks, I feel better already."

"So, what really happened in there?" Shelvin asked, just as Nick felt like talking.

Val had contacted him in Cutpine, Nick related. Urgent. She claimed to have vital information on the Katogoula troubles, which he also explained to Shelvin. She wasn't around at the agreed time and place to meet at the *Crescent Luck*, but he got VIP treatment while he waited. Val showed up. Nick got right to the point—that is, the Katogoula—but she had other ideas. She came on to him immediately, knew what she was doing. Being no saint, he saw no problem with that. At a critical juncture, she excused herself, went to the bathroom. Next thing Nick remembered, a security guard named Butch who just happened to be—*uh-oh!*—her boyfriend, was pummeling him senseless.

"Set up," Shelvin said. "Must've called mayday from the bathroom. What you done to her?"

"Nothing. I mean, except those few hot minutes on the couch. And that was more 'with her' than 'to her.' I get the feeling she and her casino company want me out of the picture. About a month ago she tried to hire me away from the Katogoula."

"Uh-huh. See it a lot down on Bourbon. Competition's fierce. Place got a good band, a fine stripper, doing too much business to suit the neighbors. All of a sudden, there's an accident. Star of the show's laid up. These Luck o' the Draw dudes are deep like that, man. Protecting their turf down at the Chitiko-Tiloasha casino. Putting up roadblocks for your Katogoula friends; you just ran into a roadblock named Butch. But what you told me about the murders don't seem like their M.O. They turn up the volume slow, do only what's necessary. It ain't no Schwarzenegger movie. When they decide some dude's got to go, you never find the body. No, what you got up there in the woods, Herald, is a killer with a message to deliver. The real sick ones do that, feel the need to tell the world what's inside their heads, teach society a lesson. Who's on the suspect list?"

Nick told him.

"Best thing to do," Shelvin said, "shock 'em. Shock 'em good with something they don't think you know."

"What if I don't have anything definite to shock them with?"

"Find it. Make it up. Rub their face in it. If they're lying, and they're not completely psycho, you'll know. Especially you, seeing as how you're such a good liar yourself."

Shelvin's idea of humor.

"See you, Shelvin." Nick opened the door and turned his windbreaker collar up against the damp river chill. He was already shivering from the pain. "Drop by sometime."

"Where you think you're going, fool?"

"Home."

"Walking in the Quarter after two A.M.? Shit, I don't do it myself. Shut that door. You're coming with me, where the cops hang out."

"Hey, I'm the one who got framed and beat up. Why are you arresting *me*?"

"Not arresting you, man." Shelvin smiled as much as he ever did. "Buying you breakfast. You need something hot in your belly, and I'll *know* you're staying out of trouble for an hour or so."

Chapter 29

The town of Cutpine had a police chief—when he wasn't running his gas station. Emery Rud—a fifty-eight year old, sun-baked, crew-cut, jump-suited heart attack waiting to happen.

Emery had little use for showering and shaving, even less for flossing his one brown upper incisor. He didn't see what the big deal was about a few more dead Indians, as he often made abundantly clear to his white customers, who wanted to know where these Katogoula got off wanting everything on a silver platter. Like everybody hasn't been screwed by the government at some time or other.

Law enforcement shared office space with the business of keeping pickup trucks running. Emery thought it was damn Christian of him to allow the town a four-drawer file cabinet, for a small fee. The rare miscreant who needed incarcerating was sent to the parish jail in Armageddon, and, if necessary, on to the state penitentiary at Angola. There were no stop lights to run in Cutpine, and speeding wasn't much of a problem, since Emery's garage helper did most of the repair work, and that badly.

Before the recent rash of unsolved violent crimes, the chief had found it no problem to juggle his many responsibilities. A substantial distraction had come up two weeks before, however: he was caught fudging school-bus safety inspections. His scheme had brought in a nice income for him; he was sorry to see it go. How could a man live on what the town paid him for being chief? he would ask his sympathetic but tight-fisted customers and fellow citizens. He hadn't had a raise in ten years.

The scheme was this: bus drivers from all over central Louisiana came to Cutpine to get a safety sticker, because they knew the chief would do the inspection with one eye half open. He made a little from the inspections themselves, but his profit came from the obligatory incentive to squint when necessary. Drivers knew to leave the payment—cash only—under the chief's outdated desk-pad calendar.

Now he was in lots of trouble. Some school board member horny for re-election was swinging her moral ax, and Emery's enterprise was the vice she was determined to shatter. He really didn't have time for sleuthing.

Sheriff Big John Higbee felt like whistling the theme from *The Andy Griffith Show* every time he spent a few minutes with Police Chief Emery Rud, as he was doing this afternoon, accompanied by Lieutenant Ray Doyle Sprague, his chief of detectives. Sprague had promise—a towheaded country boy proud of his mostly peach fuzz mustache, reluctant to get tough with people he'd known all his life.

The three men sat in the office of Emery's service station, enjoying cans of soda. Big John had paid for all three. The customer bell clanged as a vehicle rolled across the black hose by the pumps. Emery hollered, "Luther!", and eventually a surly young man with slicked back hair sauntered from the garage in filthy overalls.

Emery had no love for Native or African Americans, Big John knew. The police chief was renowned for his repertoire of racist jokes, and among friends he'd always referred insultingly to the Katogoula as *sabines*, *redbones*, *griffes*, or *zambos*. Sheriff Higbee, only partly out of professional courtesy, a few days before had delivered the summons for Emery to appear in district criminal court in Armageddon. Payback like that doesn't come along every day.

Big John hoped to get a lead from Emery. Many Katogoula lived in the city limits of Cutpine; and if the killer was a member of the tribe, or someone else with a grudge against them, Emery just might have picked up some loose talk while adjusting a fan belt. The sheriff knew that most criminals have a compulsion to blab or brag about their crimes.

But Emery had nothing helpful to say about the murder of Carl Shawe, the arson at the museum, the resulting deaths of Grace and Irton Dusong, and the assaults on the Shawe twins and the genealogist. Big John had another unsolved case: a troublemaker by the name of Travis Corbett had been reported missing. A regular crime wave, something you'd see in New Orleans or Shreveport, not around here.

The Sangfleuve Parish DA demanded action. Big John wanted answers, too. Emery was more worried about his upcoming hearing before the State Police inspection-sticker committee. He showed Big John various administrative orders to appear in Baton Rouge, and picked his nose with a greasy finger while the sheriff explained what was expected of him.

◙

After the fruitless meeting with the police chief of Cutpine, Sheriff Higbee and Lt. Sprague drove out of the sleepy town, onto the highway leading past closed Tadbull Mill, and along the privately owned enclaves of planted or harvested fields carved out of Tchekalaya Forest. Mostly Katogoula small farms, traditional lands occupied long before the arrival of the European powers. It was cotton-picking time. Soybeans and corn had already been harvested. Sugar cane was ready for cutting. Pecans were just popping out of their big green cases.

Big John hoped the fall harvest would be a good one. The idea of serving foreclosure papers on Katogoula farmers who'd lost their main source of income—Tadbull Mill—saddened him. Though a casino in the parish would inevitably bring more bankruptcies, broken marriages, and petty crime, he wished the Katogoula could get their act together.

Fall so far had been fairly pleasant, with no killer hurricanes charging up from the Antilles. Now the days were reliably below eighty and the nights getting into the low fifties. The early teal season had already closed. Real hunting weather only a duck and duck hunter could love—gray, rainy, and cold—was just a few weeks away. Football weather. He would never forget the cheers from the bleachers of floodlit podunk ball fields on cool November nights....

Uninterrupted dense pine forest hugged the road here. Big John tuned out Ray Doyle, who hadn't stopped blabbing about the forensics conference he'd just attended. He was all fired up, which, Big John, reflected, was a pretty good reason to send someone.

He was heading to the scenes of the crimes, Lake Katogoula and the remains of the museum, hoping to put Ray Doyle's enthusiasm to use, to discover some new angle for investigation. Later he would send Ray Doyle and his other detectives to canvass the Katogoula again. As an experienced lawman, Big John knew that changes in stories often broke cases. A second or third visit from a detective usually riled people and sometimes goaded perpetrators into incriminating admissions. Interviewing was an art; Lt. Sprague would have to get over his excessive politeness if he wanted to solve crimes outside of textbooks and seminars.

Big John had the cruise control at fifty. With a lot on his mind, and nothing for miles ahead, he didn't register the movement at the verge of the forest for a split second. Before the thought activated his muscles, he realized what was happening: an animal, a large one, breaking from the trees, heading fast for his lane. Too fast.

"Hold on, Ray Doyle!"

Big John stomped the brake pedal to the floor with both huge feet. Tires screamed and smoked. Even so, the ABS on the big cruiser wasn't going to stop him in time. The animal entered his lane. There was nothing to do but grip the steering wheel and pray for the animal's soul, if it had one.

He felt the sickening thud. The windshield shattered but remained intact.

"Gawd! what the—" was all Ray Doyle could say before the air bags inflated with loud pops like gunshots and then several milliseconds later deflated.

A dark-yellow blur had glanced off the bumper and the passenger-side windshield, over the car, heavily onto the trunk, and then had disappeared.

The car skidded to stop after what seemed like years. Big John looked over at Ray Doyle: he was all right except for blood running into his precious mustache. The young man had already switched on the interior emergency lights and now spoke to the dispatcher on the radio, dabbing at his nose with a tissue.

This boy might make it after all, Big John was thinking as he grabbed the shotgun, heaved himself out of the car, and looked back at the thing that lay on the faded centerline.

The road was quiet. No other vehicle in sight. Big John jogged the hundred and fifty feet to the heap of mangled fur. No sense letting the poor thing suffer.

He slowed about six feet from the animal, holding the shotgun at hip level, ready to end the misery or to protect himself if it suddenly attacked him in its dying pain. He could see that it was still breathing. Blood had started to fill a pothole.

Now his own breath left him. It looked like a cougar—but the strangest one he'd ever seen. The skin and fur seemed to have come off the body. Had the impact literally skinned the beast?

And then it moaned. *A human moan!*

Big John knelt down and warily, gingerly pulled the cougar's head away, and then the rest of the skin. It was a costume, a damn hokey costume, at that!

Below was a sweat-drenched, bloodied young man, with black hair and the complexion of an Indian. Although the man's mouth was a red mess, Big John could see that he wore braces. Probably late teens or early twenties. He didn't recognize the victim as Katogoula, who in general were indistinguishable from whites.

He made a quick inventory of the obvious injuries: facial and oral damage, both legs broken, an arm, too. Then he ran through the scary possibilities: concussion, broken hip, broken back, organ injuries. Most of the visible bleeding came from the left leg, where the tibia had punctured the skin. That, at least, he could do something about.

Running back to his car, Big John traded the shotgun for a comprehensive first-aid kit and some flares. The victim was feeling what had happened to him by the time the sheriff returned and set two flares out; his moaning was low and constant, pitiful. Big John worked skillfully to stop the bleeding. The splint he made for the leg satisfied him. Shock was a danger now. He called to Ray Doyle for blankets.

And then he noticed, in the back pocket of the boy's jeans, a crumpled, leaking can of lighter fluid. Big John removed it and set it aside.

The boy kept looking at the forest edge, stark fear on his dazed face. As if something horrible were pursuing him, he tried to crawl away.

"It's okay, now, son." Big John held him down effortlessly and spoke in a calming tone. "Ambulance is coming. Everything's gonna be fine, you hear? What's your name? Can you tell me your name, son."

The boy kept repeating Chief Claude's name. "You ain't Chief Claude, son.... Is he the one you want me to call? Is that it?"

"Chief. Yes. Oh! Oh! Hurts..."

"Yeah, I expect it does. You took a bad thumping, there. What's your name, son? Can you tell me?"

"Stu—" he coughed, spluttering blood, crying now from the pain. "Stu George. I saw it. The real one! Eating a man! The real one!"

Lt. Sprague put a blanket under the boy's head and another over his torso.

When Big John had done what he could to quieten Stu George, he stood up and forced his mind into detective mode through the fading adrenaline rush. Biting his lower lip, tasting his sweat, he critically took in the scene.

His eyes traced the probable path of the victim. Was this just a young idiot drawn to mischief by the press reports, or had he been running from someone else, there, where the grassy shoulder of the highway met the dense tree line?

The real one. The tribe had been upset by reported sightings of the mythical cougar. Maybe it wasn't a myth, after all. What was it that had forced Stu George to run heedlessly in front of a moving car? The boy was terrified, even now.

Lt. Sprague, standing next to him now, said: "This costume, Sheriff. Got me thinking. The twins, only eyewitnesses we got, say a cougar attacked them. Cougar that acted mighty funny. Walked upright. We found cougar signs where Carl was killed. And that lighter fluid the boy had. The museum fire. You think maybe we done run down our killer?"

"I think we just stopped another murder. You get some men in there," Big John said, pointing to Tchekalaya Forest. "And be quick about it. There's more to this than a boy in a cougar suit."

◻

Big John, cradling his old Ithaca 12-guage pump, moved with watchful speed through the pines and light underbrush. He hadn't waited for more men to find out what Stu George had been fleeing. The killer was close. He could feel it.

This was state forest, a beautiful testament to intelligent natural resource management. Big John marveled at the tall longleafs, just as he did every time he hunted in these woods. The trees had spaced themselves in a natural orderly pattern older than civilization, older than human beings, who had turned the clock back for the longleafs through science and public policy.

Forests still covered half of Louisiana, and trees were the state's number one crop. Tchekalaya Forest was famous for its restored longleaf stands, though in some less intensively managed areas loblolly and slash pines predominated. With prescribed burns in the spring, Nooj and his fellow agents and foresters cleared out faster growing bushes and trees that could fuel major, devastating fires.

Even deliberately set, strictly controlled fires were something else, Big John remembered. Surreal, hellish. The fire starters would walk down roads with diesel or kerosene and gasoline in fuel cans, dripping fire that soon clawed through the tangled understory. Turpentine-sharp smoke billowed up, dimming the sun to a peculiar orange color and causing a noticeable drop in the temperature.

How they kept those fires from raging out of control was beyond him. Had something to do with backfires, firebreaks, plowed borders, and the longleaf's resistance to natural, lightning-kindled fires.

Yep, this forest was another world, Big John reflected, walking beneath a squirrel chattering maniacally; here, the laws of man must yield to a more ancient way. We may think we have it all hemmed in and prettified, but we're just kidding ourselves. There was something here, something violent and unpredictable and elemental, that laughed at laws, roads, and prescribed burns. He'd seen it in people, too, for instance when some formerly peaceable dude snapped and shot everybody in his family, including the dog and the icebox on the porch full of Budweiser. You just never know when it's going to happen. We're all at its mercy.

Different language here, too, the language of silence, that really wasn't silence. What's it saying? Made the hairs stand up on your arms.

But at first glance, if you didn't think too hard, the forest *was* beautiful, benign on the surface. Hard to believe that this thriving ecosystem had not always been here, that this area at the turn of the twentieth century had looked like the site of an asteroid impact, clear-cut of every tree. Now there was a delicate but healthy truce that benefited the whole community: loggers could harvest trees, hunters could pursue their traditional pastime, and environmentalists could savor victory on behalf of dozens of saved species.

What would happen to this truce when the Katogoula started reclaiming their rights, set up their reservation, which would surely take in some forest land they presently owned and leased to the state? Would they allow public hunting? What about logging and tourism? He'd heard stories of tribes suing for hundreds of thousands of ancestral acres wrongfully taken, and winning goodly portions.

Big John wondered ruefully if central Louisiana was about to become a battlefield over the complex issues born of Katogoula recognition. The Civil War had never ended around here; all he needed was another one. National interest groups seemingly of every stripe had put this area on their radar screens. He could see it now, disaster waiting to happen: demonstrations, spiked trees, human blockades, bloodshed, network news crews intoning judgment…he desperately needed to solve these damn murders, get back to doing positive things, nip that kind of trouble in the bud. He was justly regarded across the parish as a superb referee and negotiator of problems before they required the solutions of the courts, or of the gun.

The forest floor had begun to rise slightly, and the composition of the woods subtly changed; fewer pines, more hardwoods. He was probably on Tadbull land, now.

The sheriff knew something was wrong as soon as he stepped from the dense woods into the clearing. A flock of crows vied noisily around one of the old burial mounds. He saw more cautious turkey vultures circling overhead on the thermals. The opportunistic crows wheeled and darted and cawed in a frenzied competition for something that even from this distance the sheriff could smell. Something large and dead.

The full sun was hot, and he felt every year and every pound as he strode rapidly across the grassy meadow, scanning for any suspicious movement. The Shawe twins had been attacked near here.

He stopped as soon as he saw the charred designs in the dry grass. *They were letters!* One row about three feet tall, the shorter one below it twice that:

CASI

NO

Touching a finger to the black grass, sniffing, he concluded the letters had been burned very recently. Was that lighter fluid he smelled? He glanced at the patient vultures circling in the hazy blue sky. You could probably see this from ten-thousand feet up. Somehow, word would have gotten around about this strange telegram to the tribe at this remote but sacred place. A turboprop puddle-jumper on the way to Dallas, Houston, or Atlanta, an A-10 from Barksdale Air Force Base, a forestry plane, or a crop duster would have spotted it soon enough.

Big John concentrated now on the mounds. The crows watched him but kept on tearing at the carcass. He fired off a shell into the ground a few feet ahead, pumped a new one into the chamber, fired, pumped again. The black birds scattered, suddenly quiet, yielding to the superior predator. After the sound of the shots ceased reverberating around the meadow, nothing seemed to move.

He stepped around the letters to approach the mound.

The clothed body of a large man, an atlatl spear through his chest, hung from the trunk of a gnarled oak; sneakers just touched the ground. This spear looked longer than the one that got Carl Shawe.

Big John had a sickening feeling he recognized the build, in spite of the decomposition, bloating, and damage done by the birds. This was no recent death, but the crucifying—if you could call it that—seemed a recent act. The body seemed to have been buried; the clothes and hair and skin were caked with dirt.

He climbed the mound. Travis Corbett. Had to be. The bark of the old oak tree was scarred and scraped on either side of the body, as if by some sharp-clawed animal. No question about it: the killer of Carl Shawe had struck again. All in all, about the strangest thing he'd ever seen.

He gagged, struggling to hold down lunch. "My Lord! What did you get yourself into, Travis?"

Big John called in on his radio. He gave rapid-fire instructions, starting the well-oiled machinery for processing a murder scene.

Chapter 30

"Did you hear gunshots?" Nick stopped on the Golden Trace.

"This isn't New Orleans," Holly chided. "Don't be so jumpy on such a gorgeous day. Hunting season, remember? It's perfectly legal to blast all those cute little squirrels and rabbits and doves.... Exercise! Fresh air! Sunlight! Move it, buster!" she commanded over her shoulder.

With drill sergeants who looked like her, the armed services would be shooing recruits away.

Plaid flannel shirt tied around her waist, skimpy sleeveless T-shirt hanging untucked, flapping up now and then to show the muscular slopes of her lower back, cutoff jeans like a second skin.

She noticed he was staring and smiled. Was there a note of sadness and regret in that brief glance?

Get over yourself, Herald, as Shelvin would say. She loves Wooty. End of story.

They followed the old Katogoula hunting and trading trail winding through the towering pines, a comfortable six feet at its usual width. In the thirties, the Civilian Conservation Corps had made the path accessible to city slickers like him. Dusty red earth, pine needles, deciduous leaves. An easy hike, if you kept an eye out for the rock-hard pine roots, huge rusty fingers of a subterranean beast groping across the path to twist an ankle of the unwary. Railroad ties formed steps where the forest floor occasionally rose or fell precipitously; concrete-and-boulder bridges marked "CCC-1938" traversed small bayous. The Louisiana

Office of Forestry was doing a creditable job of keeping the place up. Nick was tempted to revise his low opinion of bureaucrats.

"*Tcheyak* means 'pine,' and *falaia* means 'long or tall.'" Holly had been trying to teach him the elements of Mobilian Jargon. "Tchekalaya, 'tall pine forest.' In sentences, word order expressed grammatical function. Object-subject-verb was the usual form. So, you'd say, 'Forest tall we go.' Simple, really."

"If you ask me, the Katogoula were better at war than language. They whipped every enemy around but surrendered their native tongue without a fight."

"How disgustingly chauvinistic and unicultural. Just what I'd expect from a politically incorrect boor like you." She stopped and squirted water from a plastic bottle into her mouth. "A broader-minded person would say they showed commendable adaptation to changing circumstances."

"Let's get to the cemetery," Nick said, passing her, "so I can listen to my favorite rabid talk show on the radio I brought."

She squirted him. "You didn't bring a radio. I'm the pack mule of the expedition, so I ought to know. Here, give me your sling, if you're not using it. You're going to strangle yourself."

He slipped it off and she stowed it in her backpack. Then she offered the bottle to him; he squeezed his mouth full of cool water several times. Holly, the consummate organizer, had a backpack with a cold pouch.

His ribs and face ached from the beating two days before at the *Crescent Luck*, but, oddly, his arm and shoulder felt almost normal. Holly was right: the exercise *was* doing him good, spreading warmth throughout him, soothing even the more recent pain. His body was repairing itself, obeying a recuperative power beyond his comprehension or control that was built into the very structure of things, like the renewing forces keeping the forest alive.

Evil, too, was built into the structure of things, according to the ancient Katogoula beliefs. And when evil was loosed on the tribe, only someone granted special power from the spirit world could restore the balance.

Did he have that power? He wasn't sure. If he did, it would manifest itself in the same process he followed in his genealogical work: examine sources, identify evidence, prove hypotheses as facts—and sometimes, wing it.

Nick had asked Nooj for the promised tour of the old Katogoula cemetery in the forest, but the wildlife agent said he had other duties. Hunting season was almost in full swing; licenses needed to be checked, kills counted, violators ticketed, usage fees collected. Sounded reasonable, but Nick couldn't shake the idea that Nooj was avoiding him until he gave up and returned to New Orleans for good.

The cemetery wasn't indicated as a feature on public maps, because the tribe discouraged tourism there. That morning at Three Sisters Pantry, Miss Luevie, too, had snubbed him. She'd refused even to leave the kitchen to see Nick and Holly as they ate breakfast; Royce Silsby gave them the map, apologizing quietly for his wife's stubborn temper. Tommy Shawe was tied up with a guiding job that day, a couple of rich men from Texas who'd bow-hunted deer regularly with Carl, his late brother.

Nick's last legitimate genealogical excuse for remaining here was this visit to the old Katogoula cemetery; he'd gathered all the information from local sources he would need to complete his tribal history and the stories of the six core families. This considerable mass of work, he felt sure, the tribe would compensate him for, if only out of a sense of fair play; and certainly once they saw the impressive presentation Hawty would produce using the professional-grade publishing programs she kept adding to the fairly new but already outdated office computer. And then, unless Tommy became chief again, the Katogoula would be through with him, and he would have to take Hawty's advice: leave the detective work to Sheriff Higbee.

Any genealogist worth his salt bravely confronts the unknown every day. He is obsessed by it, even in his dreams; with an emotional masochism he returns to the arena to face it, over and over, only certain that he can never prevail, and at best fight it to a draw. Until he knows *exactly* who did what, when and where, beyond the shadow of doubt, he'll carry each impossible gap, in an individual life or a family's story, with him as if it were his wounded comrade.

Nick couldn't give up or stop theorizing about suspects and motives, even though it wasn't in his best interests, even though snooping around had already proved nearly fatal.

"We're almost to the branching of the trace." Holly was studying the single copied sheet they'd picked up from Three Sisters Pantry. "Too bad Nooj didn't come. I wanted to see your famous interrogation methods at work."

"Yeah, too bad," Nick said, eyeing the faint and, to him, indecipherable map. "You sure you know where we're going?"

"Of course I do," Holly replied indignantly. "Only about two kilometers now…or is that miles?" The map went back in her jeans pocket. She was off again.

A few minutes later she shouted back to him, "There it is!" She plunged down one of three indistinct paths that meandered into the thick shady woods, shot through with shifting spears of afternoon sunlight. "I think," Nick heard her add as the trees swallowed her.

◫

"Not the easiest place to find," she said.

"Maybe that's the point."

For the next few minutes they stood without speaking. It was a serene place, alive with secrets. Nick had visited other holy sites, natural or man-made: Delphi, Jerusalem, Rome, Tikal, Stonehenge, Giza…where he'd also felt this indefinable wonderment, the invisible tug of transcendence, like a subtle physical force you don't notice until you isolate it from the background buzz of sensation.

A woodpecker's staccato laugh rattled from somewhere deep in the sighing shadows of the scaly pines. Sunlight flooded down from the opening in the trees above the enclosure of grassy graves; a black iron fence surrounded the enclosure; around the roughly rectangular area was the ubiquitous pine straw; and then trees forming a ragged, encroaching circle about two hundred feet in diameter

Nick thought of an auburn-haired Katogoula goddess, with eyes of radiant green, forever holding the reflection of her returned children in a loving, unblinking gaze.

Holly unharnessed herself from the backpack. "I could rest in peace here," she said, her voice dreamy and distant.

Were the two redheaded, green-eyed goddesses communicating in some silent way? Confirmed skeptic that he was, Nick nevertheless felt the modern certainty of what was magical and what was real beginning to slip away. More vividly than ever before, he understood what the Katogoula were feeling, sitting atop the long-slumbering dragon of their mythology as it shook itself awake.

Snap out of it, pal! Hard facts, that's what you need. Before you start seeing mythical cougars and sacramental deer!

"What are we looking for?" Holly asked, flexing her shoulders and rotating her neck.

"Everything. Genealogists get excited about going to cemeteries. One of the high points of a research trip. You never know what you may find."

"Okay, if you say so. I was here a few weeks ago for Carl's funeral. Touching. They put sand on the grave and corn seed in little packets of foil. But everybody was looking at everybody else, like, 'Was it you who killed him?'"

Nick mentioned that he'd visited the church in Cutpine that served the Katogoula and other Catholics in the area. The church had a nice, quaint graveyard; but now the parishioners used a commercial cemetery a few miles from town. Carl's burial here in the forest signified the tribe's tacit admission that part of the old identity had to perish for a new one to survive. The ancient ways of living off the land were lost to all but the sociopath, a throwback like Carl.

"I used the Cutpine church's graveyard in the documentary," Holly said. "Remember? The shot of the green corn ear placed on the old cross headstone? I thought that was a pretty good symbol of the cultural mix. But I sure would love to work this place in somewhere." Her eyes swept the area with a director's alertness to cinematic possibilities. "It's so beautiful, without all the people—well, living people, anyway.... I only brought my still camera today; you think they'd let me come back and shoot some video?"

"I doubt it. Royce asked us not to take any pictures at all." Nick unzipped the backpack and found his notebook. He took out a Fig Newton bar. "Want one?"

"I'll take an apple, though."

He found one a bit deeper in the backpack and then tossed it to her. She snagged the apple one handed.

"It's fairly common to find multiple cemeteries for a group of people living in one place for a long time," he said. "There might be a family graveyard on ancestral property, and the family sells it; burial then is done somewhere else. Congregations split or merge, families, too, which is why you'll sometimes find members of the same family in cemeteries miles away. Graves and whole cemeteries get relocated. Or plowed under."

"I had no idea it could be so complicated. Just when you think, okay, now I know where they all lived and died, they're all over the place. Genealogy's like blindman's bluff. You know the answers are close, but you have to grab them and make them sing out."

She chomped on her apple and moved toward the green enclosure of graves.

Nick, meanwhile, walked the perimeter of the iron-spear fencing, counting his steps. "First thing is to measure, get an overview...ninety-eight, ninety-nine, a hundred...." He counted a few more feet to a corner; then he stepped off another side. "One hundred nine by eighty-seven," he said, writing. Now he moved inside the glossy black fence, through a gate that opened without a squeak.

The place was well tended. The Katogoula had not forgotten their dead.

Holly followed him in. Squatting down to read a headstone, she said, "Oh, Nick! Look at this one. It's so neat..."

"Wait a second. Not so fast. If you get sidetracked by the first thing that catches your interest, you'll never get anything done, or remember anything later, when you need it. Come take a look."

"Yes, teacher. Do I have to scrub the blackboards after class."

Advice he himself rarely followed; he could spend an entire day in a courthouse or a library, happily browsing through material that had nothing to do with the project at hand.

He was sketching the aisles and sections of the cemetery. Holly watched him, inches away.

She bit into her apple viciously. He could tell she was peeved, hated to be corrected. She reminded him of Hawty: headstrong, precocious, like students he'd taught who couldn't wait to match wits with the most difficult writers, who propelled the class at a pace too fast for the lesser intellects, prodigies who kept the professor from fuzzy thinking and dumbed-down compromise.

Suddenly, he felt an almost overwhelming compulsion to touch her, kiss her, squeeze her, roll the bouquet of her skin across his tongue, tumble with her in the soft, thick grass, wallow in her scents and juices, dive into the ecstatic depths of her ocean, worship at her altar...but he kept writing.

She finished the apple and threw it into the trees with a fast underhand pitch.

"Pan-Hellenic softball at LSU," she said, in answer to Nick's look of astonishment at her unexpected skill. "Our sorority won, four years straight."

He finished the sketch and then told her of the wealth of clues an old graveyard could provide.

The positioning and composition of memorials might suggest ancestral nationality; Germans, Poles, and Scandinavians, for example, placed their markers in distinctive ways. Sometimes the original Old World spelling of a name was on a headstone or in a sexton's records, crucial because census takers garbled foreign names. On badly eroded markers, the date could often be inferred from the style, which changed according to public taste. Inscriptions, designs, workmanship, layout, upkeep…such subtle indicators might provide important leads lacking in printed sources.

"A gravestone can sometimes tell you more than a census," Nick said. "Or even courthouse records." He bent down, brushed some lichen away from a sandstone slab. "For a nineteenth-century woman like this one, it may be the only written record of her existence. Who was she? What was her maiden name? Did she have special talents? What did she believe in? What was her financial situation? Who's buried nearby? Who loved her, missed her after she died?"

Holly no longer pouted; she was hooked on the secrets of cemeteries. "Have you heard of those computer programs forensic anthropologists use?" she asked. "You know, the ones that build the victim layer by layer, until you can see what she looked like alive. That's what you do, isn't it, sort of, with all these scattered facts?"

Nick slowly nodded. What a pity he'd lost her. For a moment, he pictured them lecturing together at genealogical conferences, all eyes drawn to her mesmerizing beauty instead of her slide show. What a pleasant change she would have been from the normal female contingent, which, to be charitable, was generally a more mature bunch.

"Get a pad and pencil," he said. "Help me transcribe these stones."

"Hasn't that been done yet, after all these years?"

"Not that I can find. I've checked around. There's no printed source for this cemetery. Thousands of cemeteries around the country are in the same boat. The priest at the church can't even locate the old burial records. But he did tell me the Katogoula had an older church here. So, it seems we're about to break new ground."

"Har-har," she said, returning with a yellow legal pad. "Oh boy, you genealogists are real riots. Next you'll tell me you dig up remains for those really, really difficult cases, for jewelry and DNA, whatever. Oh, please! Like I'm that gullible." She held her pencil poised over the yellow pad. "Where do I start?"

Nick didn't think it necessary to say he'd tried a bit of unsanctioned archaeology and other unorthodox—not to mention unlawful—strategies in the quest for genealogical truth.

About an hour later, they'd documented one hundred sixty-three headstones. There were eighteen unmarked sunken areas, most of them two or three feet in length, indicating unnamed children, or stranger burials. Nick had once seen a small grave for a man's severed arm, and one for a woman's prize recipes, which she'd vowed to take with her when she died.

回

"What is it?" Holly put a warm hand at the back of his neck. "Are you all right?"

"Yeah, I, uh…" he managed to get out. He swallowed with difficulty and cleared his throat. "Just feeling a little chilled."

He dropped to his knees to read an unpolished, weathered marble headstone:

Adolicia Hastard Coux

Gray Wing, Our Dear Birdie
Beloved Mother, Wife, Daughter, Wise Woman
Born: 1838 Died: June 18, 1951

Above the name were two chipped hands, barely distinguishable, the fingers seemingly interwoven in some ritual placement he'd never seen before.

Countless facts, past and present, which had swirled around him in a funnel cloud of randomness, now settled before him, individual grains taking their ordained places in a marvelous sand painting. He was no longer looking at a memorial headstone carving, darkened and damaged by time, the elements, and perhaps human effort. He saw instead the hands on the stair railing at the courthouse, the day someone tried to kill him; and the hands in Grandfather Tadbull's drawings hidden away in the attic; the sand shifted to reveal the hands of Luevenia Silsby, the first time he met her at Three Sisters Pantry; and again it shifted, becoming Luevenia's hands offering cash in front of the smoldering Katogoula museum.

And then the magic sand painting blew away as phantasmagorically as it had formed. He was back in the illusory peace of Tchekalaya Forest, a strange clarity allowing his mind to peer into depths of the past. As if old Gray Wing herself had cured him of doubt and confusion.

Nick never forgot a name—for very long. Coux was the maiden name of Luevenia Silsby's grandmother, Adolicia's daughter; it was the name blotted out on the back of Grandfather Tadbull's drawing. Adolicia Coux, known as Birdie and Gray Wing, whose hands were the subject of that drawing, was Luevenia's great-grandmother on her mother's side. And the small French Bible from the attic of Tadbull Hall established Adolicia's link to the hereditary Vulture Cult line.

Long Black Feather, Black Wing, Gray Wing...*Little Wing*. Luevenia Silsby was Little Wing! Even long after the adoption of Western naming ways, private Katogoula names were given at birth. Luevenia would have received one. Adolicia's great-granddaughter could well be of Luevenia Silby's age. Luevenia had no sisters, but Adolicia might have had many other great-granddaughters....

His hunch had to be right; more things fit than didn't as a result. Luevenia *was* Little Wing, and the Bible had belonged to her, at one time. A gift from her great-grandmother. Two questions occurred to him again: what was it doing up in the attic of Tadbull House, and how long had it been there?

Great-grandmother Adolicia/Gray Wing/Birdie had written the dedication in the old French Bible to remind her great-grandchild of the family's distinguished Vulture Cult heritage. Luevenia could possibly be the last living standard-bearer of a noble line. Did she remember and realize the significance? And if not, how would she take it?

But she does know, and she fears unmasking!

Contemporary Katogoula didn't look at this aspect of their ancestry with pride. They had a new, updated religion with its own wonders—Catholicism leavened with the most durable and generally most wholesome aspects of Katogoula beliefs. Their culture had mutated into a hybrid species. The Vulture Cult was the senile old relative who touched himself and slobbered in public—an aspect laughable, unsavory, unheroic, even horrifying, not part of the rehabilitated past.

"You found something, didn't you?" Holly asked, now down beside him, in a catcher's squat. "Something important. Is that why you have that cute stupid grin on your face?"

"This, lovely Holly, was Luevenia Silsby's great-grandmother, herself the great-granddaughter of maybe the last high priest of the Vulture Cult."

"Wow!"

He sprang up, ignoring small stitches of pain, and tried to walk off some of his excitement. "We've just awakened the dead, and they have tales to tell. Listen. This is what I hear."

When he'd finished his rapid-fire scenario five minutes later she said, "You're crazy. Are you really telling me that shame over Vulture Cult heritage drove Miss Luevie to...?" She shook her head. "No way. That sweet, sweet woman?"

"Hey, all I'm saying is, it's something to think about. I hope it's not true. If you have a better idea—"

She wasn't about to admit she didn't. "*I refuse to think of my friends as murderers. It's crazy, just crazy!* Falling down the stairs dented your good sense, obviously. Nick, listen to me." She was up now, too, standing before him, his father's well-worn gabardine Army dress shirt bunched up in her hands.

"This made it through WWII," he said. "I'd hate to lose it now."

"Oh. Sorry." She let go of his shirt. "Miss Luevie's no murderer. I know her. I've spent months with her. She's one of the kindest, most principled people I know." But suspicion had crept into her green eyes, and she grudgingly made room for it. She forced herself to add: "Generous, well adjusted."

Nick said, "At the museum, you told me the Katogoula always held mixed feelings about the Vulture Cult. Her reasons for keeping this heritage quiet may never make sense to us. Is it vanity, fear of social ostracism, a concern for her business? The irrational needs very little, if any, justification."

"Okay. I'm just giving you the benefit of the doubt here. Why Carl? You at the courthouse and the Dusongs at the museum I can see. You're digging in the past, and the Dusongs were preserving it. All of you could have stumbled on a clue that would have exposed her...like you apparently did today, here. And how did she do it? She's a frail little lady."

"I don't know about that. She's on her feet twelve hours and more a day. And there's a lot of elbow grease expended in that kitchen of hers. How frail is that?"

"Well," Holly began, searching for some contradictory fact, "why don't the others already know Adolicia was Luevenia's great-grandmother?"

"What's the name of your best friend's great-grandmother? And I don't mean Wooty. Quick."

"Hmmm. I see what you mean."

"Look at these sculpted hands," Nick said, indicating the headstone. "I doubt anyone today connects them with Vulture Cult heritage. No one knows very much about it. Like most people, they've been more concerned with the grocery bill than extinct customs. What they do know is pretty much guesswork."

"Maybe this Adolicia woman wasn't closely related. If she died in 1951—which would have made her awfully old, by the way—shouldn't she be buried with the rest of Miss Luevie's family, over at the Cutpine church? Coux. I bet that's a common name."

Nick touched the grass of the grave on the right. "This is probably her husband." The headstone was all but illegible. "They probably bought adjacent plots. He died decades before, in the 1880s, from the look of this marker. Of course, I'll have to try to verify who this woman was, and look into those unusual dates, but…are you hungry?"

She was mauling a pickled peach, her hands and chin slathered in syrupy juice. "Starved. I can't listen to any more of your ridiculous ideas on an empty stomach. No more work from me until I get my fill of fried chicken and potato salad."

"Hey, as I recall, you transcribed those names and dates like a veteran genealogist. Ever consider joining our merry band? I'll teach you the secret handshake."

"If it means hanging around cemeteries and accusing innocent people of murder, no thanks." She wound up an underhand pitch, and sent the peach pit into a tangled mass of underbrush, a few yards into the trees.

With a chime, the pit slammed into something solid beneath the vines.

"What was that?"

"A piece of the old church?" Nick suggested. "Sounded like stone in there."

"Let's find out!" Holly charged into the shadowy woods, hungry for something else now.

Chapter 31

They tore through thorny vines, tough saplings, and fallen branches, all of which formed a matted, shoulder-high clump the size of a small church's altar. Blood and sweat and squashed mosquitoes smeared their scratched arms. Raised, pink tracks of fingernails marked Holly's sun-toasted legs. The scent of fresh blood drew more mosquitoes wiser in the ways of tormenting them.

Nick imagined he could already feel the runny rash of poison ivy, and the swollen welts from ant, red bug, and tick bites—hazards of cemetery research, and the reasons why he always wore long pants and high-top shoes, and brought several pairs of gardening gloves. Holly, in her lust to tear into the mysterious tangle, at first had laughed at his pants tucked into his socks and scoffed at his insistence on wearing gloves. Now she understood.

It was hot, dirty, hard work, and Nick's mind kept replaying lines from Yvor Winters' poem "Sir Gawaine and the Green Knight," warning of the dangerous seductiveness of the physical world, in the form of a beautiful forest spirit who transforms herself at will to snare those unwise enough to wander into her savage net.

Something moved abruptly, noisily within the foliage. Holly, closer to the movement, uttered a cry of warning and jumped back, into Nick's chest. For a lingering instant he buried his face in her hair. The heat and smell of her were intoxicating. He forgot about the murders, the Vulture Cult, the Spanish *Legajos de Luisiana*, the French clerk's account, the

Bible from the attic of Tadbull Hall, the flashes along the lakeshore, and whatever it was that had startled her.

"A snake," she said through the slow, deep breaths of an athlete. She gently pulled away, averted eyes aware of her effect on Nick and maybe of an equally powerful urge she was having difficulty suppressing. She wiped away a sweat-soaked wisp of hair from her forehead with the cuff of one glove. Then she picked up a stick and stirred an area of underbrush. A fat snake made a break for it, slithering rapidly away.

"Copperhead," she said, with complete equanimity.

Nick wasn't so calm. "Kill it!"

"It's just as scared of us." She tossed the stick away. "Would you rather have a thousand rats around? Predators and death are facts of nature."

"Hey, I'm all for natural balance, as long as mankind is part of the equation. I may not have the bumper stickers to prove it, but I'm a liberaltarian."

"That means"—two handfuls of stubborn foliage finally gave way to her determined yanking—"you get to do whatever the hell you want and feel good about it, huh?"

"That's about right. Having an active ecological conscience is fine by me, as long as it doesn't get me killed." Nick cast a worried glance at the spot where he thought the snake had entered another area of dense undergrowth. "I wonder what balance our murderer wants to maintain."

"The murderer's a human being," Holly said. "We traded in our instincts for self-awareness. Our motives aren't controlled by nature anymore. The snake has no choice. Call me radical environmentalist or whatever if you want, but that doesn't make me a wimp. I wouldn't hesitate to defend myself against a man—or a woman—who should know better." She put her weight against another wiry mass in her hands. Vines twanged and snapped and whipped about. She staggered backward. "Are you going to stand there and yak all day or can you give me some help here?"

"Timber!" he shouted, grabbing a hank of knotted forest entrails, letting his good left side handle most of the heavy lifting. He hoped she was right: that the killer *was* a human being, who could be fought with a big enough stick. A poisonous snake or a deranged killer he could handle. *But an angry spirit? No thanks!*

After a few more minutes of work, they were able to see vertical stone slabs, regularly placed to form two-and-a-half rows.

Nick said, "Doesn't look the ruins of a church to me."

"More graves."

He pushed a large rotting pine limb to the side; it fell with a thud, splitting into pieces, sending a swirl of insects and chaff into the humid air as much of the remaining underbrush went crashing over and down with it.

Holly said, "What's this cemetery doing so close to the other one?"

"I wonder. Let's get these inscriptions down first. There's no substitute for accurate written notes. What do you think, twenty, thirty graves? Why don't you start here and I'll go to the other end—"

"No way, Jose. I'm not writing down any more names or dates or anything. I'm getting my camera. Images, not words—that's what I do best."

While she went to her backpack for the camera, Nick cleared away more debris and began to read the inscriptions that were legible. She'd obviously had enough of his preaching; he decided not to harp on the fact that good old-fashioned notes from a field trip could serve as backup for genealogical information otherwise lost to a malfunctioning camera or tape recorder. So he transcribed as he read anyway, just in case the film didn't come out.

There were few surnames on the headstones in sight that he recognized. That was good: more ancestral Katogoula lines, more possibilities for living descendants, a more viable tribe with more members. The birth dates were, for the most part, in the early nineteenth century, with only a few crossing beyond the 1800 line. Death dates were all over the map, extending into the 1890s. Three generations, maybe four.

Was this where the Katogoula first started burying after they fully embraced Christianity, and ceased to bury their dead in mounds? Not a lot of graves for that amount of time, Nick thought. The dates were earlier than those of the larger cemetery, just a few yards away in the clearing—but not by much. Why two graveyards, if the time frames were roughly parallel? Could there have been some structural impediment separating them, a part of the old church, no longer here? Maybe this little graveyard held the last traditionalists, who followed the matriarchal clan-centered ways instead of the Western patriarchal family structure.

Nooj Chenerie had been wrong about finding graves no more than about a hundred years old. Nick wondered why?

Holly unzipped the protective case of the camera. She knew what she was doing. He stopped worrying about a photographic mishap.

"Our friendly wildlife agent may write us up," Nick said, ribbing her. "The tribe doesn't like tourists taking pictures of the gravestones, you know."

"We're not tourists," she replied, aiming the camera, making adjustments. "I was corrected once at another tribe's pow-wow for taping during the eagle-feather dance. They were very polite—after they took my tape."

"I've run into that a few times, myself," Nick said, ogling his companion with impunity as she fussed with the camera or ripped foliage from a headstone. "The prohibition on cameras. Some groups consider it sacrilege, some a violation of privacy; others just want to sell their cemetery lists without competition."

When Holly was satisfied with the settings, she began snapping close-up shots of individual headstones from various angles. "We'll be through here in no time," she said. "Who'll know, except the trees?"

And the dead. For Nick, the clicking of the shutter and the whirring of the auto-wind seemed a gross affront to the beauty and peace of this natural setting...a serene mirage that was a phantom of human sentimentality, a soothing human delusion masking an eternal bloody struggle. Maybe he was still a bit rattled from seeing the snake, maybe it was his long-standing distaste for technology, the merciless automaton-god worshipped nowadays, but each time the camera clattered and the film advanced, he winced.

Holly said from behind the viewfinder, "Do you always do what other people tell you?" She moved to another headstone and crouched down. "Where's your sense of adventure?"

Then she lowered the camera.

"These names," she said, still working on a half-submerged thought. "Nick, I read some of these surnames in the *Legajos de Luisiana*.... They're Quinahoa!"

He'd wandered to the end of the small graveyard. "Are you sure?"

She walked along the stones, reading them out. "Oh, absolutely! Most of them were in the *Legajos*. Spelling's not quite the same, but the Kentucky trader or the Spanish who wrote this stuff down might have screwed up the French surnames they heard. Nick, I think the people in these graves were descendants of captured Quinahoa enslaved by the Katogoula. The earliest ones maybe only a generation or two away from the big war. Wow, this is the cemetery of the slave caste!"

"That's why it's separated from the larger one," he said. "Putting on my sociologist's cap, I'd say the actual slavery and the attached stigma had long since evaporated. They'd become part of the larger Katogoula tribe, but considered themselves distinct. Maybe this isn't a place of humiliation, at that. Could it have been that the Quinahoa were still fighting for their identity, even in their burial customs?"

"Like the Katogoula in white society," Holly said, snapping shots again. "Now I *really* want this on film."

As she moved through the small graveyard recording their find, she told Nick that Indian slavery was, in major respects, unlike black slavery in the antebellum South. The Southeastern Indian culture didn't rely on a one-crop plantation system, so there was no need for massive cheap labor. Life was still relatively simple, pastoral, with communal farming and hunting. Possessions and practices promoted survival, and material luxuries weren't much of a factor, until the Europeans came. There was little real difference between the life of the slave and of the master. Slavery was more a mental construct, a matter of enhanced honor for the captor, of lost dignity for the captive. A powerful tribe could boast many slaves; and though warriors often were tortured to death, or maimed so that they couldn't escape, in time manageable slaves were treated as pets.

The Quinahoa who survived the war—some were rumored to have vanished into the forest—became Katogoula and Yaknelousa chattel; a few were probably traded to other tribes or to the whites. If the general pattern ruled, the Quinahoa served as menial laborers and artisans; some were forced into prostitution; the exceptional ones no doubt gained respect for special skills, like hunting or fishing. The passing of years, then of generations, made the distinctions less noticeable. Daily contact led to increasing familiarity and acceptance. To respect, friendship, matings. And then came the day when no one remembered who had been a slave, who a master. Finally, the truth became another legend on the tribe's dusty shelf.

Nick said, "It seems that the last to care about their glorious degrading past were the Quinahoa descendents themselves. I guess it became a matter of ethnic pride, in the end. But eventually they stopped using this graveyard. The headstone dates tell the story. Sometime before the turn of the twentieth century, they stopped thinking of themselves as separate and became Katogoula in spirit, Katogoula in death."

"Maybe they all died out," Holly said.

"Yeah, maybe." Nick stood before several partially hidden headstones fifteen feet away from her, carefully clearing lush poison ivy from them with his gloves. "These are interesting," he said, more to himself than to Holly.

"What is it?...Oh, boy, there you go again."

He stared at the headstone directly in front of him, his mouth gaping slightly, catching mosquitoes, feeling the old familiar chill of the eureka moment. He shook off his gloves and began to scribble feverishly on his yellow pad.

"Well, whatever happened," Holly said, curious now, starting to walk toward him down a line of old graves, "now they're one big happy family up in the sky somewhere."

A headstone shattered into stone splinters to the right of Nick with a loud crack like close lightning. Then another headstone fell decapitated to his left.

Stone dust filled the air. He instinctively ducked his head. "What the hell!..."

A brown streak whooshed by his face and stuck in a thick pine behind him. *An atlatl spear!* Thrown with such force that the sharp stone tip protruded from the other side of the tree.

"Run!" Holly screamed. "This way! Get out of here!"

Holly in front, they ran up the narrow path that had led them into the denser woods and to the graveyards, and then left and onto the Golden Trace again, the ancient hunter's path through the life-giving, death-concealing forest.

Now they were the hunted, and Nick felt the terror of a rat in the coils of a snake. If this was the natural order at work, survival of the fittest in action, he didn't feel nearly fit enough!

Holly was a good runner, keeping her arms close to her sides, pumping them in alternating rhythm with her stride. Somehow she'd managed to secure her camera bandoleer style; it flopped between her shoulder blades. She looked back at him and then beyond him. Fear replaced concern on her face.

Almost at his feet fat shapes exploded in every direction. Quail.

"I see...something!" she shouted. "Faster, Nick! Come on, stay with me! It's still back there!"

He felt off balance, lame like a captive, intentionally hamstrung Quinahoa warrior, his bad arm and shoulder becoming more and more of a painful hindrance. A vicious cramp burrowed below his ribs, spreading, gnawing, making his breaths come shorter and shorter. His body suddenly weighed many tons. He seemed to be walking against an undertow pulling him toward the center of the earth. Panicked, he glanced down to make sure he wasn't up to his hips in quicksand.

He'd skipped his jogging for a few weeks before his courthouse fall. A teenager could lay off for almost a month and remain in top shape; a forty-two-year-old man couldn't.

They weren't heading back the way they'd come. Nick had no idea where they were, where they were going. He thought he could hear footsteps behind him, gaining. Skilled footsteps of a hunter who knew these pine thickets, a hunter whose deadly pursuit made scarcely as much noise as a pine needle falling.

The Golden Trace made a sharp curve.

Nick looked back, grimacing in pain. He wasn't sure, but he thought he detected in the dark green-and-brown shadows a large animal in pursuit. *A cougar?*

He faced forward again, peering through the telltale tunnel vision of oxygen deprivation. Sparks fired in his peripheral vision. Holly had really turned on the speed; Nick struggled to keep up. He couldn't do this much longer.

The voice of reason upbraided him: *Fool! Coward! Stop, turn, face your enemy.* The more ancient voice of his pre-human ancestors screamed: *Run! One more step, one more step, and another one! Run! Run or die!*

Something thwacked into a tree where a moment before Holly's head had been. Seconds later Nick was even with the tree—an atlatl spear had skewered it. And then the tree was a blur as he pushed his body beyond exhaustion.

Suddenly they broke from the trees into a bright openness. A field? Nick had a vague sense that he knew this place, or had dreamed of it. The world bounced wildly as if through a shaky lens attached to his befuddled consciousness. A meadow, those rounded grassy hillocks so old they looked natural. The ancient Katogoula burial mounds, on Tadbull land!

And there are people over there. Men in uniform. Lots of them. Why? Forget it. Must make it to those men! Must make it to the mounds, must make it! Faster, faster!...

Now everything was upside down and he fell into bluebonnet immensity.

◉

When he opened his eyes, he saw an eclipse.

No, that wasn't quite it.

A large, round, dark face. Sheriff Big John Higbee, looking down at him. Holly's smaller face floated beside the sheriff's head, in the blue and yellow and white of the afternoon Louisiana sky.

Holly's head grew larger and blotted out everything else. Nick felt lips on his sweat-streaming forehead. In another moment, he realized he was flat on his back in tall, yellow grass. Something had been burning nearby, possibly the grass, he was thinking.

"We're safe now, Nick." Holly's face was even lovelier from her recent exertion. Half dreaming, half awake, Nick called up a vision of her after their lovemaking. *A week ago? God, it seems like centuries!*

"One of you men bring this man some cold Gatorade," Big John called out. And then to Nick: "Son, you better take up something safer, like alligator wrestling. This genealogy's getting to be a hazardous line of work."

Nick sat up.

"Looked like that movie with Cornel Wilde," Big John said. "What was it, *Naked Prey?* Uh-huh, just like that. I always rooted for the Africans, you know what I'm sayin'. Yep, that's what you two looked like to me. 'Cept I didn't see any Africans chasing after you. Fact, I didn't see *anyone* chasing after you. You two out for a jog?"

Holly explained what they'd been doing, and what had happened.

"Sheriff," Nick said, "you asked me to tell you if I found anything in my genealogical research pointing to a motive for murder. Today I—"

"We," Holly said.

"*We* found something important."

"Well, seeing as how you picked the middle of my crime scene for your siesta, I guess you could say you're officially part of this investigation. Give the man a hand, Ray Doyle."

"Crime scene?" Nick said, getting to his feet with the help of Holly and a young plainclothes detective.

Nick had collapsed on top of the final two letters of the puzzling protest burned into the grass. "'Casi-NO,'" he read aloud. "What does it mean?"

"He'd like to know," Big John said, pointing to the corpse being lowered from the tree. "And so would I."

"Oh, damn!" Holly said, slapping her back.

"You hurt, miss?" asked Ray Doyle, with flirtatious eagerness.

"I'm all right, Lieutenant Sprague. Thanks. It's just that I dropped my stupid camera back there in the woods."

Nick gave a drunk's loud laugh that turned into a lurching cough. When he could stand up straight again he unclenched his right hand and showed Holly the sweat-soaked ball of yellow paper he'd clutched during their flight through the forest.

Nick grinned. "See. Nothing beats good written notes." He was too weak and nauseated to gloat any more.

Holly snatched the ball of limp paper and carefully opened it. She read the inscription from the headstone Nick had transcribed just before the attack:

> Amalie Chenerie Madeul
>
> Wife of Vincent, Sr.
> Born 1835
> Died Feb. 5, 1893
>
> Sadly Do We Bid Goodbye
> But Know Her Spirit
> To Heaven Will Fly
> No More A Slave Submit.

"I really hate it when he's right," Holly said to Big John.

Chapter 32

Two mugs of coffee in his huge hands, Sheriff Higbee shut his office door with a shoe, muting the tumult of his busy staff outside. He handed Nick a mug and walked to a window.

Outside, protesters marched in antagonistic counter circles at the foot of the broad, gently rising front steps of the Sangfleuve Parish Courthouse. A live-remote truck from one of the local television stations had arrived and now the crew was setting up for a report in the six P.M. news. A sectioned aluminum pole topped by an antenna rose in slow jerks as a young technician scurried around the truck.

Otherwise, the late Friday afternoon was calm in downtown Armageddon; traffic lights changed over deserted streets.

"Yep, nothing like a few murders and the smell of cash to get the wheels of democratic dissent rolling," Big John said. He pointed to a corner of the newer combined parking garage and jail annex attached to the rear of the courthouse. "At least it'll give the prisoners something to watch besides Columbo and *COPS*.

"That marcher there, the one pumping the sign about money-changers in the temple," Big John continued, "he's the prime mover of our anti-gambling group—former gambling addict and convicted embezzler. The pro-gambling group giving him dirty looks is headed by a pawnshop owner; now, he expects to get rich from hocked family microwaves. The black man there leading his little flock is a firebrand preacher who once marched with Dr. King—so he claims; says a casino'll victimize us poor, powerless black folk, and incidentally take money out of the church till, which buys his fancy cars and clothes. And over on the side, well, that's our local white supremacist loudmouth; throws his hood into most elections. Wants a reservation for the white people. Gets about twenty votes, mostly his in-laws and cousins—far as I can tell, there's not a frog hair's difference between those two groups."

Murder was the topic of their meeting. Nick felt a bit guilty enjoying Big John's cutting analysis of the protesters. But the sheriff seemed to appreciate the cathartic value of humor, and Nick, unwinding for the first time after his wild day, didn't hesitate to laugh along. He suspected, in fact, that putting him at ease was the sheriff's intention.

Big John lowered the great bulk of his body into the oversize highback executive chair behind his desk—the desk of an important man who each day presided over a non-stop assembly line of thick files affecting many lives. "Where were we? Oh, yeah. You were dishing out some pretty powerful accusations. You say you found possible motives—and I stress *possible*—in the family histories of two upstanding citizens in my jurisdiction: Luevenia Silsby and Nugent Chenerie."

"They're both hiding something," Nick stated with assurance. "I believe I know what it is in each case."

"Let me see if I got this straight. Miss Luevie is a descendant of the Vulture Cult, the ancient caste in charge of rites for the dead, to see them on to the next world, and so forth. The Vulture Cult wasn't even originally Katogoula, you've discovered, but some tribe called Yaknelousa."

"Correct," Nick said.

"But Miss Luevie's all hung up about this, right? Doesn't want anyone to know, 'cause she thinks it might bring dishonor on her, her husband, her business, what have you. And she thinks if she scares everybody enough with all these supposedly supernatural doings that the tribe will just pull down the blinds and tell all these Nosy Parkers—like you—to skedaddle. That about sum it up for dear Miss Luevie?"

"Perfectly. I have convincing documentary evidence of her family connection to the cult. We found the crucial link in the Tchekalaya Forest cemetery, just before we were attacked. And I have reason to believe she was the one who ambushed me on the stairs."

"It's a big leap from throwing a trash can to killing someone. All right, let's move on to subject number two, then. Nooj Chenerie." Big John leaned back, cocking his massive arms behind his head. Nick thought of some huge crossbow shooting the sheriff's keen mind across the centuries of the wildlife agent's heritage. "Nooj holds some twisted allegiance to another tribe altogether. Help me out here."

"The Quinahoa," Nick said. "Around two hundred and fifty years ago, the Katogoula, allied with the Yaknelousa, defeated and enslaved the Quinahoa."

"Nooj is still pissed off about that, is he? So much so that he could be the one running around dressed up like a cougar, taking revenge for the disgrace his extinct people suffered at the hands of the other two tribes, lo those many years back. And his family has a tradition of using poisons to hunt, you say?"

Nick agreed enthusiastically, impressed that the sheriff hadn't missed a word. "Most of the Quinahoa died in the battle, along with lots of Yaknelousa. Some Quinahoa escaped into the woods, where they plotted a counterattack for a while. The captive Quinahoa were made slaves, but over time they assimilated with the other two tribes to form what the Europeans called the Katogoula Tribe.

"Nooj has Quinahoa and Katogoula ancestors on his paternal and maternal sides," Nick continued. "We found compelling evidence at the Quinahoa cemetery in the forest. A woman with the last name Madeul is buried there; she was born a Chenerie. There were other Cheneries and a few Bellarmines—his mother's family—but I didn't have time to record them. There's little question both lines of his family had Quinahoa roots; this was a source of pride as well as festering resentment for generations."

"That's sure a lot to infer from a poem on a headstone," Big John observed skeptically.

"A rare public moment of emotional sincerity from Nooj's family."

Big John rubbed the back of his neck. "I got to hand it to you, Nick, you make the improbable sound almost convincing. Nooj sure could handle one of them kerosene fire cans without incinerating himself; and he and Miss Luevie both know the forest better than most. But here's where I get a little lost. Why'd either one of them pick Carl Shawe and the Dusongs? And why is Travis Corbett part of this?—he's not even Katogoula. He was the poor bastard we found speared to a tree at the Indian mounds. You might not remember that, considering the state you were in. The spear didn't kill him, but it was a different design altogether. Authentic in every detail, but newly made, bigger, like the ones aimed at you and your pretty redhead in the woods. Tommy says these spears were probably flung from a more serious atlatl than the one stolen from his garage closet. Again, Miss Luevie or Nooj could've managed that just fine...if you're not just barking at the moon."

"This is where my facts end and speculation begins," Nick said. "As a genealogist, I've learned to keep those ideas to myself, until I can prove them. A murder investigation has different rules. It's more than just filling in some empty spaces on a pedigree chart."

"'Speculation,' huh? And here I thought you been makin' up the whole thing!...Just kiddin' you, man. I have great respect for what you do, this family-tree business. So go ahead, climb out on that limb."

"I keep coming back to the idea we talked about at Three Sisters Pantry a few weeks ago," Nick said. "Carl was a black sheep, a loner. The Dusongs were childless. This murderer feels part of the tribe and is making careful decisions about his victims. The Shawe Twins survived their attack, as did their father, Tommy."

"Maybe our Sacred Cougar saw a chance to send another warning at the burial mounds on the cheap," Big John suggested, "without killing anybody else. Travis had been dead for weeks, broken neck. That part of it was an accident, coroner thinks, but he's sending the corpse off for more lab work just to be sure. Could be the killer knew about the body buried there, and figured out a way to use that young Chitiko-Tiloasha fool as his messenger of fear to the Katogoula.... This warning theory would make sense for Miss Luevie, but what ultimately would Nooj want from the tribe? Is he playing some weird game or is he just going to slowly wipe them out, one by one?"

"Who's speculating now?" Nick asked wryly. "In genealogy, you go to the original source to get as close to a fact as possible. Someone needs to ask Miss Luevie and Nooj those very questions."

Big John laughed loud enough to startle the protesters outside into momentary silence. "I ought to reassign some of my detectives to my convict vegetable farm and just hire me a genealogist or two!" He snatched up his phone and ordered a potentially superfluous detective to prepare two search warrants for him to complete. He made another call to a secretary.

Nick, seated in a chair facing the sheriff's desk, took the opportunity to survey the office.

Academic and professional diplomas and awards covered a couple of walls. Neat stacks and rows of books and periodicals on tables and shelves around the office spoke of a well-informed student of many disciplines, a man not too proud to learn new things. Near the phone, Nick noticed a popular genealogical paperback primer, the top cover arching up from use. This sheriff was a hands-on guy.

"Now, if I convince a judge to give us search warrants, what do you expect us to find, exactly?" Big John asked after hanging up the phone.

"Maybe the spear-thrower, a blowgun, a cougar skin...hell, I don't know. You're the forensic experts, I'm just a genealogist who may have uncovered a motive." Hawty would second that, Nick thought. "What's the story on that young man you, uh, apprehended with your front bumper today?"

"The Chitiko-Tiloasha kid? He's spillin' all the beans he's got. Says a woman by the name of Val put him up to the stunt. She's some kind of manager down at the Bayou Luck Casino who wanted to spook the Katogoula out of opening up their own casino. She been giving him a little of the good thing, you know, to get him wrapped around her finger. Ain't never met a man who could turn it down. More powerful than dope, and I ain't lyin'!"

"Val," Nick said with distaste, probing the tender parts of his ribcage. "You pay big time for thrills with her."

"So you know Val, do you?"

"Oh, yeah, we've met." Nick explained his short, unhappy friendship with Val and Butch.

"I'll be chattin' with Miss Val directly," Big John said, jotting down something of what Nick had told him. "Apparently, her idea was to capitalize on all the weird stuff happenin' around here. Sends out young Stu dressed up like a cougar, with some lighter fluid to write an anti-casino billboard from the other world. He makes sure some folks hereabouts see him in his costume.

"But the way he tells it, something went wrong. He's doing his artistic arson in the grass, looks up, and there's the *real* cougar, or spirit, whatever you want to call it, on the burial mounds, doing something God-awful with a body. Travis Corbett, you know? So he takes off and runs smack dab into me, or my car, to be more precise. He swears up and down he had nothin' to do with the other cougar sightings, the murders, or the fire."

Big John glanced down at the genealogical book and then grinned slightly, realizing that Nick had seen it. "Why all of a sudden? That's what puzzles me. How come our killer laid low until now? Fact is, both Miss Luevie and Nooj been your all-star Katogoula."

"It must have something to do with federal recognition," Nick said, "the plans for development, all the attention. These events were the psychological trigger. You've seen it before, haven't you, Big John? The famous preacher caught in a hotel room with a hooker; the great doctor who kills his terminal patients with a secret injection; the family-values politician busted in drag in a seamy French Quarter bar. The commendable behavior is a front for a powerful, suppressed desire to do the opposite. And it's always some great life crisis that opens the cage door for the evil twin of the psyche."

"Reaction formation, as I recall from my psychology courses."

"The Katogoula believed in an essential duality of creation long before Freud. The good keeps evil in balance, until something—human conflict or an external force like drought or disease—disturbs the balance. You'll see this idea in their Twins of the Forest myth."

"Say, you're not a half-bad profiler, you know that?" Big John said.

"Thanks."

The phone rang. Big John listened to the caller, smirked, shook his head, and replaced the handset. "I shoulda known. It's Friday, after five o'clock, and hunting season, to boot. Still hunting for deer starts tomorrow. Won't find a judge within fifty miles of this courthouse. They're all out at their camps. But I'll keep on it; maybe one of our judicial big shots'll get his limit early and come on home; somebody's got to be on call, you would think, right? Well, at least I'll send young Ray Doyle out to talk to Miss Luevie and Nooj first thing tomorrow." He glanced over at his holstered pistol on a credenza. "I do believe I'll go with him myself."

回

Nick didn't wait for the search warrants or the promised visit from the sheriff and his head detective. There was too much at stake. The killer's evil side was winning the battle. The cougar could strike again at any moment.

After he left the courthouse, he stopped at a gas station. From a pay phone he called the Wildlife and Fisheries toll-free poaching hotline. In a passable local drawl—he imagined his tongue as a boot stuck in mud—he reported that he'd seen a hunter using live decoys, baiting the water around his Lake Katogoula duck blind, taking pre-season ducks, spotlighting deer, and committing many other infractions he'd found in the official hunting-regulations booklet he'd picked up at the courthouse.

Easy as pulling the fire alarm at his high school. Grinning like the mischievous teenager he once was, he tickled his arthritic MG to life and pointed it toward Three Sisters Pantry.

Chapter 33

The squeal of the screen door at Three Sisters Pantry obliterated any notion of a stealthy visit. It didn't matter. "Shock 'em," Nick's detective friend Shelvin Balzar had advised. Nick intended to do just that.

Luevenia stood behind the counter, tallying purchases for two men—three six-packs of beer, a big bag of pork cracklings, cigarettes, lottery tickets. She looked up at Nick. Instantly, her congenial manner drained away. Her pine-bark brown eyes seemed to grow rounder and intensify in color, telegraphing hate and anger so unmistakably that Nick almost turned around and left.

Flustered, she returned her attention to the register and her waiting customers; three times she counted out change incorrectly. The two black men were construction workers, just ending a long day of sweaty, grimy, grueling labor. Yellow hardhats tilted back rakishly on their heads. They nodded at Nick as they left, their expressionless faces showing their fatigue. Nick listened to their company truck drive off through the gravel.

He'd heard there was a "truck stop" going up not far from Three Sisters Pantry. A huge affair, a veritable mini-casino, much too large for the trickle of traffic that heretofore had used the crumbling road. The Bahamian-based company building it—a narcotics outfit, the sheriff suspected but couldn't yet prove—was betting on an expected invasion of gamblers heading for a future Katogoula casino. The truck stop would hold ten times as many video poker machines as diesel pumps.

And miraculously, the legislature had found money to resurface and widen the rural highway!

There were no other customers in the store now; the ceiling fans were immobile in the serenity of the fall evening. From the back of the store, plates and pots clattered in the kitchen.

"Help you?" Miss Luevie said, her curt question bristling with animosity. She walked around the counter and past Nick to shut the door against the coolness of the blue dusk.

"That's what I was hoping," Nick replied. "It's up to you."

"Well, you were hoping wrong," she said, almost shouting in sudden rage, "because I got nothing to say to you. None of us do. We've said it all. So why don't you leave, like we asked you?"

From the back of the store, the clamor in the kitchen ceased momentarily, and then resumed.

Nick followed the small woman to the counter. Luevenia turned her back and busied herself with straightening cigarette cartons and liquor bottles.

"The tribe hired me to bring the past to life," Nick said. "I haven't held up my side of the bargain; in fact, through something I may have done I've brought death to the present. Look, this has gone beyond simple genealogical research; I'm still here because it's personal now. It's my responsibility to figure this out, to stop the killing. I won't sleep at night until I do figure it out. Remember, I'm a target, too; I may not have another chance to sleep at night if I can't get to the bottom of these murders and strange events."

His rational argument thus presented, he took out the small blue velvet French Bible from his coat pocket and laid it on the well-worn dark wood of the counter.

Luevenia turned. She stared at the book. A visible shudder rippled through her. She involuntarily stepped backward until she made gentle contact with a shelf of bottles. The clinking seemed to snap her out of her initial terror. Her eyes rose to search Nick's face, as if trying to detect some malign presence hiding within his skin.

"I know who tried to hurt me," he said, "the first time, at least. And I know why."

Her voice was scarcely above a whisper: "Where did you find that Bible? You got no right to it."

"You can't hide anything from a good genealogist. That's what worried you, wasn't it? That's why you tried to warn me off, that day at the courthouse? You were there. I talked to the blind snack man. You'd just delivered some baked goods. I don't think you planned it, though. You were desperate, did a rash thing."

Luevenia drew a long breath and let it out shakily. She removed her thick glasses and set them on the clean counter. Her artist's hands trembled as she rubbed her eyes and then smoothed her perfectly placed gray hair all the way back to the bun.

The fierceness in her demeanor had faded by the time she spoke again. "Looks like you're better at finding secrets than I am at hiding them."

"Did you kill Carl Shawe, or poison Tommy?"

She looked directly at Nick. "No."

"You didn't burn the museum, scare the Shawe twins, murder Travis Corbett, or try to kill Holly and me today?"

"No. I threw that trashcan at you, and I'm sorry for it. That's all I done in this whole mess." Her gaze dropped to the Bible again. "But not all I done wrong."

She was telling the truth. As he often did in his genealogical work, Nick had trusted his instincts in coming here and confronting her. Now he felt justified in his belief in Luevenia's innocence. The evidence was there on her face to read, as legible as any long-sought document proving with certainty another generation further back into the murky past.

"Miss Luevie, help me catch the murderer. Nobody knows more about the tribe's history than you do. Knowledge is our best weapon, our atlatl spear to throw at this enemy of the tribe."

Luevenia walked to the door and turned the "CLOSED" side of the dangling sign toward the front. "Come to the trailer," she said.

回

The Silbys' trailer was every bit as nice as a house in a middle-class neighborhood. Spotless and comfortable, projecting a feeling of permanence that belied the usual itinerant image of mobile-home living. Apart from historical interest, Nick's French Quarter apartment didn't compare favorably at all, he decided, as the two of them sat on the couch in the small den at the front of the trailer. Luevenia sat stiffly with the Bible in her lap; her hands covered it protectively.

Nick could sense the marital amity that existed here, just from the arrangement of furniture and accessories. He often could imagine the emotional state of a family from the odd accidental detail in a deed or probate file; such impressions sometimes helped explain a problematic property transfer, an unusual bequest, or an unexpected disinheritance. Genealogical facts were the exterior of the edifice of a life; the family historian who hoped to truly understand his subjects had to walk into that house and live there, if only for a moment.

Nick mentally noted the details that gave him this impression of mutual happiness, compromise, and consideration patiently developed over decades. Luevenia's baskets, quilts, pillows, wall hangings, and beadwork; the western novels Royce liked, his hunting, fishing, and crossword magazines, his half a dozen shotguns and rifles in the gun cabinet.... *No wonder she was desperate to preserve her marriage, her way of life. It is enviable.*

"How did you come by this?" she asked, meaning the Bible.

"I, uh, borrowed it."

"You borrowed it, huh?" Luevenia was no fool. "Does he know? Does he know that…"

"That you're his mother?" It was a long shot. He'd run different scenarios through his mind to explain the presence of the Bible in the attic of Tadbull Hall. Finally, he'd amplified a faint hunch into a ringing conjecture: Wooty Tadbull had his mother's hands.

"Yes. That I'm his real mother." It wasn't easy for her to say; quite probably, these were words she'd never spoken aloud. "Does he know?"

Nick shook his head negatively.

Luevenia placed the Bible on the coffee table and stood up. She walked toward the closed door of the trailer. Nick hadn't noticed the shotgun she now picked up from the corner; it had been out of view when the door opened.

Had he made a fatal miscalculation? He'd just confirmed that her secret was still safe. *Killing me would keep it that way.*

The shotgun was a small side-by-side double barrel, the mellow umber stock satiny from many years of use. She smiled slightly—a smile tinged with sorrow.

"Tried to shoot myself after I gave that Bible to Wooty. My thumb just wouldn't work, had no strength at all. Everything else I can hit. Ducks, dove, quail, rabbit, even deer…you name it. If it walks or flies and it's legal to hunt, I've probably shot it, gutted it, skinned it, and cooked it. But me? Shoot myself? No. Couldn't do it." The gun was clearly a trusted companion; she rubbed a hand over the stock. "Just a .410, but I'm good with it, like all us Katogoula. Been using it since I was a girl. Reminds me of good times, when the old ones were alive and it seemed like nothing could happen they didn't have an answer for."

"You're not cut out for suicide…or murder."

"I don't guess I am," she said, seeming resigned to that fact, almost as if she wished it otherwise. "Would have been the easy way out."

"But you would have accomplished nothing," Nick said. "You realized you could never kill the truth. And your suffering? Well, you and pain are old adversaries, aren't you? You strike me as the type who doesn't like to lose. Living became a greater victory, and a greater sacrifice, than dying."

She replaced the shotgun in the corner. Nick started breathing normally again.

For a half hour, Luevenia explained, holding the Bible resolutely in her lap. Her husband Royce, who poked his head into the trailer, was promptly sent packing to the store with a novel.

Some of her story Nick had already guessed. Some was new to him.

Thirty-eight years before, Wooten Tadbull was a balding playboy who had just been married at his father's insistence, after four disrupted arranged engagements to other daughters of Louisiana's gentry. It was a loveless match. The bride despised the backwardness of Sangfleuve Parish and the drunken boorishness of her husband. Within two months, there was a pregnancy neither young Wooten nor his wife wanted—but the couple's growing mutual hatred bowed to the will of the man who controlled the family purse strings, Mr. Tadbull II. An heir had to be provided.

Wooten took solace in the company of a budding beauty of the Katogoula tribe, Luevenia Dejeune, who visited Tadbull Hall often to perform her manicuring tasks, and to deliver herbal remedies which her mother and she were skilled in preparing. The wife knew about Wooten's infidelities, which were manifold. She sought refuge in alcohol and prescribed drugs. One night she overdosed on an herbal concoction, deliberately, the family knew, in an effort to kill herself or her fetus or both.

A rumor began to circulate that the wife had been poisoned; and she allowed the suspicion to grow as a way of striking back at Wooten and Luevenia. The attitude of the whites of the area became dangerous;

Luevenia, of course, was blamed without further investigation. There was even talk of a lynching, until it was discovered that Luevenia, too, was pregnant. The whispers hinted that Wooten was the father; sentiment turned against him, instead, and the women were seen as his victims.

Mr. Tadbull held almost feudal power in the area. The sheriff of the day did his bidding unquestioningly. Louisiana was a lot like medieval Italy, with its own versions of Medicis, Malatestas, and Sforzas. Luevenia was whisked away to a convent home for unwed mothers in Arkansas, where some months later she gave birth to a healthy son.

The Tadbull child was premature and grievously sick; he didn't survive long. Mr. Tadbull laid down another law: Luevenia would give up her child to the family, in exchange for lifetime financial security for her family. The official story would thenceforth be that one of two Tadbull twins had died.

And that is what the public records reflect. The memories of those who were alive then tell another tale; but their number declines with each passing year.

Luevenia returned to her Cutpine family not long after her son was brought home; she'd been visiting relatives in Oklahoma, her parents reported. She was a changed woman: quiet, introspective, mature beyond her years. Her hair had started to turn gray. No one talked of the controversy; Mr. Tadbull saw to that, with money or threats. Royce Silsby was completely unaware of the late trouble when he returned to Cutpine after a stint in the Army and service in Vietnam.

Royce proclaimed his love for the still beautiful Luevenia. She accepted his proposal. But the first love of her life was the son she'd held in her arms so briefly, the boy who was given the Tadbull name: Wooten Tadbull IV, called Wooty.

Two years later, Wooten's wife, disgusted with her reprobate husband, and already a long way toward the derangement that would make her a zombie by the time she was thirty, fled back to New Orleans. The divorce was arranged in absentia.

◻

Nick said, "I saw the small grave in the Tadbull family cemetery. The real son of Wooten and his wife?"

She nodded. "Wooty took his place."

Luevenia gave no warning before crying. Her tears fell suddenly, fat raindrops from a sky that had been clear only a moment before. And just as suddenly, her crying jag was done.

"I would like Wooty to know about me, that I'm his birth mother. But it wouldn't be good for him, as much pleasure as it would give me. Wouldn't be right." Her teary eyes filled with joy. "He's so handsome. Been to college, you know. Played football, got degrees. I'm real proud of him."

"Holly loves him."

"Yes, I heard that. She's a good woman. He could do worse. Could set his heart on someone like Mrs. Tadbull. I went to every high school game he played in. Told Royce it was for the child of some friend of ours. He has a good future waiting for him. I don't want to spoil it."

If she knew what he was into, she wouldn't be so sure of Wooty's future.

Nick tried to bring her back from her fond memories to the dangers of the present. "If there are no records in the courthouse proving he's your son, why did you throw that trash can at me?"

"I don't know much about courthouse records; I was scared of what you might find, there or somewhere else. Like you said, I didn't want to kill you. Just make you go away. Make you think it was dangerous to poke around in the tribe's past. I run off a few genealogists that way already, long time ago. You turned out to be more stubborn, smarter. Couldn't even buy you off. I could've shot you though pretty easy, if I'd wanted."

"Miss Luevie, you're not leveling with me. Your past holds another secret, doesn't it?" For a second, Nick thought she would bolt for the shotgun again. "The Vulture Cult."

She gave him that look of astonished fear bordering on raw panic. "You—you know about the Vulture Cult?"

"Enough to understand your anxiety. I know that they were priests and undertakers, but much more. Figures of awe. Tribe members honored them—"

"And feared them," said Luevenia, gazing intently at a space where Nick saw nothing. "The others shunned them when they were...unclean. They put the dead person on a scaffold of wood gathered by the family. They covered it with skins, left it to smoke over a fire for six days. The mourners and the Vultures sat around the scaffold and cried out their grief. Then the Vultures picked the body clean to the bones, in front of the mourners. And they buried the bones of the dead one in baskets in the mounds."

She let go of the ancient vision of her ancestors and focused on Nick again. "After each time, the Vultures who did the ceremony had to cleanse themselves. The mourners went back to their house, the Vultures went to the woods. They didn't eat for days and made drinks from plants that made them vomit and sweat. A Vulture couldn't perform another burial until one month had passed; and during all that time, he—or she, there were women ones, too—they couldn't be anywhere near the preparation of food, or have...relations. The tribe left meals for them outside the village, like they pass trays to prisoners in jail."

"Do you think the others still believe in the old taboos?"

She gave a one-shouldered shrug. "I didn't want to find out. Probably a lot of Katogoula don't really know what the Vulture Cult was, the young ones especially. You might not think they care. We're good Catholics now, you know?" She gave a slight chuckle. "Have been for more than a hundred years. I wonder, when it comes down to it. We've spent all them years forgetting, but when we start to remember, and find out which families were in it...well, I think you see what I was afraid of. Still am. Old Odeal Caspard—you know, the old man who's always telling the same foolish jokes—he might be able to tell you some of the families, if his mind wasn't half gone. I wanted to keep it that way. Selfish, I guess. I'm not sure how my Royce will take this."

She had begun to squeeze her hands white, wringing them as if trying to unscrew them from her wrists.

"We were doing just fine until that recognition letter came from Washington," she said, exasperation at the incidents beyond her control making her voice quiver. "Nobody expected it, not many would've wanted it if they knew all the trouble it would bring. The attention and meanness and lies. Would have been okay with just us as the tribe, just the few of us families looking out for each other, like always. But then they want to go poking around in the history of the tribe, like you did. Getting all kinds of folks we never heard of in here with their hands out. And sooner or later, I knew it, somebody was going to find out about me.... I'm glad I didn't hurt you too bad. Went a little crazy."

Nick asked himself how he would feel if he were to find out his ancestors picked rotted flesh from the bones of corpses? The idea would take some getting used to, at the very least.

"Wooty was gone to me. I just couldn't bear to lose my husband, too," Luevenia said. "And who's going to want to eat in my store, with that awful thing in the back of their minds? That's all we got, that store. I wouldn't blame him if he didn't sleep in the same room.... You forgive me?"

"Sure, I forgive you. From what I've seen of Royce, my guess is he will, too."

"You haven't told anybody else? Please say you haven't!"

"Oh, no. I wouldn't do anything like that." Lying was the ignoble course to take, but Nick didn't consider himself hero material anyway. "I think I can explain things to Sheriff Higbee without mentioning the

Vulture Cult. And as far as Wooty goes, that's a matter for you and him to work out, if you decide to. But you *can* help me on another matter of tribal history. The Quinahoa. What do you know about them?"

"Well, my great-grandmother—"

"Adolicia Hastard Coux?"

Luevenia gave Nick that uneasy look again, but it passed quickly. "Yes, that's her. She used to tell me the chief of the Quinahoa swore his warriors to vengeance before the Katogoula and the Yaknelousa tore off his flesh and burned him alive. Some of them lived in the woods, watching their women…serve the Katogoula warriors."

Comfort women. Like the Korean and Chinese women forced to "serve" Japanese soldiers in World War II. Nothing really ever changes; search far enough back, and we've all got something to be ashamed of.

"When I was coming up," Luevenia continued, "it wasn't something we talked about a lot. The Quinahoa. Oh, there was some name-calling in school, and one or two mothers wouldn't let their children play with children from those families; but most of us didn't take it no more serious than that." She thought about it a moment and then shook her head. "No. I'm sure we all thought of ourselves as Katogoula by then, in our hearts."

"Do you know the families that are supposedly descended from the Quinahoa captives?"

"I think Altrice Mateet had one in her family; but she don't live here anymore. And I recall poor Grace Dusong's cousin's first husband was one. Nooj, too, they say, way back on one side or the other. But all of us got a little of another tribe in them. Me, I'm part Yaknelousa. But you know that, like you do everything else." She seemed to grasp what Nick was thinking. "Why are you asking me about the Quinahoa?"

"You were driven to extreme measures by your concerns with the past."

"You mean Nooj?" Luevenia laughed tensely. "But he's always been so involved with the tribe, since he was a boy. When we have a Trade Days or a mini pow-wow, Nooj dresses up in the traditional feathers and skins. He's so good with the white and black children, teaching them the dances and all. Knows more about the old ways of hunting and the forest than anybody now, since Carl is dead. Nooj, he don't go in for this gambling and development, either, like me—and I do think it's wrong, even without my secrets. He voted against it. No, Nooj wouldn't do nothing bad to his own people he loves," she said, with wilting conviction.

Nick had discovered feuds that lasted centuries for less substantial reasons. That Luevenia remembered who had Quinahoa ancestors proved to him that the old prejudices weren't quite dead yet. But he wasn't looking for Luevenia's agreement. He'd gathered important facts from her, and in so doing had eliminated her as a suspect in the murders. That was all he'd hoped to accomplish here.

"How did you first find out about the recognition?" he asked.

"Brianne called and told me the good news, that very afternoon the sawmill closed. Well, I didn't think it was so good at the time. All kinds of things was going through my head."

"Did Nooj visit the store that day?"

"How'd you know?" But she answered her own question, nodding at this further proof of Nick's omniscience. "Nooj stopped by not long after Brianne called. He don't get too worked up about much, even that. But he did buy a Lotto ticket. He let the machine pick the numbers; I remember, because he usually marks his own. Maybe his way of celebrating."

He had ample time to plan Tommy's framing ambush and Carl's murder.

"I think it would be best if you didn't mention our conversation to anyone. I could be wrong, of course. In that case, we wouldn't want to spread false suspicion, or show the real killer our hand."

"Yes, I understand."

"There's one more thing, Miss Luevie."

She nodded and reluctantly held out the Bible over the coffee table.

He put up his hand to refuse it. "No, you keep that. My job is to help clients find their heritage, not rob them of it. Actually, I was thinking of dinner."

A big smile bloomed across her face. "You're hired again."

Chapter 34

The sun had plunged into the depths of the earth; the great deity of daylight had called back his myrmidons to his molten court.

Crouching behind a thick pine tree, disoriented in the profound darkness, Nick found it easy to believe in the gods Stone Age humans had worshipped. He, too, was feeling curiosity, wonder, and fear as he witnessed elemental forces battle for control of the forest.

For all our science, the primitive endures, and ever will.

He wouldn't have much time to search Nooj's fire tower; the wildlife enforcement agent would soon figure out that someone had a reason for distracting him, calling him out on a wild goose chase for phantom violators.

Nick listened to the crickets searching for each other in the darkness. Then he moved toward the tower.

A cone of glare from a bare bulb illuminated the foot of the stairs. Nick had brought along a small flashlight, but decided not to use it for the climb. The light would be a dead giveaway to someone approaching the tower, visible for many yards even in the dense forest. He preferred not to confront Nooj, especially considering his recent injuries and his recollection of the game warden's formidable physique.

The sunset had faded to a lavender glow in the west. He climbed the first flight within the steel frame of the tower, pausing on the pine-plank stairs to give his eyes time to adjust. It took concentration to sort real from floating false images, but he was beginning to get the hang of it. The dark square of the living quarters loomed above. He resumed his ascent.

With each flight the stairs changed directions. The forest slumbered around and below him. He glanced down and a sense of his altitude sucked his breath away for a moment. When his mind shook off its bout of acrophobia, he thought he detected a star pattern in the shadowy stair angles below.

Patterns reveal themselves, in human lives as in the physical world, only from the right perspective.

Nick emerged on a mesh deck that surrounded what had once been the tower's fire-observation room. The wind was stronger up here at the level of the treetops. The door to Nooj's quarters was locked. Nick recalled that one of the Shawe twins had broken a window, but Nooj apparently had repaired it.

Genealogy wasn't all paperwork; Nick sometimes needed to resort to the unorthodox, and, well, the slightly illegal. He'd acquired a lock pick that resembled the innocuous Mini Maglite he also carried on such questionable missions. The screwdriver-like, wavy-tipped blade extended, the lock pick became a different animal. He inserted the pick blade and the companion tension wrench into the doorknob keyhole. Working the pick with inexpert jiggles, in-and-out, up-and-down, he simultaneously turned the tension wrench…the knob yielded and the metal door opened.

Nick was careful to point his flashlight down as he assessed the roughly twenty-by-twenty room. A monkish place, a bit warmer than outside but not welcoming to visitors. He thought of Henry David Thoreau, building his cabin by Walden Pond "to transact some private business with the fewest obstacles," making use of only the "necessaries of life." If Nick was right, Nooj parted with Thoreau over the idea of nonviolent civil disobedience; his style was a more active form of protest: murder.

A couple of tables; three chairs; a squat cast-iron wood-burning stove; a kitchenette; a bed on the upper level of a prison-issue iron bunk set, the lower level converted into an open closet for Nooj's uniforms and a few other belongings. Three shotguns and two rifles filled a gun rack on one wall. He saw no evidence of running water but noticed a clear plastic water jug, three-quarters full, upended in a dispenser. Except for the electricity that powered the small but obviously adequate space heater cooling in a corner, the wildlife agent could have been living in the nineteenth century.

The storage area below the bed seemed the logical place to start. Nick pushed aside Nooj's uniforms. Shoes, boots, fishing rods, stacks of *Louisiana Conservationist*, *National Geographic*, and *Penthouse*…could have been a Boy Scout's closet.

Nick moved to the middle of the room. Something wasn't right. A million ice ants charged up his back and neck and into his scalp. *The wood-burning stove!*

Why did he need a wood-burning stove? The kitchenette, the lights, the space heater…all electric. Could it be a heat backup, for outages, which probably happened here often as a result of falling limbs? Nooj was much tougher than that. Maybe it was a relic from a time when the place wasn't wired. Why was there no visible chimney pipe exiting through the wall or ceiling?

In the capacious, ash-less belly of the stove Nick found three bundles carefully wrapped in what appeared to be deerskin suede.

In the first thin bundle he found an atlatl. Was it Tommy Shawe's childhood toy, stolen from his garage the evening of the day Nooj and the rest of the tribe learned of federal recognition? Yes: a child's hands had carved the word "Tommy" in the wood. Just a simple, forearm-sized stick, really—with an un-toy-like rock strapped by leather cords at the base below the spear socket. Nick envisioned an ancient hunter, in the company of other similarly armed men, snapping his atlatl forward and hurling a spear with deadly accuracy at that evening's tribal entrée.

He was careful not to touch the atlatl. There could possibly be Nooj's incriminating fingerprints on it. He knew full well that he was tampering with evidence; but he wasn't a cop and didn't have to follow the official, complex code. Not that cops always did, either. A lot could happen with evidence between crime scene and courtroom.

The second deerskin bundle contained an assortment of unmatched notebooks. Nick used the supple deerskin like a glove to flip pages. Four books were of relatively modern vintage, from the last fifty years or so. The fifth and others were much older, of worn canvas and peeling leather. Many different hands had written in them; the earliest entries were in poor French.

Death dates. Only death dates. Spanning a period of perhaps two hundred years. In each book the old core families had separate sections, the Bellarmines, Nooj's mother's family, included. There was also a section for the Cheneries. It was clear to Nick that the Cheneries should be considered the seventh core family; though elusive in official records, they had in fact maintained a constant local presence. Other pages handled more numerous non-core families who moved in and out of the Cutpine area, including many names Nick hadn't encountered in his research. When the last member of a family died, the chronicler used the same transliterated phrase, in the Roman letters of the white conquerors: *BAH-UA CU-BISH-NAW-A*. Nick presumed that these words were Quinahoa, some expression of triumph from the lost ancestral language of the defeated and enslaved tribe, though he had no inkling of the exact meaning.

The pen strokes of each of the writers infused the phrase with exultation. That needed no translation. He understood the human emotions that crossed ethnic boundaries and millennia, that seemed to make the notebooks glow with oppressed pride and hot vengeance in the murky fire tower. The Cheneries were ghoulish reverse family historians, not celebrating the triumph of life through the generations, but watching with silent, bitter satisfaction as the Katogoula tribe staggered toward extinction.

Nooj was apparently the last archivist of the Quinahoa blood grudge, the lonely guardian of his lost tribe's honor, the keeper of the flame of hate. *And in a stove, at that.* Nick scanned one of the oldest notebooks and saw the handwriting of one chronicler give way to that of the next, the passing of the torch confirmed by death dates in the Chenerie section. Nooj was continuing the tradition, with a new twist: no longer watching with passive detachment, but helping along the slow process of gradual death of an entire tribe. And the question formed in his mind: had past Cheneries merely watched, and nothing more?

Tommy and Brianne and their three children were recorded, with a dash after their names; so too were all the other living Katogoula in the Cutpine area. Nooj had duly noted the death dates of Carl Shawe and the Dusongs; he'd judged them for a past they had no hand in creating, using collective guilt to sentence them all to death.

No one should have such power, Nick thought, a hot surge of anger causing him to rip a page as he turned it.

Nick let his imagination touch and probe the discovery he had made. He surmised that some Cheneries apparently wished even for the disappearance of their own name, as they secretly reveled in the larger tribal decay. In the minds of the true believers of the family—Nooj's father's line, the keepers of these notebooks—they had been polluted by the Katogoula, even though against their will, and no longer felt deserving of life. Other Cheneries, ignorant or scornful of the sick vigilance of their kin, had insisted on reproducing, continuing the line. Thus Nooj was born. He'd written his own name and a dash in the most recent Chenerie section—confirming his own contract with oblivion.

Where had it started? With a Chenerie Katogoula warrior who fell in love with a Quinahoa concubine, ten or more generations ago? Was it she who injected the venom of vengeance? From then on, had this Chenerie branch devoted itself to uniting with other families having

Quinahoa blood? Nick felt the truth of his theory: in Nooj, the bloodline had been bred back to pure hatred.

Nooj surely knew his ancestors by heart, probably to a time even before these written records. Nick remembered their conversation at Three Sisters Pantry; he'd had the feeling then that the wildlife agent was selling him a bill of goods in claiming that his grandfather was "kind of an orphan." Was he observing the ancient Quinahoa naming taboo? Hoping to put the snooping genealogist off his trail? Probably both.

Stacking the notebooks in order and rewrapping them, Nick wondered how the Chenerie sentinels had felt about Katogoula who left the Cutpine band and entered other cultures. He supposed they had their own qualifications for tribal disaffiliation, just as all tribes have rules for joining. Once a Katogoula married outside the tribe, left Cutpine and surrendered his Katogoula heritage by jumping into the mainstream, he was lost—and the ancient debt was paid—as surely as if he'd died childless. Nick had noticed many names with lines drawn through them, sprinkled throughout the notebooks; these must have been the Katogoula who turned their backs on their ancestral way of life.

The third bundle, a very fat one, contained the cache of Katogoula records that Tommy's father had assembled, also stolen from the Shawes' garage closet. There couldn't be much doubt about that, now. Nick recalled Tommy saying that Brianne had forgotten to look for the papers that wild afternoon, as he had asked her to do just before rushing off to meet with Chief Rafe Claude at the Chitiko-Tiloasha casino. Nick was wowed: this was a crucial collection of family-history documentation the BIA either had never received or had lost, for he had had no luck obtaining copies from the agency.

Nooj must have seen the certainty of the tribe's humiliating destruction snatched away from him the day word came of recognition. This blew his small private flame into a raging forest fire. And it was then that he began his last-ditch campaign to break the spirit of the tribe and halt its progress toward growth and prosperity.

He robbed the Katogoula of priceless genealogical material, terrorized them with impersonations of an angry spirit, framed the tribal leader with the death of his own brother, burned the museum and in the process killed the Dusongs, extinguishing two more Katogoula lines. It almost worked, too. The tribe members by now were terrified and interpreted their recent luck as the reason for the plague of misfortune. Who would join a tribe so cursed? Luevenia Silsby, motivated by her own secrets, unintentionally aided Nooj's plan.

Nick wondered if Nooj, undetected, never satisfied with his psychological warfare, would have murdered the whole tribe in time, as Sheriff Higbee had suggested.

The sound of a truck engine echoed distantly through the dark forest.

Nick quickly rewrapped and replaced the last bundle in the stove, killed his flashlight, and groped his way toward the open door, straining to listen over his incredibly noisy breathing.

He'd never noticed how much racket the human machine makes.

What were his options? Stay in the tower, try to find a phone or radio in the darkness? No. He'd be trapped, on Nooj's home turf. Help would take too long to arrive at this desolate place. He'd take his chances down there on the ground—chances he made a bit more even by grabbing a pump shotgun from the wall rack and a handful of shells from a box on the table below. A shell dropped on the pine-plank floor; the noise boomed through the forest.

Great. You're going to get yourself killed, klutz!

He fumbled with three shells until the gun swallowed them. The hunting regulations booklet had mentioned something about a magazine "plug" that limited the number of shells. *Nooj, law-abiding homicidal maniac.*

Outside on the catwalk, he heard nothing alarming, a fact which failed to put him at ease. He started down the stairs. Nick hadn't fired a gun in thirty years. His father, who'd fought into Germany with General

McAuliffe—of Bastogne and "Nuts!" fame—had always tried to familiarize him with guns, "In case we get another Hitler," he often said. Nick hated hunting and thew up the first and only time he killed anything with a gun—a turtle.

He prodded sleeping pathways of memory, hoping to awaken some boyhood shooting lesson that might save him.

Starlight and a silver sliver of moon rising in the pines guided his steps. Halfway down, now. *The light at the bottom of the tower!* It was not casting its feeble illumination. Through his racing heartbeat, he heard nothing but calming insect cadences.

He took the final steps down and crept watchfully into the pine-straw covered clearing where Nooj probably parked his department pickup. No truck. That was good.

He glanced up at the dark tower behind him and let out a breath of relief. Nothing to worry about, he decided, chuckling at his earlier skittishness. He was alone, except for the spirits of departed Katogoula, Yaknelousa, and Quinahoa warriors, fighting their bloody battle until the end of time.

Now his main problem was getting back to his car, which he'd hidden in the woods on a rutted logging trail that split off from the well-maintained gravel road between the parish highway and the fire tower.

He wouldn't need the shotgun, after all. Lucky thing; he'd probably just end up shooting himself. Maybe he should go back up, search a few minutes longer, and return the gun, the absence of which would surely alert Nooj that—

Something thwacked into the gunstock, very close to his hand. Nick instinctively crouched low. He looked down: a feathered blowgun dart the size of a pencil had burrowed itself into the wood of the stock. He heard another dart whiz past his head.

Then the pine curtains of darkness parted and a large animal raced toward him. It was cloaked in strange blue phosphorescence from the sky, moving rapidly but in jerks, as if in a video missing every tenth frame. In an awful moment of recognition, Nick knew this was the Sacred Cougar!

Animal, man, or spirit?...Nick didn't have the luxury of time to find out. He fired once and tried to pump the next shell into the chamber. But the thing already had him by the throat. They both went down on the pine straw. The shotgun went flying.

Using his good left arm, Nick punched, clawed, and poked his attacker with every ounce of strength he could muster.

Liquid, metallic and hot! He felt and smelled blood on his hands and face. Whose, he didn't know.

Nick and the thing rolled over several times. The heavy beast crunched down on him, compressing his injured collarbone, shoulder, elbow, and ribs into a throbbing nucleus of agony. He yelped reflexively and lashed out savagely with his left fist, hitting a whiskered, toothy snout. The animal seemed stunned—but only for a moment.

A moment was all it took for Nick to realize he had a weapon within reach. *The lock pick!* And then he had the tool in his hand, driving the sharp shaft over and over again into the furry back of his attacker.

More hot, slippery blood leaked onto his hands.

The cougar shook him off, stood up abruptly, and then fell backward. Panting and groaning, it got to all fours. Nick was certain he'd hurt it.

"Nugent Chenerie!" he shouted, frantically searching the straw for the shotgun. "I know it's you. Nooj, listen, it's over! We know what you're trying to do, and we're not afraid anymore. Stop the killing! Don't add to the tragedy of the Quinahoa with the death of more innocents. The battle ended long ago. You can't change it!"

Nick saw the glint of Nooj's badge below the cougar skin...or was it his pistol? Was it Nooj? Such questions were academic now. He kicked at the threatening metal and felt thudding contact.

On his feet now, he ran blindly into the unimaginable evil of the dark forest.

Chapter 35

Deep in Tadbull woods, Wooty nervously waited in the night's inscrutable blackness on the porch of his family's disused, rustic hunting cabin. He heard something.

A backfire? A shot?

He couldn't be sure. "Damnit!" he muttered. He'd chosen the instant before the distant noise to lay his pistol and flashlight beside him on the dusty boards. Now he sat on the porch ledge, his back to a thick old cypress post, tapping his shoes in the pine straw, listening, his jumpy right hand ready to grab for the gun. Though he'd given up smoking, he now drew deeply from the fourth cigarette of his vigil. When that one burned down to the filter, he used it to light the next one.

It was thirty-three minutes past nine o'clock. He'd pressed the nightlight on his watch so many times the battery was weakening. Except for that noise a few minutes ago, Tchekalaya Forest slept restlessly.

His contacts were already an hour late. Three guys—he knew only the first name of one who'd made the trip before—were supposed to pick up the marijuana he'd stored in the old cistern here at the cabin, and then drive it on to a secret airfield, God knows where. He didn't want to know that, either.

The cylindrical cistern hulked on stilt legs in the shadows to his right. Wooty imagined it as a fat, fifteen-foot-tall forest jester chuckling quietly at all the things that could go wrong.

He'd made some stupid decisions in his life, but this took the cake. He hated this drug-running idiocy, and it had taken external events to open his eyes. That bothered him, that he still lacked the maturity and savvy to figure things out for himself. He would have to get smart fast, if he wanted to run with the big dogs, Bayles and his crowd.

Anyway, this would be the last time, thanks to Nick and Holly.

Holly...he'd almost lost her today, on the Golden Trace. Earlier tonight, holding her naked body against him, he vowed to himself never to let her go again. They would leave this place of stagnation and death, he promised her; and she said she wanted only to be with him, wherever he went, whatever he did. Together they would chase the dream held out by state senator Augustus Bayles.

And then she'd raised holy hell when he wouldn't let her join him on this final job. Luckily, she was exhausted and didn't have all of the usual fight in her. She'd played gin rummy with his father, who was delighted to have a beautiful woman in the house, even though she beat the pants off him in every game; and now she slept in Wooty's bed at Tadbull Hall, the television her babysitter. He ached to return to her strong embrace.

He lit another cigarette, upbraiding himself for all this self-pity, which was getting him nowhere and changing nothing. Regardless of his emotional dilemma, the dope had to move tonight. That's one of the things he hated most: they called all the tunes, and he had to dance to them. He just hoped they held up their end of the bargain, and let him and Holly go their own way.

In the old days, when Wooty was just a boy, his father had used this camp every fall, for weeks at a time, entertaining politicos and moguls from all over the country in a blood-sport marathon. That's how he first met Representative Rufus Girn. The men shot anything that moved, occasionally even a hapless guide; Tchekalaya Forest became a battle zone. Lots of drinking, great open-air eating, and a good bit of whoring. The adult Katogoula of the time—most were gone now—worked the annual event as guides, cooks, and bartenders. He remembered a half dozen Katogoula round palmetto huts, constructed amid the trees every year to house the reveling men who didn't rate a bunk in the cabin.

The place looked pretty good back then, and invitations were treasured things.

Wooty shook his head and laughed as he recalled one unfortunate guest—some Yankee lobbyist—who fell off the porch while taking a piss, right into the campfire. No major harm done, just minor burns. The Yankee said he'd had worse damage to his pecker, and less fun, with a few congressmen's wives.

Thinking back to those heady times over twenty-five years before, Wooty recalled a different Mr. Tadbull: a dynamic, good-looking, irresistible man, who could spin a tale for hours in a duck blind on a slow day or laugh at your joke until he cried.

No, he didn't really hate his old Pop. How could he hate a part of himself? But there was another part of his soul that he'd inherited from someone else in the family, he didn't know who. He'd seen heredity at work in horses, cows, and dogs; why not in humans, why not in feelings and personality and character? Sometimes he thought he was almost a new species. Unlike Mr. Tadbull, Wooty had a vision of larger horizons, a hunger to escape the anonymity of ordinary life, a hatred of the chains of somebody else's rules.

He wondered if his yearning blood came from his great-grandfather Bascove Tadbull, the artist, or from his mother, who was supposed to have gone crazy and been sent back to her family in New Orleans in a straight jacket? Maybe she had hot French or Spanish blood in her. He could conjure up only the vaguest images of his mother, based mainly on old photos he'd since lost track of and on one or two very early visits to New Orleans. But he knew his father well enough to suspect he'd unfavorably embellished her real nature and ultimate fate.

The faint sound of movement snapped Wooty back from his ruminations. He felt a difference in the forest. Someone was there, in the pitch blackness. He snuffed out his cigarette on a floorboard and took up his pistol, clicking the safety off.

Whoever it was out there knew the forest, knew how to move at night like a stalking animal. Definitely not his clumsy contacts, who were supposed to be tough city guys from New Orleans, but surely complete idiots in this environment. He would have heard their vehicle bouncing along the primitive road to the camp long before they arrived.

Wooty remembered the night several weeks before, when his buddy Travis Corbett had fallen to his death, the same night he had later seen the apparition of the deer and the cougar in the moonlight. Was this the same person, or entity, who'd led Travis on his fatal pursuit?

He aimed both his pistol and shining flashlight in the direction of the subtle rustling of pine straw fifteen feet in front of him.

"Identify yourself! Now!" he said, louder than he'd intended.

"No need to shout." It was a woman's voice. A familiar voice. "I can hear you, Wooty. If I was two miles away, I could hear you."

The beam of light locked onto Luevenia Silsby, emerging from the scaly pine trunks toward an astonished Wooty. As if cradling an infant, she carried her shotgun propped over her left arm.

"What the...Miss Luevie, listen, you can't stay out here. I've got...business. Visitors, uh, friends coming. It's very confidential."

"Turn that light out of my eyes, if you please."

"Oh, sorry." Realizing he was still pointing his pistol at her, he hastily uncocked it and put it in his hip holster. He then laid the light on the porch behind him and covered it with his camouflage jacket. The two looked at each other in the soft green glow.

Miss Luevie had always been so nice to him, growing up. Boy, the stuff she'd treated him to at her store in his youthful years! He had never had to pay a cent for anything at Three Sisters Pantry; he would just take whatever he wanted to the counter, and Miss Luevie would smile and nod. Surely she wouldn't have just given him all that merchandise; she must have charged it all to his father's account. And he couldn't even remember where he'd put that old Bible she'd brought the other day. It must have been very important to her.... He felt rotten about his thoughtless ingratitude toward Miss Luevie now and over the years, but he had to get rid of her, pronto.

"You have to leave," he said, trying to keep it plain and polite, but firm. "Right now, you understand? Any other time, Miss Luevie, and I'd be...what are you doing in these woods at night, anyway?"

"Well, I told Royce I had a taste for fried coon."

Oh God, here we go. He shouldn't have asked.

"Thought I'd go out and find one." Smiling, she held up her little double barrel. "That explains this; but I don't reckon you ought to be walking in the woods alone at night without something a little better than coon shot. My second shell is a slug. There's all kinds of strange things that go on out here. Might even bag me a cougar." She gave an enigmatic snicker, as if over a private joke. Her steel-frame glasses twinkled in the moonlight. "I see you got your gun, too. A man needs to watch out for hisself. You never ate my coon stew, have you, Wooty?"

"No, I haven't had the pleasure."

"I brown it in a skillet first, with some bell peppers, onions, celery, and red pepper. Then I—"

"Miss Luevie, please, I don't have time to visit at the moment. Like I said, I have some—"

But she had other things on her mind and paid no attention to his protestations. "You're supposed to use dogs and a .22 at night for coon, you know."

The simple old gal must be afraid I'll turn her in. "You can trust me. I won't tell," he said. "Now, you better get on back or Royce'll be worried."

She glanced off into the darkness, and then her eyes found Wooty's again. "I really didn't come out for coon. I come looking for you."

"Me? Well, why? And how'd you know where I was?"

"Even this forest can't keep secrets forever. I learned that the hard way. That's why I'm here. To let you in on a secret of mine. And yours."

Chapter 36

Nick ran at full sprint through the tangled gauntlet of woods. It was worse than any nightmare. At least in dreams, the mind's stage lights illuminated even the most surreal horrors.

Unseen tentacles battered, garroted, and lacerated him. Like an addict going through withdrawals, he imagined giant spiders looping silken ropes around him, turning and turning him until his helpless immobility made him an easy living meal. Then he was a human pinball, bouncing off tree trunks, to the accompaniment of flashes and bells in his stunned brain.

A solid snarl of vegetation stopped him cold. He changed course to bypass the wall. He tripped and rolled, endlessly it seemed to him, down a steep slope that in the utter darkness felt worthier of the Himalayas than the modest hills of Tchekalaya Forest.

At last he came to a stop. He rested, trying to catch his breath in the sudden silence, using his shaky good left arm to prop himself up on his knees.

He tried to swallow, but his throat stuck together like flypaper. He'd inhaled too many bugs and leaves and pine-straw bits and dirt in his flight from whatever it was, whoever it was, chasing him. Was it Nugent Chenerie, after all?

His attacker had grunted and snarled but hadn't spoken in an identifiable voice. Could he be wrong? Suppose Nooj didn't know about the three incriminating bundles in the stove. Suppose someone was attempting to set up the wildlife agent, just as someone had attempted to frame Tommy Shawe for his twin's murder.

His mind cleared a little. No time now to play detective. He had to get himself out of this maddening labyrinth.

Looking up, he could see gleaming knifepoints of stars above him, in a narrow indigo river between pine trees. Had he fallen onto the Golden Trace? Yes, this had to be it! Which way should he go? The Shawe property was somewhere on the trace. So were the lake and the burial mounds and the cemeteries and the burned museum and Tadbull Hall. Anyplace would be better than here. He stood up, turned around and around in an attempt to get his bearings until he forgot where he began, and started running again.

Above and behind him, he heard his pursuer crashing through the woods, making even more noise than he had. No point in stealth now. The thing behind him was wounded and just as desperate as he was. Nick could hear labored breathing and groans as it fought pain and the forest to catch him. The shotgun blast must have been merely a glancing hit. What damage had the fairly puny lock-pick blade done?

But this was still far from an equal contest: his pursuer had a gun. Nick had convinced himself that it was a gun he'd kicked during the scuffle with the bizarre man-like cougar.

Every joint and bone and muscle of Nick's body, every inch of exposed, bleeding skin, screamed in agony and begged for just one moment of rest; but he commanded himself to run, run, faster, faster, faster!

Before the sun came up, he would unmask this killer, or be the next victim.

Chapter 37

A black van, parking lights on, bounced slowly along an old logging trail. The three men inside hadn't spoken for ten minutes. Limbs and bushes screeched against the windows and doors. The driver fought the steering wheel through ruts and stomped the brakes when the van dove unexpectedly into water-filled craters. Four times already, two of them had pushed the vehicle out of thigh-deep, cold mud holes. No one looked forward to another one. Green light from the dashboard splashed across the grim faces of the two big men in the front.

"You sure this is the right way?" said the man strapped in the passenger seat.

"Yeah, don't worry," the driver replied. "Could get to that camp with my eyes closed."

From the back of the van the third man, who sat on a stack of tarpaulins, said, "Our eyes *are* closed." He was getting the worst of the rough ride, with nothing to hold on to except the metal ribs of the large van's cargo area. "This ain't just dark, boys. This is D-A-R-K."

The men spoke with the languorous, droll, exotic accent of native New Orleanians.

"Turn on the lights," the front-seat man said to the driver. "Ain't nobody around for miles."

They'd taken the precaution of disabling their brake lights.

"Yeah, yeah, okay, you wimps. What, you afraid of the dark, dawlin'?" said the driver, laughing.

He switched on the headlights. The Golden Trace was visible a few yards to their right.

"There's the road, you dumb fuck," said the third man.

"Who you callin' 'dumb fuck'?" The driver slammed on the brakes and twisted in his seat belt. "Thas not the way we supposed be goin', asshole. Thas the scenic route, a hiking trail for yuppoes and other upstandin' junkies."

"Don't talk bad about our customers," said the second man. "You two should shutup arguin', so we can pick up the shit and get out of here.... Whazat?!"

"Whaz what?" The third man in the back lifted a compact submachine gun to his chest. "I didn't see nothin'. Kill the lights! All of 'em. Quick!"

The van idled as the three men inside watched the dark figure of a man coming nearer on the Golden Trace.

"Help!" The man stumbled off the trace, into the thickening brush, toward the vehicle. "Someone's trying to kill me! Help! Can you hear me? My name is Nick Herald. Help me!"

"What do we do?" asked the driver.

"I'm gonna tell the weirdo to beat it, okay?" said the second man from the passenger seat.

But before he could, the three couriers saw another figure enter their slice of view, roughly thirty yards down the Golden Trace from the first man.

Gunshots popped and echoed. Three shots, spaced for careful aim. The muzzle flashes strobed the pursuer in three instants of white light.

After the first shot, Nick resumed his flight, and after the third, his pursuer went after him.

All was quiet again.

"Whathefuck!...you see that?" the third man asked. He had muscled the front passenger aside and had stuck his head and upper torso out the window. He held his stubby automatic weapon at his shoulder, ready, his elbows propped on the door.

The second man said, "Am I nuts, or was that some kinda lion walking on two feet? Shooting at that guy in front of him?"

"Get back in," the driver said. "This ain't our fight. We're gettin' outa here." He gunned the van.

"No shit," said the second man. "The rest of this parade I don't want to see."

◙

The three couriers were nervous when they arrived. And so was Wooty when they explained what they'd witnessed.

"Said his name was Dick," said the driver.

"No, fuckwad, it was Gerald," the second courier insisted.

"You're both nuts," the third man insisted. "He wasn't even speaking English. It was Russian...or something."

"Oh, right," the second man said, "like you know Russian!"

Wooty and Luevenia had been startled by the gunshots; now Wooty realized that the couriers had seen Nick Herald, running for his life. But who was chasing him?

The three couriers were still arguing about what they'd seen. Wooty grabbed his gear. "Something's come up," he said rapidly to the driver. "You know where the stuff is. Been nice working with you guys."

"Hey, we could use some help here," the third man protested.

But Wooty had already disappeared into the dark embrace of the pines.

Luevenia waited out of sight in the woods a few yards away. Wooty called softly to her.

"Did you hear what they said?" he asked her.

Luevenia materialized in front of him. "Yes. Sounds like Nick."

"Got to be. That guy gets into more trouble. What about the…thing following him? If I believed in the Katogoula ways"—he corrected himself—"in *our* ways, I'd say that was the Sacred Cougar hot on his trail."

"It's a man, Wooty, not a spirit. Nick thinks it's Nooj behind all the killing, behind that cougar mask."

"I just can't get my mind around that," he said, shaking his head. "Holly told me about Nick's theory. He had you down as the murderer, too, I hear."

"I have a lot more to tell you, when this is all past us."

"There's a lot I want to ask you. I'm glad you told me what you did. But right now we have to help Nick."

"Please, my son, be careful."

He kissed the top of her head. "Try to get to a phone, call Sheriff Higbee. My cell phone won't work out here; the whole forest is a"—Wooty paused—"a dead zone. Tell the sheriff to take some deputies out to where the Golden Trace hugs the lakeshore."

"Just about where Carl got killed?"

"Yeah, I guess it is," Wooty said, picking up her unspoken fear. "Anyway, I'll meet him there and we can start searching. If they're on the trace still, maybe I can cut through the woods and gain on them before the sheriff gets there. If it's Nooj, Nick won't last long against him. And don't worry too much about me…Mother. Feels funny to say that."

"Feels good to hear it."

Wooty cleared his throat and after a moment said, "I know these woods as good as Nooj does. Must be the Katogoula in me."

His pistol drawn, he sprinted off like a quarterback rushing for the goal line.

Luevenia Silsby walked fast along the Golden Trace to reach the Shawe place and a phone.

She stopped, looked down at her old hunting companion, the .410, and reversed course.

Chapter 38

Lake Katogoula yawned before Nick, a ravenous mouth of death.

The black surface of the water glimmered with white shards of reflected celestial light.

Limp with exhaustion and slightly delirious, Nick believed he saw in that light every mythos in history, broken into final, fatal, jagged beauty, a tragic testament to mankind's hopeless quest to touch the infinite. It called to him, this light, and then he saw transcendent dancers in a magic ceremony moving to a magnificent, frightening requiem of all the prayers ever sent into the starry blackness to all gods. How he wanted to join these dancers in their celebration! He was so tired and the light and the dance and the sound were unbearably alluring.

No! You can't dance with them and live!

Duck blinds floating on the water seemed to Nick to shoot holes in the scintillating skin covering the lake. On the far shore, in the orange glow of a lone sodium-vapor security light, Nick could just discern oil tanks, pipes, and pumps siphoning liquid prehistory to the surface, from wells drilled into the lakebed. This lot across the lake was where the duck hunters parked, and where Holly had taken much of her evocative background footage for her documentary. The rest of the shoreline that he could make out offered merely the suggestion of darker trees at the dark water's edge. Mourners at his funeral?

Nick lurched over to a mammoth old cypress tree, a few feet from the softly lapping water, and leaned back on it. He was dizzy and shivering.

He wasn't thinking right; maybe one of those drugged darts had actually hit him.

He didn't see a way out of this. His breath condensed before him and rose into the cold night sky. He envied its freedom from the doomed prison of his body.

Was he going to end up like Carl Shawe and Travis Corbett, nailed to a tree, a martyr to a murderer's genealogical obsession? Or like the Dusongs, but smothering in another elemental force, water in place of fire? He'd rather take his chances swimming. His pursuer, though probably injured, had the advantage in these woods. Yeah...it seemed worth a shot. He was a good swimmer, or used to be. Maybe he could make it to the closest duck blind—fifty, seventy-five yards?—without being detected. Did he have the strength? How cold was the water? What if his attacker followed him?

He'd always heard that drowning was peaceful, as ways of death go.

He waded in, and the frigid shallows crawled up his calves.

A hand covered his mouth. He felt himself being spun around.

"Quiet! I don't know how close he is," Wooty said, his voice scarcely a murmur above the lake sounds. "You okay?"

"Yeah, I...I think so, aside from the fact that I'm running on empty. Nooj, or whoever, is chasing me. He's wounded. I shot him and stabbed him."

"What the hell you need me for then?" Wooty asked sarcastically. "Miss Luevie—my mother—told me about how you uncovered her secret. I'm beginning to think *you're* the spirit walking these woods.... We were together when we heard you were in trouble. Let's get to some cover. I'm hoping the sheriff'll be here soon."

"No spirit," Nick said through chattering teeth. "I'm very human tonight, and I want to keep it that way. What about hiding in one of those duck blinds?"

"I got a better idea."

Wooty told him that Carl Shawe usually kept several pirogues hidden around the lakeshore, to accommodate his illegal activities. Wooty confessed that he had sometimes hunted, fished, and trapped with Carl, outside of the law. Their best bet was to find one of the dugout canoes and head for the landing on the far side of the lake, about a mile's journey. They could then make a run for the highway and the nearest residence.

Wooty pointed to some brush nearby. "Come on. It's shallow enough to walk. Hasn't been enough rain this year. There! There it is!"

Nick saw the vague shape of the crude wooden boat, wedged into the grass and clay of the shoreline. If walking across the water was out of the question, he'd settle for a less spectacular miracle that kept him alive.

A gunshot shattered the darkness. Wooty crumpled.

Nick crouched down, searching the shore. He saw the shadowy shape of the cougar and the gleam of a handgun in its extended arm. It began splashing unsteadily toward him.

"My gun," Wooty gasped from the water. "In the...holster. Gun." He was silent.

Nick yanked off his Russell chukkas and arranged them under Wooty's head. High-tops: a bit stodgy in the fashion department and bearing scorches from the museum fire, but right now they seemed positively brilliant! The extra inch or two would keep the injured man's mouth and nose above the water—*if* he was still alive.

Then Nick found the holster and Wooty's pistol. It was wet, slippery, unfamiliar. He tried to pull back the slide, but this was too much for him. The cold, his exertion, and his aggravated old injuries had turned him into a veritable infant, lacking adult strength. He cursed the frailty of the human body as he fought to make his hands and arms obey.

He looked up. The cougar was standing fifteen feet away, staggering from side to side on rubber legs. Like a drunk tightrope walker struggling for balance, the cougar waved its gun arm in a wild meaningless pattern, which tightened and tightened until the oscillations ceased.

Nick stared into the deadly void within the silver ring of the barrel.

Using both thumbs against the hammer of Wooty's pistol, he finally was able to cock it. Was there a bullet in the chamber? Was the safety on or off?

He raised the gun and drew a wobbly bead on the advancing cougar.

Chapter 39

Luevenia Silsby dropped to her knees in the muddy clay of the lakeshore. She had never seen a god before, and here was one thirty feet in front of her.

She stared through tears at the Sacred Cougar walking on the surface of Lake Katogoula, standing over the carcass of the deer it was offering to the wandering, weary tribe. She'd heard the story hundreds of times, but it had never moved her as the real thing did now.

Was this the real thing? Had she traveled back centuries, millennia, to the era of her ancestors? Was this a sign that she'd been chosen for some special role, like her priestly forebears of the Vulture Cult? Devout Catholic though she was, no saint's tale or church service or claim of a weeping garden statue had ever made her feel this way, thrilled by the immediate presence of the divine.

And if the ancient gods were not dead, then maybe Nick Herald was wrong about Nooj, wrong about many things. What if…what if he was indeed the evil that had turned everything upside down, as she'd once suspected?

No. This is all illusion.

She shook her head and closed her eyes, blotting out the false vision on the sparkling lake. As much as she wanted to believe in this epiphany, she knew it was a lie. Love cleared her mind, steeled her certainty. Love for Wooty. She had come to the lake to protect her son. He was her religion now. And he was out there, too. Which was he, the moving one or the stretched out, motionless figure?

She stood up and aimed the shotgun two inches above the cougar, high enough, she calculated, to avoid scattering shot on the two shapes in the water below. The first shell held pellets intended for small game. But it could kill.

She squeezed the trigger. The gun barked and she leaned into the mild kick of recoil.

The cougar jolted forward, but righted itself and turned toward her.

This time she aimed only fractionally above the cougar's head. Her second shell was loaded with a slug, a lump of lead that could fell a deer at fifty yards. At this short distance, gravity would pull the quarter-ounce projectile down only slightly.

She fired.

The cougar fell backward into the water.

回

Immemorial peace, like omnipotent death, settled again upon the lake, as bloody ripples murmured ancient obsequies on the shoreline.

Chapter 40

"The new Katogoula Tribal Center," Tommy Shawe said, spreading his arms out as if to embrace the future. The circles under his eyes were as dark as ever, but a pure childlike joy radiated from the eyes themselves.

Nick thought about the contrast of sadness and elation Tommy's face presented, and decided it was a perfect metaphor for the Katogoula's month of terror, which had ended with the death of Nugent Chenerie, two weeks before this cool, bright mid-November day.

Katogoula men and women hammered and wielded power tools and poured concrete and slathered mortar between bricks.

"By summer, we'll be in," Tommy shouted over the shriek of a circular saw. "In time to celebrate the Green Corn Ceremony here."

The ceremony had its roots in prehistory and once marked the beginning of the Katogoula year. It was a renewal on a personal and communal level. In the distant days when the ancient traditions still reigned, tribe members prayed to their gods for a good harvest, sought reconciliation with the living and the dead, and expelled the past year's demons.

Nick particularly liked the expulsion-of-demons part.

Tommy turned away from Nick and Sheriff Higbee and gazed at the burial mounds, not far away across the grassy meadow. The tribal center would face the ancestral graves. Tommy rubbed his eyes now and then, and Nick and Big John noticed his stubby pony tail shaking as he tried to regain control of his emotions. He had let his fair hair and beard grow; as with the rest of the tribe, his outward appearance was evolving, mirroring the growth of Katogoula identity inside. He looked like a sane version of his brother, Carl, people said teasingly around Three Sisters Pantry.

The foundation of the center was still only pipes and lumber sticking up. Circular, following archaeological studies of traditional Katogoula village architecture. Nick and Big John walked with Tommy around the perimeter of the large complex. Tommy explained enthusiastically where the meeting rooms, infirmary, new museum, and library would be.

"That Atlantic City company wanted to put the casino here. Right here!" Tommy said, his tone a mixture of exasperation and wonder at how close they'd come to selling their souls for a few casino chips. "I called them right after I got re-elected tribal president. Those Vegas and Tahoe folks, too. Collect. Told them all to shove it up their ass. It took the deaths of my brother and the Dusongs and all the other bad things that happened to show us our blood is way more than just a jackpot."

Nick didn't want to spoil the moment by mentioning the dark debt owed to Nooj Chenerie. Through his rampage of retribution, Nooj, descendant of proud warriors as well as humiliated slaves, had taught his enemies to fight for their heritage, but not to live in self-destructive bondage to the past. Nooj, as, in a way, the most recent incarnation of the Sacred Cougar, proved to the Katogoula that they could provide for themselves in the modern, alien land of twenty-first century America. His deadly masquerade had been as true and instructive as any myth.

"It took their suffering," Tommy was saying, "for us to learn who we want to be. And a big part of that is knowing who we were, the good and the bad of it. For that, we thank you, Nick."

"Hey, you can bet I'll take advantage of my honorary tribal membership, too. Count on me shaking a leg at every pow-wow."

The three men laughed.

"Well, Tommy, you sure didn't make many friends in the Louisiana Legislature and the U.S. Congress," Big John said. "I understand they're especially pissed off at your tribe 'cause you upset a cozy little relationship they had with the gambling interests."

"They'll just have to find another cow to milk. We don't need to beg and bargain anymore. The FBI can worry about those guys, from now on. I'm sure not."

"From what my sources tell me," Big John said with the steely innuendo of a prosecutor ready to press charges, "that's not at all unlikely."

Then the sheriff, giving Nick due credit for his brilliant hunches and damning, if sometimes improperly gathered, evidence, sketched out the still-evolving picture of Nooj's deadly crusade from the moment the BIA envelope arrived.

That afternoon, the wildlife agent heard the devastating news while visiting Three Sisters Pantry, that his ancestral enemy, the Katogoula, would be rescued from oblivion through federal recognition. He also learned that Tommy had driven to meet with Chief Claude. He began to set his first devastating murder in motion, a crime that would implicate Tommy. Circumstances aided Nooj, and his night of terror developed better than he could have hoped.

Nooj must have remembered Tommy's atlatl from their childhood together; he stole it and the genealogical records—the records perhaps a lucky find—from the Shawes' garage, after dark. On his way to ambush Tommy, Nooj inadvertently caught the attention of Wooty Tadbull and his two partners; and even though he was a supremely skilled woodsman, he almost didn't escape the raging Travis Corbett. Nooj led poor Travis into a pit trap he knew was there.

Having shot Tommy with the blowgun dart, Nooj led the drugged man into the woods, stationing him out of sight while he put on a spooky cougar show for Wooty, engaged in his gruesome task on the burial mounds—a show that got the unexpected cooperation of the trophy deer Carl Shawe had been hunting for several nights. Carl probably would have bagged that buck, had Nooj not shown up first and impaled him with an atlatl spear.

Nooj, from his fire tower aerie, spotted more and more opportunities to sow fear. He swooped down on the Shawe twins, set fire to the museum, and scared Stu, the cougar impostor, with the corpse at the mounds, all with maximum dramatic effect that served to heighten superstitious panic among the tribe. He attacked Holly and Nick at the forest cemeteries when they got too close to the truth of his Quinahoa lineage and the undying Chenerie grudge.

Big John, like Tommy Shawe, had made up his mind about casinos, too: he didn't want one in his jurisdiction. No transparency, no accountability, too slippery, he confided to the two other men. He hadn't even been able to catch up with the little fish named Val. According to her company, she'd stolen some money and was now missing without a trace; so was her boyfriend, Butch, who worked at the company's riverboat property in New Orleans. Nick had nothing definite to offer on their fate, but in his imagination he saw a Luck o' the Draw helicopter hovering low over the Gulf, dropping chunks of something into the water.

"Tommy, there's a new space on your pedigree chart I need to fill in," Nick said. "What did you and Brianne name the baby?"

"It was twins again! Girls, this time. We named one Carlotta Shawe, after my brother. And the other one Talinda, sort of after the Tadbulls."

Nick turned to the burial mounds in front of the planted seed of the new tribal center. This was the meadow he and Holly had run across to escape Nooj Chenerie, the day he'd attacked them in the Katogoula cemetery. Then it had been Tadbull land; now it belonged to the Katogoula again.

Big John and Tommy walked ahead to the latter's new truck.

Nick lingered behind, breathing in the fresh breeze blowing from Lake Katogoula and Tchekalaya Forest and across the meadow and the burial mounds. He thought he heard an ancient song up there where the pine needles danced in the golden sunlight, the voices of Katogoula spirits assuring him that the good twin of the forest was at last ascendant.

For now.

◘

Nick strolled alone along the Golden Trace toward Tadbull Hall. He thought of early morning in the French Quarter, when a similar sparkling calm sometimes allowed the willing listener to hear the local gods who'd temporarily vanquished the cackling demons of the treacherous Quarter night.

The Golden Trace was a necklace strung with totems of the Katogoula past. One of these totems was Tadbull Hall. The trace ran right into the elliptical cart path in front of the house and picked up again on the other side. Nick stopped to read a newly erected marker explaining that the original Tadbull patriarch had deliberately interrupted the sacred trail with his front yard to demonstrate his power to the Katogoula.

Nick stepped onto the bright shell driveway and headed for the house. The tribe had finally broken free from this purgatorial loop the white world had imposed, to find its traditional path once again; and the Tadbulls had received a painful lesson in the limits of earthly posturing.

As he reached the porch, he noticed two people on the driveway, making their way toward the bayou. Holly's hair glowed in bronze glory, even from a couple of hundred yards away. A thin man walked slowly beside her; he used a cane to do most of the work healthy legs should have done. Nick could see that the man turned his head frequently toward Holly, as if she were the source of the only heat keeping his limbs from frozen immobility.

Holly waved animatedly at Nick, made the motions of shouting something at him, and then the two resumed their walking. "We'll be there in a few minutes!" the words said, reaching him finally.

Nick waited for them.

Wooty seemed to have aged twenty years. He was gaunt and ashen. In his eyes, their size exaggerated by his body's frailness, the vibrant cockiness had been replaced by the dazed, distant wariness of the man who's awakened more than once to find death, like a beautiful succubus, jumping impatiently up and down on his chest. Wooty's encounters with a surgeon's scalpel had left scars the color of raw veal, beginning just below his now prominent Adam's apple.

"This is our first day all the way around," Holly said, her face and voice proud of their joint accomplishment. She guided Wooty up the steps, onto the porch, and into one of the big rockers.

Holly patiently helped the sick man when necessary, but didn't pamper him. Wooty clearly appreciated not being treated like a child.

They would do well together for the rest of their lives, facing their problems with mutual dignity, Nick was thinking.

Holly hugged Nick, pressing close with her body, her head turned outward against his shoulder. Today her hair smelled of nectarine. The deep, quavering breath she took and released told him better than words what hell she and Wooty had been through.

"They broke me open like a boiled crab," Wooty said, attempting a little laugh that obviously hurt. "I wonder which parts of me they took out, white or Katogoula? Nothing I can't live without, anyway. Besides, I got a few good parts left." He winked at Holly.

She sat on the arm of his rocker and held his hand. "At least they removed that defective get-rich-quick gland. We're going to do honest work for our living, from now on, right? And no more of that illegal stuff. No more Senator Augustus Bayles, either."

Wooty nodded capitulation in a war he no longer cared to fight, leaned his head back, and closed his eyes. Holly tucked a Katogoula quilted throw around him, from chest to knees, and he fell into instant open-mouthed slumber below the geometric tree-of-life pattern.

"As soon as he gets well," Holly said softly, "we're opening the mill again. And the tribe's hired me as cultural director; they made me an honorary member, like you. Me, a Scottish lassie through and through, a Katogoula Indian! Best of all, I get to run the new museum. Bascove Tadbull's paintings and drawings and photos will be the first things up on the walls."

"How's Mr. Tadbull?" Nick asked. "He had something of a breakdown?"

"Doctor says it's depression that'll probably pass eventually. Or maybe not. Doctors! Come on, I'll show you," she said, pulling him by his slightly sore right arm inside the house. "Smell that cooking? Miss Luevie's in charge of the grub around here; it's a regular Three Sisters Pantry. She tells Verla what to fix—much to her annoyance. They're planning a major bash for Thanksgiving, out on the front lawn; the Katogoula don't make a big negative thing out of it, like some tribes. I'll make sure you get an invitation. Miss Luevie made me promise not to let you leave until you've had lunch. Don't make a liar out of me."

They walked to Mr. Tadbull's den and stepped back into the dining room across the hall to observe the old man framed by the doorsill.

"His casino deal fell through, of course," Holly whispered, "after he put all those people out of work and wasted all that money sprinkling payoffs around. The sad story of his affair with Luevenia came out. And then his son nearly gets killed. I think he did some soul-searching, and didn't like what he found. Even his old buddy Representative Girn abandoned him."

Girn was now the head Washington lobbyist for a political action committee advocating a congressional assault on all American Indian tribes for allegedly introducing tobacco to the colonists.

In his last real conversation with Holly, shortly after Wooty's brush with death, Mr. Tadbull had told her he was a selfish old goat for keeping

Wooty subservient and ignorant of his true origins. Though he hadn't been responsible for Nooj's mad acts, he felt that his son's harrowing experience was a judgment from God, and a last chance to do something worthwhile. Mr. Tadbull had arranged for his son, when sufficiently recovered, to take over all family business, exercising complete, unquestioned control. As a final penance, he sold half of the family's land and a half interest in the sawmill to the Katogoula Tribe for the grand sum of five Sacagawea dollar coins, a buffalo nickel, and an Indian-head penny.

Mr. Tadbull sat at the pearwood gaming table in his study; a lamp made from a miniature slot machine cast more shadow than light on the relics of the room. An inviting blaze crackled in the fireplace. Wristwatches were spread out like cards on the fuchsia baize in front of him. A cigar box to his left contained a heap of eviscerated timepieces.

"Oh, he eats and sleeps and all that," Holly said. "He's healthy physically. But this is what he does. After he signed everything over to Wooty, he just retreated into a shell. Miss Luevie sits with him a lot, since Royce runs the store now mostly. She buys those cheap watches for him. He likes her to do his nails. That's about the only thing that makes him smile. Just a little." She walked to the door of the den. "Hi, Wooten. Nice day out there. Want to take a walk with me?"

He hunched over the watch he was working on, doubly intent on his meaningless task.

"Come on," Holly said to Nick. "He'll start crying in a minute. Have you ever seen an old man cry? I hate it when they do that."

Miss Luevie and Verla made sure Nick ate too much delicious lunch.

And later, Holly, reluctant to let him step on the gas and go back to New Orleans, stood beside his car at the driver's-side window. She held his extended hand in both of hers at her warm, firm stomach, against her evergreen cashmere sweater.

"You know," she said, "Chief Claude had you only half figured out: you're the Midwife-of-Tomorrow Man, too."

The world of Sangfleuve Parish and Tadbull Hall fell away from his view, and he was a holy man a thousand years in the past or in the future—he couldn't tell; and his hand on this goddess's belly was a blessing of life for the Katogoula Tribe, and mankind, forever.

The next second he was back. His eyes misted and he had to swallow hard a few times before he could say, "Thanks."

"I called one of my anthropology professors at LSU," said Holly. "About the phrase in Nooj's notebooks: *BAH-UA CU-BISH-NAW-A*. She was pretty excited. Only a handful of Quinahoa words have survived. It's more like Caddo than anything else. She translated it as 'war blood.' The Quinahoa might have been one of those tribes that drank their defeated enemy's blood or"—she made a disgusted face—"ate them. We're going to make the Chenerie notebooks available to the public. I'm sure Nooj and his Quinahoa ancestors didn't realize their death lists would help future genealogists trace their enemy's ancestry."

She told him of another project: assembling a list of Quinahoa and Yaknelousa names from the memories of living Katogoula and from written sources.

"Just think," Holly said, "if enough Quinahoa and Yaknelousa descendants turn up, maybe they'll want to start their own tribes? And I know the perfect genealogist for the job."

"Oh, no, not me," Nick said, jamming the MG into reverse. "I've had enough Indian genealogy for a while. I'm taking some time off."

"Actually, I meant Hawty. We chatted via e-mail this morning. She's raring to go. We'll be glad to offer all the help she can use. The old hatchet's finally buried now—"

"You mean the old atlatl?"

"We plan to display Tommy's atlatl in an honored place at the museum. Now it's part of our common history—Katogoula, Yaknelousa, and Quinahoa—just like the war. We would welcome the Quinahoa into our tribe, but we'd also understand their desire for their own identity.

After what we've been through, though, I can't say I recommend it.... Hawty's a good gal, Nick. Don't let her get away from you."

◫

Yeah, he said to himself, braking and looking back at Tadbull Hall in the afternoon sun. *A talent of mine.*

◫

The drive home was long and lonely, except for Doc Cheatham and his horn. Flush with Katogoula cash, and more to come, Nick decided to double Hawty's salary, then triple it, and finally compromised with himself and cut the tripling in half.

Judge Hilaire Chaurice had pleaded to be reinstated as a client. The throwing justice had decided to document his maternal line instead, certain—or perhaps just hopeful—that there were no colonial prostitutes on that side. His son's marriage was scheduled for May, but he was now worried the fiancée's rich family was getting cold feet. He needed something very impressive in the way of ancestors to tilt the scales his way.

A raise and a bonus. He would give Hawty the judge! *Perfect.*

Nick turned up the music and the heat a bit, savored the earth-scented cobalt and vermilion Louisiana dusk flowing in through his half-open window, and imagined the pleasures of a month in Italy with Veronique.

Chapter 41

Requirements for Membership in the Katogoula Tribe of Cutpine, Louisiana

Resolved, by the Katogoula Tribal Council:

Individuals may seek enrollment in the Katogoula Indian Tribe of Cutpine, Louisiana, and thus participate in the Rights, Obligations, and Honors attaching to such membership, by means of at least one of the following criteria:

1) For those living at the effective date of this document, proof, through verifiable genealogical research, of descent from one of the Katogoula kinship groups residing in the Cutpine area during the time of the Removals to Indian Territory, Oklahoma, 1825–1855. Seven groups have been documented.

2) For those living at the effective date of this document, proof of descent from any individual identified as a Katogoula Indian—whether of the core groups or not—before 1825. Admissible evidence shall include, among other things, written accounts of explorers, missionaries, military and administrative operatives, and traders. Those proving descent from any member of the Yaknelousa and Quinahoa

tribes, both amalgamated with the Katogoula Tribe before historical times, shall be entitled to admission.

3) Adoption, at the discretion of the Tribal Council, taking into consideration special circumstances:
   a. Honorary membership for meritorious service to the tribe,
   b. For humanitarian reasons, or
   c. For any other reason the Tribal Council may deem appropriate.

   Adoption, in all cases, shall be for a lifetime term only, and shall entitle the individual to all privileges except tribal monetary allocation and heritability of enrolled status. Certain federal aid programs may not be available to adoptees of the tribe.

4) Individuals born after the effective date of this document who seek admission to the tribe must have either parent as an enrolled member, in good standing—or so enrolled at time of death—of the Katogoula Tribe of Cutpine, Louisiana. There is no blood-quantum requirement imposed by the tribe with respect to enrollment of individuals covered by this section.

Prospective enrollees have the responsibility of providing all necessary genealogical proof. The tribe's History and Genealogy Department may be able to offer suggestions and limited assistance. The materials listed below provide excellent general background information on the Katogoula Tribe and its struggle to preserve its heritage:

1. Herald, J. N. and H. Latimer. *People of the Sacred Cougar: The Katogoula Tribe of Louisiana.* New Orleans: Coldbread Press, forthcoming.

2. Herald, J. N. and H. Latimer, eds. *The Chenerie Katogoula Death Lists*. New Orleans: Coldbread Press.

3. Worthstone, Holly. *Wind through the Pines: A Visual Journey with the Katogoula Tribe of Cutpine, Louisiana*. Baton Rouge: Tadbull Hall Productions. DVD.

4. Worthstone, Holly and Lovenia Dejeune Silsby. *The Art of Bascove Tadbull: Forest Gothic*. Baton Rouge: Tadbull Hall Productions, forthcoming.

5. On the Web: <httz:\\www.freretu.edu/hawty/katagoula>. Here we have provided complete contact information. Additionally, you can learn about the ongoing research into Katogoula topics and download a free genealogy starter kit, featuring family charts, a research log, and questionnaires for relatives. Links to relevant genealogical and governmental sites and to specifically American Indian resources are added frequently. A separate Katogoula tribal site is presently under construction.

All decisions regarding membership suitability, and changes in the requirements for membership, shall be the sole province of the Katogoula Tribal Council, which, per the Tribal Constitution and treaties with the Government of the United States of America and with the State of Louisiana, is in its own affairs sovereign.

Tommy Shawe	Luevenia Dejeune Silsby	J. N. Herald
President	*Chairwoman, History & Genealogy Dept.*	*Consulting Genealogist*

0-595-30886-4

Printed in the United States
74033LV00004B/55